AGAINST THE TIDE

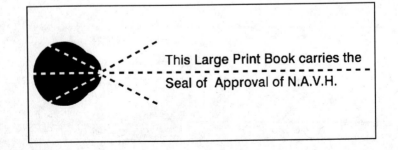

This Large Print Book carries the
Seal of Approval of N.A.V.H.

THE BRODIES OF ALASKA

AGAINST THE TIDE

KAT MARTIN

THORNDIKE PRESS
A part of Gale, Cengage Learning

GALE
CENGAGE Learning·

Farmington Hills, Mich • San Francisco • New York • Waterville, Maine
Meriden, Conn • Mason, Ohio • Chicago

GALE
CENGAGE Learning·

LIBRARY OF CONGRESS CATALOGING-IN-PUBLICATION DATA

Martin, Kat.
   Against the tide / Kat Martin. — Large print edition.
     pages cm. — (The Brodies of Alaska) (Thorndike Press large print core)
    ISBN 978-1-4104-8438-3 (hardback) — ISBN 1-4104-8438-6 (hardcover)
    I. Title.
   PS3563.A7246A766 2015
   813'.54—dc23

                                   2015028284

Published in 2015 by arrangement with Zebra Books, an imprint of Kensington Publishing Group

Printed in Mexico
1 2 3 4 5 6 7 19 18 17 16 15

AGAINST THE TIDE

CHAPTER ONE

Valdez, Alaska

The piercing ring of the cell phone lying on his nightstand didn't bode well. There was no such thing as good news at three o'clock in the morning.

With a sigh, Rafe rolled over and grabbed the phone, scrubbed a hand over his face as he pressed it against his ear. "Brodie."

"Police Chief Rosen here. We've got a problem, Rafe, and it's a bad one. I need you to meet me down at the harbor. How soon can you get here?"

Rafe swung his long legs to the side of the bed and sat up. "Ten minutes. What's this about, Chief?"

"It's Scotty Ferris, Rafe. I'm afraid he's dead. I'll fill you in when you get here. I'll be waiting on the dock next to the *Scorpion.*" The police chief hung up the phone.

For several long moments, Rafe just sat

there. His chest felt tight. Scotty Ferris was twenty-four years old, a handsome, hard-working kid who was engaged to be married. His June wedding to Cassie Webster, one of the local girls, was only three weeks away. Cassie was going to be crushed.

Rafe swore softly. What the hell could have happened?

But in this rugged country where the climate, wild animals, or just bad judgment could get you killed, accidents happened all the time.

Shoving himself up from the bed, Rafe grabbed a pair of worn jeans off the chair and jerked them on, drew a sweatshirt over his head, pulled on his heavy socks, and shoved his size-thirteen feet into a pair of high-topped, rubber-soled boots. Since the temperature at night even in late May was still in the thirties and it had rained during the night, he grabbed his jacket as he headed for the steps down to the garage.

The boat harbor wasn't far from his house, a brown bi-level with an oversized two-car garage that sat a few blocks north on Mendeltna, a street off Hazelet Avenue there in Valdez. *Sea Scorpion* was his flagship charter fishing boat, a thirty-eight-foot Mac, his pride and joy. It was the boat he usually captained himself, one of three that made up his fleet. Scotty Ferris was part of *Scorpion*'s crew.

Rafe thought of the young man as he parked his dark green Ford Expedition in a spot in front of the harbor, climbed out, and closed the door. Puddles from last night's rain sloshed against his boots as he made his way toward the dock. The occasional streetlight burned into the darkness, but quiet surrounded him, along with the familiar salty tang of the sea.

Ringed by the snowcapped Chugach Mountains, gleaming white glaciers, and the turquoise waters of Prince William Sound, Valdez was considered one of the most beautiful places on earth.

But the climate was a major drawback for most people, being wet, cold, and snowy much of the year. Rafe couldn't imagine living anywhere else.

Which brought his thoughts full circle to Scotty. With year-round residents numbering less than forty-five hundred, everyone knew everyone who lived there. And everyone knew and liked Scotty. The kid had been born in Valdez. He thrived on the rugged lifestyle, planned to marry and raise kids here, probably never would have left.

What the hell had happened? Rafe thought again as he walked toward his boat.

And why did Chief Rosen want to meet him at the *Scorpion*?

A few spaces down from where he'd parked, Rafe spotted a black-and-silver Ford police SUV. In the distance, the familiar antenna above the wheelhouse of the *Scorpion* marked where the boat bobbed near the middle of the dock.

Rafe started down the long wooden walkway, his gaze on the group of people gathered next to where the *Scorpion* was moored. The area was cordoned off with yellow crime scene tape, the boat clearly off-limits until the police were finished collecting evidence.

Police Chief Clifford Rosen, a stout man in his fifties, bald head ringed by thinning gray hair, stood next to a figure lying on the dock, covered by a long, white cloth. Knowing Scotty Ferris lay under the cloth made Rafe's stomach burn.

Two other officers quietly conversed while a doctor he recognized as Karen Ward, a woman who worked at the local clinic and served as medical examiner, knelt next to the sheet-draped body.

"What happened?" Rafe asked the chief.

"Looks like he was robbed," Rosen answered. "Wallet's missing, jewelry's gone. Car keys. Cell phone's missing. Single blow to the back of the head. Blunt instrument. Baseball bat seems the most likely, something that size that would be easy to handle."

"Jesus."

"I asked you to come down because I need someone to identify the body. With his parents both dead, I figured better you than his fiancée. Soon as you do that, I'll break the news to the Webster girl."

Rafe just nodded. Cassie was going to be devastated. She and Scotty were crazy in love, the kind Rafe figured had a good chance of lasting. Sometimes fate could be a real bastard.

"Who found him?"

"Young couple wandered out this way from the Fisherman's Catch Saloon. Found him lying right there. Shook 'em up pretty bad."

"What time?"

"Two a.m. The M.E. makes preliminary time of death between eleven and two."

One of the officers, a red-haired young cop Rafe recognized as Rusty Donovan, leaned down and lifted the edge of the sheet. As the cover rolled back, Rafe's gaze fixed on Scotty. The boy's brown eyes were open, staring sightlessly into the black night sky. His handsome face was frozen in a look

11

of surprise.

He was wearing a jacket but it was unzipped, revealing a long-sleeved blue T-shirt that read FISHERMEN DO IT DEEPER. Rafe could almost see the grin on the kid's face when he'd put it on.

"It's him," he said darkly. "Scott Ferris."

"You know what he was doing down here?"

"No." But once he got his head wrapped around Scotty's death, he intended to find out.

"As soon as we check for any forensic evidence on the boat, I'll want you to take a look inside, see if anything's missing. At first glance, there's no sign of a break-in. Probably took him out before he went aboard."

Rafe just nodded.

"That's it then," the police chief said. "We'll wrap things up here and I'll talk to Cassie Webster."

Rafe looked down at Scotty and clenched his jaw. "You're going to catch the sonofabitch, right? You're going to find the guy who killed him?"

"If he's in town, we'll catch him. If he's some loser just passing through, might be a whole lot harder."

Rafe frowned. "You don't think he was killed by a local?"

"Wouldn't be my first guess. Hell, we haven't had a murder here in years. But violent crime's been creeping up lately — assaults, thefts, burglaries. These days anything's possible."

"Either way, you're going to get him," Rafe repeated, making it clear there had better not be any doubt.

Rosen just nodded. "Thanks for coming down."

"Keep me posted, will you?" When the chief made no reply, Rafe shoved his hands into his jacket pockets, turned, and started back the way he'd come.

It was almost dawn. If he had a fishing charter today, he'd be at the dock by five, getting ready to take the boat out at six. He did half-day cruises; nine hour; or full-day, twelve-hour charters that lasted till six p.m.

He wasn't taking a group out today, which meant he wouldn't be seeing Jaimie Graham, the nineteen-year-old girl who crewed for him along with Scotty. She dressed like a man, worked like a man, but under her determination to prove herself in the world of men, Jaimie had a bad crush on Scotty. She was going to take the news damned hard.

Rafe got into the Ford and started driving toward the house Jaimie lived in with her parents. He needed to speak to her, break the news before she found out from someone else. He hated to wake up her folks, but he didn't have any choice.

Rafe sighed into the darkness. He wished he could just go back to bed, get some badly needed sleep, but there was no chance of that.

Not with his mind circling around, going over what had happened, trying to make sense of the senseless murder of Scotty Ferris. Trying to think why Scotty might have been down at the *Scorpion* in the middle of the night. Wishing he knew who had killed him.

Thinking how much he'd like to wrap his hands around the bastard's neck and squeeze till he paid for what he had done.

CHAPTER TWO

The breakfast crowd at the Pelican Café had begun to arrive, as people did every morning when it opened at six a.m. The café had opened its doors in the fifties and been going strong ever since. Of course, it had passed through a dozen different owners, had its ups and downs, and been near financial ruin more than once.

Having purchased the restaurant six months ago, Olivia Chandler was the most recent person to step into the driver's seat. Unlike the previous owner, who had let the place sink into disrepair, Olivia had been making changes, most of which had been heralded with great enthusiasm by the local customers.

The bell above the door rang as a young mother and her little girl walked in and headed for one of the light blue vinyl booths. Melissa Young, Olivia remembered, was her name. Liv made a point of getting to know her customers — just not too well.

While Melissa grabbed a child's high seat and settled one-year-old Suzy in it, the waitress, a slim little blonde named Katie McKenzie, grabbed the coffeepot off the burner behind the counter and headed for the booth. Katie smiled as she filled Melissa's mug and handed her a menu.

"I'll give you a minute to decide," Katie said, hurrying off to another table to refill an earlier patron's cup.

One of the changes Liv had made was to hire a new cook — one who wasn't high on marijuana half the time. Wayne Littlefish was Alaska Native, reliable and great in the kitchen. An older man, Charlie Foot, worked the dinner shift.

Liv had also hired two part-time waitresses instead of one full-time worker, which gave each of the girls a more flexible schedule and made taking time off easier for all of them, including Olivia and long-time employee, Nell Olsen.

A buxom woman with thick, silver-streaked black hair, Nell had worked at the café for more than ten years. She was as much a fixture as the sky-blue interior, the ocean theme, and the anchors and fishing nets on the walls.

Nell had been invaluable in helping Liv

take over the business since, aside from waiting tables for the past couple of years, being a fairly decent cook, and a very fast learner, Liv had almost no experience in running a restaurant.

Still, in the last six months she had managed to keep the old clientele happy and add new customers. The tourist season was just starting, so business was getting even better.

"Well, look who's coming," Nell said, staring out the window at a tall man in jeans and a sweatshirt crossing the outside patio. The brick patio was empty now while it was still cold, but with summer approaching, soon would be noisy with people. "If it isn't Mr. Tall, Dark, and Handsome."

Katie walked past Liv just then, a platter of bacon and eggs riding on the flat of her hand. "I just call him Mr. Freakin' Hot."

"Shame on you," Liv teased. "You just turned twenty-one. Rafe Brodie's got to be at least a dozen years older."

"Just means he's a man not a boy. And I like a guy with a little experience."

"From what I hear, he has plenty of that," Liv said dryly as Katie sailed off to deliver the food.

Nell chuckled. "I'm fifty years old and that man can still make me swoon."

Olivia busied herself wiping off the long Formica-topped counter as Rafe shoved through the door, ringing the bell above. Seating himself in his usual booth, he stretched his long legs out in front of him. Rafe was a regular in the café, which sat on North Harbor Drive right across from the boat dock.

"Katie's busy," Nell said with a match-making glint in her eyes. "Why don't you wait on him?"

Olivia shook her head. "I'm busy, too. You go ahead."

Knowing there was no persuading her, Nell sighed. "Probably better you don't. Everyone in town knows Rafe's a dedicated bachelor."

As the owner of the café, Olivia caught most of the local gossip. According to Cassie Webster, the other part-time waitress, Rafe Brodie had dated a woman named Sally Henderson for nearly three years, until she dumped him four months ago because he refused to marry her.

Apparently, he'd made his intentions — or lack thereof — clear from the start, but Sally hadn't believed him, poor girl.

Dedicated bachelor or not, Nell and Katie were right. With the thick, dark brown hair curling just over his collar, the faint shadow of beard that usually lined his hard jaw, and those hot, whiskey-brown eyes, he was one of the best-looking men Olivia had ever seen.

Which was exactly the reason she had avoided him since the day she had met him.

Oh, she'd been pleasant enough when she had to be, spoken to him for a moment when she'd been introduced to him at a chamber of commerce mixer right after she'd bought the café, but she always managed to be too busy to wait on him.

No use putting temptation in her path. It was simply too dangerous.

Still, as she worked taking orders and delivering meals to the patrons at the counter, she couldn't help an occasional glance in his direction. He had always reminded her of a dark-haired lion, powerful and dangerous yet fascinating in some primitive way. He looked different today, the shadow along his jaw darker, as if he hadn't had time to shave, his handsome features set in grim lines, and faint shadows under his eyes.

She watched as Nell chatted with him a moment, then Liv watched the easy smile Nell usually gave him slip from her face.

The coffeepot wavered. Rafe grabbed the glass pot to keep her from dropping it and

19

spilled hot coffee over his hand.

Olivia didn't hesitate, just grabbed a towel, wet it with cold water, and hurried in Rafe's direction. He was sitting down again, Nell fussing over him, relieved to see Olivia approaching.

"Here — wrap this around your fingers." She handed him the wet towel. "It's cold enough to ease the pain and keep the burn from getting worse."

"I'm all right," Rafe said. "It's no big deal." But he accepted the wet cloth and looped it over the back of a big, suntanned hand.

The man was all of six-four, two-hundred-plus pounds, with a solid, athletic build and very wide shoulders. Liv was five-nine, but Rafe was more than half a head taller. She tried not to stare at his mouth, which seemed harder this morning without the smile he always had for Nell.

She glanced in her friend's direction, sucked in a breath as Nell's pale blue eyes filled with tears.

"Oh God, what is it?"

Nell blinked and the tears rolled down her cheeks. She wiped at the wetness with a trembling hand. "I could tell something was wrong. It was stamped all over Rafe's face."

Liv glanced from one to the other, saw

the same grim expression on both of their faces. "Tell me what's happened."

Nell swallowed. "It's . . . it's Scotty. He was killed last night."

Olivia felt the blood seeping out of her head. She found herself sinking down on the bench opposite Rafe. "Oh God. That's why Cassie didn't show up for work this morning." The reason Olivia had had to call Katie.

Rafe's towel-wrapped hand unconsciously fisted. "I'm sorry, I shouldn't have said anything. I figured since Cassie works here, Nell already knew."

"I'm glad you told me," Nell said. "I need to go to her, make sure she's okay."

"I'll cover while you're gone," Liv said. "We'll be fine."

Nell wiped fresh tears from her cheeks. "This is going to break her heart. She loved Scotty so much. Everyone loved him."

"I can't believe he's dead," Liv said, aching for the young woman whose future had been shattered. "What happened?"

"The police think it was a mugging," Rafe said. "Whoever did it stole his wallet, jewelry, cell phone."

"Where did it happen?"

"On the dock next to the *Scorpion*."

"Last night?"

"That's right."

Liv frowned. "What was he doing down at the dock at night? He's usually home with Cassie."

"I don't know. I talked to Jaimie Graham before I came over. She had no idea what he was doing down there."

"Jaimie had an awful crush on Scotty," Nell said. "She must have taken the news real hard."

"Jaimie isn't good at hiding her feelings," Rafe said. "She ran out of the house as soon as I told her, took off so no one would see her cry."

Nell shook her head, moving the thick, salt-and-pepper hair that came to her shoulders and was clipped back on each side. "Poor thing."

"I still can't figure why Scotty was down at the dock," Olivia said.

Rafe's brown eyes swung to her face. "I'm hoping once things settle down, Cassie'll be able to tell us."

Olivia thought of the young woman who worked for her, imagined her pain, and her throat went tight. In the six months she had been running the café, she and Cassie had become close friends. Or at least as close as Liv could allow.

She looked over at Nell, whose face was

still pale. "You go on. Go to her. As soon as the breakfast rush is over, I'll join you at Cassie's house."

Nell just nodded. Picking the coffeepot up off the table, she headed for the breakfast counter, set the pot on the burner at the back. Removing her sky-blue Pelican Café apron, she slipped out through the side door near the rear of the building.

Liv glanced across the table at Rafe. His jaw looked iron hard, his eyes so dark she could barely see a hint of gold. For the first time it occurred to her that Rafe was hurting, too. Scotty was his first mate and they were friends. Cassie had said Scott idolized Rafe, had thought of him as an older brother.

Reaching toward him, she settled a hand over the fist he rested on top of the table. "Are you okay?"

His dark eyes flicked down to her hand, then moved up to her face. "Scott was a good man. One of the best. Whoever killed him is going to pay."

A little shiver ran through her. It wasn't a statement. It was a vow. "Surely the police will find the man who did it."

"There're eleven guys in the Valdez department. Eleven police officers to cover two-hundred-seventy square miles, including the pipeline terminus." Valdez was the end point of the Alaska pipeline. The huge oil shipping facility at the edge of town was one of the things that made Valdez famous.

Along with the *Exxon Valdez* oil spill. Eleven million gallons killed 250,000 seabirds and hundreds of otters and seals, a disaster it took thirty years to recover from. That and the biggest earthquake in U.S. history.

More recently, the tiny town was a place known for its majestic scenery and fabulous fishing.

"What about the State Troopers?" Olivia asked.

"I don't know. Maybe. Rosen is a good man, but cops can be pissy about their territory. He may think he can go it alone."

"Maybe he can," Liv said, but she didn't really trust the police. Hadn't since she'd been forced to run for her life and couldn't count on the police to help her.

"Maybe," Rafe said. "I guess we'll see."

Liv watched his jaw settle into a determined line and thought of the vow he had made. Clearly it was a promise he meant to keep.

As she slid out of the booth, she realized her legs still felt shaky. "Would you like something to eat? You look like you could use it."

Rafe rubbed a hand over the bristles along his jaw. "Lost my appetite. I just need some coffee. That's what I came in for."

She noticed the china mug in front of him had never gotten filled. "I'll take care of it." She headed across the café, grabbed the pot off the burner, and returned, poured his mug to the brim. "It's on the house today."

"Thanks . . . Liv." Rafe's gaze fixed on her face. It was the first time he had used the more familiar version of her name.

Olivia didn't like the way her stomach lifted at the way he said that single, softly spoken word.

Rafe leaned back in the booth as Olivia walked away. Beneath her light blue apron, she wore black leggings under a black skirt, and a black turtleneck sweater. She wore black a lot, he'd noticed, and with her heavy, dark hair, pale complexion, and striking features, it suited her.

The café was beginning to fill with customers, both locals and the first of the tourist crowd. Besides deep-sea fishing, the area offered helicopter sightseeing, wildlife cruises, glacier cruises, kayaking, hiking, camping, and a jillion other things visitors thought up to entertain themselves in a place so rich in natural beauty.

By the first of May, as winter slid into spring, the local hotel and restaurant businesses jump-started into high gear. So did Rafe's company, Great Alaska Charters.

His fleet was composed of a thirty-two-foot Armstrong; a Glacier Craft thirty-five; and his thirty-eight-foot Mac, all of which worked from April through October, depending on the weather. Scotty had made a place for himself in the company, had become an important part of the business, and it was going to be damned hard to replace him.

Scott Ferris had become Rafe's right-hand man, and more than that, a very good friend. There was no easy way to lessen the personal loss Rafe felt at Scott's death. He needed to go see Cassie, find out if there was anything he could do to help her get through her grief.

Rafe knew from experience it was going to take a helluva long time for her to heal.

He looked over at the tall, slender woman moving around the café. She was the real reason he had come to the Pelican this morning. Just watching her eased some of the tightness in his chest. Trim and lithe, she moved like a dancer, in more of a glide

26

than a pattern of steps, so light on her feet she was there one moment, then she wasn't.

With her high cheekbones, wide forehead, and unusual gray eyes, Olivia was a beautiful woman. Her chestnut hair, twisted into a knot at the nape of her neck, glinted with vibrant highlights. By midmorning, a few strands escaped around her face, softening the severe appearance she seemed determined to maintain.

And there was that mouth. Lipstick was the only real makeup she wore, a glossy dark red on lips so plump and perfectly curved they could have been in a magazine ad. That mouth made him think of dirty sex and taking her to bed, or anywhere else he could have her.

Maybe she could read his mind; maybe she knew what he was thinking and that was the reason she never waited on him. And though she was always polite, she spoke to him only if she had to and rarely by name.

For the first couple of months after she'd taken over the business, he'd figured she was just too busy to notice him. Besides, he was still dating Sally, and he wasn't the kind of guy who cheated on a woman he was involved with.

Four months ago, Sally had moved on, and Rafe had discovered he was glad. He cared for Sally Henderson, but he wasn't in love, never had been. He'd told her from the start he wasn't interested in marriage. At the time, she'd convinced him she wasn't either. But relationships changed, and Sally was ready to settle down.

Sally was ready. Rafe wasn't.

It wasn't until after they'd parted that he started to take an interest in Olivia Chandler. Besides her striking looks and porn-star mouth, there was just something about her, something that began to intrigue him. She was always friendly to the other customers, though according to Nell, she had no close friends outside the people she worked with, and no family in the area that anyone knew of.

At first he'd told himself he just wasn't the lady's type, but the more she ignored him, the more intrigued he became. She rarely went to the local pub, he discovered, just kept mostly to herself in the apartment she lived in above the café. She was a runner, he knew, having seen her jogging early in the mornings with the big, black-and-brown German shepherd she called Khan.

Every time he went into the Pelican, which was often since he was a bachelor and a lousy cook, he watched her, and eventually a funny thing happened. Over the days and weeks that passed, Rafe became more and more certain Olivia Chandler wasn't avoiding him because she wasn't attracted to him.

She was avoiding him because she was.

Liv Chandler was a beautiful mystery, one Rafe no longer intended to ignore. He meant to unearth her secrets, and in the process, if luck was on his side, maybe he'd discover the fierce attraction he felt for her was returned in equal measure.

Rafe damned well hoped so.

Rising from the booth, he tossed a dollar bill on the table for the waitresses' tip jar and started for the door. Olivia Chandler was a mystery he meant to solve.

But another mystery needed solving first.

His jaw hardened. Rafe wasn't about to let the man who murdered one of his best friends go unpunished.

Whatever it took, he was going to see justice done.

CHAPTER THREE

Olivia knocked on the door to the wood-frame house Cassie Webster shared with Scotty Ferris. Cassie's mother, Lois, opened the door. She was a petite woman, a little too thin, and her narrow face looked ravaged.

"Olivia . . . Please come in. Nell said you were going to stop by. She just left to go back to work a few minutes ago."

Liv handed the woman the mac-and-cheese casserole she'd had Wayne put together, figuring there was no better comfort food in the world than mac and cheese.

Lois took the dish from her hand. "Thank you. I don't think Cassie could hold anything down at the moment, but sooner or later, she'll have to eat something."

"All of you will," Olivia said, walking into the living room as Lois closed the front door. Cassie sat on the sofa, her face bone white, her chin-length brown hair still sleep tangled, hazel eyes staring out at nothing. She was petite like her mother, but curvy, the kind of person whose glass was always half-full instead of half-empty.

"Cassie, honey, I'm so sorry." Olivia walked toward her.

The girl's head turned toward the sound of Liv's voice and her eyes filled. "Thank you for coming."

Liv sat down beside her, reached over and took hold of her icy hand. "I wish there was something I could do."

"I know. I just . . . I feel sick all the way to my soul. My heart says Scotty can't be dead. I tell myself it can't be true, but I know it is."

Liv squeezed her hand. "The police are going to find the man who did it. I know that won't make the pain you're feeling go away, but it's something to hold on to."

Cassie swallowed. "I don't . . . don't understand what happened. Why was Scotty down at the harbor?"

"I thought maybe you'd know the answer to that."

Cassie just shook her head. "It was his regular poker night. Scotty went over to the Seaside Motel to play with Ben Friedman and some of the guys." Ben was the owner

31

of the motel. He lived in an apartment behind the office. Cassie had mentioned that Scotty played with the same group of men every week.

"I knew Scotty wouldn't be home till late," she continued, dabbing a Kleenex against her eyes. "But it got later and later and he didn't show up, and I got worried. Then the police arrived and Chief Rosen said he was . . . said he'd been killed. That Scotty had been murdered." She started sobbing, and though Olivia wasn't much of a hugger, it was all she could think of to do.

"I'm so sorry." She rubbed Cassie's back and just held her, let her cry out some of her grief.

Eventually the girl raised her head and blew into the Kleenex. "I have no idea what Scotty was doing at the harbor. Or why someone would try to rob him. Scott never carried much money. A little more tonight, maybe, since he was playing cards. But not enough for someone to kill him. Whoever did it couldn't have gotten away with very much."

Cassie sniffed into the Kleenex. "He had a smartphone, but it was an old one, probably not worth very much."

Olivia sifted through the information, which made absolutely no sense. "Maybe it wasn't about the money," she heard herself saying. "Maybe it was something else."

Cassie looked up. "Maybe it was just some rotten piece of filth who likes to hurt people."

It happened. These days it happened way too often. "Or maybe Scotty was just in the wrong place at the wrong time." Olivia knew only too well how badly that could turn out. It was the reason she'd wound up in Alaska.

"He was such a great guy," Cassie said, grabbing a fresh Kleenex out of the box and wiping at the wetness that kept rolling down her cheeks. "I'll never find another man like him."

Olivia made no reply. Good men were hard to find. As far as she was concerned, they mostly didn't exist. Scotty Ferris was a rare exception, and it was going to take Cassie a long time to get over him. Liv was going to miss him, too.

They sat together in silence, Cassie holding on to her hand. The lunch crowd would be arriving at the Pelican soon. She needed to get back to work, but she wasn't ready to leave the younger woman with her sorrow.

Liv looked up as Lois walked into the living room carrying a tray with cups and a carafe of coffee. Olivia reached for one of the cups, let Lois fill it with the strong, black brew. Nell would be back at work by now.

Olivia could stay a while longer.

Rafe couldn't put it off any longer. He headed for Cassie Webster's small wood-frame house, dread churning in the pit of his stomach. He knew what it was like to lose someone you loved. He and his family had been living in Anchorage when his mother died of breast cancer. Being the oldest, he'd had to step up, help his dad raise Dylan and Nick. Then a few years later, his father died, another tough blow for him and his brothers.

Little by little, Rafe had learned to steel himself, ignore the pain and get on with his life. After his younger brothers had both turned eighteen, he enrolled in college and met Ashley Richards.

Ash was sweet and pretty, and he was crazy about her. They dated for a year before he decided to ask her to marry him. The afternoon it happened, he'd gone to look at rings in a jewelry store not far off campus. Two hours later, he got a phone call from Ashley's brother. Ash and her best friend had been killed in a car accident. Bad weather and icy roads had sent her little Volvo careening off the hill into a tree.

The diamond ring never left the store.

Rafe finished out the school year, then joined the Coast Guard. He'd become a Rescue Swimmer, stayed in the service for the next five years, and aside from his family, had done his best not to let himself get too deeply involved with anyone ever again.

He thought of Scotty, and the tightness in his chest reminded him why he was better off keeping his emotions in check and his heart locked up good and tight.

Rafe parked the Expedition in front of the house. As he glanced over at the front door, his chest clamped down so hard, he could barely breathe.

He knew what Cassie was feeling.

Exactly what Cassie was feeling.

Stepping out of the vehicle, he walked up the sidewalk onto the porch and rang the bell, took a couple of deep breaths while he waited for the door to open.

"Rafe." Lois reached out and took hold of his hand, gave it a gentle squeeze. "Thank you so much for coming."

He just nodded, glad Cassie's mother was there. "How is she?"

"A little better. Olivia Chandler stopped by. She's in there with her now."

Rafe looked over the petite woman's head, saw Olivia sitting on the sofa next to Cassie. For an instant their eyes met and held.

Even with the weight of Scotty's death pressing like a boulder on his shoulders, he felt a little tug of awareness.

He walked directly to Cassie, crouched in front of where she sat on the sofa, and took hold of both her hands. They were ice-cold and trembling. "I'm really sorry, honey. Scotty was one of the good guys. We're all going to miss him."

The girl just leaned forward, slid her arms around his neck, rested her head on his shoulder, and started to cry. Rafe hung on to her hard, wishing there was something he could say, something he could do.

Knowing there wasn't a single damn thing.

She finally eased away, wiped her eyes as he rose to his feet. "It'll get better, I promise you," he said. "It just takes a lot of time."

She looked into his face and he could tell she understood what he was saying. Understood that he'd felt the same kind of loss and survived it.

"Have you talked to the police since you saw them at the dock?" Olivia asked. "Have they made an arrest?"

"No word yet. I called Chief Rosen before I came over. He wasn't in, but I left a message. I'll call again as soon as I leave."

"They've got to find the killer," Olivia said with such conviction, Rafe blinked. "People get away with murder and it just isn't right."

Cassie dashed away the tears on her cheeks. "I want to know who killed him, Rafe. I want to know why whoever did it picked Scotty. I want that animal brought to justice."

"The police are doing their best. Valdez is a small town. Odds are good they'll find him."

"What if they don't? I can't stand to think of it. I can't stand to think that Scotty is dead and someone is walking around free, walking around as if killing him means nothing."

The muscles tightened across Rafe's shoulders. He'd had the same thought, kept telling himself to let the authorities do their job. Knew that with every passing hour their chances of finding the killer were growing slimmer.

Before his brother Nick had quit his job last year, he'd been a homicide detective with the Anchorage PD. Which meant Rafe knew more about police work than the average guy and had a brother willing to help in any way he could.

Rafe also knew too many crimes went unsolved.

"Whoever did it isn't going to get away with it," he said. "I'm not going to let them." He fixed his gaze on Cassie. "If you're up to answering some questions, maybe we can work together, help the police figure things out."

She took a deep breath, sat up a little straighter. It was good to have something to do, he knew.

"Yes, that's a good idea." She turned to Olivia. "Maybe you could help us. You know a lot of the locals. Most of the tourists who come to town are in and out of the Pelican at one time or another. You could keep an eye out, see if any of them looks or acts suspicious."

Olivia started nodding. "Yes, I can do that."

"He was killed at the harbor," Rafe said. "Do you know why he would have been down at the *Scorpion* last night?"

Cassie shook her head. "It doesn't make sense. He was supposed to be playing poker with Ben Friedman and a bunch of the regulars. That's where he was headed when he left the house."

"What time was that?" Rafe asked.

"Seven o'clock. *Scorpion* only had a half-day charter, so he was back in town early."

"That's right," Rafe said.

"The guys always have pizza and beer on poker night. So he left before supper." She blinked hard, dabbed at her eyes. "Scotty kissed me good-bye at the door and took off walking. God, Rafe, it hurts so much to know I . . . I'll never see him again."

She started crying and Olivia reached over and hugged her. "We won't let whoever killed him get away with it," she said determinedly, bringing Rafe's attention back to her. "We'll make sure the police catch the guy who did it."

"I need to talk to Ben," Rafe said. "Maybe Scotty never showed up. Or if he did, maybe Ben knows why he went back to the *Scorpion.*" Rafe leaned down and brushed a brotherly kiss on Cassie's cheek. "I'll let you know what I find out. Take care of yourself, okay?"

She nodded.

Turning, Rafe started for the door. He was out of the house, striding down the walk toward the Expedition, when he felt a hand on his arm. When he turned, Olivia stood on the sidewalk. He hadn't heard her approach.

"Would you mind if I went with you?"

"You want to go with me to see Ben Friedman?"

"That's right."

Would he mind? *Hell no.* He'd been looking for an excuse to talk to her for weeks, though this was a rotten way for it to happen. "Did you walk over?"

She nodded.

"Get in. I'll drop you off when we're done."

Rafe almost couldn't believe it when he pulled open the door and Olivia Chandler climbed into his SUV.

It took the death of someone she cared about for Olivia to let down her guard enough to follow Rafe Brodie out of the house. For six months she'd been avoiding him.

Now Scott Ferris was dead and she couldn't get Cassie's haunted features out of her head. Cassie wanted Scotty's killer caught. So did Liv. Wanted it bad enough to risk helping Rafe Brodie make certain it happened.

Why she believed he could handle the job, she wasn't sure. Maybe it was the hard glint in his eyes when he'd promised Cassie that whoever had done it wasn't going to get away with it. Maybe it was just that everything about Rafe Brodie said he was an extremely capable man.

"I don't think the police have talked to Ben yet," she said as he drove his SUV toward the Seaside Motel. "Lois told me

Cassie got completely hysterical when Chief Rosen told her Scott was dead. Her mother drove over and gave her a Valium. The chief promised to come back later, after she was a little more in control, but he hasn't been back yet."

"I'd like to know what the medical examiner found out," Rafe said. "She should be able to give us the official cause of death, maybe come up with a more exact idea of the murder weapon."

"She?"

"Dr. Karen Ward. Works at the clinic. Town this size isn't big enough for a full-time forensic examiner."

"That isn't exactly good news. Someone who only works part-time could miss something important."

"She's a good doctor, but you're right. It's not exactly like having some hot-shot CSI on the case like you see on TV."

"Speaking of forensics, maybe Scotty left something on the boat. Have you been back aboard yet?"

"No. It's part of the crime scene. As soon as it's cleared, I'm supposed to take a look, see if anything's missing."

Olivia leaned back as he turned the SUV at the corner and drove up in front of the Seaside Motel.

"In the meantime, we'll see what Ben has to say." Pulling into the parking lot of the two-story clapboard structure, he turned off the engine and Olivia climbed out of the vehicle. The motel was inexpensive but clean, with two dozen sparsely furnished rooms, six upstairs, six down.

Rafe held open the motel office door, and Liv preceded him inside and walked up to the counter. When Rafe leaned over and rang the service bell, his big, hard body brushed hers, and her breath caught. Just standing next to him was making her heart beat a little too fast.

Olivia couldn't remember a man affecting her the way Rafe did. She'd noticed him the first time he'd walked into the café and every time since. She'd told herself it was just that he was such a handsome man and she hadn't had sex in years. It was just that he was tall and good-looking, with a lean-muscled body that filled out his long-sleeved thermals in exactly the right places. Any normal, red-blooded female would be attracted to a man as sexy as Rafe.

Whatever the reason, she needed to keep her guard up.

Then again, Rafe Brodie was the most eligible bachelor in town. Half the women in Valdez were in love with him. Since he had never shown any real interest in her, maybe she was worrying for nothing.

She latched on to the thought as Ben walked out of the back and spotted them on the opposite side of the counter. He was a short man, a little rotund, with a receding hairline and a cheerful disposition. She could tell by the grim set of his features that Ben had heard about Scotty.

"I guess you know," Rafe said, coming to the same conclusion.

"It's all over town. Goddamn the bastards. I can't believe he's dead."

"Did you see him last night? Did he show up for the poker game?"

"He was here. Scotty rarely misses."

"Have you talked to the police?"

"Not yet. I'm surprised no one's come round asking questions."

"Rosen wasn't able to question Cassie. She was too upset. The chief doesn't know Scottie was here last night before he was killed. You know why he went back to the boat instead of going home?"

Ben shook his head. "No idea. We were all feeling real good with the tourist season kicking in and business picking up. We decided to raise the limit a little, and Scotty started winning. The kid was on a roll, cleaned us all out. When he got up to leave,

Marty ragged him about staying, thought he should give the guys a chance to win back some of their money. But Scott wanted to get home. Said something about buying Cassie a real nice wedding gift with his winnings."

Ben shook his head. "Damn shame is what it is. Goddamn shame, nice boy like that."

Olivia looked up at Rafe. Scott had left with more money in his pocket than he usually carried. Maybe that was the reason he'd been mugged. But how would anyone except the other players have known?

Rafe asked the question she was thinking. "Besides you and Scott, who else was in the game?"

"Like I said, Marty Grossman was a player. Sam King and Chip Reed were the other two guys."

"Reed used to date Cassie," Rafe said. "They were pretty hot and heavy at one time. Then she met Scotty and Chip was out the door. How did Reed and Scotty get along? Any animosity?"

Ben shrugged his rounded shoulders. "Chip used to goad Scotty once in a while. Joked about him being henpecked. Told him to grow a pair and keep Cassie in line. Stuff like that. But you know Scott. Rolled off him like water off a duck's back. Scotty liked everyone and everyone liked him."

"Not everyone," Olivia said darkly, drawing Rafe's sharp gaze back to her.

When she said nothing more, he returned his attention to Ben. "Soon as the police find out Scott was here last night, they'll want to talk to you and the other players."

Ben nodded. "I'll call and let them know. If there's anything I can do to help catch that murdering bastard, believe me I will." He let out a weary sigh. "Thing like this . . . makes me wish Alaska had the death penalty."

A muscle tightened in Rafe's jaw. "I know what you mean."

"What time did Scotty leave?" Liv asked.

"Guess it was a little after midnight."

"Coroner puts time of death between eleven and two," Rafe said. "If Scotty left around midnight, he must have been killed sometime not long after. What time did the rest of the players leave?"

"Game broke up maybe ten, fifteen minutes after Scotty took off. Hell, he had all our money."

"Are you sure he didn't say anything about going back to the boat?" Liv asked. "Mention some errand he needed to run or something?"

"Not that I recall."

Rafe flicked a glance in her direction. "Anything else?" he asked her.

Liv shook her head.

"Thanks, Ben," Rafe said. "If you think of anything that might help, you know where to find me."

"You got it."

Olivia turned and started for the door, and Rafe fell in behind her.

"Rafe?" Ben called after him. Rafe stopped and turned. "You won't let this drop, will you? You'll keep after them till they find the guy who did it."

Rafe's jaw turned iron hard. "I won't stop until the sonofabitch is arrested — or he's dead."

CHAPTER FOUR

Once they were back in the Expedition, Rafe pulled out his cell and phoned the police department. The SUV was equipped with hands-free, so Olivia could hear the conversation.

Rafe asked for Chief Rosen, but Rosen wasn't in. "How about Rusty Donovan?" Donovan was one of the officers he'd seen at the dock. His dad, Jim Donovan, was a dedicated fisherman. Rafe knew both of them fairly well.

After a few moments, Rusty answered. "Donovan."

"Rusty, this is Rafe Brodie."

"Hey, Rafe. Sorry about your friend. I met him a couple of times when I was helping Dad work on his boat. Seemed like a real nice fella."

Rusty was only a few years older than Scott. "He was a good kid. You guys got anything new to report?"

"We're waiting for the autopsy. The body was taken to Anchorage. We won't have the official results until at least tomorrow."

"What about the crime scene? Can I go back aboard my boat?"

"You should have gotten a call. You can go ahead. They dusted for prints, but Scott worked aboard, so his fingerprints are bound to be all over. They probably found yours, too. Could turn up someone you may have had on a charter. They're running what they've got through AFIS right now."

"What about security cameras? Have they had a chance to look at those yet?"

"Not yet."

"I'd take it as a personal favor, Rusty, if you'd keep me posted on the case."

"I can do that. Sure."

"Give my best to your dad."

"Will do."

Rafe hung up the phone, reached down and started the engine.

"AFIS? That's the way they match up fingerprints, right?"

He nodded as he put the SUV in gear, pulled out of the lot, and started back toward the restaurant. "Automatic Fingerprint Identification System." When her eyebrows went up, he felt the pull of a smile. "My brother was a homicide detective. He loved to spout off stuff like that."

"Does he live around here?"

"Used to live in Anchorage. Recently got married and moved to Seattle. But he'll help us if we need him."

Olivia glanced away. Instead of being impressed, she looked as if that wasn't the best news she could have been given. Made him wonder if the mystery of Olivia Chandler went deeper than he'd thought.

"So what do we do next?" she asked as he drove back to the Pelican.

"I want to talk to Marty Grossman, Sam King, and Chip Reed, and I want to go aboard *Scorpion,* see if anything's missing."

"When you talk to the men, I'd like to go with you. But I've got to go back to work for a while. I don't want to leave Nell alone too long during the lunch hour."

"All right. I'll go down to the boat and check things out, then come back and get you."

"If you need addresses for those guys, I can get them off my laptop."

He angled the Ford into a slot in front of the café. "Grossman works for Orca Charters. Their boat's docked not far from *Scorpion.* I know where to find him. And I know where to find King, but not Reed."

"I'll take care of it. I'll see you when you

get back."

He nodded.

"And Rafe . . . thanks for letting me help on this. It's really important to me."

"Why? Because Cassie's your friend? Or is it more than that?"

She glanced away, giving him his answer. He'd noticed her reaction earlier and wondered if her motivation came from more than just wanting justice for a friend.

"Scotty didn't deserve to die," she said. "It isn't right for his killer to get away with it."

"You don't have much faith in the police."

"If they catch him, great. In the meantime, I'm going to do everything possible to make sure he's found."

Unease rolled through him. Searching for a killer could be dangerous. Still, odds were the police would catch the killer fairly soon. If not and things got dicey, he'd keep Olivia out of it.

"I'll be back in a couple of hours," he said. "Get me that address."

Olivia nodded, jumped down from the SUV, and closed the door.

Rafe left the Expedition parked in front of the Pelican and crossed the street to the boat harbor. As he walked along the dock, headed for the slip where *Sea Scorpion* was moored, he thought of Scotty and a chill slid down his spine.

Scott had been walking this same path last night. Why hadn't he heard his attacker come up behind him? Why hadn't he realized he was being followed? Or was the killer waiting up ahead, hiding somewhere in the shadows?

The crime scene tape was gone when he reached the boat. Rafe climbed aboard, pausing on deck for a moment to take a look around. At first glance, nothing seemed out of place. Nothing had changed since he had returned the boat to the dock yesterday noon.

He headed below. Unlike his other two boats, *Sea Devil* and *Sea Dragon,* which were set up strictly for fishing, *Sea Scorpion* had a galley with a sink, refrigerator, and stove; a dining area with enough seating for customers to get inside out of the weather; a larger head with a shower; and a cabin with a queen-size bed. *Scorpion* was equipped with state-of-the-art electronics and even a thirteen-inch color TV.

The Mac was his personal boat, and though he used it mostly for charter fishing, he also used it for wildlife and glacier cruises. Toward the end of summer, he booked a couple of weeks for his own personal use and took off for parts unknown, used it off and on much of the year.

He made a cursory examination of the pilothouse, let his gaze wander over the equipment, but the minute he had stepped on deck, he'd known the boat hadn't been boarded since he had left it yesterday afternoon.

Scotty Ferris never made it onto the *Scorpion* last night. What Rafe couldn't figure was why the hell the kid was even on the dock.

Olivia worked through lunch, grateful the restaurant was crowded and noisy. Being busy helped keep her mind off Scotty, Cassie, and particularly Rafe Brodie.

Scotty, a sweet boy who would never hurt a soul, had been brutally murdered. The young woman who loved him wanted his killer arrested and thrown in jail — or worse. Olivia had her own personal reasons for wanting justice for Scott.

It was hard to believe only three years had passed since she'd witnessed a brutal murder in an apartment in New York City. Just a case of wrong place, wrong time. She'd been in the bathroom that night when the first shot rang out. Heart pounding, certain it was a robbery, she had opened the door a crack, enough to see a pistol being emptied into her ex-husband's already lifeless body.

Terrified she would also be killed, she had stayed hidden until the murderer was gone, finally had come out and called the police.

She'd told them exactly who had murdered Stephen Rothman and why, but instead of arresting the killer, the entire incident had been covered up. High-powered people were involved, people willing to silence a witness who knew too much — no matter what it took.

Instead of being the accuser, Olivia had become the main suspect. Instead of arresting the murderer, the authorities had come after her.

Once she was out on bail, she'd escaped. With the help of an expensive attorney, time, and careful planning, she'd gotten out of Manhattan. It had taken three long years to erase her trail completely, three years of moving from place to place, changing her looks and her identity, three years to immerse herself in a new life as Olivia Chandler in a remote part of the world that she was coming to love.

She hadn't been able to find justice for

Stephen, whose murder had officially never been solved.

She was Olivia Chandler now, and there was no way to go back, no way to set things right. But if she could help the police catch Scotty's killer, maybe it would erase some of the guilt she'd felt since the day she had packed her most essential belongings, boarded a train out of Grand Central Station, and left Manhattan for good.

The crash of shattering glass and Katie's muffled curse ended Liv's unwanted musings. The lunch crowd was thinning. The meaty aroma of burgers on the grill had been eclipsed by the scent of fresh-brewed coffee. Liv was refilling a patron's mug when Rafe walked back through the door.

For an instant, she lost her concentration and almost overfilled the cup. Dear God, with his thick, dark hair and strong jaw, the man was handsome. She gave the customer an apologetic smile. "Sorry."

Big and rugged. Strong and capable. When it came to virile males, there wasn't a man in New York who could compare to Rafe Brodie.

Though she had often admired his height and the solid build beneath his heavy winter coat, Liv had never allowed herself to imagine him naked. But since she'd arrived last fall, she had come to believe that whatever was underneath those warm clothes was just as attractive as the rest of him.

"You ready?" he asked as he walked toward her, the perfect picture of tall masculinity and temptation.

She swallowed, set the coffeepot back on the burner, managed to force out the word "Almost," and hoped it didn't sound as breathless as she suddenly felt.

It was ridiculous. She was one of the most grounded women she knew. Had learned to be in order to survive. She was strong and capable, not the type of woman who went giddy in the presence of a hot guy.

Dammit, her reaction to Rafe was way out of proportion and the very reason she had avoided him for so long. She had rarely felt this kind of attraction to a man, and never a pull this fierce. She wished there were a way to solve Scotty's murder on her own, but she was still a newcomer in town, and more importantly, she needed to keep a low profile.

There was always a chance, no matter how remote, that someone from her past might track her up here to Valdez.

"I need to check on Khan first. I'll be right back." Leaving Rafe at the counter, she removed her apron and made her way toward the rear of the café. Grabbing a couple of dog treats out of the bag next to the back door, she walked out on the porch above the backyard.

Khan, her big, black-and-brown German shepherd, trotted up to greet her, ears forward, hoping for a treat. When he sat down politely in front of her as he had been trained to do, she held up an organic dog biscuit. Though she put it right in front of his nose, he didn't try to take it.

"Okay," she said, giving him permission, then handed him the treat. "Good boy."

Khan was a professionally trained guard dog. She had paid a small fortune to buy him from a training facility in Texas and immediately fallen in love with him.

But there were rules to owning a dog like Khan. Maintaining discipline at all times was extremely important, and feeding him a careful diet, in his case Purina Dog Chow supplemented with vitamins, and foods like rice, meat, and eggs.

At the sound of the back door opening, Khan's head turned, his ears went sharp, and a low growl came from his throat. Liv felt an instant of alarm before she turned to see it was only Rafe Brodie standing on the porch.

The ruff at the back of Khan's neck was up.

"Hold," Liv said, though the dog wouldn't attack unless she gave the command. Still, Rafe was smart enough not to make any hostile moves. "Friend," she said, and Khan sat back down. His attention returned to her, awaiting her next command.

"This is Khan," Liv said to Rafe. "Come and meet him."

Rafe walked toward her, stopped right beside her. "Beautiful dog."

"Yes, he is."

"I've seen the two of you jogging in the mornings. I could tell he's well trained." He held out a hand, let the dog sniff, get familiar with his scent, then smoothed his hand over the dog's thick coat.

Rafe's gaze returned to her. "Woman couldn't have much better protection than a dog like that."

Except for the Glock 18 she kept upstairs next to her bed, and the million-volt stun gun she carried when she went jogging.

"Khan would protect me with his life."

Rafe's mouth edged up. "I'll remember that should I ever decide to turn caveman and carry you off over my shoulder."

Heat flashed through her and her stomach muscles clenched at the image. Dear God,

Rafe Brodie carrying her off over a powerful shoulder, doing things to her she refused to imagine. "Have you considered it?"

"Off and on," he said, a faint smile tugging at his lips and no way for her to tell if he was kidding.

"We'd better get going," she said, opting for a quick change of subject, and turned back to Khan. "Go play. I'll take you for a walk when I get back."

The dog barked as if he understood, which he did. Though he had his own large, private yard behind the café, Liv took him for a walk every morning no matter the weather, and whenever she could break away. Khan looked forward to it and so did she.

Moving past Rafe, she went back inside, darted into the office, and grabbed her black wool pea coat off the rack beside the door.

"I'll be back in time to help you get things ready for the dinner crowd," she said to Nell as she walked past.

"You just do what needs to be done," Nell said, casting a glance from her to Rafe.

Wondering if she'd caught a hopeful gleam in Nell's pale blue eyes, Liv headed for the door.

CHAPTER FIVE

A light mist was falling as Rafe walked Olivia down the street.

"So where are we with the investigation?" she asked. "Have the police come up with anything?"

"Not since I saw you last. Rusty's promised to call if something new turns up. I haven't heard from him since our last conversation."

"Did you find anything missing on the boat?"

"Not a damn thing. Scotty never made it aboard. Everything was exactly the way I left it yesterday afternoon. Whoever did it must have followed him, taken him out right there on the dock."

"If the guy was a robber, you'd think he'd at least have gone aboard and taken a look around, seen if he could find something valuable."

"It was locked."

"Wouldn't Scotty have a key?"

"He had one. His keys were missing just like his wallet, but no one went aboard." And the *why not* was something he'd thought about himself.

"Interesting. So who are we talking to first?"

"The *Orca* wasn't in its slip. Probably a full-day charter. Grossman's part of the crew, which means we won't be able to talk to him until the boat gets back."

"What about King and Reed?"

"Sam'll be at work this time of day. He's a packer over at the Easy Breezy fish-processing plant."

Olivia looked up at him and grinned, and that same shot of awareness hit him. " 'You reel 'em, we seal 'em,' " she said.

Rafe laughed. "That's their motto, all right. We do a lot of work with those guys."

"Sometimes tourists bring in some of the fish they've caught that Easy Breezy has flash-frozen for them. They ask us to cook it, then rave about how good it is. But then, what fisherman doesn't brag about his catch?"

"True enough. But the company does a good job, ships the fish all the way home for the customer. In those commercial-grade bags, it'll stay fresh for more than a year."

She smiled. "You sound like a walking commercial."

He chuckled. "Fishing's my business."

Olivia's smile slowly faded. "You'll be fishing most days from now on. Who are you going to hire to replace Scotty?"

A grim memory of the kid lying dead on the wooden dock next to the *Scorpion* flashed in his head. "I don't know. Scotty was great with the customers, efficient, trustworthy, reliable. Finding someone won't be easy." Though he was thinking he might already have the problem solved. He'd give it a little more thought, then move forward.

It didn't take long to reach the single-story wooden building with the EASY BREEZY FISH PACKING sign on top. With its false front, double doors, shingled porch, and wooden boardwalk, it looked like something out of an old Western movie.

Rafe pushed open one of the doors and they walked inside. A big bald Russian named Ivan Petrov came out of the back, a white apron tied around his substantial girth. There were lots of Russians up here since they'd once claimed the territory that was now Alaska, and Russia was just across the Bering Strait.

"Hey, Rafe," Ivan said. "Sorry to hear about Scotty. Sam told me he was killed last night."

"Murdered," Rafe corrected, since there was a helluva lot of difference between dying and having your life stolen from you. He flicked a glance at the woman beside him. "Ivan Petrov, this is Olivia Chandler. She's the new owner of the Pelican." Here *new* could be anything from a week to five years.

The Russian nodded. "I've seen you around. Nice to meet you."

"You too, Ivan."

"I need to talk to Sam," Rafe said. "If you can spare him for a couple of minutes."

"Sure. No problem. I'll go get him." Ivan sauntered toward a door leading to the back of the building and disappeared. A few minutes later, Sam King walked up behind the service counter.

Half Alaska Native, half Russian, Sam was only a couple of inches shorter than Rafe, with thick arms and a muscular body. At twenty-five, with his gleaming black hair and handsome face, he was a favorite of the ladies, pretty much had his pick during tourist season.

Spotting Olivia, he removed the

bloodstained white apron he wore, a sign of the job he did in the fish-packing operation.

The first words out of his mouth were, "Have they caught the bastard yet?"

"Not the last time I called the station, which was about half an hour ago." Rafe tipped his head toward the slender woman in black standing beside him. "Sam, this is Olivia Chandler. She owns the Pelican Café."

"Hi, Sam," she said. "We've spoken a couple of times in the restaurant."

Sam, being the ladies' man he was, let his gaze travel over Olivia in a far-from-subtle appraisal that made Rafe's jaw go tight.

"I remember." His eyes dropped to those long dancer's legs. "Hard for a guy to miss. Or maybe I should say you just make it har—"

"Sam —" Rafe warned, cutting off the rest of the sexual innuendo the kid was about to deliver.

Olivia said nothing, but Rafe didn't miss the faint thinning of those amazing X-rated lips. Apparently Rafe wasn't the only guy who got the cold treatment from Liv Chandler. He almost smiled.

"So what's going on with the case?" Sam asked.

"From what I know, Chief Rosen has officers out knocking on doors all over the area. They're checking the RV parks, the harbor, and the roads leading out of town. Ben Friedman called the cops and told them Scott was at the poker game last night."

"He was there. When he left, I thought he was going home. What was he doing at the harbor?"

"I was hoping maybe you'd know. You were one of the last people to see him alive."

Sam blanched, his face going pale beneath his dark skin.

"Scotty didn't say anything about going back to the boat?" Olivia asked.

"No, never mentioned it."

"The police haven't talked to you yet?" she asked.

"Actually, Lieutenant Scarborough was here about an hour ago. He asked me about the poker game. I told him we wound things up about midnight."

"Did the lieutenant ask where you were between midnight and two?" Olivia asked. "That's when Scotty's body was found."

Sam's black eyes darted away then sharpened on her face. "I went home and went to bed. That's what I told Scarborough."

"Did anyone see you there?" she pressed. "Can anyone verify your alibi?"

Sam's jaw subtly tightened. "Why would I need an alibi? I was home in bed when he was killed. You aren't trying to pin this on me?"

"Olivia didn't say that," Rafe soothed. "We're just doing a little digging, seeing what we might turn up. If you were home, then you were home."

Sam tossed a hard glance at Olivia. "That's right."

"If you think of anything that might help us catch this guy," Rafe said, "I'd really appreciate a call, Sam."

"Hey, no problem." Sam turned to Olivia. "You know, you really need to work on your pancakes. They're too thin. A man wants his cakes nice and thick."

One of Olivia's dark eyebrows arched up. "I'll look into it," she said dryly, clearly not meaning it.

Since Rafe liked her pancakes just the way they were, he bit back a smile, walked to the door and pulled it open. "Time to go," he said, figuring he was doing Sam a favor getting her out of there.

Olivia cast the kid a final disapproving glance and sailed past Rafe out the door.

As soon as Liv was out on the walkway, she flashed Rafe a look. "That guy is flat-out lying. Surely you could see that. You must have noticed the way he cut his eyes —"

"I noticed. You're right. Sam didn't go home after the poker game. Doesn't mean he killed Scotty."

Somewhat mollified, she reined herself in, glad Rafe was as perceptive as she had hoped.

"So if King didn't kill Scotty, why was he lying?"

"I don't know, but we're going to find out. In the meantime, let's talk to Chip Reed."

She dug her smartphone out of her pocket, pulled up the address and the other information she had found and dumped into a file she'd labeled *Scotty*.

"Chip lives in an apartment on Jago Street."

"Let's drive. It'll be faster."

They walked back to the restaurant, climbed into Rafe's SUV, and he started the engine. Once they reached the apartment on Jago, which turned out to be unit A of a duplex, she let him guide her to the door.

No one answered the bell. "Chip works at C & J Trucking," she said. "It's out on Richardson Highway."

Rafe's gold-flecked eyes swung to her face and she felt a little hitch in her chest. "I didn't think you knew Chip," he said.

"I don't. Reed's got a Facebook page. Posts all kinds of selfies. From the looks of it, he's got an ego the size of Mount McKinley."

Rafe chuckled. "Maybe that's the reason Cassie dumped him."

"If it is, I don't blame her."

Rafe turned the big Ford onto the highway.

"Maybe we should call ahead," Liv said, "see if he's there. Save us a trip."

"I'd rather just drop in. If Reed isn't around, we'll catch him tonight after work."

Alarm bells went off in her head. Sweet God, she hadn't imagined spending the evening with Rafe. Her gaze shot in his direction. With all that male virility wrapped up in such a gorgeous package, the man could make big money in the advertising business.

He caught her watching him, jarring her out of her Rafe-imposed coma. "What is it? You have to work?"

"Sorry, just thinking." But the truth was, she hadn't thought past this afternoon. She and Nell alternated evening shifts. She would be available if she wanted to go with him.

Which she did.

And she didn't.

She was tempted to lie. But her entire life was a lie. She didn't want to add to the list unless she had to. "I don't have to work. Nell and I alternate evening shifts. I just . . . I guess in the back of my mind, I was hoping the police would catch the killer and we would be done with all this."

"It may happen soon. Rusty says they've been knocking on doors all over town. Lots of tourists around. That seems to be where Chief Rosen is focusing the investigation."

"If it's someone from out of town, he probably took Scotty's money and hit the road."

"The troopers will be watching the highways, looking for anything out of the ordinary. They might get lucky, pull someone over on a traffic stop, find the murder weapon or something that connects to the murder. It happens."

"Not that often."

"No. Which is why, at the moment, I'm doing everything I can to help."

So was she. It would be easier if she wasn't trying to do it while sitting next to Rafe Brodie. "And if the police don't find him?"

"If they don't — I will," Rafe said, and the way his jaw settled into a hard, determined line, Olivia believed him.

■ ■ ■ ■

When they arrived at C & J Trucking, they discovered Chip Reed had left that morning on a two-day run through Anchorage up to Fairbanks. Liv hoped if Reed had killed Scotty, he wouldn't just keep driving.

With the interview postponed, Rafe took her back to the restaurant, promising to return and pick her up for their conversation that evening with Marty Grossman.

Grossman was the big loser at the poker game. Maybe he wanted his money back. Maybe he was just mad at Scotty for beating him so badly. Mad enough, maybe, to kill him.

As Olivia headed into the restaurant, she didn't tell Rafe she wouldn't be downstairs working when he got back, that she would be upstairs in her apartment. She didn't want Rafe and all his masculinity invading her personal space. And she didn't want to give him any more insight into her life than he had already.

They were only working together for a very brief time. Surely the police would pick up a vagrant desperate for drug money or some runaway teenage psychopath who just wanted to find out what it felt like to murder someone. Once the killer was in custody, things could go back the way they were. Rafe would come into the restaurant to eat, and Liv would ignore him.

Which she hoped wouldn't goad him into turning caveman and carrying her off over his shoulder.

Her stomach muscles contracted at the thought. Damn, this wasn't good.

Once everything was set for supper, she turned the restaurant over to Nell and headed upstairs. Her apartment was completely different from the café's ocean theme and cozy atmosphere.

This was her personal space, the interior gutted when she'd bought the building, newly remodeled and modernized, though the breathtaking view over Prince William Sound couldn't possibly be improved upon.

The place was all clean lines, white walls, and dark wood, a compact, state-of-the-art kitchen with stainless appliances, a powder room off the entry, guest bedroom with bath, and a spare room she used as an office and gym. The master suite had a king-size bed and dark furniture, a bathroom with black granite countertops, a separate shower and tub. The fluffy white designer towels she had ordered online from Neiman Marcus were to die for.

She might have had to give up her expensive Manhattan lifestyle, but during the years she'd been working, she had saved plenty of money. She could afford to bring some of the better parts of her old life all the way up here.

There were drawbacks, of course. Since the apartment hinted at a different side of herself from the one she showed the people in the restaurant, few were invited upstairs. She told those few the same story. Her husband, a wealthy older man, had died and left her a large inheritance. She had decided to change her life, bought the café, and moved to Valdez.

It was total fiction, of course, but it seemed to be accepted. There were hundreds of reasons people came to Alaska, so no one pressed for more information. Privacy was respected here. It was one of the reasons she liked it so much.

She checked her wristwatch. The days were already eighteen hours long, which meant the sun wouldn't be setting till after eleven p.m.

Rafe would be arriving at eight. Olivia went downstairs to check on Khan, played with him for a while, practiced commands, then went back up and did some work on the café ledgers.

As she sat in front of her laptop, she tried not to think of Scotty or Cassie.

But it was a difficult thing to do.

CHAPTER SIX

It was seven forty-five p.m. when Rafe's cell phone rang. He had just angled the Expedition into a parking space in front of the Pelican Café and turned off the engine. Pulling the phone out of his pocket, he pressed it against his ear. "Brodie."

"Chief Rosen, here. I know how close you were to Scott, Rafe. I thought I'd touch base, bring you up to speed on the investigation."

"Appreciate it, Chief."

"I gather you know Ferris went to a poker game last night."

"Cassie told me."

"So far our people have talked to three of the men at the card game. None of them know why Ferris went down to the dock after he left the motel. All of them have explanations for their whereabouts at the time of the murder. Sam King and Ben Friedman are bachelors. They say they were

73

home by themselves. Can't be verified, but at this point, no reason not to believe them. They'll stay on our suspect list, though, until this is over."

"What about Grossman?"

"Home with his wife. She verified he came right home after the game. We haven't talked to Reed. According to his boss, he's out of town on a job. Won't be back for a couple of days, but to tell you the truth, I don't think any of Scotty's friends were involved."

Neither did Rafe, even though he was pretty sure Sam King wasn't telling the truth. Whatever King was up to, it probably involved a woman, not murdering Scotty. Eventually, he'd run the story down.

"So you're thinking it's someone passing through," Rafe said.

"That's right. We posted a man at the ferry terminal. Checked the passenger list for those who were boarding. A number of locals with round-trip tickets. If anyone doesn't return when he's supposed to, we'll have his name. Still early in the season, so there weren't many folks traveling one way. Lieutenant Scarborough questioned them. Didn't turn up anything suspicious."

"Anyone down at the harbor see anything last night?"

"A guy staying on a transient boat in a slip in another area says he heard something a little after one o'clock. Got up and took a look, saw a man walking away from the area."

Rafe's interest sharpened. "Did he give you a description?"

"Tall, thick-shouldered, wearing a hooded sweatshirt, boots, and gloves. White guy, he thinks, but it was raining and by then it was dark. He's definitely a person of interest, though."

"What about the security cameras? Did the guy show up there?"

"None of them were aimed in exactly the right direction. Got a shadowy glimpse of someone matching our suspect's description walking away from the crime scene. Timing's about right. One thirty-three a.m. Couldn't see the face, though."

"What about boats leaving the area after the murder?"

"We're talking to as many people as we can. Far as we know, no private boats left the harbor till this morning. The charters have all gone out, but they'll be back. I take it you didn't have a group this morning."

"No. Not till tomorrow. What about the roads? Guy could have hitched out of town."

"Troopers have been covering the

highways since last night. We're doing every-thing we can, Rafe, I promise you."

Rafe scrubbed a hand over his face. "Anything else?"

"We've put a BOLO out on the guy who was spotted at the harbor. But we don't have enough of a description for a sketch. As I said, troopers are keeping an eye out, but there isn't anything they can do here that isn't already being done."

Rafe didn't argue. For the most part, he figured the chief was right. At least they had a lead. Someone had been seen in the area around the time of the murder. Law enforcement would be watching for him.

Didn't mean Rafe intended to stop search-ing for the bastard himself.

"We should have the autopsy report back tomorrow or the next day," the chief continued. "If anything new turns up, I'll let you know."

"Thanks, Chief. I appreciate everything you're doing."

"Just doing my job." Rosen hung up the phone.

Rafe had planned to pick Olivia up and go talk to Grossman. Was losing at poker, even if it was more than a normal amount, enough motivation for murder? Probably not, but he'd wanted to check it out.

Now he knew Marty had been home with his wife, a solid alibi that at least for the moment eliminated him as a suspect.

He glanced toward the café. Olivia would be waiting. She was as determined to find Scotty's killer as Rafe was. His conscience warned him he had to tell her there was no need to interview Grossman tonight. If he did, she wouldn't spend time with him. She would dodge him the way she'd been doing for weeks.

With a sigh of resignation, he cracked open the door and had started to get out of the SUV when the passenger door flew open and Olivia climbed into the vehicle.

She buckled her seat belt and turned toward him. "I'm ready. Let's go."

Rafe's gaze ran over her slender curves, disguised completely in black, returned to those plump, dark red lips. He imagined those full lips parting under his, then burning against his skin as her mouth trailed hotly down his body.

His groin tightened. Until today, she'd avoided him. But today wasn't over.

His conscience be damned. Rafe started the engine.

Turning the key in the lock, Trent Doyle opened the door and stepped inside the rented house. In front of him, two men stood waiting, grim-faced, exactly where he'd told them to be.

"I hear you ran into a little trouble last night," he said evenly, pulling off the expensive lambskin gloves he was wearing, tossing them down on a table in the entry. He shrugged out of his raincoat, opened the closet, very carefully hung up the coat and closed the door.

The first man cleared his throat. "I know it wasn't part of the plan, but it couldn't be helped." Lee Heng was Asian-American, five-ten, slight, muscular build, with buzz-cut black hair combed straight up. "We did what we had to."

"That's true," the second man said. Mikal Nadir was bright, from a wealthy family, educated in England. He was tall, lean, and strong, with a narrow face, high cheekbones, and a dark complexion.

"The man must have heard us through the window," Nadir said. "Cain was outside smoking when he spotted him. He had to kill him. One blow, very neat. We were lucky no one was around."

"Where is Cain now?"

"Back at work," Heng said. "He won't be making contact again."

Trent's eyes fixed coldly on the Asian. "He

wasn't supposed to make contact in the first place. Why did he?"

Lee shrugged his lean-muscled shoulders. "It was his night off. He's been working for weeks, staying in that trailer out at the RV park. He said he hadn't heard from anyone lately. He stopped by to check things out, make sure nothing had changed."

"Cain has a job to do. He needs to remember that. So do you. From now on, I expect you all to do exactly what you're told. Nothing more. Nothing less. Is that understood?"

Both Nadir and Heng nodded.

"I asked if you understood."

"Yes, sir," they said in unison.

"Where's the body?" Trent asked.

"Cain dumped it," Lee said. "Made it look like a robbery. We'd seen the guy before. We knew he worked on one of the boats at the harbor, so Cain took him there. It was late. Dark. No one was around."

"You had better hope you're right."

"So what do you want us to do?" Nadir asked. "Do you want us to change locations?"

"No. You stay right where you are. Hide in plain sight. If you made it look like a robbery, they'll be searching for a local or someone on the move, someone heading out of town. You won't be leaving. Not until this is over."

Trent pinned each man with a long, pointed stare. They were expendable and both of them knew it. They wouldn't ignore his orders again.

"You can go," he said. "I'll be in touch." Trent watched the two men walk out of the house and close the door. He heard the motor start on their rented Jeep, then watched through the window as they backed up, turned around, and headed down the road the way they had come.

Trent glanced toward the bedroom. He had a friend waiting. And a very pleasant evening planned — the rest of which did not include disciplining his unruly men.

Sitting next to Rafe, Olivia settled back as the big Ford rolled down the road. To her surprise, the vehicle didn't go far, just turned and went around the block, then turned back onto North Harbor and pulled up in the lot in front of the Fishhook Grill. It was the nicest place in town with a great view out over the harbor.

Liv glanced at Rafe as he turned off the engine. "What are we doing here? Is Grossman meeting us or —"

"No." Rafe got out of the Expedition,

rounded the hood and opened the passenger door. "We don't need to talk to Grossman. The police say he was home with his wife at the time of the murder. His alibi checks out."

He extended one big hand to help her down, and since she still didn't understand what was going on, she reluctantly accepted it, feeling his workingman's calluses as his fingers wrapped warmly around hers.

"So what are we doing?" she asked, ignoring a little shimmer of heat as she stepped down out of the vehicle.

"We're having dinner and I'm bringing you up to speed on the investigation."

"Why do we have to do that here?"

"Because I'm hungry. You have to eat something, too, and I thought it would be a nice change from eating at the Pelican. Plus you won't be jumping up all the time to handle some problem." Before she could argue, he set a hand at her waist and started walking, urging her toward the door.

With no real option short of making a scene, she walked inside the restaurant, into a big open room with lots of wood and glass. It was still full daylight and would be for three more hours, showing off the spectacular view of the boats in the harbor and the mountains heavily capped with snow along the distant shoreline across the water.

"So I guess you talked to the police," Liv said as the waitress, a pretty little blonde, all goggly-eyed over Rafe, seated them at a table in front of a window. Probably the reason they got the best spot in the house.

"Would you like something to drink?" the girl asked, smiling all the while at Rafe.

He turned to Liv. "How about a glass of wine? I've seen you drink an occasional glass. Would you rather have red or white?"

She started to say she didn't want a drink, but it had been a long, exhausting day and a glass of wine sounded fabulous. Occasionally she enjoyed a glass in the Pelican at the end of the day. Obviously Rafe had noticed. She wondered what else he had noticed about her. "Red."

He nodded. "Bring us a bottle of that Wild Horse cab you've got on the menu."

"Sure." The blonde grinned so big a dimple dug into her cheek. "I'll be right back." She sashayed off, giving her hips a little extra wiggle for Rafe's benefit, but he didn't seem to notice.

"You must come here often," Liv said.

"What makes you think so?"

"You didn't have to look at the wine list. And, of course, you knew the little blonde."

He chuckled. "I come in once in a while. I never get tired of looking at the ocean, and the food's pretty good. As for the blonde . . . she's Mo Blanchard's daughter. He captains one of my boats. Even if she wasn't just a few years out of her teens, she'd be off-limits. Add to that, she isn't my type."

Olivia felt an eyebrow creeping up. "What type is that?"

"Smart and sexy. The rest I leave pretty much open."

She found herself smiling. "I heard through the grapevine you were seeing Sally Henderson for a couple of years. I guess that's over."

"Been over for a while. What about you? You seeing anyone?"

She laughed. "I'm too busy for romance — even if I were interested, which I'm not."

His eyes ran over her face. "That's too bad," he said softly.

Her pulse gave a little leap. "Why? Are you looking for a replacement for Sally?"

"Sally's her own person. I'm not looking for someone to replace her. There isn't anyone quite like Sally. Just the way there's no one quite like you."

She didn't know why his answer pleased her, but it did.

The wine arrived. The blonde opened and poured. It wasn't an expensive bottle. There wasn't a wine on the menu that cost as much as the cheapest bottle on a Manhattan wine list, but it tasted just fine to Liv.

The waitress took their orders. Both of them chose prime rib.

"A meat eater," Rafe said, taking a drink of the dark red liquid in his glass. "Good to know."

"Why is that?"

"I might want to cook you supper sometime, and I have a freezer full of game. Some of my friends trade meat for fish. You wouldn't mind eating a nice moose steak, would you?"

She grinned. "Never tried it, but my customers tell me it's very good."

"Then we've got a date. After this is over, I'll make you supper. I'm a lousy cook, but I'm a helluva griller."

She laughed before she could catch herself. "I don't think supper is a good idea."

"Why not?"

"I told you, I'm not interested in dating."

"Yes . . ." he said, those whiskey-brown eyes on her face. "So you did."

She couldn't help a twinge of regret when he didn't pursue the subject.

"You said you were going to fill me in on the case." She took a sip of her wine, surprised at how much she was enjoying herself.

A trickle of guilt slipped through her. A friend had been murdered. It wasn't a day for any sort of enjoyment.

"The police have a lead," Rafe said, putting things back on track as they should be. "Someone on one of the visiting boats at the harbor said he saw a man in the area around the time Scotty was killed. Security camera may have caught a glimpse of him as he was leaving."

"Oh wow, that's great. Do they have a name? At least some kind of description?"

"No name. Not much of a description. Tall, thick-shouldered, wearing a hoodie. He appeared to be on foot. No sign of him since. But they've put out a BOLO. That's cop talk for —"

"Be on the lookout." Liv knew exactly what it meant since she'd had one put out on her. She managed to smile. "We have Dish TV up here, you know? Plus I like action movies."

The corner of Rafe's sexy mouth edged up. "From a man's point of view, that's a definite mark in the plus column."

"Are you keeping score?"

"So far just taking notes."

Liv made no reply. She didn't want Rafe Brodie making notes on her. She didn't want him cooking her supper.

But dear God, she was attracted to those dark good looks and hot brown eyes. She wanted him, she realized, admitting it to herself as she had refused to do before. She'd wanted him for weeks.

She couldn't let it happen.

It was too much of a risk.

Then again, a single night with Rafe Brodie might be worth the risk.

Rafe dropped Olivia back at the Pelican and headed on home. He had a half-day charter in the morning. He'd need to be up early and he hadn't slept much last night.

He parked the SUV in the garage next to the silver F-150 he used as summer approached, good for hauling gear for the boats. There was a shed out back that held his ATV, a UTV, and a pair of snowmobiles. With sixty-four inches of annual rainfall and three hundred inches of snow, they were way more than toys up here.

The house was cold when he walked up the steps into the entry. With the garage below, living room and kitchen on the main floor, he had great views of the mountains.

There was a deck off the living room and one off the master bedroom, which was up half a story from the entry.

He kept the heat turned down when he wasn't home. He walked over and turned it up, then headed upstairs to the bedroom to strip off his clothes. After the day he'd had, he looked forward to a soak in his big Jacuzzi, which sat in the sunroom he'd built at the end of the upstairs hall.

Too bad Olivia wasn't there to share it with him.

He thought of the evening he had spent with her. She was good company. A little too reserved, but he was pretty sure the lady had secrets she was guarding.

Still, she was quick and not afraid to spar with him, unlike a lot of women. And he'd been right about the attraction. Rafe knew women. Knew when one felt the same pull he did. The quickening in the blood. The need that gnawed at your insides and wouldn't let go.

She'd said she wasn't dating. He'd watched her enough to know that was true. But Olivia was a woman and women had needs.

One thing for sure. The lady clearly needed a man.

Rafe was surprised how much he wanted to be that man.

CHAPTER SEVEN

By the time Rafe reached the dock early the next morning, the sun was up and shining over an ocean as smooth as glass. A reflection of the far-off, jagged, snow-covered peaks shimmered on the surface of the water.

Rafe pulled in a lungful of cold, crisp air. It was a beautiful time of year. Perfect, if he didn't have to think of his dead friend, lying murdered, his killer still walking free.

Rafe rubbed a hand over his jaw as he headed down the dock toward *Sea Scorpion*. Now that the fingerprint crew had finished their work, the boat would need to be cleaned all over again, and even more thoroughly than usual. Today was a sightseeing excursion, not a fishing trip.

There would be coffee and donuts for the passengers when they arrived, sandwiches and soft drinks for later. Jaimie Graham, the youngest member of the Great Alaska

Charters crew, would be picking the food up before she came aboard.

Rafe had spoken to Jaimie again last night, told her she could take as much time off as she needed, but she had insisted on working — which Rafe figured was a smarter idea.

Doing something was always better than sitting around grieving, unable to find a way to make the hurting stop. On a sightseeing trip, he didn't really need an extra hand, but he figured Jaimie needed something to do, so he'd find a way to keep her busy.

Today's trip would also include a new member of the crew. Zach Carver, who'd been working on *Sea Dragon,* would be taking Scotty's place as first mate. It was a tough decision since Zach was only twenty-one, but Scott had been the same age when Rafe had brought him aboard.

Zach was just out of college, still trying to decide what he wanted to do with his life. But he was responsible and smart, and always eager to learn. Rafe figured, in time, Zach would be able to handle the first mate's job as well as Scotty had.

As Rafe climbed aboard, he spotted the kid's dark head at work in the galley, wiping off the black fingerprint powder the police had left behind.

Aboard early and hard at work. Rafe took it as a good sign.

"Morning, Captain."

Rafe reached out and they shook hands. "Welcome aboard, Zach."

"Thanks. I'm . . . ahh . . . really sorry about Scotty. I know it gives me a chance to work for you, but —"

"You don't have to say it. We all miss him."

"I hope I can do half as good a job as Scott did."

"You just need a little time. You'll be fine. Today should be easy enough. We're only doing a little sightseeing. Give you a chance to work on your guiding skills."

"You're letting me give the tour?"

"You're taking over Scott's responsibilities. Narrating the trip is one of them. Can you handle it?"

Zach smiled. "I know the landmarks and the history of the area. In the summers, I did tours for another company before I started working for Mo. I can handle it."

He'd seen that information in Zach's résumé. It was one of the reasons he'd decided to give him the position. "Do a good job and you'll be handling the job from now on."

"Cool. I mean . . . thanks."

Rafe felt the pull of a smile. It was good

91

having Zach aboard, someone to help keep his mind off Scotty. For the passengers' sake, the crew needed to stay positive, give their paying customers a good trip to remember.

Jaimie arrived with the food a little before six. She was tall and curvy, though she rarely allowed those curves to show. She kept her auburn hair cut short, wore jeans, rubber-soled boots, and heavy sweaters. She usually wore a wool cap pulled down over her ears, the way she did today.

She set the coffee and donuts out in the galley. Rafe saw the instant she recognized Zach Carver and realized he was taking Scotty's place.

Her mouth thinned. "What are you doing here? Why aren't you on *Sea Dragon*?"

Zach gave her a hard-edged smile. He was several inches taller, with short, black hair and dark eyes. A trace of Alaska Native somewhere gave him an olive complexion. His mother, who'd once competed in the Miss Alaska beauty pageant, gave him the good looks that set him apart from other guys his age.

In a darker, less all-American-boy way, Zach was even more handsome than Scotty, though Jaimie never seemed to notice.

"I work here now," Zach said. "I know

that jacks your jaws, but you'll just have to get used to it."

Jaimie turned to Rafe, her eyebrows climbing. "He's just here temporarily, right? You aren't bringing him aboard as first mate?"

Rafe poured himself a cup of coffee, blew over the top to cool it. "You don't think he can handle it?"

"Scotty's only been dead for a day. It isn't right —"

"I've got a business to run, Jaimie. I need a first mate and Zach has earned this shot. Now I'd suggest you tend to your own business if you want to keep your job."

Jaimie tossed a hard glance at Zach and stomped out onto the deck.

"I figured she'd take it hard," Zach said. Like everyone else, he knew the feelings Jaimie carried for Scott.

"They were friends," Rafe said.

Zach scoffed. "Yeah, they were friends, all right. Only because Scott wasn't interested in Jaimie that way. He was in love with Cassie."

Rafe made no reply because it was true. He felt sorry for Jaimie. But it was time she faced facts and got on with her life.

Rafe finished his coffee and went to work, checking and rechecking equipment, preparing for the passengers who had booked a half-day sightseeing charter: a family of three from Minnesota and a couple from Connecticut.

Ten minutes later, the Carsons arrived, a boy about nine and his parents, all of them a little overweight. They were warmly dressed and clearly excited.

"Welcome aboard," Rafe said, and introductions were made all around.

The woman turned to her husband. "Oh, isn't it just the perfect day, George?"

"It is, Betty, it surely is."

The family was settled inside, drinking coffee and eating donuts, when the couple from Connecticut arrived. Trent Petersen was a little over six feet tall and solidly built, with perfectly groomed medium brown hair and blue eyes.

His wife was average height, wore glasses and very little makeup. Long, straight black hair showed beneath the wool cap pulled down over her head. There was nothing about Anna Petersen that stood out, nothing about either one of them, really, except for the man's blue eyes.

"It's a pleasure to meet you, Captain," Petersen said.

"You, as well. Welcome aboard."

"Thank you. Please call us Trent and Anna." The pair sat down at one of the tables inside the cabin and the couples introduced themselves. George Carson introduced his son, Bobby.

Once everyone was settled, Rafe powered up the big twin Cummins diesels, and Zach made his way onto the dock to toss off the lines. He jumped back aboard, and they eased out of the slip.

They were on their way. Rafe was grateful for the beautiful day that, in some small measure, helped to lighten his dreary mood.

As *Scorpion* roared over the water, Zach could feel the hostility simmering off Jaimie in waves. They were standing out on deck, enjoying the wind and the sun and the sea. Soon the temperature would warm, the passengers would wander outside, and Zach would take over the mic and narrate the sights along the coastline.

He gave Jaimie as much space as he could, but the hostile look she wore was beginning to get on his nerves.

"I can't believe you'd take advantage of Scotty's death the way you did."

He turned to where she'd walked up next to him at the rail. "What the hell are you talking about? Captain Brodie came to me, not the other way around. I didn't take advantage of anything."

"You always wanted to be *Scorpion*'s first mate. Every summer when you came back here to work, you were looking for a way to get Scotty's job."

"You are so full of it I can't believe it." She was nineteen, he knew, and she was pretty, though she did everything in her power to hide it. He had known her since high school. He'd been a couple years older, but there had always been something about her. She was smart and she was fearless.

And even though her wealthy parents spoiled her like crazy, he could tell Jaimie Graham was special. Seemed like she was the only one who didn't know it.

"Look," he said, "I get that you're hurting. I know you had a big thing for Scotty. Everyone knew it, including Scott. But he was in love with Cassie. She was right for him and you never were."

Fury tightened the lines of her pretty face. "What do you know? You don't know anything about it. Scotty had to marry her. She's pregnant!"

He'd heard the rumors. He was fairly certain they were true. It didn't make a damn bit of difference. Scott loved Cassie and he made sure everyone knew it.

"You really think that was it? You don't think he loved her? Because I think he was crazy in love with her. I think you were just determined not to see it."

"You don't know anything!" She tried to turn away, but Zach caught her arm.

"Your parents spoiled you, Jaimie. They gave you everything you ever wanted. You thought you could have Scotty the way you've gotten everything else, but you couldn't. Once you accept the way things really are, you'll be a whole lot better off."

"Leave me alone!"

"Gladly." Turning, he left her standing at the rail, so furious she could hardly breathe. Anger was better than tears, he figured. Still, Zach wished that anger wasn't directed at him.

CHAPTER EIGHT

It was three fifteen Friday afternoon, the lunch crowd pretty much gone, when Liv took off her apron and headed upstairs to her apartment.

In the bedroom, she dragged the clip out of her hair, shook the dark mass free, then used a scrunchie to pull the heavy strands into a ponytail. The ponytail went through the hole at the back of one of her many baseball caps.

She owned dozens; most she'd purchased, some had been given to her, a few she'd had since the night she left New York City. Everything from Superwoman to Daisy Duck.

She rarely wore her hair down. For years, she'd been doing her best not to be noticed. The ball caps had started as a necessity, but over time had become a kind of private rebellion against the austere life she'd been forced to live. She had fun, playful caps;

dark, black-mood caps; a few with swear words across the front.

Today, with Scott and Cassie weighing heavily on her mind, she chose a black cap with EARTH SUCKS printed in sapphire blue. It went with her black running pants with the blue stripe down the side and matched her dismal mood.

She kept her stun gun in the top dresser drawer. Liv took it out, carried it into the entry, grabbed her Windbreaker, and stuck the stun gun into the pocket. Eager to get outside, she locked the apartment door and set the alarm, headed downstairs and out to the backyard.

Khan barked once and ran toward her. She held up his leash, which was *nuff said* in dog speak.

"Wanna go for a run? What do you say, big boy?"

He barked once. *Walk* and r*un* were among the many words he understood. "Okay, let's go."

Liv hooked the leash into his collar and they headed out the gate. Khan fell immediately into position beside her, his dark eyes scanning the area for threats. Liv's hand unconsciously slid into the pocket of her jacket. At the comforting feel of the stun gun, she relaxed and picked up her pace.

Eventually, she figured, she'd feel safe enough to leave the weapon behind, but so far that time hadn't come.

Lengthening her stride, she moved into a steady jogging rhythm, and Khan matched her pace, running effortlessly along beside her. With the day so gloriously sunny, she headed up Meals Avenue. Stretching her legs felt great and she had plenty of time. She jogged north for a while, then cut over to Hazelet and decided to go all the way up to the end of the road.

She was enjoying herself. She loved the tangy smell of the sea, the crisp, chilly breeze against her skin, loved the feel of the warm sun soaking through her clothes. Since the night she had left New York, Valdez was the first place she had allowed herself to call home. She felt safe way up in Alaska, thousands of miles from the trouble she'd left behind, a place where the climate and harsh conditions created a protective barrier from the rest of the world.

She had finally begun to feel safe, and that feeling grew stronger every day. She had even made a few friends, like Nell and Cassie and Katie. Scotty had become a friend, too. Memories of him with Cassie brought a fresh jolt of pain, but Liv pushed it away, determined not to think about it now.

Instead, she continued her easy run, figured she had covered a little over a mile when a tall man rounded the corner a block in front of her. She recognized those wide shoulders and long, purposeful strides.

Rafe Brodie.

He hadn't noticed her behind him. Clearly his mind was somewhere else. She'd been hoping to hear from him all day, but so far he hadn't called. She knew he'd had a charter early that morning, but he would have been back at the harbor before now. She'd been hoping something new would turn up on the case or the autopsy report would come in. Positive news of some kind.

She wondered where he was going, wondered if his destination might have something to do with the investigation. Or maybe Sally Henderson lived somewhere close by and he was actually still seeing her. Or perhaps he was seeing someone else. The thought made her mouth tighten.

When he turned onto Robe River Drive, she decided to follow him. She needed to speak to him, right? It was as good an excuse as any.

The high school was just up ahead. She watched him striding toward the big building that housed the Valdez High School swimming pool. When he reached the entrance to the building, opened the door and disappeared inside, her curiosity hitched up another notch and she followed.

School was out for the weekend and there weren't any students around. Even if one appeared, Khan was great with kids. He was only a threat when she gave the command, which so far she had never needed to do.

Pulling open the door, she and the dog slipped quietly inside and Khan sat down at her feet. She had read somewhere that the pool was seventy-five feet long, with six swim lanes. She glanced around the big open space, searching for Rafe, didn't see him till she heard a splash as he dove into the water.

She should leave, give him his privacy, but some little demon just wouldn't let her.

She watched him swim the first ten laps with a skill that clearly showed years of practice. On the eleventh lap, he started doing butterfly strokes from one end of the pool to the other, his wide shoulders breaking the surface, his lean muscles bunching and stretching.

Something lifted in her stomach. *Time to go,* she told herself, seeing him slow toward the near end of the pool. *Leave before he catches you standing here watching him like a teenager with a crush.*

But it was already too late. That lean, hard body lifted out of the water onto the decking. Water rushed over all those beautiful muscles as he came to his feet and started toward her. Droplets streamed off a chest that was lightly furred and rippling with muscle, down a ridged abdomen, over the sexiest little black Speedo she had ever seen.

She couldn't breathe.

Rafe grabbed a towel off the bench and kept walking, mopped his face and chest, towel-dried his hair, then tied the towel around his hips.

"Keep looking at me that way and I'm going to do something about it," Rafe said.

Liv jerked her gaze to his face, embarrassed that she'd been caught staring. "Sorry. I just . . . Khan and I were getting a little exercise when I saw you turn onto the road. I wanted to talk to you so I . . . umm . . . followed."

She fought to keep her eyes from wandering over that amazing body again. "You're a very good swimmer," she said. "I guess that's how you got so . . . ummm . . . so . . ."

"So . . . what?"

"Ripped," she said, and he laughed.

"I was in the Coast Guard. Rescue Swimmer. It was important to be in top condition. Swimming helps me stay fit and I like the water, so I've kept at it."

"I'd say it's working."

"I don't usually parade around half naked in front of a woman — unless there's a reason."

She felt those dark eyes on her face, felt the heat creeping into her cheeks, and tried not to think of sex, which after seeing him in that tiny swimsuit and going three long years without a man, seemed impossible to do.

When no words came out, Rafe just smiled. "I'll get dressed. We can talk when I come back."

As he walked away, she got another eyeful. Wide back tapering to a tight butt, and those long, sinewy legs. A swimmer's body. Olympic swimmers had bodies like that. Good Lord, the guy was hot.

He returned a few minutes later in jeans and a lightweight V-neck sweater, his damp hair looking almost black. A gym bag hung from one big hand. "We might as well head back."

She just nodded. They left the indoor pool and started back down the hill toward town.

"I was hoping to hear from you," she said as they walked along. She set a good pace and he matched his long strides to hers. "When I saw you, I figured now was a good time to find out what's happening. Have you heard anything?"

"Afraid not. The only thing we can do is wait for the autopsy, see if anything turns up there, or the police come up with another lead."

"What about Sam King? We're both pretty sure he was lying."

"I figured I'd talk to him again tonight. He usually heads for the Catch after work." The Fisherman's Catch Saloon was a local favorite. "Get a couple of beers in him, he might open up."

"But you don't really think he's involved."

"No, but we need to cross him off our suspect list and we can't do that until we know for sure where he was at the time of the murder."

"Chip Reed should be back tomorrow," she said. "He and Scotty weren't exactly best buds. Maybe they argued and it got out of hand."

"Could be. I'll call his boss, see what time he's due back, but I'd rather speak to him at home. He'll be more relaxed. Might be easier to get him talking."

"Makes sense," Liv said.

"I've got a full-day charter tomorrow. We can talk to Reed after I get back. I'll call, let you know what time I'll pick you up."

She bit her lip. She wanted to talk to Reed. And she and Rafe seemed to be working well together. She shouldn't be spending so much time with him, but she'd worry about that after Scotty's killer was found.

"What about King?" she asked. "I want to be there tonight when you talk to him."

"You might recall your last conversation with Sam. You two didn't exactly hit it off. He'll be more likely to open up to another guy."

"Or maybe not." She looked up at him. "How about good cop, bad cop? You can guess which one I'll be."

He chuckled, seemed to be thinking it over. "Might work. Okay, we'll give it a try. I plan to drop in about eight."

"Fine, I'll meet you at the Catch at eight."

They walked at a brisk speed, moving easily together, Khan trotting along at Liv's side. "You live around here?" she asked.

"I've got a house on Mendeltna. I bought it at the right price and remodeled. Did a lot of the work myself over a couple of winters. Kept me busy, and it turned out pretty much the way I wanted. You ready for that supper I promised to fix you?"

She quickly shook her head, then realized it was an automatic response to a man asking her out. Rafe was a good-looking, sexy male, and no matter how much she tried to suppress her feminine nature, she was still a woman.

"Not yet," she finally said, still trying to decide how to handle the dangerous attraction she felt for him. "Maybe once this is over."

He just nodded. She liked that he didn't press her. Sort of.

They reached the corner of his street. "If I hear anything, I'll call you," he promised. "Otherwise, I'll see you at the Catch." Turning down his street, he started striding away.

Khan made a whimpering sound, reminding her it was time for them to go home. With a sigh, she started walking on down the road toward the café.

Rafe reached his front yard and started up the steps to the porch. As often as he could manage and nearly every afternoon in the winter, he spent time at the swimming pool. Certain days were open to the public. He and some of the locals paid a fee for access when the pool wasn't in use.

Water was his domain, had been since he'd joined the Coast Guard. A Rescue Swimmer had to be in top physical condition, able to endurance-swim in the roughest seas, in the worst possible weather.

Now he swam to stay in shape. Still loved doing it.

His iPhone sounded as he walked into the entry, playing the Coast Guard theme, "Semper Paratus." The song reminded him of an especially good time in his life and always made him smile.

He dragged the phone out of his jeans and pressed it against his ear. "Brodie."

"Chief Rosen here. Autopsy came back. Medical examiner says *Scorpion* wasn't the primary crime scene. Ferris was killed somewhere else. His body was dumped on the dock after he was dead."

Fresh anger rolled through him. "Why didn't the coroner pick that up?"

"Rained that night. At the time, we figured there wasn't more blood because it had been washed away. We've started looking for the actual murder scene. Scotty walked from his house to the motel. He was probably on his way back home when he was killed. We'll be searching along a couple of possible routes."

"Any news on the suspect?"

" 'Fraid not."

"Any chance I could take a look at that security cam photo you've got? Maybe I could pick up something."

"Sure. I'll have my guys send it to your

e-mail address. What is it?"

"Rafe Brodie at g-mail dot com."

"Got it."

"Thanks, Chief."

Rosen rang off. As Rafe climbed the half flight of stairs to the master bedroom, the photo arrived on his iPhone. He took a quick look, but needed to examine a larger image. Heading down the hall past the guest room, he entered the bedroom he used for an office, went in and booted up his computer.

The photo was as shadowy as the chief had said. The rain was coming down hard, the camera angle was wrong, and the image was extremely blurry, just the outline of a figure, the head mostly covered by what appeared to be some kind of hooded outerwear. The shoulders hinted at a muscular build, but it was just a guess.

No sign of the murder weapon in his hand, but if the crime scene was somewhere else, the weapon had probably been disposed of before the killer arrived with the body at the dock. They needed to find the weapon and they needed to find the primary crime scene.

He'd let the police look for a while. But if they came up empty-handed, he'd take a whack at it himself.

In the meantime, he had work to do to keep his company running. Once he finished, he'd have time to think of his rendezvous with Olivia tonight at the Fisherman's Catch.

His mouth edged up as he remembered the baseball cap she'd been wearing today, one of a dozen different caps he'd noticed. EARTH SUCKS, that one had said, relaying her mood, and pretty much summing up his feelings at the moment, as well.

In all the times he had been in the café, he had never seen her hair down. But damn, he wanted to. Wanted to see if it was as silky as it looked. Wanted to wrap his fist around it and drag that sexy mouth up to his.

Maybe tonight he'd convince her to come home with him.

Probably not.

More importantly, maybe tonight he'd come up with information on Scotty Ferris's murder. Rafe's jaw hardened as he sat down at the computer to work.

CHAPTER NINE

The Fisherman's Catch was jam-packed on a Friday night. It was one of those locals' joints with a couple of flat-screens on the wall playing ESPN, an L-shaped bar with black-and-chrome bar stools, and small, round, Formica-topped tables scattered around the interior.

Pitchers of Alaskan Amber flowed like water out of a Valdez gutter in the rainy season. Rafe spotted a table off to one side that had just been vacated, walked over and took a seat. He scanned the room but saw no sign of Sam King or Olivia. It was early yet. From where he sat, he could watch the door, keep an eye out for both of them.

He ordered a beer and leaned back to wait. At exactly one minute to eight, Liv pushed through the door. Several male heads turned and Rafe sat up straighter in his chair.

Holy Mother of God. His wish had just

been granted. Well, one of his wishes.

Liv had set her dark hair free, letting it hang in long chestnut waves down her back, and in the neon-lit bar, it gleamed. In a short — and he meant short — black skirt that barely covered her sweet little ass, a hot pink top with a bare midriff that exposed a glimpse of pale skin, and high black heels, she was a knockout.

Some of the other women in the bar wore dresses on Friday nights, so she didn't look completely out of place.

She just looked incredible.

She spotted him and waved, and heat exploded in his groin. Beneath the table, he went hard to the point of pain. Rafe took a calming breath and thought of icebergs as she hung her coat on the rack beside the door and started walking toward him.

By the time she got there, he was once more in control, his brain in gear enough for him to stand up and pull out a chair. "For a minute, I didn't recognize you," he said with the hint of a smile.

"I hope that's a compliment."

"Darlin', you look delicious. Good enough to eat."

She glanced up, saw the hunger in his eyes he made no effort to hide, and colored at his choice of words. A good sign, he thought.

"You should dress up more often," he said as they sat back down.

"Are you kidding? In Valdez?"

His gaze fixed on her mouth, those perfect, plump red lips that never failed to turn him on. She was wearing makeup tonight, including a trace of eye shadow that made her big gray eyes stand out. He was amazed at the change. Olivia wasn't just a good-looking woman. She was over-the-top beautiful.

And clearly the lady went out of her way to make certain no one noticed. Which was nearly impossible to do.

"Be my pleasure to take you somewhere else," he said. "Anchorage has some nice places. We could fly up. Go out for supper, go dancing. I've got a hunch you're a very good dancer."

The color slid out of her face. "What . . . what makes you think that?"

He shrugged. "Nothing in particular." Though he figured he had just touched on one of her secrets. "Maybe the way you move."

She relaxed a little, glanced around the crowded pub. "Is King here yet?"

"Not yet." He lifted a hand, and the waitress moved toward them, a chunky little brunette named Donna. "What're you drinking?" Rafe asked Liv as the waitress walked up to the table.

"I'll have a beer. Alaskan Amber."

"Got it," Donna said with a smile and hustled away.

"A woman who drinks beer," Rafe said. "Another mark in the plus column."

Liv smiled. "I guess I'm doing pretty well so far."

"I'd say you're doing just fine. How am I doing?" He took a sip of his beer.

"If I were interested in dating — which I'm not — you'd be at the top of my list."

"Not bad, then. I'm still in the running."

"I said *if* —"

His mouth edged up. "I know what you said."

Olivia glanced away. She understood what he was saying — that he wasn't about to give up. Not by a long shot. He had a feeling she was glad.

Donna showed up with Olivia's beer and headed off to another table. Olivia slid the glass a little closer. "Do you think King will show?"

"It's Friday night. Odds are he'll be here."

"Unless he killed Scotty and he's already left town."

"King's still on our suspect list, so it's possible, but it's better not to jump to conclusions."

"True enough." When she took a sip of her beer, Rafe's gaze went to that porn-star mouth and his groin pulsed. He needed to get a grip.

"Anything new on the case?" Liv asked.

Rafe took a drink of his beer. "Actually, there is. The autopsy arrived. Scotty wasn't killed at the dock. The police say it happened somewhere else and his body was dumped next to *Scorpion.* They've been searching for the primary crime scene since this afternoon."

"Wow, I didn't see that one coming. That changes everything. Scotty would have walked to the motel, so it must have happened along the route on his way home."

Rafe nodded. "I got a look at the security cam photo, but it was raining and the lens was aimed in the wrong direction. Couldn't see much, but there was definitely an image of a big guy in a hoodie."

"Sam's big."

"Yes, he is."

"What about the murder weapon?"

"No sign of it yet."

"Why would the killer dump Scott's body next to the *Scorpion?*"

"Good question. I've been trying to figure

that out myself."

"Everyone in town knew Scotty worked for you. That points to the killer being local."

"It definitely narrows things down in some way."

They sipped their beers for a while. More people streamed in and the jukebox in the corner fired up. Nineties music. Some Garth Brooks, an Alabama tune, a few other country favorites. Someone played an old rock and roll song. Elvis was belting out "Burning Love" when Sam King walked into the bar.

"That's him. He just came through the door." Olivia tipped her head in that direction, making all that long, wavy hair swing against her cheek. Desire shot through him like a fire in his blood. Damn, he had it bad.

"I see him," Rafe said. "Let's let him settle in for a while."

Liv nodded. They ordered another Amber, sipped it slowly. King cozied up to a little redhead at one of the tables and started drinking boilermakers — a straight shot of Jack washed down with a glass of beer. He was pretty well lit by the end of the hour.

When the redhead laughed at something he said and headed for the ladies' room, Rafe stood up from his chair. "Showtime."

Liv grabbed her little handbag, hot pink in a snakeskin design, and slung the strap over her shoulder. He didn't know much about fashion, but the bag looked anything but cheap. *Interesting.* He was beginning to amass little tidbits of information about her, but they only made her more intriguing.

Setting a hand at her waist, he guided her over to Sam King's table. "Well, look who's here," Rafe said, taking one of the empty chairs while Liv sat down in another. "Buy you and your lady friend a drink?"

Sam leaned back in his seat. He was big and good-looking. Trouble was, he knew it. "Sure, why not?"

Rafe raised a hand and the waitress went to fetch another round.

"How's the investigation coming along?" Sam asked, a trace of whiskey in his voice.

"They may have a suspect. They're trying to eliminate anyone else on their list. You're still on it, you know."

Sam stiffened. "What?"

"No alibi," Rafe said. "You told them you went home, but until you can prove it, you stay on the list."

"For chrissake, I didn't kill him. We were friends."

"I'm pretty sure you didn't go home, Sam. Which means the cops don't think so,

117

either. Be better for everyone if you just told the truth."

Sam's big hand fisted. "That's bullshit. Where do you get off calling me a liar?"

"I don't think you're lying. I just don't think you're telling all the truth. You can rectify that right now."

"I told you I went home."

Olivia leaned across the table and got right in his face. "You went home — eventually. Where were you after you left the poker game, Sam? Did you follow Scotty, maybe the two of you got in an argument? Maybe it got heated and you picked up something and hit him in the head. Is that how it happened?"

Sam's face turned beet red. "Back off, lady, or you'll wish you had."

Rafe felt the heat at the back of his neck. "Take it easy, Sam." The warning was clear in his voice.

"You believe what she's saying? Or are you just trying to get in her pants?"

Rafe came up out of the chair. He had Sam by the front of his shirt and dragged out of his seat before he even realized what was happening. "Watch your mouth, kid. Or you'll be dealing with me, not her."

Sam's thick shoulders vibrated with tension. The look in his black eyes could have

118

sliced through steel. He was big and strong, but he was a hothead. Guys like that went down hard.

Rafe let go of Sam's shirt and some of the younger man's tension eased. He sat back down in his chair and so did Rafe.

Sam blew out a breath, raked a hand through his shaggy black hair. "So that's what the cops think? That I followed Scotty down to the dock and killed him?"

"Turns out he wasn't killed at the dock. He was murdered somewhere else and dumped there. Where were you, Sam? You need to tell us. If you do, I'll straighten things out with the police."

Sam sighed. "I was with a woman. She's married. Her husband'll go crazy if he finds out we were together."

"What's her name?"

"I don't want to cause her trouble, okay?"

"What's her name?" Rafe repeated, leaning toward him.

Sam's shoulders slumped. "Heather. Heather Polson. Promise me you'll keep her out of this."

"The cops'll want to verify your story, but I'll talk to the chief, fill him in on the circumstances. That's the best I can do."

Olivia's voice came out softly. "You did the right thing, Sam."

The kid's features softened. "I'm ah . . . sorry about the comments. This whole thing with Scotty . . . it's really got me freaked, you know?"

"I know," she said.

A smile flickered over Sam's lips. "No offense meant, but, fact is, you are one smokin'-hot babe."

Olivia's pretty mouth edged up. "No offense taken."

Sam turned his attention to Rafe. "So we're good, then?"

"Long as your story checks out, we're good. If you think of anything that might help, give me a call."

"Count on it," Sam said. "I want this prick as much as you do."

Rafe just nodded, glad to have the kid on his side.

They were just leaving when the redhead walked up. "What do you say we blow this joint and go somewhere a little more . . . private?" she said.

Sam winked at Rafe. "Good idea." Draping a thick arm around the girl's shoulders, he headed for the bar to pay his bill and the two of them slipped outside.

Rafe waved to Donna, left enough money on the table to cover his check, grabbed Olivia's coat off the rack next to the door, and they walked out of the bar.

The night chill had set in and the air felt damp against his skin. Stars glittered like diamonds above his head. Rafe held the coat and Olivia slipped into it.

"We still haven't talked to Reed," she said as she tied the sash around her waist.

"He's due back late tomorrow afternoon. I'll pick you up at seven thirty if that works for you."

She nodded.

"Did you walk down here?"

"I drove." She smiled. "I wasn't dressed for walking."

He glanced down at the vamped-up, come-fuck-me shoes she was wearing and felt another shot of lust. No, she wasn't dressed for walking. She was dressed to stir a man's blood, and it had worked on half the men in the bar, and especially him. "Where's your car?"

She turned. "Over there." She pointed toward a little white Subaru. Good car for this kind of climate.

"You look so pretty it seems a shame for you to go home this early. Maybe you should come up to the house and let me fix you a nightcap."

Liv shook her head, setting her long, dark hair in motion. "Not a good idea."

"Maybe not," Rafe said, trailing a finger down her cheek. "But I'm pretty sure this is." Liv gasped as he pulled her into his arms and his mouth came down over hers. For an instant, she stiffened, pressed her hands against his chest to push him away.

Then those full lips softened under his and she kissed him back, a hot, wet, open-mouthed kiss that sent a fresh rush of heat straight to his groin. Hunger burned through him, sharp and fierce, and the kiss went deeper, hotter. That sexy mouth tasted like ripe, dark cherries, and her floral perfume filled his senses. Heat and need battered at his control and his erection throbbed against the fly of his jeans.

A heartbeat later, she was gone.

Rafe groaned.

Breathing too fast, Liv backed a couple of steps away. In the lamplight, her pretty gray eyes looked big and uncertain. "I have . . . have to go," she said, sounding slightly breathless. "I have to get back to the café. Good night, Rafe."

He didn't try to stop her. As he opened her car door and she slid in behind the wheel, he didn't remind her he would be seeing her again tomorrow night. "Good night, Liv."

He hadn't missed that deer-in-the-headlights moment when she'd ended the kiss, and he didn't want to scare her away. He'd been patient for weeks. He could wait a little longer.

One thing was certain. The next time he kissed Olivia Chandler, he wasn't letting her run away.

CHAPTER TEN

Liv spent a restless night, tossing and turning, thinking about Scotty, going over the
clues, trying to solve his murder. When she
wasn't thinking about finding the killer, she
was remembering Rafe Brodie's scorching
kiss.

She'd never felt anything like it, nothing
remotely similar to the heat that had rushed
through her body, the hungry craving for
Rafe that dragged her under and refused to
let go. She remembered the moment she'd
given in to it, let herself feel the intense
power of the man, the lure that called to
her so strongly. For a few brief seconds,
she'd been on the verge of completely giving herself to him.

In her other life, as she thought of it now,
she had enjoyed sex with her husband, but
it had always been more about satisfying
needs than a fire burning out of control.
Her divorce from Stephen had been

amicable. He'd been unfaithful, had betrayed his marriage vows. He knew it, felt somewhat guilty about it, didn't try to stop her from leaving him.

After a time, she had even managed to set aside her resentment and return to being his friend, which she should have remained instead of marrying him in the first place.

The few sexual relationships she'd had before Stephen were mostly the same, more about companionship than the burning lust Rafe made her feel.

Liv sighed as she lay in the darkness staring up at the ceiling. She shouldn't have given in to the little demon who'd convinced her to throw caution to the wind and dress the way she had. Dress to impress Rafe Brodie.

But she couldn't resist giving him a glimpse of the woman she kept hidden inside. She thought of that blazing hot kiss and knew her plan had worked a little too well.

Liv closed her eyes and tried to fall asleep, but it wasn't until well after two in the morning that she finally fell into an exhausted slumber, only to awaken three hours later, groggy and ill-tempered.

It was after five, the sun up but hidden beneath a layer of clouds, when she pulled on a hooded sweatshirt and a pair of running pants, grabbed her stun gun, and took Khan out for a run. As soon as they got back, she went up to her apartment and showered, changed into black skinny jeans and a turtleneck sweater, and headed down to the café.

Nell was already hard at work. Katie was tying a light blue Pelican Café apron over her clothes, and Wayne Littlefish was firing up the grill in the kitchen, getting ready for the early morning customers to arrive.

Unconsciously, Liv glanced toward the door. Rafe had a full-day charter, she knew, and berated herself for thinking about him again. She would be seeing him tonight when they talked to Chip Reed, a thought that actually made her stomach flutter.

It was ridiculous. For heaven's sake, she'd be thirty years old on her next birthday. She wasn't some infatuated teenage girl.

Determined not to waste any more time, she went to work. Breakfast turned into lunch, then the lunch crowd thinned and the café settled down, giving the crew a bit of a breather.

"So how are things going with Rafe?" Katie asked, appearing next to where Liv worked behind the breakfast counter.

"If you're talking about the investigation,

not very well. We need a lead, something that will point us in the right direction."

Katie smiled. "I was talking about you and Mr. Scorching Hot." She grinned. "I heard you and Rafe went to the Catch last night."

One of Liv's dark eyebrows went up. "Did you? Then you probably also know I met him there and we left in separate cars. We went to talk to Sam King. We're trying to help the police. That's all it was."

Katie rolled her eyes. "Yeah, right. Like any woman with a vagina could sit in a bar with Rafe Brodie and keep her mind off sex."

"Katie!"

"Hey, I say go for it! I would."

Liv shook her head. "You know I love living in Alaska, but I don't like the part where everyone knows everyone else's business."

Katie just shrugged. "Like you said, you both went home in separate cars." She grinned. "Unfortunately."

Liv just smiled.

"By the way, Cassie is coming in for the dinner shift. She called and talked to Nell. Cassie says she's going crazy just sitting around the house thinking of Scotty. She begged Nell to let her work tonight."

Liv nodded. "That's probably a good idea. Besides, you've been taking double shifts."

She cast Katie a look. "Maybe you can go down to the Catch and see if there's anyone interesting around."

"Maybe I will."

"As long as it isn't Sam King."

Katie scoffed. "You're right about that. The guy is a total hound dog." Katie sailed off when a customer walked in, and Liv went back to work.

She was busy refilling saltshakers when Nell ambled up. "Been busy all day," the older woman said. "Kind of nice to see the place jumping like it used to."

"I'd definitely rather be busy."

"Plus you might actually make a profit."

Liv smiled. "Actually we're doing better than my original projections."

"Good to hear. Means I'll be able to keep my job."

Liv impulsively leaned over and hugged her. It was a little out of character, or at least out of character for Olivia Chandler. But maybe it was all right to start letting her guard down a little.

"I couldn't do it without you, Nell. Which reminds me. I've got to go out again tonight. We're going to talk to Chip Reed. I hate to ask you to work for me, but —"

"I want that bastard caught as much as you do. I don't mind working. We can trade shifts and you can work tomorrow night."

"That'd be great. Why don't you go home for a while, get a little rest and come back for the supper shift?"

"I think I will." She lifted her apron off over her head. "So you're meeting Rafe again tonight?"

"He's picking me up at seven thirty."

"You think Chip Reed could be involved?"

"Cassie dumped Chip for Scotty. Maybe that finally got to him. Maybe they argued about it. Who knows?"

"Could be, I guess. So what do you think of Rafe?"

Liv shrugged, but she couldn't keep the color from creeping into her cheeks. "He's nice enough."

"Nice!" Nell hooted. "We're talking about Rafe Turn-Your-Body-Into-A-Furnace Brodie here. Describing a man like that as *nice* ought to be a criminal offense."

Liv laughed. "All right, but if I tell you something, you have to take an oath of silence."

Nell drew a cross over her heart. "And hope to die," she added.

"He's the best kisser on planet Earth."

Nell's salt-and-pepper eyebrows shot up. "I knew it! Lord, I'm starting to feel faint." She waved a hand in front of her face. "I can't believe you waited this long to find out."

Liv sighed. "Unfortunately, it can't go any further. I'm not looking for a relationship. I'm still trying to get my life in order." Which was true, since she had been moving around the country trying to stay alive for the past three years.

Nell seemed to ponder that. "Maybe you're right. Rafe's not a good bet for the long haul." She smiled. "On the other hand, if you could get your mind wrapped around it, a little fling might be something to consider."

Olivia laughed. "I don't think I'm that brave." But after last night, she'd begun to give the idea some thought. What could it hurt?

Sally Henderson had survived, post Rafe. Why couldn't Olivia Chandler?

A dull, leaden sky hung over the water. It had rained a couple of times that afternoon, but the squalls hadn't lasted long. The weather had finally eased up, the ocean smoothed into great, flat, undulating sheets. Gulls screeched overhead, circling the boat in the hope of carrying off a few scraps of food.

Rafe was nearing the end of a full-day

charter. He had six fishermen aboard today, a group of four friends who'd flown up from Los Angeles, and two guys who were spending a few days in town, then driving back to Anchorage.

They were an interesting pair; one Asian, a kid named Lee Wong, was maybe five ten, hard-muscled and athletic, kind of a young Jet Li. The other, Michael Nevin, was taller, dark-complexioned, thin-faced, with a trace of an accent Rafe couldn't quite place.

Both were in their midtwenties. Wong had explained that the two were former college roommates, getting together for a long-overdue reunion/vacation. Both were intelligent, but neither was much of a talker, nor particularly good at fishing.

Rafe smiled at that. A lot of the younger guys were more into Facebook these days than fishing. But everyone had to start someplace. Today was their second day on the water. The men had fished with Mo aboard *Sea Dragon* a couple of days ago. But today one of the engines was giving Mo trouble, so Rafe had split the charter passengers between *Sea Scorpion* and *Sea Dragon.*

The two men were getting a full-day charter for the price of a half day, though Rafe wasn't sure they were all that pleased to get the extra hours for free. Aside from the discomfort of a little rain, which the group had dodged by taking a coffee break in the cabin, the fishing had been excellent.

And on a trip like this, work for the passengers was minimal. Besides the captain, all Great Alaska charters included two crew members to take care of the fishermen's needs. Zach and Jaimie baited their hooks, provided rods and rigging for different kinds of fishing, helped the men reel in and land their catches and gaff the bigger fish aboard.

Being the low man on the crew, Jaimie handled the grunt work, the dirtiest job on the boat — cleaning the fishermen's catch.

The breeze freshened and a bait boil churned the water, beginning to attract the birds. Soon the gulls were dive-bombing the ocean, and black-and-white Dall's porpoises broke the surface of the sea not far away.

Earlier in the day, the men had been rigged for halibut, but the big fish hadn't been biting. Zach and Jaimie had changed out their rods and reels, rigged the men for fishing rock cod, lingcod, and snapper, and the fish had been hitting like crazy.

Once that happened, the passengers had begun to laugh and joke and enjoy themselves. Even the two greenhorns seemed to be having fun.

Before he headed back to the harbor, Rafe planned to change locations, move the boat to a spot he favored, and try for barn-door halibut again. Even a smaller size would be welcome.

He looked out over the bow, toward the snow-topped mountains across the water. As much as he was enjoying the day, he'd be glad when the trip was over. He wanted to talk to Chip Reed. He wanted to know if the police had located the actual crime scene, or the man in the security cam photo, or any other damned thing.

If the engine on *Sea Dragon* wasn't fixed by the time he got back, Rafe was handing *Scorpion* over to Mo for tomorrow's charter. Instead of working, Rafe could spend the day digging, nosing around, doing whatever needed to be done to find the cowardly scum who'd killed Scotty.

He'd make a run at Reed tonight — a thought that brought him full circle from where he'd started this morning. Thinking about Liv Chandler and reliving that hot, mind-blowing kiss. Jesus, the lady made his blood boil. He wanted more of her and he wanted it soon. He was tired of waiting, and he had a hunch, deep down, Liv was tired of it, too.

As Jaimie and Zach worked to change out

the rigs, he started the engines and headed for the spot where he'd had good luck fishing halibut before.

Though he usually enjoyed every minute he spent on the water, Rafe couldn't wait to get home.

"Need some help with that?" Zach's deep voice rolled over her and tension settled in Jaimie's shoulders.

"I can handle it." Ignoring him, she continued to rig up one of the halibut outfits. It was weird being out here with Zach instead of Scotty. Where Scott was always laughing and joking, treating her like one of the guys, Zach's mood was dark and brooding. He did his job and he was polite and helpful to the paying customers, but he wasn't an outgoing kind of guy.

Jamie remembered him from high school, though he was a couple of years older. He'd been reserved back then, too, but his dark good looks made him popular with the girls, who thought of him as the strong, silent type, kind of an Alaskan Johnny Depp. He wasn't an easy guy to read back then and that hadn't changed, though he made it no secret he thought of her as a woman, not a guy.

Jaimie wasn't sure how she felt about that.

When he looked at her from beneath his thick, black lashes, her stomach kind of lifted and she felt oddly unnerved.

He liked the ocean, though, and he knew what he was doing when it came to fishing. He gave good advice and it didn't take long for him to earn the customers' respect.

She wasn't sure yet, but maybe she would cut him some slack — as long as he left her alone.

Jaimie almost smiled. She figured the way she looked in her rubber coveralls and knee-high rubber boots as she gutted a big, bloody fish, leaving her alone wouldn't be a problem.

CHAPTER ELEVEN

The sky had begun to clear but the wind had started blowing by the time Rafe parked the Expedition in front of the Pelican that evening. The door opened as he turned off the engine and Liv walked out, shrugging into her pea coat against the fifty-degree weather. She was wearing a pair of those black skinny jeans he'd seen her in so often, but had changed out of her comfortable work shoes into low-heeled, knee-high, black leather boots.

He took in those long, long legs, thought of what they would feel like wrapped around him, thought of that sexy kiss last night, and heat slid into his groin. Even with her hair twisted up and very little makeup, she was one good-looking woman.

He got out of the vehicle, rounded the hood and opened the passenger door as she approached. He could tell by the way she was avoiding his gaze, she was remembering that hot kiss, same as he was, wondering if he would bring it up. Which he wouldn't.

She climbed into the seat, and he closed her door, went around and slid in behind the wheel.

"Have you heard . . . umm . . . anything?" she asked as he fired up the engine.

"Not today. But I just got in a little over an hour ago. Let's talk to Reed, see if he has anything new to add."

"Do you know if the police have tried to track the killer through Scotty's cell phone?"

He flashed her a look, wondering how it was she knew so much about police work.

"I saw it on TV," she said, answering his unspoken question.

"I'll ask the next time I talk to someone." They headed for Chip Reed's duplex apartment, pulled up in front. A light burned in the living room window. Looked like Chip was back from his long haul to Fairbanks.

"You think the cops have talked to him yet?" Liv asked.

Rafe cracked open his door. "I guess we're about to find out."

They walked up on the porch and Rafe rang the bell. A few minutes later, Chip Reed opened the door. Medium height and build, blond hair and brown eyes. Kind of a pretty boy, Rafe had always thought, and way too full of himself, which Cassie had finally figured out.

One of Chip's golden eyebrows went up. "Brodie. What are you doing here?"

"If you've got a minute, we'd like to talk to you about Scott Ferris. This is Liv Chandler. She owns the Pelican Café."

"I know who she is." He turned his attention to Liv. "Cassie Webster works for you."

"That's right." She smiled up at him. "May we come in, Chip? We're really hoping you can help us find out what happened to Scotty."

Rafe bit back a smile at her sweet tone of voice. Now she'd decided to play good cop. Maybe she actually had been in law enforcement.

"Come on in," Chip said, giving Olivia the once-over as they walked through the door into the living room. It was sparsely furnished with a beige-and-brown tweed sofa and chair, and dark brown carpet. There were a couple of empty beer bottles on the coffee table, and the flat-screen TV was on, though the volume was turned down low.

"I just got home about an hour ago," Chip said. "Been on a haul up to Fairbanks. My boss told me what happened to Scotty. I've been expecting the cops. I was one of the last people to see the poor guy alive, you know."

"See, that's the thing." Liv gave him a sugary smile. "We were hoping you might remember something he said, someplace he was going that night."

"Boss said he was killed down at the dock." A hint of smugness touched his lips. "I figure maybe he went down there to meet up with Jaimie. She had the hots for him bad. I mean, Cassie's a nice girl and all that, but the guy's only human. I figure he had to be tapping Jaimie on the side."

Rafe fought a rush of anger, felt Liv's hand on his arm, and clenched his jaw to keep from grabbing Chip Reed by the back of the neck and tossing him across the living room.

"Turns out what you heard is old news," Rafe said, forcing his back teeth to unclench. "Scotty wasn't killed at the dock. He was killed somewhere else. Cops think it happened somewhere between the motel and home."

"But it could have been anywhere," Liv put in, flashing Chip another sweet smile. "We were hoping — for Cassie's sake — you might be able to help us figure out where it happened."

Chip shrugged. "Scott was the first one to

leave the game. If he didn't go straight home, maybe he was headed for the Catch, see if he could pick up a little action there."

At Olivia's warning glance, Rafe kept his voice even. "You think he was seeing someone else?"

"He's a man, isn't he? He liked to play Mr. Nice Guy, but deep down, he wasn't any better than the rest of us. Even if he wasn't screwing around, it was only a matter of time. Cassie never understood that."

"Is that the reason the two of you split up?" Rafe asked. "Cassie found out you were cheating on her?"

He shrugged. "I tried to tell her it didn't mean anything. Didn't mean I didn't love her."

Liv moved into Chip's space. "You are sooo full of shit!" she barked at Reed, and Rafe grinned. So much for role-playing. She was better at bad cop, anyway.

"Where did you go when you left the motel?" Rafe asked.

"Not that it's any of your business, but I drove back here. I had to be at work early the next morning."

"Anyone see you?" Liv asked.

"How would I know? I left the motel, got in my pickup, drove home, and went to bed."

"You'll continue to be a suspect until you can verify your whereabouts," Rafe said. "Are you sure you didn't see or talk to anyone before you got home?"

Before Chip could answer, a knock sounded at the door. "That's probably the police right now," Rafe said, wondering if it actually could be, since the cops hadn't talked to Reed yet. "Be careful what you say, Chip."

"What? I'm telling the truth!" He pointed at Liv. "Both of you — get the hell out of my house!" He stomped over and threw open the door, found a plainclothes policeman — Lieutenant Richard Scarborough — and two uniformed officers on the porch. Rafe recognized red-haired Rusty Donovan as one of them.

"Charles Reed?" the lieutenant asked. Rick Scarborough was a fisherman. Rafe had known him for a couple of years.

"That's right. I go by Chip."

"We need you to come down to the station. We have some questions we need you to answer."

Chip straightened. "You have questions, you can ask them right here. I'm not going anywhere."

"If you don't come willingly," Scarborough said, "I'm going to have to arrest you."

"What? Are you crazy? I didn't do anything."

"We found the murder weapon, Reed. It washed up this afternoon."

"What does that have to do with me?"

"It was a baseball bat. The name C. Reed was carved into the handle. Since your dad's been dead for a couple of years, we figure the bat must be yours. Now let's go."

Reed's face went bone white.

"Read him his rights, Officer Donovan."

Rusty came forward. "You have the right to remain silent," he started, repeating the Miranda warning as he locked a pair of handcuffs around Chip's wrists. "Anything you say can and will be used against you in a court of law."

"I didn't kill Scotty! If the guy used my bat, I don't know how he got it! I don't believe this!"

Rusty was finishing his recitation as Rafe and Olivia walked outside. Rusty made eye contact and gave him a subtle nod, while the other officer turned off the lights in the apartment, took Chip's keys, and locked the front door.

Rusty urged Reed down the path to the waiting police SUV, then shoved his head down as he settled him into the backseat of the vehicle.

Scarborough approached the Expedition, where Rafe stood next to Olivia. "What are you doing here, Brodie?"

"We came to talk to Reed, see if he had any useful information about the night of the murder." He tipped his head toward Liv. "This is Olivia Chandler. She owns the Pelican."

"I've seen you in there," the lieutenant said. "How are the two of you involved in this?"

"We aren't," Liv answered. "Cassie Webster works for me. Scotty was a friend of Rafe's. We just want to help the police in any way we can."

"In a town this size, we can always use the help. Did Reed say anything that might be useful to our investigation?"

"We just got here a few minutes before you arrived," Rafe said. "We didn't really get a chance to talk to him. Chip didn't deny the bat was his. Are you sure it's the murder weapon?"

"No fingerprints. The bat had been in the water for a couple of days, but there was enough blood left in the cracks to be identified as belonging to the victim. A few strands of hair should confirm DNA."

Rafe's stomach knotted at the gruesome image. Olivia swayed a little and he drew her against him to steady her. "Even if the bat belongs to Reed, doesn't seem like enough to charge him with murder."

"We can hold him for forty-eight hours without filing formal charges. Who knows, maybe he'll confess."

"Maybe," Rafe said.

"We've got a warrant to search this place and his vehicle. His pickup is parked in the garage. A couple of forensic guys from Anchorage will be here tomorrow morning. We'll know more after that." He handed Rafe and Olivia each a card. "If either of you think of anything that might be useful, I'd appreciate a call."

Rafe just nodded. He helped Olivia climb into the Expedition, then went round to his side and got in behind the wheel. They sat watching as the police vehicle rolled off toward the station. Both of them were belted into their seats before either of them said a word.

"Well, that's it, I guess," Liv said.

Rafe turned in her direction. "You think so?"

For an instant, her eyes slid closed. "I don't know. I don't have a clue why, but I'm just not sure Chip Reed killed Scotty."

"The weapon belonged to him."

"He just . . . he seemed totally flummoxed, you know? Like he was in absolute shock."

Rafe sighed into the quiet. "Reed's a complete dickhead, but it's hard to see him as a killer."

"Stuff like that happens, though."

"Unfortunately, it does." Rafe started the engine.

"We have to talk to Cassie. Let her know what's going on. She's working the supper shift at the Pelican."

Rafe nodded. "Good she has something to do."

"That's what Nell thought."

Rafe glanced over at Liv as he drove off toward the café. The minute the police had arrested Chip Reed, he'd known the night wasn't going to end the way he'd planned.

There'd be another night, he told himself. He just hoped it would be soon.

Olivia walked in front of Rafe back into the café. People mostly ate supper early up here. The café was usually closed by nine, sometimes sooner, unless they had a large party or someone had made special arrangements.

Cassie was busy helping Nell with the last few customers and starting the cleanup.

Liv walked toward her, set a hand gently

on her shoulder. Cassie turned. Being so much shorter, she tilted her head back to look up at Liv. "What is it?"

"Cassie, honey, Rafe and I need to talk to you a minute."

The rag Cassie was wiping the table with paused in her hand. Some of the color washed out of her face. "What is it? Did they catch him? Did they catch the man who killed Scotty?"

Rafe took her arm. "Come on, sweetheart, let's sit down where we can talk."

Across the room, Nell's eyes met Liv's in silent question. Liv cast her a glance that said she would fill her in, but Cassie needed to hear it first.

They sat down in a booth near the corner, Cassie on one side while Rafe slid in next to Liv on the other. She could feel his iron-hard thigh pressed against hers and tried to ignore the sudden uptake in her heart rate.

"Tell me," Cassie said, her hazel eyes fixed on Rafe.

"This afternoon they found the murder weapon," he said. "It was a baseball bat, just like they figured. The thing is, it belonged to Chip Reed."

Cassie glanced from one of them to the other. "That doesn't make sense. How did the killer get hold of Chip's bat?"

Liv reached out and covered Cassie's cold hand where it rested on top of the table. "They think Chip did it, Cassie. They arrested him just a few minutes ago."

She started shaking her head, her chin-length hair swinging against her small ears. "No. That can't be right. Chip . . . Chip is a jerk but he isn't a murderer. He would never do something like that."

"The police think he did," Rafe said.

"I don't believe it." She let her head fall forward, covered her face with her hands. "God, this is just getting worse and worse." She looked up. "He didn't do it, Rafe. If they charge him with Scotty's murder, it just means the real killer is going to get away."

Liv reached for her hand. "Sometimes people do things we don't expect them to. Maybe Chip followed Scott after he left the card game. Maybe they had a fight, Chip got mad and hit Scott with the bat. Maybe he didn't mean to kill him, it just happened."

"Then Chip would've had the bat with him, right? He plays softball so maybe it was in his truck. That would make sense. But he would have had to go after Scotty on purpose. Hit him in the head on purpose. That just isn't Chip. And if you want the

147

truth — Scott wouldn't have let Chip get the best of him that way. Scott could take Chip Reed any day of the week."

Liv exchanged a look with Rafe.

"We'll let the police handle it for now," he said. "If you're right, they'll figure it out and start looking again. But you have to know, Cassie, there is always a chance Chip is guilty."

Tears welled in the girl's hazel eyes, making them more brown than green. "You won't stop looking, will you? You won't let Chip take the blame while the real killer gets away?" She turned to Liv. "You'll keep helping, right? I'll do anything you want me to, but I don't know where to begin and I . . ." She swallowed and more tears welled. "I'm pregnant."

Liv's heart squeezed. She'd heard rumors, hadn't been sure if they were true. She figured Cassie would tell her when the time was right. Now the girl had lost the man she loved and her baby would grow up without its father.

Cassie wiped away the wetness on her cheeks. "We . . . we didn't tell anyone but my mom. I'm only a few weeks along and Scotty said he didn't want anyone to think he was marrying me for any reason except that he loved me. Please, Liv, say you'll keep helping Rafe."

"Of course I will. I'm not stopping, Cassie, I promise you. You just worry about taking care of yourself and your baby."

"We'll keep looking," Rafe promised. "We're going to make sure the police find the right man. You need to believe that, honey."

Cassie swallowed. Wiping fresh tears from her cheeks, she nodded.

"I'll drive you home," Rafe said. The glance he cast Liv told her he had hoped for a different ending to the evening, but from what Liv knew about Rafe, he wasn't a man who shirked his responsibilities. With Scotty gone — and now that there was going to be a baby — as far as Rafe was concerned, Cassie was in his care.

They all slid out of the booth and Rafe walked the petite young woman to the door. "I'll call if I hear anything," he said to Liv.

"No matter what time," she told him.

"All right. I'll see you tomorrow."

She watched the two of them walk outside, feeling strangely deflated. Some part of her had actually imagined Rafe taking her home with him, making mad, passionate love to her. It wouldn't be a smart thing to do. She would be letting down her guard even more than she had already.

Chip's arrest had ended any chance of that happening. For tonight at least, she'd been granted a reprieve.

But with each day that passed, Olivia was less and less sure a reprieve was what she wanted.

CHAPTER TWELVE

Rafe walked Cassie to the front door, then went inside and checked the rooms to be sure no one was there. The man she lived with had been murdered. Until Rafe was damned sure the right man was locked up in jail and the motive was clear for Scotty's death, he wasn't about to take any chances.

"Thanks, Rafe," Cassie said as he headed back out the door. "I really appreciate what you're doing. We all do."

He just nodded and returned to the Expedition. Chip had been arrested. The cops believed he was the man who'd killed Scotty. So why did Rafe have this nagging suspicion they were wrong?

As he started driving home, he thought of the evening he had planned, a night that ended with Liv Chandler in his bed. But nothing was more important than finding Scott Ferris's killer. He wished he could convince himself that arresting Reed had solved the problem, but he just didn't buy it.

Restless energy churned through him. Too jacked to go home and sleep, he drove past the café and saw the lights had all been turned out, the restaurant closed for the night. Telling himself to keep driving, he turned instead at the corner and pulled into a space near the front of the apartment upstairs. Liv's single-car garage behind the café took up space underneath.

There was an intercom next to the gate at the fenced-in area that led to the outside staircase, and stickers warned the place was fully alarmed. The lady was nothing if not careful.

Rafe pressed the buzzer, heard Khan begin to bark in the yard out back. The big dog couldn't get into the entry, but he was letting his mistress know someone was outside. With recent events, Rafe was glad Liv had the dog for protection.

He pressed the buzzer again. He wasn't sure what Olivia was going to say when she realized he was there, but he wasn't leaving until he knew. Rafe pushed the buzzer again.

Liv stood next to the intercom in the entry of her apartment, her heart pounding from the shot of adrenaline Khan's barking had

152

sent through her. She rarely used the front entrance, mostly came in through the back. The front door was for deliveries, the postman, and the few guests who visited who didn't work in the café.

The buzzer sounded again, and Liv pressed the reply button. "Who is it?"

"It's Rafe. I need to talk to you."

Relief trickled through her. It was Rafe. Nothing to be afraid of. He probably had some sort of news. "Come on up." She pushed the release buzzer, disabling the alarm and allowing the gate to swing open. A few seconds later, his heavy footfalls pounded up the stairs.

A fresh shot of adrenaline hit her. Dear God, what was she thinking? Rafe Brodie was coming up to her apartment! Had she gone mad?

Then he was there, rapping on her door. She glanced around. She kept the place neat and clean. It was simply her nature. He rapped again, a little impatiently, she thought. No time to retrieve the boots she'd pulled off to give her feet a rest after such a long workday.

Barefoot and slightly disheveled, Liv took a deep breath and pulled open the door. "Hi. Has something happened?"

Rafe stepped into the apartment, making

it seem suddenly smaller. "No, darlin', not yet." Those dark eyes zeroed in on her mouth. "But it's way past time it did." Closing the door behind him, he pulled her into his arms, bent his head and his mouth came down over hers.

For a moment, Liv just stood there, feeling the heat of those firm male lips and a rush of desire so fierce her knees went weak. Calling herself ten kinds of a fool, she slid her arms around his neck and kissed him back.

The kiss went wilder, hotter, deeper, a demand that seemed to have no end. Pressed against him, she could feel his hard-muscled body, feel his heat and his rigid arousal. Her fingers slid into the thick, dark hair at the nape of his neck and she bit back a moan. She moved anxiously against him, wanting more.

She thought he'd be as impatient to take things further as he had been to get in the door, but instead, he slowed, began to taste and coax, his lips softer than she remembered, melding perfectly with hers.

Bending his head to the side of her neck, he kissed her there, nipped an earlobe, took her mouth in one of those deep, burning kisses again.

A whimpering sound escaped from her

throat. Rafe kept kissing her, pausing only long enough to shed his jacket and toss it away, then his mouth was on hers again.

Her heart was hammering. She kept forgetting to breathe. Her fingers dug into the heavy muscles across those swimmer's shoulders. Rafe's hands slid down to cup her bottom, and he pulled her into the vee between his legs, letting her feel his erection.

He was big and he was hard. She wanted to rip off his clothes and just look at him. She wanted to touch every inch of that perfect male body. Her fingers shook as they moved to the front of his denim shirt and she started unfastening the buttons.

Rafe grabbed the bottom of her black turtleneck sweater and peeled it off over her head, knocking her hair clip loose, sending it spinning across the hardwood floor. Her hair tumbled free and he grabbed a fistful, wrapped it around his hand and dragged her mouth back to his for another burning kiss.

A sob caught in her throat. She was hot all over, her nipples hard, her breasts aching. A soft, relentless pulsing throbbed between her legs.

"God, I want you," he whispered between fiery kisses.

"Rafe . . ." The sound of his name on her lips seemed to enflame him.

The gold in his eyes glittered as he unsnapped the front of her black lace bra, dragged it off her shoulders and tossed it away. Then his mouth was there, taking the fullness, sucking hard, torturing the tip with his straight, white teeth.

Pleasure tore through her. She felt dizzy and on fire. She couldn't think of anything but touching him. He dragged off his shirt, and her hands slid over the bands of muscle on his chest, through the light furring that arrowed down to his narrow waist. She skimmed kisses over his sun-darkened skin, let her hand glide down to the front of his jeans to cup his hardened sex.

Rafe groaned low and deep. She felt his hand at her waist, felt the snap pop on her jeans, then he slid them down her legs and they disappeared. Kissing her again, he backed her against the wall, parted her legs and began to stroke her through her panties. She heard him open his belt, heard the buzz of his zipper sliding down, vaguely realized he had freed himself.

His hands skimmed over her hips, his fingers curled around the tiny, bright-pink lace thong she was wearing, and his hot, brown eyes followed, sliding down her near-naked body.

For the first time, he paused. "Jesus, Liv, those are just too damned pretty to rip off."

She was hot and she was wet and he was driving her insane. Liv reached down, grabbed hold of her lacy pink thong and ripped it away, tossed it across the room.

Those molten eyes darkened, turned almost black. The lion was free, she thought as his mouth crushed down in a deep, erotic kiss that sapped the last of her will. Vaguely it occurred to her the lion had been stalking her for weeks.

Lifting her up, he wrapped her legs around his waist and cupped her bottom in his two big hands. Liv cried out as he buried himself to the hilt, then gritted his teeth and suddenly went still.

"You all right, baby?"

She was tight and she felt unbelievably full, but she was okay. She made a little sound and nodded.

"I don't want to hurt you."

"You aren't hurting me. Please, Rafe, forgodsake don't stop."

His mouth faintly curved the instant before he claimed her lips in another searing kiss and started to move. Long, deep thrusts had her tingling all over. The feel of his hard length made her insides go tight and hot.

Rafe kissed the side of her neck. "I've never wanted a woman the way I want you." And then he was driving deep, thrusting hard, carrying her higher and higher, closer and closer to the peak.

"Rafe . . ." she whispered, clinging to his neck, her body strung tight, bowing, hovering near climax.

Rafe didn't stop, just kept up the hard, relentless rhythm that had her whole body shaking with need.

"Come for me, darlin'," he softly commanded, and the words, spoken in that deep, sexy voice, sent her over the edge.

Her body tightened around him, and deep, saturating pleasure rolled through her, washed out through her limbs.

"Rafe . . ." she whispered as he drove into her again; then his big body tightened, his muscles went rigid, and he followed her to release.

For long seconds they just stood there, her arms around his neck, her head against his shoulder. When he finally let go, her legs slid down to the floor, but they felt boneless and numb, and she wasn't sure they were going to hold her up.

Rafe kissed her briefly and left her a moment, and she realized he was taking care of the condom she hadn't realized he'd put on.

He returned, wordlessly lifted her into his arms, and started striding down the hall. "Which one?" he asked.

"First door on the right."

He turned into the master bedroom, his belt buckle clanking, and it occurred to her that she was totally naked while Rafe still wore his jeans and heavy leather boots.

Embarrassment washed through her. Dear Lord, she'd been so hot for him she hadn't bothered to let him get undressed. He sat down on the edge of the bed and settled her in his lap. She wasn't a small woman but he made her feel that way.

"You okay?"

She nodded. "I just hope I didn't make a fool of myself. I didn't even wait for you to take off your clothes."

He chuckled, lifted her up, turned and settled her in the bed. "That's all right. I'll take care of it now."

Her eyes widened as he sat back down, bent over and untied his laces and took off his boots, stripped off his jeans and briefs.

"Wait a minute," she said. "What do you think you're doing?"

Hot, hungry eyes fixed on her face. "You didn't think we were finished?"

159

"Well, I —"

He reached down and cupped her cheek. "Not by a long shot, darlin'." Leaning over, he started kissing her, stirring the long-buried need she'd felt before, making her ache for him again. It wasn't supposed to happen this way. It was too dangerous.

But her body didn't seem to care. Liv slid her fingers into his thick, dark hair and kissed him.

He was hers, at least for tonight. Tomorrow was still a day away.

Liv awakened to the sound of pans clanging in her galley kitchen. For an instant, she went tense. Then she remembered that Rafe had come to her apartment, that he had made mad, passionate love to her, just as she had imagined.

No, that wasn't right. There was no way in hell she could ever have imagined a night in bed with Rafe Brodie. The man was insatiable. She hadn't realized it was possible to make love three times in one night and again in the morning. Multiple orgasms, she had wrongly believed, were a myth. Ha!

A soft smile curved her lips. She sat up in the bed, feeling boneless and content in a way she never had before.

She heard him moving around in the

kitchen, thought of what that implied, and her smile slowly faded. Last night had been amazing. More than she ever could have hoped for, but it was over.

When Rafe appeared in the doorway, dressed once more in his jeans, denim shirt, and work boots, carrying a tray with a tall, white porcelain mug steaming with rich, dark coffee, a buttered, perfectly toasted English muffin, and a dish of strawberry jam, she nearly bolted out of bed.

A glance at the clock told her she'd overslept, dear God, by almost two hours. Well, part of the morning she'd been asleep, the other part . . . She tried to block the memory of Rafe's hard body spooned behind her, his soft kisses against the back of her neck. She tried not to think how he'd felt moving inside her.

"I overslept," she said lamely. "I can't remember the last time I did that. I have to get to work. Can you please hand me my robe? It's in the closet." She pointed in that direction, the sheet pulled up over her breasts, which still carried patches of pink left by his late-night beard.

"It's all right, baby, I talked to Nell." Rafe set the tray on the dresser. "I told her we had some work to do on the case. She said not to worry. She and Katie have everything under control."

"You . . . you . . . talked to Nell? She knows you spent the night?"

He shrugged those wide shoulders, looking amused and not the least repentant. "The Expedition's out front. Didn't take a brain surgeon to figure I was up here with you."

Her chest felt tight. She should have sent him away. Now half the town would know she had slept with Rafe Brodie. "Don't you have a charter today? Surely you must have some kind of work to do."

"One of the engines on *Sea Dragon* is out. Mo's taking *Scorpion,* combining my charter with his."

"Well, I have to work," she said tartly. "Please hand me my robe."

He didn't, of course, just stood there watching her for several long moments. "I should have known you'd run. You've been doing that for weeks."

"What are you talking about? I'm not running from anything."

"Did you think after I had you, I was just going to walk away?"

Her breath hitched. *After I had you.* The words made her think of sex all over again. After the hours she'd spent in bed with him, it was impossible. Surely. Wasn't it?

"You don't own me. Just because we made love —"

He moved closer. "We had sex, Liv. You want it to be more than that, don't try to push me away." That sexy mouth edged up. "It won't work anyway. What happened between us last night . . . it isn't always that way, and you know it. We're good together. You want more, and so do I."

"You're wrong." She tipped up her chin, feeling vulnerable as she huddled naked beneath the sheet. "You fucked me, and now we're done."

One of his dark eyebrows went up. "You think talking tough is going to work? You want me to come over there and prove I'm right?" He took a step toward her and she shot backward in the bed, dragging the sheet along with her.

"Or would you rather get dressed," he said mildly, "so we can go out and try to find the bastard who murdered Scott Ferris?"

Some of the tension left her body. He was letting her off the hook, putting things back on an even keel. Because both of them knew if he came over there and started kissing her, pressed her into the mattress beneath his big hard body, she would want him all over again.

"Okay. That . . . that sounds good."

He opened the closet door and grabbed her robe, tossed it onto the bed.

"I'll be downstairs when you're ready to go. I've got one hell of an appetite this morning." Rafe winked at her and then he was gone.

Liv just sat there. What in God's name had she done? But deep down that little demon inside was doing handstands. Rafe wanted more of her. And the simple truth was, Liv wanted a whole lot more of him.

CHAPTER THIRTEEN

Rafe sat in one of the blue vinyl booths in the café, sipping a cup of coffee and eating a plate of bacon and eggs. He glanced over at the woman working behind the breakfast counter. After leaving her apartment, he'd gone home, showered, and changed, left the Expedition in the garage, and driven his Ford F-150 back to the restaurant. Once the snow stopped falling, the pickup was great for hauling gear.

He watched Olivia working. She'd mellowed a little since he'd left her. Liv wanted to catch Scotty's killer or prove Chip Reed was guilty as much as Rafe did, though he had a suspicion her motives went deeper than just being Scott and Cassie's friend.

He wasn't the least surprised by her hostile greeting this morning. The woman had kept to herself since her arrival in Valdez. No one knew where she came from or anything about her. Nell had told him the story of her dead husband and her inheritance. He figured it might be true, might not. Until last night, he hadn't really cared. People had a right to their privacy — as long as it didn't pose a problem for him.

Last night had changed things. Every fantasy he'd ever had about Olivia turned out to be mild in comparison to the real thing. Sex with Liv was ten times better than any dream he'd ever had. A hundred times better.

They were good together in any number of ways and perfectly suited in bed. Liv liked a man who took control. Maybe because she was so in control of herself at all times. Maybe once in a while it felt good to give up the reins, let a man take charge.

Rafe enjoyed a woman who responded to that control but wasn't afraid to take the lead herself. He'd told Liv the truth. He'd never wanted a woman the way he wanted her, and he still did.

Whether she admitted it or not, Liv had surrendered to him last night, and that wasn't something a woman as strong as Olivia did lightly. She'd surrendered, and that made her his.

At least for as long as it lasted.

Thinking of her, Rafe picked up the last crisp piece of bacon on his plate and crunched it down, wiped his hands on a powder-blue napkin, and stretched his long legs out under the table.

Nell walked over to pick up his empty plate and refill his coffee cup. "Everything okay?" she asked, pouring the mug to the brim.

He didn't pretend not to understand. "It will be. Might take a little time for the lady to get used to the way things are now."

Nell's hand went to her heart. "Oh, dear Lord, I don't like the sound of that. And to think I encouraged her. You listen to me, Rafe Brodie. You hurt her and you'll answer to me."

He smiled. "She looks like a pretty tough lady. You don't think she can handle me?"

Nell eyed him sharply. "If anyone can, it's Liv. But tough? Liv's exactly the opposite. Under that protective shield she's built around herself, she's so vulnerable, sometimes it scares me."

He'd had the same thought. It was the reason she had avoided him for so long. She was afraid of what might happen if she let down her guard, let him see the woman she was inside.

"I know that, Nell," he said softly.

"You just mind my words, you hear? You hurt her and you'll answer to me."

He chuckled, glad Olivia had a friend like Nell. "Yes, ma'am."

He watched the older woman's hips sway as she walked away, then opened the newspaper he'd found on the table when he'd sat down, the *Valdez Star.* As he read the headlines, he sat up a little straighter.

MAN KILLED IN ACCIDENT AT PIPELINE TERMINAL

The article went on to say that sometime after midnight last night, one of the workers had been killed when he'd fallen off a big oil storage tank at the facility. At the time the paper went to press, it hadn't been determined whether the man had committed suicide or if the fall was an accident.

Rafe finished reading the article and set the paper aside as Olivia walked out of the kitchen into the dining room. She was wearing another pair of those stretchy black jeans. When she turned to say something to Nell, he noticed the hot pink roses embroidered on her hip pockets.

His mind shot back to the little pink thong she'd been wearing last night, the way she'd torn it off so he could have her. His body clenched at the memory and desire washed hotly through his veins. He wondered if

Olivia realized the effect she had on him, but Rafe didn't think Liv completely understood her sexuality. He planned to make the exploration one of his top priorities.

"You hungry?" he asked, rising as she arrived at the table.

She shook her head. He didn't miss the wary expression in those big gray eyes.

"Everything's gonna be okay, darlin'. You're going to have to trust me a little on that."

She didn't answer. Rafe was pretty sure she didn't trust anyone, particularly him.

She was wearing a pair of hiking boots, her hair pulled into a ponytail that came out through the hole in a black baseball cap. This one said BADASS in bright red letters outlined in yellow.

He almost smiled. She was putting her wall back up. Didn't matter. Soon as he got her back in bed, he'd just tear it down again.

As she slid into the booth across from him, she happened to glance at the headlines on the paper lying across the table. "Oh no. It looks like someone else died this week."

"It happens up here."

"Alaska's a hard place to live. It didn't take long for me to figure that out. People freeze to death or drown or get attacked by bears."

"So why'd you move here then?"

Her glance strayed out the window. "In a different way, the city's far worse. They've got robberies and shootings, rape and murder." She looked back at him. "At least here you have clean air to breathe and you don't feel trapped the way you do in a city."

"You got that right." Pulling out his wallet, he left enough cash for the bill and a tip, then guided her to the door and outside onto the patio.

"You were talking about life in the city," he said. "Sounded like you were speaking from experience."

She shrugged her slender shoulders. "I've lived in a few different places."

"With your husband?"

"Umm . . . yes." She shook out the lightweight jacket she was carrying, shoved her arms into the sleeves. "What are we doing first?"

"As of last night, the police haven't found the primary crime scene. We're going to give them a hand, see if we can come up with something. We'll cover every route Scotty might have taken from the motel back to his house. Maybe we can find something the cops missed."

"The police claim the bat belongs to Chip. Unless someone stole it out of his apartment, he must have had it with him that night. Chip mentioned driving to the card game, so it could have been in his pickup, like Cassie said. If the bat was in his truck and he left the doors unlocked, the killer could have taken it out of the truck and used it to kill Scotty."

"Or Chip could have."

"Cassie doesn't think so."

"Maybe the bat was in the bed of the truck instead of inside," Rafe said. "The killer spotted it there, grabbed it and hit Scott in the head."

"Makes sense. Either way, the murder would likely have happened near where the truck was parked."

"According to Rusty Donovan, they searched the area around the motel the next morning, but it was raining hard the night of the murder. The water would have washed away most of the blood or any sign of footprints. Unless the police got lucky, finding the actual spot where it happened would have been nearly impossible."

"The ground's dried up since then," Liv said. "The motel is the best place for us to start looking."

Rafe nodded. "I brought my pickup. It's

over there." He pointed toward the silver Ford he drove this time of year. "Easier to haul equipment once the snow is gone."

Rafe led her in that direction. "I'd rather have brought my Razor," he said. "A UTV would be perfect for this kind of thing, but off-road vehicles can't be made street legal up here."

"UTV? That's one of those all-terrain things where you sit side by side?"

He chuckled. "That's right. You've never driven one?"

"No, but I've always thought it would be fun."

"First chance we get, we'll take Khan and go out riding."

She hesitated, searching, he figured, for a way to politely say no.

"Come on." He caught her hand and tugged her over to the truck. "We need to get moving."

Resigned, Liv followed him to the pickup and they climbed in. Liv buckled herself into the passenger side of the comfortable, upholstered bench seat.

"What about snowmobiles?" he asked as he started the engine. "Or a four-wheeler? Ever done that?"

"Never tried either. What, you've got those, too?"

"Sure, why not? In case you haven't noticed, we pretty much make our own fun up here."

She rolled her eyes. "You know what they say, the only difference between men and boys is the size of their —"

He cast her a bawdy glance.

"Toys," she finished dryly.

Rafe grinned. "Well, that, too."

The V-8 engine rumbled as he drove past Cassie's home, then continued slowly toward the motel, taking a route Scotty might have walked coming back. The windows were down, allowing them to lean out a little, feel the breeze drifting in off the sea. Both of them kept their eyes on the side of the road, looking for something. A scrap of paper, a piece of clothing. Anything.

But the rain that night had erased any footprints that might have been along the road and it only took a couple of stops that turned out to be nothing to realize they were on a fool's errand.

Hoping to have better luck closer to the motel, Rafe kept the pickup crawling along the edge of the road.

"So what do you do for fun in the winter?" he asked when he came to a stop sign.

"I used to ski," Liv said wistfully. "I was

pretty good, but I haven't done it in a while."

"Why not?"

She made a frustrated sound in her throat. "I was busy trying to get the café up and running, okay? Are we doing this or not?"

He didn't press her, just stepped on the gas. He didn't want her clamming up on him, finding another excuse to push him away. After last night, he realized he wanted more from Olivia than just her beautiful dancer's body. He wanted to know her secrets. He wanted her to trust him. He wanted to be able to trust her.

A surprise waited for them when they reached the Seaside Motel. Three black-and-silver police SUVs were parked in the lot, and several uniformed officers prowled the grounds.

Rafe pulled into one of the spaces, and he and Liv climbed out of the pickup. He spotted Richard Scarborough, waved, and the lieutenant walked toward them.

"What's going on?" Rafe asked. He knew Scarborough some, not a lot. And they had spoken briefly during the arrest at Reed's place last night.

"We've located the primary crime scene," the lieutenant said.

"I figured it was somewhere close by."

"Once we positively identified the murder weapon as belonging to Reed, this became the most likely place to look."

"So Reed's being cooperative?"

"He hasn't confessed to the murder, but he's answered our questions, admitted the bat was his. He left it in the bed of the truck that night. Reed says he drove to the card game and parked in front of the motel. The owner's unit, where the game was held, sits right behind the office. We initiated another search this morning, and now that the ground has dried up, we found the evidence we were looking for."

"Which was?"

"Bone fragments. Ferris was killed just a few feet away from where Reed's truck was parked."

Rafe glanced down at Liv, saw her face had gone deathly pale. Sliding a hand around her waist, he drew her closer, felt her lean slightly into him.

"Doesn't look good for Reed," Rafe said.

"No, it doesn't."

"Have they found anything in the truck? Blood or fabric evidence, anything like that?"

"Forensics is still working on it."

"Anything on the security cameras?"

"There aren't any. This isn't exactly a five-

175

star motel."

"Not exactly," Rafe agreed.

"What about Scott's cell phone?" Liv asked. "Did it ever show up? Anything show up on the GPS?"

"Apparently the phone was turned off or dumped in the ocean. Never got a thing. I pressed Friedman a little harder about the game that night. He admitted Reed and Ferris got into it over Ferris's fiancée. Reed made some innuendo about what a disappointment Ferris's girlfriend was in bed and Ferris got in his face, threatened to kick his ass. Reed was the second guy to leave the game. Next thing you know, Ferris is dead."

Rafe nodded.

"That gives Reed means, motive, and opportunity," Liv said, drawing the lieutenant's attention.

"She watches a lot of crime TV," Rafe explained.

"She's right. We're still building a case, but Reed's our primary suspect. The district attorney's office in Palmer is filing formal charges today."

"I appreciate you keeping us in the loop about this, Lieutenant."

"Everyone in town knows how much you thought of Scotty. And how much he thought of you. I know how I'd feel if he'd been one of my friends."

Scarborough turned to Liv, tugged on the brim of his dark blue VPD ball cap. "Take care, Ms. Chandler."

"You too, Lieutenant."

Scarborough returned to his men. Rafe and Liv watched the officers walking the area, looking for any other evidence they might have missed.

"I wonder how much longer they'll be here," Rafe said.

"They've already searched the area once. I doubt they'll be here much longer. Why?"

"According to Rusty Donovan, Scarborough interviewed the motel guests the morning after the murder. But now that we know this is where it happened, it might not hurt to talk to them again. Press them a little, see if anyone might have remembered something about that night."

"Most of them have probably checked out and left." She flicked him a glance. "You're still thinking Chip might not be our guy."

He shrugged. "I like to be thorough."

Liv nodded as they headed back to the truck. "We could talk to Ben, find out who's still staying at the motel."

"I'll call him once the cops are gone, ask him about it. I'll ask him to let me know when the police are finished."

"I've got to get back to work," Liv said as she climbed into the truck.

"All right, I'll drop you off. If you want to come with me when I return to the motel, I'll pick you up after I hear from Ben."

"I want to come," Liv said.

Rafe flicked her a glance, clamped down on the erotic image that popped into his head. Reaching down, he started the engine and drove back to the Pelican Café.

CHAPTER FOURTEEN

"So how was it?" Katie asked as she sailed up to where Liv was working behind the breakfast counter. "We're all living vicariously through you. You have to dish, give us at least some juicy little morsel."

"I don't know what you're talking about."

Katie rolled her big blue eyes. "Pul-eeeze. His SUV was parked out back all night. We know he was up there with you. Come on. Just one little detail."

Liv inwardly groaned. She hated people knowing her business. She couldn't afford for them to start speculating about her. The bell above the door rang as a patron walked in. *Saved by the bell,* she thought.

"You've got a customer." Liv tipped her head toward the heavyset older man who slid into a booth.

"I've got it." Katie whirled away to wait on him, one of the last three customers in the café. This time of afternoon the place was mostly empty, just a few patrons sitting here and there. Katie took the customer's order, then brought him a piece of berry pie and a cup of coffee. A few minutes later, she appeared where Liv was stacking dishes under the counter.

Katie set a dirty plate in one of the plastic bins on its way to the kitchen. "Come on, Liv, dish."

Olivia shook her head. "I'm not dishing anything. Rafe and I are trying to help the police find the person who killed Scotty. That's it."

"I thought Chip Reed killed Scott," Katie said. "It was in the paper this morning and that's what everyone's saying. He and Scotty got into it over Cassie."

"That's the current theory. But Cassie doesn't think it was him."

"Yeah, that's what she said. She stopped by a little while ago. She's with Chip now, down at the jail. She thinks he's innocent. She was always too naïve for her own good."

Liv's stomach twisted. "Cassie's down at the jail?"

Katie nodded. "She should be back any minute. She's working today. Ought to be interesting to hear what Chip has to say."

"I'm sure it will." It bothered her to think of sweet little Cassie visiting her ex in the local jail. Olivia didn't like to think the police might have arrested the wrong man.

"Whatever he tells her, it doesn't mean it's going to be true," Katie said. "He was a big fat lying cheat when he and Cassie were dating."

"There is that."

The rattle of a lunch plate sliding under the heat lamp drew Katie's attention. "BLT and a Cobb salad. I gotta go." Katie picked up the plates and headed for a man and his wife two booths away just as Liv looked up to see Cassie coming into the restaurant.

Though she was wearing makeup, her face still looked pale, and dark crescents smudged the skin beneath her eyes. She looked as if she hadn't slept in days, which she probably hadn't. Liv felt guilty for letting her work, but if it helped her cope with her loss, then that was okay.

Cassie spotted her the minute she entered the dining room and hurried in Liv's direction. "Can we talk?"

"Of course." Liv glanced around. Everyone had been served, and Katie was a really good waitress. Liv tipped her head toward an empty booth. She walked in that direction, and she and Cassie slid in on opposite sides.

"I heard you went down to the jail," Liv

said. "If I'd known you wanted to see Chip, I would have gone with you."

"I know you would have. I just . . . it was something I had to do on my own."

Katie showed up just then with a couple of cups of coffee. Cassie gave her a grateful smile as she accepted the cup. Katie smiled back and took off to check on the man who had ordered the berry pie.

"Chip didn't do it, Liv," Cassie said. "I'm more certain than ever. He says he didn't even see Scotty after he left the card game. Chip doesn't have the money to hire an expensive lawyer. He's terrified, Liv. He actually cried when he saw me walk in. Chip isn't a guy who cries. I know he has his faults, but he isn't a killer. He says he's innocent. He says he doesn't know anything about Scott's murder, and I believe him."

"You don't still have some kind of a thing for him, do you? Because I thought —"

"Good Lord, no! But I know Chip. We went together for nearly two years. Even after we broke up, he and Scott were never enemies. He made some stupid remarks once in a while, but in a strange way, I think Chip respected Scotty."

Olivia made no reply. She knew what it was like to be accused of a crime you didn't commit. She knew how terrifying it could be and how hard it was to prove your innocence.

"Chip's telling the truth," Cassie continued. "I could always tell when he was lying."

"Even when he lied to you about other women?"

Cassie glanced away. "Embarrassing as it is, yes. I was just so naïve, I thought I could make him love me enough to change."

Olivia thought of Stephen. He had cheated before they were married but convinced her he would never do it again. "I can tell you from experience that doesn't work."

"I know that now. Thank God I met Scotty. Being with him showed me how good a man can be."

Liv took a sip of her coffee just to have a moment to think. She set the mug back down on the table. "So that's it then. You believe someone else killed Scott and the police have arrested the wrong man."

"That's exactly what I think." Cassie's eyes welled. "God, I miss him. The house is so empty without him."

Liv reached across the table and caught Cassie's hand. There was nothing she could say to make her friend feel better. Only time could do that.

She glanced up to see Rafe shove through

the door. "Rafe's here to pick me up. We're still working on this, okay?" She slid out of the booth and took off her apron. "If Chip's innocent, we'll find a way to prove it."

"You and Rafe . . . you're the best friends I've ever had. Thank you."

Liv managed a smile for Cassie as she headed toward the door. Rafe held it open and she walked past him out onto the front patio. Another week or so, with a few propane heaters, it would be warm enough for customers to sit outside. She liked that idea. A lot.

"You called Ben?" Liv asked.

He nodded. "He doesn't believe Chip killed Scotty. He says he knows it looks bad, but according to Ben, Scott and Chip have been jabbing each other over Cassie ever since she dumped Chip and took up with Scott. Ben says Chip knew it was his own damn fault. Basically he blamed himself, not Scotty. Plus, according to Ben, he just doesn't have it in him to murder someone."

"Cassie talked to him at the jail. She's completely convinced Chip's innocent."

Rafe blew out a breath. "Reed's damned lucky to have her on his side. Most women would tell a guy who hurt her the way he did to take a flying leap."

"Yeah — out of a plane without a

parachute." Liv stepped back as Rafe opened the passenger door and she climbed into the cab. He smiled as he shut the door, then rounded the truck and slid in behind the wheel.

"Ben says he's got three rooms still occupied by guests who were there the night of the murder. The cops talked to everyone in the motel and came up with nothing. Over the last few days, all but the people in those three rooms have checked out and left the area." He started the engine and put the pickup in gear for the short drive to the Seaside Motel.

"You realize the odds of us getting a lead are slim and none," Liv said.

"No question."

"The killer could even be one of the guests who've left Valdez."

"Could be."

"But it's worth a try, and I appreciate you taking me with you." She could still see the grief in Cassie's face. The girl wasn't going to be whole again until Chip's guilt or innocence was proven without a doubt. Until Scott's killer was locked up in jail.

Liv glanced over at Rafe as he pulled up in front of the motel. She needed to do this, and Rafe was her best chance of getting it done, but each time she was with him, her attraction grew. She wanted to spend time with him, get to know him, make love with him. But the more she let down her guard, the more she let him in, the more danger she put herself in. Put both of them in.

It wasn't fair to either one of them.

And yet when the passenger door opened and Rafe reached up and set his hands at her waist, swung her to the ground as if she weighed less than nothing, she gave herself in to his care as she had done before.

Together they walked toward the motel.

Rooms two, five, and twelve all had guests who had checked in before the murder and hadn't yet checked out. Ben's apartment was behind the office, where Chip's truck had been parked. Beneath an overhanging roof that ran the length of the corridor, all the rooms faced the parking lot. Room number two was closest to the office. Rafe knocked on the door but no one was there.

Moving along the corridor, he knocked on room five, and a feeble-looking gray-haired woman came to the door. Seeing her, Rafe eased Liv a little in front of him, not wanting to intimidate the older lady.

Liv immediately understood. She smiled. "Hello. My name is Olivia Chandler and this is Rafe Brodie. We're friends of the man who was killed here a few nights ago. You were a guest here at that time, right?"

"That's right. My daughter Gwen and I."

"We were wondering if you might have remembered something about that night that would be helpful."

"Already talked to the police. So did my daughter. We're here visiting my sister. She's in a nursing home."

"So you didn't hear anything unusual that night?" Rafe asked.

"Heard men talking, people going in and out of their rooms. Told the police that."

"Do you remember which rooms?"

"We were inside with the TV playing. Just heard some footsteps, doors opening and closing, that kind of thing. But it was earlier, before midnight. I hear midnight's around when it happened."

"That's right," Liv said. "And your daughter? Do you think she might remember something that would help?"

The woman shook her head. "She's a real sound sleeper, is Gwen."

"Well, thank you, ma'am." Rafe set a hand at Liv's waist. "We appreciate your help." The door closed and he urged her down the corridor.

"Not worth much," Liv said.

"Not much."

They climbed the outside stairs and spoke to the man in room twelve, which was above the office. A traveling salesman, bald and overweight, he said he'd heard laughter downstairs, undoubtedly the card game, but by midnight he was asleep and hadn't heard anything else.

The afternoon was waning. They were heading back to the truck when a dark-blue Jeep Cherokee pulled into the parking lot, took a space in front of room two.

Two men got out. One was Asian. Rafe recognized him immediately as Lee Wong, the man who'd been aboard yesterday's charter. The other man's name was Michael Nevin. Former college roommates touring the area.

"Come on," he said to Liv, his hand at her waist. "I know these two." He guided her toward the Jeep.

Wong recognized him as they approached, gave him a casual smile. "Captain Brodie. Nice to see you."

Rafe returned the smile. "How did you enjoy the fishing trip?"

"It was great. We'd never tried ocean fishing before we came up here. We had a lot to learn, but we had fun."

Nevin was looking at Liv and there was something in those onyx eyes Rafe didn't like. He didn't introduce her.

"We went sightseeing today," Nevin said. "We took a lot of pictures. This is a beautiful area."

"Yes, it is. I hate to bother you. I know you spoke to the police about this, but a friend of mine was killed here in the parking lot a couple of days ago. I was hoping you might remember something about the night it happened."

"The newspaper said a man was arrested for the murder," Nevin said.

"That's true. We just want to make sure the police have enough evidence to convict him. Valdez is a very small town. We've been doing some digging, seeing if we could come up with something that might help them. Were you here the night it happened?"

"We were here, yes. We told that to the police."

"Scott was killed around midnight, maybe a little later. You're close to the office. It happened right out front." He turned, pointed. "Your room would have been the closest to the murder scene. Maybe you heard some sort of scuffle, something like that?"

Wong shook his head. "We had a couple of drinks earlier. Crashed pretty hard, you know?"

"I barely remember getting home," Nevin added.

"But you were here. You were in your room by midnight?"

The Asian's jaw subtly tightened. "We were here. Like I said, we crashed pretty hard. I wish we could be more help, but —" He shrugged.

"Well, thanks anyway. Enjoy the rest of your vacation." He started to walk away, then turned back. "How much longer did you say you'd be staying?"

"We will be leaving the end of the week," Nevin said.

Rafe summoned a smile. "Maybe you'll decide to go fishing again."

The Asian smiled back. "Maybe."

"Thanks for your time," Liv said.

"No problem," Wong said.

Rafe waved and started walking, helped Liv into the truck, then got in and fired up the engine, pulled out of the lot and drove off toward the café.

"What are you thinking?" Liv asked.

"I don't know. Nothing, I guess. Those two guys . . . there's just something off about them. I noticed it when they were aboard *Scorpion* the other day."

"They were on one of your charters?"

"That's right. The thing is, they've been

fishing twice this week, once with me, once with Mo, but they didn't really seem that interested in the sport."

"They're tourists. People like to try different things."

"You're probably right." He glanced back toward the Jeep but the men were already inside their room. "Nevin sounds foreign. He looks Middle Eastern. I didn't like the way he was staring at you."

She grinned. "I don't think that counts for much."

His mouth edged up. "Maybe not to you."

She laughed. "So besides the fact the guy was giving me the eye, what else bothers you?"

"More like the stink eye, and I'm not sure. It just kind of felt like they were holding something back."

"They could afford two charters and they're nicely dressed. I can't imagine they'd need to kill someone for money."

"No."

"Maybe they heard or saw something that night but don't want to get involved."

"That's what I was thinking."

"So what do we do about it?"

"I'm not sure yet. The forensics report hasn't come back on Chip's vehicle. Maybe the cops will find something conclusive in his truck or apartment, and we won't have to worry about it."

"Maybe."

Rafe pulled up in front of the café and turned off the engine. "We've done all we can for now. How about I fix you supper tonight?"

Liv shook her head. "I can't. I've got the dinner shift. Nell switched with me last night."

"All right, then I'll come over to your place after you close."

She looked up at him with those big gray eyes. "Please try to understand. I'm not used to spending this much time with anyone. I need some space, Rafe."

He didn't miss the wariness in her face. Being this close to someone was clearly new to her. Hell, it was new to him. He and Sally had dated for three years, but he was already in deeper with Liv than he'd ever been with Sally.

He reached up and ran a finger along her jaw. "I know that, darlin'. I'll give you your space." He leaned down, brushed her lips with a kiss, settled for a moment, felt her tremble, and backed away. "You can have tonight, but tomorrow I'm cooking you that supper I promised, yes?"

Her features softened. "All right." She

smiled. "Grilling, right? You said you couldn't cook."

"That's right. I'm a lousy cook, but spectacular on the grill."

She laughed. "Tomorrow, then."

He didn't say more as she cracked open the door and slid out of the pickup, hurried inside the café.

Rafe blew out a breath. He was still faintly aroused from that single brief kiss. Damn. He needed a long night in bed with Liv. Either that or a good, long swim. Rafe turned the truck up the hill toward the pool.

CHAPTER FIFTEEN

Afternoon slid into evening, grew later. A black night sky hid behind a dense layer of fog outside the windows. Stillness shrouded the single-story house, hidden off the road above Valdez. Trent listened to the sound of heavy work boots coming up the front steps, followed by a sharp knock on the door.

"That's him." Tatiana Valenchenko tossed her blunt-cut, straight, black hair over her shoulder. She was average height, average weight; at first glance, nothing out of the ordinary. But a set of perfect curves hid beneath her unimpressive gray slacks and dark gray sweater. And with very little makeup, her face went from plain to striking.

Tatiana was a true chameleon, able to quietly blend in without being noticed. Here she called herself simply Anna.

"Shall I let him in?" she asked. "Or would you rather he wait out in the cold for a while to demonstrate your displeasure?"

"He knows why I want to see him."

Anna was beautiful, brilliant, and deadly. She was Trent's current mistress and the only one of his associates he completely trusted. And only then because she had as much to gain from their endeavor as he did.

"You realize Cain has become more of a liability than an asset."

"Yes." Trent's fingers tightened around the folded-up *Valdez Star* in his hand. The headline, MAN KILLED IN ACCIDENT AT PIPELINE TERMINAL, was stamped into his brain. He tossed the paper onto the side table in the entry. The vague text message Cain had sent had been enough to alert Trent to the latest problem the man had caused.

"Unfortunately, we need him. Open the door."

She did as she was told, but only because she knew he was right. Anna wasn't one of the women who bowed and scraped at his every command. She didn't have to. She had a sharp mind and a beautiful body. She commanded men, not the other way around. That was what he liked about her.

The door opened and Darius Cain walked into the rented house in the hills. He was a big man, muscular through the chest and shoulders. He was part African American, though his features were more Caucasian. He was handsome and refined, his skin a light coffee-with-cream. Yet an air of menace clung to him like a dirty shirt.

In Illinois, where he'd grown up, he'd recently adopted the name Khalid Ahmad. His half brother, Jamal, had converted to Islam while he was in prison. Since Darius worshipped Jamal, who'd been killed in a gang-related shooting, he'd decided to follow in his brother's footsteps.

That Cain, like Jamal, was a sociopath without the slightest conscience, made him an asset to the operation.

"You killed a man out at the terminal," Trent said, without inviting him into the living room or offering him any sort of refreshment. "How did that happen?"

Cain's mouth thinned. "It wasn't my fault. The stupid ass stumbled onto a cache, found some of the explosives, then tried to blackmail me." He scoffed. "Wanted me to pay him a hundred grand to keep quiet. I told him I'd meet him at the top of the storage tank with the money." Cain laughed. "Poor fucker never did get paid."

Trent strolled toward him. Darius was smart, but he was a loose cannon, had been from the start. He was there because he more than met the criteria for the operation. Tough, savvy, no arrest record — a must for anyone involved — and he had worked in the Texas oil fields.

"This is the second time you've deviated from the plan," Trent said. "Each of those times, you've compromised the mission. If the authorities find out you're involved in either of the murders, our entire operation will fail. Do you understand that?"

"What was I supposed to do? The guy would have gone to the cops. You saying I shouldn't have killed him?"

A muscle tightened in Trent's jaw. Unlike his brother, Cain had completed high school and a couple of years of college. He spoke well, knew how to dress. Cain had almost made it out. *Almost.*

Trent worked to keep his voice even. "This is going to be over soon. If everything goes as planned, we'll all achieve our goals. All you have to do is keep your head on straight until we can make this end. Do you understand?"

"Yeah, but if someone else gets wise to what's going on —"

"You make sure they don't. And you do it without committing another murder. Can you do that?"

"Well, I —"

"Can you do that, Darius? Because you said you were doing this for your brother, doing it for Jamal. Can you manage to do what you're told long enough for our mission to succeed?"

Cain shifted his weight onto his other foot and stood up a little straighter. Jamal was the key to handling Darius Cain. His love for his dead brother was his Achilles' heel. Trent used it ruthlessly.

"What about Heng and Nadir? What are they doing?"

"They're playing the roles they were assigned. They're acting like tourists till it's time for them to do their jobs. Now answer my question. Can you do what you're supposed to without any more problems?"

Cain's mouth tightened. "I'll do my part," he said grimly. "You just make sure everyone else does theirs."

"Let me worry about that." Trent walked over and opened the door. "You can go. I don't want to see you again until the meeting."

Cain flicked a glance at Tatiana, but made no comment, just turned and walked out of the house. Trent listened to his fading footsteps, then the engine started on the older model, beat-up brown Chevy that had been purchased for his use. The sound slowly disappeared into the mist.

"I don't like him," Tatiana said. "And I don't trust him. He enjoys killing too much."

"If everything goes smoothly from now on, we won't need him anymore. Ever. Darius Cain will be as expendable as the men he murdered."

Anna walked up to him, slid her arms around his neck, leaned in and kissed him. "I do not wish to think of Cain. Let us talk of something more pleasant."

Trent nodded. He'd already dealt with one problem today. Lee Heng had phoned on the burner Trent had given him. Apparently there was a new problem with the first mess Cain had created. The police had located the original crime scene, knew the murder had been committed outside the motel.

The good news was, an arrest had been made.

The bad news was, a couple of locals, friends of the victim, were digging around, asking questions. A woman and a guy named Brodie said they wanted to be sure the police had the evidence they needed to convict the man.

Rafe Brodie was the owner of the charter boat fleet Trent had been using, the man who had captained the boat the day he and Anna had been aboard to recon the area as part of their tourist cover.

Trent had told Heng to find out who the woman was, and keep an eye on both of them. And do it without being caught.

Christ, all he needed was a few more days. Just a little more time without someone screwing up.

Tatiana took his hand and started leading him toward the bedroom. At the doorway, she paused, slid her arms around his neck, and kissed him.

Only a few more days, he thought. In the meantime, he had Tatiana to please him. Trent was hard before he closed the bedroom door.

It was going to be a long day aboard *Scorpion.* A storm was moving in. With any luck it would be brief, but the seas were going to be rough, which meant some of the fishermen might get sick. Rafe had a nine-hour charter today. Since it was paid in advance, the passengers would show up no matter the weather. It was the captain's job to keep them out of the roughest parts of the Sound and still give them a good day of fishing.

It was early, an hour before the charter

passengers were due to arrive. As he strode down the dock toward the boat, he spotted Mo Blanchard ahead of him, ambling along in his seaman's swagger, making his way toward *Sea Dragon.*

"Hey, Mo, wait up!" Rafe called out. Mo stopped and turned, allowing Rafe to catch up to him.

"Got the *Dragon* up and runnin'," Mo said. "Just a little problem with the fuel intake. No big deal. My lady's good to go." He was short and stout, a bull of a man and a veteran seaman.

"I know," Rafe said. "I talked to Pete Simmons down at the repair shop." He glanced out at the row of mostly white boats bobbing along the dock, couldn't stop a surge of pride when his gaze landed on *Scorpion.* The Mac was a real beauty, only a few years old when Rafe had bought her in Seward, a longtime dream come true.

Part of the money had come from the sale of property his family owned in Texas, enough to get him the boat, expand his business, and still leave him way more than comfortable.

"Schedule shows you've got six passengers for a full-day charter," Rafe said to Mo.

"That's right."

"I know I don't have to tell you, but try to

find a little smooth water. Always better if half the folks aboard don't get sick."

"I'll watch out for them. I don't much like cleanin' up after 'em when the weather don't cooperate."

"How did yesterday go?" Mo had captained *Scorpion* while Rafe spent the morning in bed with Liv. Of course he didn't say that. With Chip Reed in custody and no new leads, for the moment their investigation into Scotty's murder had hit a dead end.

"Halibut were biting," Mo said. "Good day all round." He chuckled. "Best entertainment of the day was Zach and Jaimie."

"That right?"

"That girl can get real salty, she puts her mind to it. Zach lets her push him till he gets tired of it, then he puts a stop to it, nice and firmlike, you know? Boy knows just how to handle her."

"I've got a hunch he's got plans for Jaimie."

"I seen the way he used to watch her when he was workin' with me. Girl couldn't see Zach for her crush on Scott, but Zach was always there, biding his time. Scotty was never right for Jaimie. She needs a man with a firm hand. Zach might just be that man."

Rafe chuckled. "Could be. I guess we'll see."

Rafe climbed aboard *Scorpion* while Mo continued down the dock to *Sea Dragon*. The third boat in the fleet, *Sea Devil,* was captained by Josh Dorset. Josh was a few years younger than Rafe, happily married with a baby on the way. He was competent and extremely capable. Rafe rarely had to worry about Josh.

As he set to work in the cabin, he thought of Zach and Jaimie, which made him think of Olivia and the dinner he was cooking for her tonight. He was facing a nine-hour charter in rough weather. He'd be tired as hell when he got home.

A memory arose of Liv in her lacy hot pink thong, and his groin tightened. Not *that* tired, he thought with the trace of a smile, and went back to work.

Liv glanced at the clock. It was already four in the afternoon. Rafe would be expecting her to show up at his house for supper at seven. Her mouth went dry. How could she have been stupid enough to agree?

"So how did it go?" Katie had a way of intruding when Liv most needed time to think. "You and Rafe went off looking for clues, right?"

Just the mention of his name sent her thoughts in his direction again. She remembered the pain she had felt at the gruesome details of Scotty's murder. How Rafe had pulled her protectively against him. How just having him there had given her a shot of strength.

"Rafe's a Scorpio, you know," Katie said as if they had been talking about Rafe all day. "Probably the reason he named his boat *Scorpion.*"

"I don't believe in astrology. I doubt Rafe does, either."

"I do. I used to date a Scorpio, and Rafe fits the description perfectly."

Her curiosity kicked in. "What are they supposed to be like?"

Katie smiled. "When I was going with Griff, I was really into that stuff. Let me see . . . a Scorpio is serious and driven. He can be overbearing and sometimes demanding. To a Scorpio, everything's black and white. I remember they like solving puzzles, finding out people's secrets. They're in ultimate control of their destiny, intensely passionate, and wildly possessive."

Katie grinned. "That's gotta be Rafe, right? I see the way he looks at you. Like you belong to him and another man better not think about getting too close."

Liv thought of what he'd said about the man at the motel, about not liking the way he had looked at her. Katie was right. It sounded exactly like Rafe. He was overbearing and possessive. He was dominating in bed and sexy as hell.

So far he hadn't asked much about her past, but the interest was there in those golden-brown eyes, a look that said he wanted to know more about her.

She shouldn't have let him spend the night. Now that she had, she needed to distance herself, put things back the way they were before. She didn't need Rafe Brodie digging into her past. She couldn't afford for Rafe to know her secrets. It could endanger both of their lives.

"Liv, are you okay? You look kind of pale."

She managed to smile. "Rafe and I are mostly just friends. One night doesn't make a relationship and that's the way it's going to stay."

Katie grinned as if she knew some deep female secret. "Good luck with that." She lifted her apron off over her head. "My shift's over. I'll see you tomorrow."

Liv just nodded. She'd agreed to have supper with Rafe. Which involved far more than just supper. Dear God, what on earth had she been thinking?

The hours slipped past. The more she thought about the evening ahead, the more she realized what a mistake she had made. She was close to a full-blown panic attack by six o'clock, though she had never had one before. She had to do something. She had to call him and she had to do it now.

Liv reached for her cell phone.

CHAPTER SIXTEEN

Rafe got the call at six forty-five. He'd been more than half expecting it. He swore softly, sure who it was before he pulled his cell phone out of his pocket. He wasn't surprised to look down and see Liv's number.

"Hello, darlin'."

"Rafe, something's come up. I can't make dinner tonight. I'm really sorry to call at the last minute, but I just can't make it."

"Actually, I've been expecting to hear from you."

"You have?"

"Of course I was hoping I'd be wrong."

"I don't know what you're talking about. A large party just came in. I need to stay and work."

"Not a problem. You gotta do what you gotta do."

"Thanks, Rafe, for being so understanding." Liv disconnected the call.

Rafe just smiled. He understood, all right. He understood exactly. Liv was running again and he wasn't going to put up with it. Grabbing his Windbreaker, he headed down to the garage and climbed into his pickup. A few minutes later, he was on his way to the Pelican.

He could hardly wait to see the look on Olivia's face when he got there.

The café was busy with the dinner crowd, and a large party sat in the side banquet room they used for bigger groups. It was busy, but Nell was working, Charlie Foot was cooking, Cassie was also on the schedule, and everything was under control.

A flicker of guilt slid through her. She had used work as an excuse to cancel her date with Rafe and done it at the very last minute. It wasn't fair and she knew it.

But she'd been frantic, worried about getting in too deep. Because the hard truth was she wanted to see him in the very worst way.

Liv blotted out thoughts of the big fat lie she had told and decided to go back to work. She was heading for her apron on the rack next to the counter when Nell walked up.

"Looks like it's gonna be a real good night."

"Yes, it does." Liv spotted a young couple who had finished reading their menus and set them down on the table. "I'll grab my apron and take care of the table in the corner."

"You worked last night," Nell said, stopping her. "This is your night off. I thought you were having dinner with Rafe."

A flush crept into her cheeks. "Well, I was, but —"

The bell rang.

Nell smiled. "Oh, good. There he is now."

Liv's eyes widened at she turned to see Rafe's tall, broad-shouldered figure filling the doorway. There was no mistaking the determination in his features, or the hard glint in those whiskey-brown eyes. She swallowed as he stalked her across the room like the lion she'd once called him.

Rafe stopped right in front of her and those hot brown eyes fixed on her face.

"I told you I couldn't come," she said. "It's busy, so I have to work."

His gaze traveled the dining room, then swung back to hers. "Looks to me like you've got things under control." He took her arm. "Let's go."

"What? What do you think you're doing?"

"I'm taking you to my house for dinner. Just the way we planned."

Liv jerked free. "I told you I'm busy. I'm sorry, Rafe, but that's the way it is."

His features darkened. "You've got two choices here, Olivia. You can come with me and I can finish making the supper I'd already started when you called. Or I can do what I've fantasized about and carry you out of here over my shoulder."

Her gaze moved down that tall, hard body, and heat rolled through her. "You . . . you fantasized about that?"

"I told you."

"You said you'd considered it. That isn't the same."

His jaw hardened. "You're right. It isn't."

Liv gasped as he bent and set himself in her middle, lifted her off her feet and slung her over his shoulder like a sack of shrimp. Rafe turned and started striding for the door, and the restaurant erupted in laughter. Several people clapped and cheered.

Furious and embarrassed, Liv pounded on his back. "Put me down, Rafe Brodie!"

Rafe, of course, ignored her.

"Damn you!" She pounded harder, but only succeeded in knocking the clip out of her hair, letting the dark strands tumble over her head. Rafe just kept walking.

They were outside in seconds. He opened the driver-side door of his pickup and tossed her roughly in the middle of the seat.

Liv scrabbled toward the passenger door and reached for the handle.

"Don't do it," Rafe warned. "You might not like some of the other things I've fantasized about doing to you."

Oh, dear God! Her face went warm as he climbed behind the wheel, leaned over and slid his arm around her waist. Hauling her across the seat, he fit her snuggly against his side. The engine roared to life and they were heading north, up Hazelet to his house.

Liv was furious. She replayed the scene in the café, remembered the determined look on his face and the feel of his hard-muscled shoulder as he'd carted her out of the restaurant. Only Rafe Brodie would dare do something like that. She was angry and embarrassed. And, she suddenly realized, ridiculously turned on.

Oh, dear God!

"At the very least we're friends," he said, casting a hard look in her direction. "Friends don't treat each other that way."

He was right. She felt like crying. He had a way of confusing her. Making her feel guilty, and angry, and on fire for him all at once.

"You're right," she said softly. "I apologize."

"That's better. Don't expect me to apologize for hauling you out of there. I liked it too much." He flicked her a sideways glance. "Were you really that afraid?"

Fresh anger rolled through her. "I wasn't afraid. Why would I be afraid?"

"Because, Liv, this thing between us . . . it's like a wildfire. You can't tell exactly which way it's going to burn, but you know you can't stop it, and it's frightening. And if you want the truth, it scares the hell out of me, too."

He couldn't have said anything that would touch her more. Her anger began to fade. She took a deep breath and slowly released it. "I'm sorry, Rafe. I really am."

"It's all right. Now you know I mean what I say. You might as well learn that right away."

"Wait a damned minute!"

Ignoring her outburst, he pulled into the driveway, opened the garage door, and drove the pickup inside.

He was standing in front of her when she climbed out of the truck.

"Are we done?" he said. "Because I was really looking forward to tonight."

She wanted to stay mad. It was always a good defense. Instead, she sighed. "We're done. What the hell, I deserved it." How did

212

you fight with a man like that? He might be overbearing, but at least he was honest.

"It's all right," he said softly, sliding his fingers into her hair, lifting it back from her face. "You're here now." Holding her in place, he dipped his head and very thoroughly kissed her. Liv told herself to push him away, but that hadn't worked before, and instead she found herself swaying toward him, clutching those wide shoulders to stay on her feet.

Rafe just kept kissing her, leisurely and deeply. She barely noticed when he lifted her into his arms and carried her up the steps into his house.

"I think food is going to have to wait," he said and kissed her again, silencing the half-formed protest on her lips. There wasn't time to look around when they reached the living room. Rafe climbed a second short flight of stairs and continued down the hall to his bedroom.

He was kissing her again and she was breathing hard when he let her go, let her body slide down his. She could feel his erection, remembered how big he was, how good it had felt when he was inside her. He moved her hair off her shoulder and pressed his mouth to the side of her neck.

"We had sex last time," he said, nibbling

an earlobe, making her shiver and her knees feel week. "This time we're going to make love."

A little whimper escaped.

Rafe trailed kisses along her jaw and took her mouth again. When he unbuttoned her shirt and unhooked the sapphire-blue pushup bra she'd put on especially for him before she'd panicked and changed her mind, she didn't try to stop him.

Rafe wanted her, and as he cupped her breasts and ran a thumb over her nipple, God in heaven, she wanted him.

In minutes he had them both naked and stretched out on his bed. He leaned over her, kissed her until she was mindless, then nibbled and tasted his way to her breasts. He was good at this, she knew, knew exactly where to touch her, how to be gentle, just when to use force. He'd already found the perfect little place behind her ear to drive her crazy.

"Please," she whimpered as he came up over her, her nails digging into his shoulders. "I need you inside me, Rafe, please . . ."

"Soon, darlin'." She heard the male satisfaction in his voice. "First, let's see if I can find something else you like."

Her eyes widened as he kissed his way down her body. The next thing she knew his talented mouth had her moaning, then tumbling into climax. She had barely returned from her trip to the stars when she felt him sliding inside her, moving with slow purpose, coaxing her body to respond again. His teeth grazed the side of her neck, nipping and tasting, then his mouth slanted over hers again. Combined with the feel of his hard length stroking her insides, she couldn't help another shivery climax.

Rafe didn't stop.

By the time they were finished several hours later, she was limp and completely sated, barely able to move.

One thing she knew. When Rafe Brodie made love to a woman, it wasn't a night she would soon forget.

It was late, well after midnight by the time they finished showering together, which included more lovemaking and lasted until they ran out of hot water. Liv pulled on one of Rafe's old, faded T-shirts with the words U.S. COAST GUARD, along with a picture of a helicopter and the words AIR SEA RESCUE TEAM, BERING SEA, AK, stamped on the front.

The T-shirt hung down over her hips while Rafe's black tee fit snuggly across his broad shoulders, powerful chest, and biceps. As they walked downstairs, it took an effort for Olivia not to stare.

In the living room, she paused, noticing the room was as male as Rafe was, done in navy blue and brown. Lots of photos of the ocean and boats on the walls, sunrise and sunset over the Valdez harbor and the magnificent Prince William Sound.

The dining table was set for two with navy-blue place mats and dark brown dishes. Everything was coordinated, which Liv found strangely intriguing.

"Everything matches," she said. "That isn't typically a man thing. How did that happen?" *Sally?* she wondered and didn't like the faint thread of jealousy that trickled through her.

"My brother Dylan's getting married to a designer from Beverly Hills. The wedding's set for July." He tossed her a look. "Maybe I could get you to go with me."

Liv glanced away. She hadn't planned anything that far ahead for the last three years. "Maybe."

"Dylan and Lane came up for a visit a couple of months back. I'd asked Lane for advice so she came prepared, brought catalogues, showed me stuff online. We picked furniture for the living room, dining room, and kitchen. Lane ordered it and had it shipped directly here."

"I like what the two of you came up with. Not too fussy, and it suits you perfectly."

"Thanks. I think you'd like her."

Liv ended her inspection and returned her gaze to his. What she saw in those dark, intelligent eyes made her want to know more about him, know the family he clearly loved.

"Maybe someday I'll get to meet her," she said softly, knowing that would probably never happen.

Rafe set his hands at her waist and drew her against him. "You'll meet them. I'm not going to let you run, darlin'." He pressed his mouth against the side of her neck. "And I won't run, either, yes?"

Liv felt the unexpected sting of tears. It sounded so good. Too good. She swallowed. "Okay," she found herself saying.

And prayed she wasn't lying again.

The late supper came off without a hitch. Along with a nice bottle of cabernet, Rafe had opted for the safer menu and broiled a couple of thick New York strip steaks instead of the moose he had in the freezer. The salad was easy enough. The baked potatoes he'd had in the oven when he'd left to fetch Liv were burnt to a crisp so he opened a can of corn and tossed in some butter. Over all, the meal was damned good. Or at least he thought so.

And after the lusty sex they'd had upstairs, Liv was finally relaxed. He wanted her to trust him. If sex was the key, he could damn well handle that.

While they ate, he was smart enough to keep the subjects neutral, what sports they enjoyed, movies they liked, a little about their respective businesses. Nothing about her past, which seemed to be the hot button that put her in flight mode.

"It was a really nice evening, Rafe," she said as both of them rose from the table.

When she reached out to gather the plates, he caught her hand. "I'll do that later. There's something I want to show you." He took her hand and started tugging her up the short flight of stairs that led to the bedrooms.

Liv pulled back. "What is it?"

One of his eyebrows went up at the note of wariness that had crept back into her voice. "You don't want me to think you're afraid again, do you?"

Her chin inched up. "I'm not afraid." He almost smiled as she let him lead her down the hall and opened the door to the sunroom. His big Jacuzzi bubbled in the middle of the room.

"Oh my God, you have a hot tub?" She walked toward it as if in a dream, stuck her face into the warm, humid air rising off the top.

"I bought it when I remodeled. Had to add a room just to have a place for it."

"It must be paradise when you get home after a long day out on the water."

He nodded. "You like single malt? I've got some Oban my brother Nick bought me for Christmas."

She turned. "I love good scotch. The smell of peat and that earthy flavor. A little goes a long way, though. I haven't had any in ages."

He walked over to the sideboard against the wall, turned over a pair of snifters, and poured a dollop of liquor into each one. Liv accepted the glass, inhaled the mossy aroma of peat. "Too bad I didn't bring my bathing suit."

Rafe walked up behind her, pushed her hair off her shoulders, and pressed his mouth against the nape of her neck. "A bathing suit, darlin', is the last thing you need."

She turned to look up at him, an interested gleam in her eyes. "Maybe you're right."

"Oh yeah, I'm right. You won't believe how good it'll make you feel."

"It? Or you?"

His mouth edged up. "Both."

A smile bloomed. He felt it like a kick in the stomach.

"After . . . you know . . . earlier, I don't doubt it for a minute." She looked at the tub, then at him. He figured she was weighing her options, telling herself she ought to go, remembering the way he'd hauled her out of the café and guessing he might do it again.

Rafe took the snifter out of her hand and set it down next to the Jacuzzi, drew Liv into his arms, and kissed her.

He figured it wouldn't take her long to figure out she wasn't going home till morning.

CHAPTER SEVENTEEN

Sunlight filtered through the curtains as Rafe crossed the bedroom, walked out into the hall, and quietly closed the door. He'd give Olivia another few minutes, then wake her. He knew she didn't want to be late for work and neither did he. But it was early yet, a little before five a.m. Making his way to the kitchen, he put a pot of coffee on to brew, went out and grabbed the newspaper off the porch.

The headlines were more the usual sort for the little town, he saw as he spread the *Star* open on the counter. FISHING SEASON OFF TO STRONG START. TOURISM PREDICTED UP 10 PERCENT. Another column read, GRIZZLY SPOTTED NEAR HORSETAIL FALLS. Just small-town news. No murder. No mayhem.

He skimmed down, saw the follow-up story on the man who'd died out at the pipeline terminal. The article said terminal security had concluded the man's death was accidental. The authorities believed it was alcohol-related.

Rafe scoffed as he read the rest of the story. Apparently the guy had been drinking and fell off the storage tank. Dumb-ass had died of stupidity. In Alaska it happened all the time.

Rafe read a few more articles and checked the clock. Ten minutes more and he'd wake Olivia — again. His mouth edged up. He'd already nudged her awake once this morning. Fortunately — and another mark in the plus column for her — both of them seemed to like morning sex.

The coffee finished brewing, the rich aroma filling the kitchen. Walking over to the cabinet, he took down two mugs, poured one for himself. He started to fill a cup for Liv when his cell phone began to play the Coast Guard song.

His brother's name popped up on the display. Rafe pressed the phone against his ear. "Hey, Nick, good to hear from you."

"Got some news. Waited as long as I could stand before I called. Hope I didn't wake you."

"I'm up and rolling. What's going on?"

"We're pregnant."

Rafe heard the grin in his brother's voice.

" 'Bout time," he said, knowing how much this meant to Nick. "Congratulations."

"Samantha's known for a while, but we wanted to wait until we were sure everything was okay."

"That's great, Nick." Having a family was his youngest brother's lifelong dream — though it was almost comic to hear his tough-as-nails, former Army Ranger, ex-homicide detective brother using the term *we* when referring to being pregnant. "When's the big event?"

"Middle of December. Samantha's already picking out baby furniture."

"And you're helping, right?"

"Well, yeah. I'm gonna be a dad, you know?" And clearly he was over the moon about it, though Nick had had to find the right woman and take on the Russian mob before he'd figured out what he really wanted.

"Boy or girl?"

"We don't know yet. Doesn't really matter."

"No, it doesn't."

"So what about you?" Nick asked. "What's happening in your neck of the woods?"

"Got some bad news. You remember Scotty Ferris, the kid who worked for me? He was murdered. Funeral's this afternoon.

I'm trying to help the cops figure out who did it."

"Be careful, big brother. Murder's my line of work, not yours."

"I hear you."

"You and Sally been over for a while. You seeing anyone interesting?"

Rafe glanced up at the ceiling as if he could see Olivia sleeping naked in his bed. "Actually, I am."

"Wouldn't be that sexy little brunette you had your eye on down at the Pelican Café last time I was there?"

"One and the same."

Nick chuckled. "Imagine that. She's a beautiful woman."

"Liv actually thinks if she doesn't wear makeup no one will notice."

Nick laughed. "She doesn't realize what a discerning eye you have when it comes to women. She as fine as she looks?"

"Finer."

"So what's her story? She's fairly new in town. I remember you told me that. She owns the café, right?"

"That's right."

"What else?"

"What do you mean, what else?"

"What else do you know about her?"

He didn't know jack, and now that she

was in his life, it was starting to bug the hell out of him.

"Not enough. I was really hoping she'd open up and tell me herself, but it doesn't look like that's going to happen. You think you could run a background check? You don't have to spend a lot of time, just give me the basics. Olivia Chandler, Valdez, Alaska. That's about all I know. Is that enough?"

"For now. I'll run with it, see what turns up, and get back to you."

"One more thing. Whatever you find, it's just between you and me. Not Dylan. Not anyone in the office. Nobody."

A moment of silence fell. "Not the police, is that what you're saying?"

Rafe didn't answer. He had no idea what his brother would find out, but he didn't want to take any chances. "Just you and me. I need your word."

"You don't have to ask."

"Thanks. Give Samantha a hug for me."

"You bet I will. Take care, big brother." Nick hung up the phone.

As Rafe walked back to the counter and filled the second mug, guilt slipped through him. He hated going behind Olivia's back, but if they were ever going to have a chance of making this thing work, he needed to know what the hell was going on. Olivia was keeping secrets. That meant she'd had problems in the past, problems that might affect her future.

For the first time, he realized making things work with Liv was exactly what he wanted. Whatever she was hiding, he needed to know, needed to find out what he was up against.

The guilt slipped away. Olivia was his now. Whether she was willing to admit it or not.

Rafe was a man who protected what was his.

At eleven thirty that morning, Liv crossed the café and turned off the orange neon OPEN sign. She turned over the hanging CLOSED sign so it showed through the half-glass front door. They were locking up for the day as soon as the customers finished eating.

Today was Scotty's funeral. Cassie had stayed home to get ready. Her mother was picking her up, and everyone who worked in the café was going. Scott's body had been cremated. The service was a memorial being held at the Community Church at one o'clock. Rafe only had a half-day charter, so he'd be back in time to attend.

Afterward, he was taking Cassie and Lois

and a few close friends, including the staff from the Pelican and the guys Scotty had worked with, out on *Sea Scorpion* to scatter his ashes.

Olivia's throat went tight. Such a useless, tragic waste of a young man's life.

She thought of Scotty, and an image of Chip Reed came to mind. He was a good-looking guy who seemed to have no lack of women. True, he had an inflated ego and was way too cocky, but a lot of young men were that way. For a while, he'd fooled Cassie into thinking she loved him, but eventually she had figured out how little he really had to offer.

Cassie had dumped him, but was that reason enough for Chip to commit an act of brutal, senseless murder? And why wait so long? Chip and Cassie hadn't been together for nearly two years.

Cassie didn't believe Chip was guilty. Ben Friedman didn't believe it. In fact, none of the other guys at the card game believed Chip was the killer.

If not, who was it? Liv's thoughts circled around to the two men she and Rafe had talked to at the motel. They'd been interviewed by the police on several different occasions, but Rafe thought something was off about them. Maybe they'd heard something that night but didn't want to get involved with the police. Maybe they knew more about the murder than they were willing to admit.

The notion had been nagging her, gnawing like a dog on a bone.

She glanced at the clock. It was time to get ready for the funeral. With a sigh, she headed upstairs to change.

Rafe steered *Sea Scorpion* out of the harbor, into the open waters of the Sound. The funeral at the church was over, a brief memorial where family and friends said good-bye to a young man they loved.

A number of those same friends filled the boat, along with Cassie and Lois, and the guys who played cards with Scotty and were there the night he was killed — all but Chip Reed, who was still locked up in jail.

The *Scorpion* crew was there, including Jaimie and Zach; and Mo Blanchard and Josh Dorset, the other two charter boat captains. The gang from the Pelican was aboard: Katie McKenzie, Wayne Littlefish, Charlie Foot, and Nell Olsen.

Standing behind the wheel, Rafe sent his gaze in search of the tall woman dressed completely in black, her glossy dark hair pulled into a severe twist at the back of her head. Standing alone at the rail, Liv stared across the water toward the high mountains rising in the distance. Rafe hadn't talked to her since he had driven her back to her apartment early that morning.

He gave the wheel over to Mo and headed in her direction, came quietly up beside her and just stood there for a while, letting her get accustomed to his presence.

"How you doin', baby?"

She turned and looked up at him, her face pale above her black sweater. She shook her head. "I feel so sorry for her. Cassie loved him so much."

Rafe's gaze went to the younger woman. Her face was paper white, her arms wrapped tight around the urn that held Scotty's ashes, her light brown hair whipping in the chilly afternoon breeze.

"I've never loved anyone that way," Liv said. "I'm not sure I ever want to."

Rafe thought of Ashley Richards, remembered the pain of losing her that had nearly brought him to his knees. "There was a woman I loved once. It was a long time ago."

Liv's gray eyes swung to his face. She must have caught the flash of grief that still lingered when he thought of Ash. "She died?"

He nodded. "Car accident. I was in college. I told myself I'd never get in that deep with anyone again. I didn't want to risk the pain. Now . . ." His gaze went to Liv. "Maybe it'd be worth it."

Olivia held his stare for several long seconds before she glanced away. "Maybe I just never met the right man."

"If you did, could you love him that way?"

Her eyes filled with tears that the wind scattered against her cheeks. "Even if I wanted to, I couldn't."

"Why not?"

She didn't answer, just shook her head. "I'm sorry . . . It's not a good day."

"No, it isn't." Rafe looked up at a sky so blue and clear, it didn't seem real. "Though God gave us the best He knew how."

She tilted her head back, followed his line of vision across the cloudless sky to the mountains beyond the glistening sea. "Yes, He did."

"You like being out on the ocean?"

"I do. My dad had a sailboat when I was a kid. I used to go out with him all the time. I loved every minute."

He liked hearing that. He liked that she was opening up a little. He liked a lot of things about Olivia Chandler. "He still around?"

"No. Dad had a heart attack the summer I graduated high school. Mom left when I was six. We never heard from her again."

"Brothers and sisters?" he asked casually, expecting her to retreat any minute.

Liv shook her head.

Rafe felt the engines slow as Mo came to the spot they had chosen. "Time to get this done."

She swallowed. "Yes."

Rafe leaned down and pressed a soft kiss on her mouth, settled a hand at her waist and drew her close.

Fifteen minutes and buckets of tears later, Scotty's ashes floated away with the current, his young life stolen, his last remains disappearing forever into the sea.

It was over. Scotty Ferris was gone.

For the first time that day, Rafe let the anger surface he'd been keeping locked away. His jaw felt tight, adrenaline pumped through his veins. It shouldn't have happened. The kid deserved to live. Cassie deserved to live the life Scotty had promised. Her baby deserved its father. Someone needed to pay.

Rafe's hand unconsciously fisted. Unfortunately, he didn't know if directing his anger at Chip Reed was where it belonged or if there was someone else. And until he knew for sure, knew without a doubt that Reed had killed Scotty, this wouldn't be finished.

Not for him.

Standing once more behind the wheel, Rafe pressed the throttle forward. The boat picked up speed as they headed back to the harbor.

CHAPTER EIGHTEEN

While Rafe did whatever captains do to their boats when they arrived back in port, Liv left with the group from the Pelican. They dispersed in front of the café, which would remain closed for the rest of the day. Most were going over to Cassie's, where half the ladies in town had left food for the group of friends who had stopped by after the service and the group who would be arriving now.

Liv sent over a couple of pies, a Pelican dessert specialty, but she couldn't work up the courage to go herself.

She'd had enough sadness for one day.

Instead, she went upstairs and put on her running clothes, shoved her stun gun into her pocket, then went downstairs and out to the backyard.

The restaurant was empty. Grabbing a couple of dog biscuits from her stash next to the back door, she walked out on the porch. Khan was lying in front of his customized, storage-shed doghouse, his best friend curled up beside him.

Liv started to smile. Tuxedo was visiting. She was the sweetest little black-and-white cat Olivia had ever seen. Tux loved everyone and apparently wasn't afraid of anything, not even a big, bad German shepherd who could eat her in a single bite.

Over the months since Liv had moved into the apartment, Tux had started to appear. The little cat had put the dog in his place right away, and Khan, like everyone else, had fallen in love with her.

The big German shepherd was mostly an outside dog, though in the coldest months, Liv brought him inside the apartment. At the neighbor's, where the little cat lived, Tux had her own swinging pet door, but she was a fair-weather cat. Now that the snow had melted, she came over a lot and loved nothing more than to curl up next to Khan out in the yard.

It probably wasn't a good idea for a guard dog to bond with a cat, but Liv didn't have the heart to separate the pair. Smiling, she went back in and got a cat treat from the bag she'd purchased for Tuxedo, went back out and walked up to where the two lay in the sun.

Khan's ears went up and he came to his feet, knocking Tux from her comfy, fur-lined perch. Liv gave them each a treat and snapped Khan into his leash.

He flicked a last glance at the cat, torn between the excitement of a run and abandoning his friend. Tux's yellow eyes flashed him a pouty, *How can you leave me?* look, then she turned away and ambled back toward home.

Liv headed for the gate, then took off running, Khan falling in beside her. The dog loved getting out, seemed to love seeing what was happening in the world beyond his yard. Twenty minutes into the run, Liv felt better, her head clear for the first time that day.

She had a bad moment when she remembered telling Rafe about her dad and that she had no brothers and sisters, but she didn't really think it was information that could get her in trouble.

Khan trotted beside her as she picked up her pace and began to move faster, letting her muscles lengthen and stretch, feeling the burn. She wasn't paying attention to her surroundings, just letting her feet carry her wherever they wanted while her thoughts wandered. When she glanced up, she saw the sign for the Seaside Motel.

An image of Cassie arose, her arms wrapped tight around the urn that held Scotty's remains. If it hadn't been for Rafe's gentle persuasion, Liv wasn't sure Cassie would have let him go.

She glanced back at the motel. A dark blue Jeep Cherokee sat in front of room number two. Unless the men had gone somewhere on foot, they were probably there. On impulse she turned and jogged toward the motel. Maybe if she talked to the men without Rafe's intimidating presence, they would be willing to tell her whatever it was they hadn't told the police.

Assuming they knew anything at all.

She slowed to a walk to cool down a little. Gave the "sit" command to Khan and told him to "stay" a few feet away as she knocked on the door. The minute her knuckles connected with wood, she realized her mistake.

What if the men hadn't just heard or seen something the night of the murder? What if they'd had something to do with killing Scotty?

As the door swung open, her hand automatically went into the pocket of her sweatshirt and her fingers wrapped around the stun gun. In a black T-shirt that fit snugly over his lean-muscled frame, the handsome young Asian, Lee Wong, opened the door. The instant before he realized who was standing in the corridor and partially closed the door, she caught a glimpse of his friend, tall, dark-skinned Michael Nevin, and a third man who quickly stepped into the bathroom out of sight.

"I really hate to bother you," Liv said, wishing she hadn't been so impulsive but determined to make the best of the situation. "I just happened to see your Jeep so I figured you were probably in your room."

"You're Captain Brodie's friend."

"That's right. Olivia Chandler. I own the Pelican Café." Ignoring the sliver of unease creeping down her spine, she managed to smile. If she'd been thinking more clearly, she would have realized how dangerous this could be. Still, she was here now and she wasn't about to miss the opportunity.

"We haven't tried your place yet," Wong said. "Heard it has great breakfasts."

She kept her smile in place. "The best. I was wondering . . . when we were here before, I had the feeling maybe you saw or heard something the night of the murder, but didn't want to get involved. I wouldn't blame you." She shrugged. "Who wants to get involved in a police investigation, right? So I thought maybe if I promised to keep you both out of it, not say I spoke to you,

you might tell me something that could be useful."

Nevin stepped forward, grabbed the edge of the door and jerked it open, got right in her face. "We told you, woman. We were out drinking. We came home drunk. We didn't hear or see a thing."

Khan growled low in his throat as Wong pushed the tall man back into the room. "Take it easy, Michael. The lady lost a friend. She wants the guy who did it to pay."

Ever the diplomat, Wong turned back to her. "I wish we could help, Ms. Chandler, but Michael's telling you the truth. We didn't see anything that night."

She nodded. She shouldn't have come. It was a stupid thing to do. "I'm really sorry I bothered you. It won't happen again."

As she turned to leave, the tall man made some remark she couldn't hear. She wondered who the third man was and why he hadn't wanted to been seen.

More suspicious than she'd been before, she started walking back to the café, Khan keeping pace beside her. Rafe had been right. There was something off about the men.

It didn't mean they'd committed a murder, but still . . .

Liv picked up her pace. She needed to put

Kahn in his yard; then she was going to find Rafe.

"I've got to call Doyle, tell him the woman was here." Lee pulled the burner phone out of his jeans. This whole mess seemed to be getting worse by the day. But the time was close at hand and all that mattered was making it happen, just the way they'd planned.

"You do whatever you want," Cain said as he headed for the door. "Just remember, I wasn't here. You understand?"

"You were not supposed to be," Nadir said darkly.

"Yeah, well, if you'd been busting your balls for weeks, you might want a little distraction yourself. I'm off tonight. I'm heading over to the Fisherman's Catch. Lots of young pussy in there. Maybe I'll get lucky for a change."

"You gotta be kidding," Lee said. "Doyle will freak if he finds out you're going out on the town."

"Doyle isn't going to find out. Make the call if you want, but keep me out of it. She didn't see me, anyway. If she did and she starts trouble, I'll take care of her."

"No way, Darius," Lee said. "You screw this up, you'll be the one who gets taken

239

care of. Doyle will see to it personally."

"Fuck you."

"Get out of here," Nadir said. "And don't come back."

Cain flipped a bird and left the motel room.

"That guy's trouble," Lee said.

"Yes, but he is the key to our entire mission."

Lee ran a hand over his short, black hair. "You don't have to remind me."

"You had better call Doyle."

"I guess."

"Doyle wanted to know her name. At least now we know who she is."

Lee nodded. But he didn't want to tell the man in charge that Cain had shown up at the room again and might have caused another problem. Doyle would freak, and shit had a way of rolling downhill.

With a steadying breath, he punched Trent Doyle's number, heard the irritation in his voice when he answered.

"What is it? And it had better not be more trouble."

"The woman came back asking questions again. Her name is Olivia Chandler. Owns a place called the Pelican Café. What do you want us to do?"

A long silence fell. "You're a computer

whiz. I want to know everything there is to know about the Chandler woman. Find something we can use, something about her she doesn't want anyone to know."

"She owns a café. What the hell do you expect to find?"

"There's always something. An extra-marital affair. Slutty reputation as a kid. Drug addiction. Alcoholism. Something. She steps in our way again, we put a stop to it. Now get to work."

The phone went dead. Lee hadn't mentioned Cain's visit. He flicked a glance across the room, got his answer in Nadir's silent reply.

They were going to keep their mouths shut and pray nothing else would go wrong.

With the funeral over, Cassie's small house was filled to overflowing with people who had been at the memorial or out on the boat. Just like everywhere else, it was a tradition in Alaska for people to gather together in times of grief.

As the afternoon slipped past, the crowd was beginning to drift away. Half-full platters of fried chicken and poached fish, scooped-out tuna casseroles, salads, and desserts sat on the dining room table.

Rafe had spoken to Cassie and Lois, made

241

polite conversation with friends, then filled a small, obligatory plate full of food, wandered out to the backyard, and sat down at the picnic table to eat.

Enjoying the chance to break away from the dwindling group of mourners, he had almost finished his last bite of the Pelican's delicious three-berry pie when his cell phone started playing. Rafe pulled it out of his pocket and saw his brother's name.

"Can you talk?" Nick asked, cutting straight to the chase.

At the tone of his brother's voice, a little thread of unease slipped through him. He glanced around. "I'm alone for the moment. What's up?"

"Looks like your lady friend isn't who she says she is."

Rafe's shoulders tightened. "If she isn't, then who the hell is she?"

"No idea. On paper she's Olivia Chandler. Born to Matthew and Cynthia Chandler in March of 1983 in Medfield, Massachusetts, that's a suburb of Boston. Graduated Medfield High School. Attended University of Massachusetts, graduated in 2004 with a 3.5 grade average. She has a driver's license, a Social Security number, even a passport."

"So what's the problem?"

"The problem, which wouldn't come up

under normal circumstances and only happened because you're my brother and I don't like the thought of some woman conning you, is that if you try to track her backward, you can't."

"I'm not getting this. What are you talking about?" His mind spun as he tried to make sense of what his brother was saying. All the while his heart was beating dully, thumping away like a big bass drum inside his chest.

"I'm telling you her parents don't really exist. Her birth certificate isn't in the courthouse records. She didn't go to Medfield High School. She wasn't at the University of Massachusetts."

Tension settled between his shoulder blades. "No husband? No marriage?"

"No. A lot of women go back to their maiden names, but that isn't the problem."

He felt sick to his stomach. "So if Olivia Chandler isn't a real person, why do the records show she is?"

"Here's the thing. If you have enough money, you can buy yourself a new identity. If you're a criminal, for instance, and you want a new life, you can pay someone to forge the documents you need, get them placed where you need them. Once you're in the computer system, you can use the information to get a driver's license, a passport, anything anyone else can get."

"Olivia isn't a criminal."

"How can you be sure?"

How could he be? He had only begun to know her. Yet every instinct told him Olivia was the strong, caring woman he believed her to be. "If you knew her, you'd know she isn't that way. What about witness protection? They do that kind of thing, right? Give people new identities. It's the only explanation I can think of that makes any sense."

"It's possible. If she's in WITSEC, that's still not good news. Means someone wants to hurt her. Long as you're with her, that puts you in the line of fire. I'm not liking this, bro."

He didn't like it either.

"Listen, Rafe," Nick continued, "I know you think a lot of this woman, but you need to be careful."

"She runs a café, for chrissake. She's not some female assassin."

"We don't know what the hell she is. We need something else, some way to find her. Get me a photo. I can run it through facial recognition. Or better yet, a DNA sample."

Rafe fell silent. Now that he knew his suspicions were correct, he wasn't sure he wanted to continue. But he knew his brother, knew Nick wouldn't stop until he found out the truth. His brother would want to make sure Rafe wasn't in any kind of danger.

"I know none of this is what you wanted to hear," Nick said a little more gently, "but if you care about this woman as much as I think you do, you need to figure out what the hell is going on. Get me something I can use."

Rafe thought of the night he'd spent in Olivia's apartment. He'd gotten up early and padded around a little on his way to make coffee. It occurred to him now that he hadn't seen a single family photo in the house, nothing on the walls, nothing on the tables. Getting DNA off a Coke can or something would be easy enough, but a photo . . . ? Probably not.

More and more, he was thinking witness protection. Maybe that was how she knew all those police terms.

"Thanks, Nick. I'll get back to you."

"Like I said, be careful."

Rafe hung up the phone.

CHAPTER NINETEEN

Liv left Khan in the yard behind the café and went in search of Rafe, heading first to the harbor across the street. Everyone was gone from the *Scorpion* by the time she got there. Mo had gone back to check on *Sea Dragon* and was now ambling along the dock in her direction.

Liv smiled. "Hey, Mo. Everyone's gone from *Scorpion.* I'm looking for Rafe. Do you know if he went home?" She didn't want to call him. She would if she had to, but she would rather talk to him in person.

"I was checking on my lady. Rafe left with Cassie and Lois, took them back to Cassie's house. The man takes his responsibilities real serious-like. With Scotty gone, he wants to make sure Cassie's okay."

She should have figured that. "Thanks, Mo." She started to turn away.

"I'm headin' there myself. You want to go over together?"

"Sure."

They walked to the house side by side, talked about the memorial service, how nice it had been, about the weather and how Scott was resting now in exactly the place he'd want to be. Then they fell silent, each lost in his own thoughts.

Once they reached Cassie's little wood-frame house, they split up, Mo going over to speak to Lois, Liv stopping to hug Cassie, then giving Lois her condolences. Olivia greeted some of the people she knew from the café, then walked into the backyard, where Cassie had told her she could find Rafe.

She found him seated at the picnic table and sat down on the bench across from him. For the next few minutes she filled him in on her trip to the motel, talking to the men, catching a glimpse of someone else. From that point, the conversation didn't go quite the way she'd planned.

"Have you lost your mind?" Rafe thundered, shooting up from the bench across the table. "What in the name of God possessed you to go back to that motel by yourself?"

She'd been afraid he'd be upset. It was the reason she hadn't wanted to have this conversation over the phone. Rafe was protective by nature. Still, she hadn't expected him to explode.

"I didn't set out to go there, it just sort of happened. I was jogging and I wound up close by, saw the motel sign, saw the Jeep, and figured the men would likely be in their room. I had my stun gun and I was with Khan, so I figured I'd be okay."

"You carry a stun gun?"

"Well, yes, when I'm running or off someplace by myself. I thought the men might tell me something they wouldn't tell you."

"Why, because you're a woman?"

"Men being men, I thought if you weren't there looking like you wanted to bash in someone's head, they might open up, give me something we didn't know about what happened the night of the murder."

"I swear to God, Olivia —"

Liv shot up off the bench, marched around to confront him. "Don't you swear at me, Rafe Brodie!" He was madder than he had a right to be, and now she was angry herself. "I can go anyplace I want — anytime I want. You don't own me!"

Rafe caught her shoulders, forcing her to tip her head back to look at him. "We're supposed to be working on this together. What you did put you in danger. That isn't going to happen. I won't let it. You do what I say or —"

"Or what?"

His jaw hardened. "Or I swear I'll lock you in my bedroom and keep you there until this is over."

"Try it and I'll just climb out the window."

"Fine, then I'll tie you to the bed, and believe me, a sailor knows how to tie a knot you won't get out of."

She arched an eyebrow. "Is that another of your fantasies?"

Amusement began to crinkle the corners of his eyes. She could feel his anger draining away, along with some of her own. His sexy mouth edged up. "Actually, it is."

A little sliver of heat moved through her. Oh, dear God! She wanted to stay mad at him, she really did. "You are the most irritating man."

He reached up and gently touched her cheek. "I couldn't handle it if something happened to you, darlin'. Promise me you won't do anything like that again."

She thought of the woman he had loved and lost, understood that he couldn't face losing someone he cared about again. "I knew it was stupid the minute I knocked on the door. I'm sorry."

Rafe slid a hand behind her neck, dragged

her mouth to his, and kissed her, a different sort of kiss this time, filled with a trace of worry mingled with relief. When he let her go, there was something in his eyes, but it was an expression she couldn't read.

"I'm sorry, too. I shouldn't have yelled at you."

"No, you shouldn't have."

"Probably won't be the last time. I can be a little overprotective."

She laughed. "A little?"

He shrugged. "I had three brothers. I was the oldest. I guess that's where I got it."

"It's not such a bad thing." How long had it been since anyone had wanted to protect her?

"No?"

"Just don't get carried away."

Rafe flashed one of his devastating smiles. "I'll do my best, darlin'." Her stomach dipped at the endearment, the way it always did when he said it that way.

"Now, one more time, let's go over what happened after you got to the motel."

For the next few minutes she filled in the details. Told him how Wong had been friendly but Nevin had been nasty and rude. She ended by talking about the third man in the room.

"I just got a glimpse, but I'm pretty sure I

saw someone."

"Pretty sure?"

She sighed. "I can't be certain. It happened so fast. He was more a shadow than anything."

"What did this shadow look like?"

"I don't know. A good-sized man, I'd say. Bigger than Wong or Nevin."

"If he was actually a man and not just a shadow."

"Yes. What do you suppose he was doing there?"

"No idea. I didn't get the impression these guys knew anyone in town."

"Should we tell the police?"

"Tell them what? That we were snooping around again, bothering the tourists? I'm surprised they haven't already warned us to back off. They will if we press too hard."

"That's what I was thinking."

Rafe looked around the backyard, but they were the only ones left outside. "You ready to go?"

"I didn't want to come in the first place. I knew I should, but I just wanted a break from the sadness, you know?"

"I know." Slinging an arm across her shoulders, he led her back through the house. Some of Cassie's girlfriends were cleaning up the mess, so Liv was able to leave without feeling guilty.

"You walk down?" Rafe asked.

"Yes, with Mo. I guess he's already gone."

"You can ride back with me."

She nodded.

They climbed into his pickup. As he drove toward the café, he didn't ask her if she wanted to come home with him. He just kept driving toward his house. When she realized the direction he was headed, Olivia sat up a little straighter in the seat.

"Rafe, I can't . . . not today. I need some time by myself."

He turned to look at her. "I know what you need, baby. Sometimes the best way to be alone is to be with someone who cares about you."

She didn't have the strength to argue. Or maybe she was beginning to trust him. Leaning her head back against the seat, she didn't tell him to turn around, and Rafe didn't take her home.

Lying spoon-fashion on the sofa, Rafe's arm draped over Olivia's sleeping figure, he kept her tucked close against him, letting her fall more deeply asleep.

Gently, he eased himself away and quietly got up from the couch. Disappearing up the half flight of stairs to the linen closet in the hallway, he dragged out a blanket, went back down and unfolded the blanket over Liv. He knew she'd thought he expected to have sex when he brought her home with him, but that wasn't what she needed. At least not tonight.

Like everyone who had cared for Scotty Ferris, Liv was grieving. Today had been physically and emotionally draining for all of them. For him sex would have been a comfort, but Liv needed something else. Instead of the bedroom, he'd led her over to the sofa and turned on the TV.

He owned lots of DVDs. He was a bachelor. Sometimes after a long day at sea, or during a freezing winter storm, he enjoyed watching a movie.

He pulled open the cabinet next to his big fifty-two-inch flat-screen and began to scan the boxes. "So what's it going to be? A Bruce Willis marathon? *The Matrix* trilogy? *Wolverine*? I've got *Star Wars, Star Trek,* got some Jason Bourne. I've got *Harry Potter* and some other fantasies, but I'm not really high on that stuff."

She was grinning, he saw, for the first time in the last few days. It made his chest feel tight. He thought of the call from his brother, thought how he wished he didn't know now what he'd wanted to know before. He needed to do something about it, but he wasn't sure what, and he wasn't about to pursue the matter today.

He dug farther into the cabinet. "How about James Bond? I've got the whole collection. We can start anywhere you like."

"I love James Bond." She was looking at him with so much warmth, his chest clamped down again.

"You got it." Rafe put on *Goldfinger.* Good a place as any to start. They watched a Sean Connery Bond, then moved on to Pierce Brosnan. They were just starting Daniel Craig in *Casino Royale,* when Liv fell sound asleep.

He'd just held her for a while, her back to his front, liking the way she fit against him so perfectly. Finally, he eased away, turned off the TV, and gently spread the blanket over her.

He had a couple of things to take care of. When he finished, he'd carry her upstairs and put her to bed, let her get a good night's sleep.

It was getting late but the sun was still shining. In the kitchen, he made the calls he'd wanted to make, starting with Ben Friedman. "Ben, it's Rafe Brodie. You got a minute?"

"Sure, Rafe, what's up?"

Rafe explained about the men at the motel and his misgivings. "There's something off about these guys. I need to know what it is. I'd like to set up some kind of surveillance, figure a way to watch them. To do that I'm going to need some help."

Ben's tone changed. "You think one of those men killed Scotty?"

"I don't know. More likely they heard or saw something and don't want to come forward, but I want to be sure. You think you could keep an eye out during the day, keep me posted as to their comings and goings?"

"Are you kidding? If they had something to do with killing Scotty, they need to be in jail. I'll be on 'em like flies on bear scat."

Rafe grinned. "Thanks, Ben."

Next he called Sam King. Sam had been cleared by the police, who had verified his alibi for the night of the murder. He'd been aboard *Scorpion* that afternoon when Scotty's ashes were scattered. He'd apologized again to both him and Liv for his behavior the last couple of days and offered to help them catch Scott's killer any way he could.

"Sam, it's Rafe Brodie. Can you talk?"

"Sure, what's going on?"

Rafe filled him in on his theory. "I want to see what these guys are up to. I'm trying

255

to put a surveillance team together. Ben's going to keep an eye on them during the day. Can you do a couple of hours at night?"

"You bet I can," Sam said darkly. "Just tell me what you need."

"I'll call you back." Rafe hung up and phoned Zach Carver. The kid was only twenty-one, but Rafe was coming to trust him more and more. And though Zach and Scott hadn't been that close, mostly because of Jaimie, he knew Zach wanted justice for Scotty.

"Hey, Cap'n, what's up?"

"I've got something I need to do and I could use some backup."

The smile went out of Zach's voice. "You got it. What do you need?"

Rafe explained again about the men at the motel, how he was trying to set up a surveillance team to see who came and went, trying to find out what the men were doing in Valdez. "I need enough guys to keep them covered twenty-four-seven. I'm going over there later to scan the area, figure the best way to keep an eye on them without being seen."

The smile was back in Zach's voice. "I've got a better idea."

"Yeah? I'm all ears."

"We set up surveillance cams. I'm kind of

an electronics geek. It's sort of what's happening in my generation."

"I'm listening."

"I've got all kinds of equipment. I use a lot of it in the wild, you know? Set up night-vision cameras to watch the bears come in to feed. Do some time-lapse on birds, watch the chicks hatch in their nests, stuff like that. I did a thing with eagles that really turned out great. It was hell getting up to the nest, but it was worth it. I put the camera up as a live feed on the Internet."

"I'm likin' this."

"Yeah, so you see where I'm going?"

"Oh yeah, I see. How long will it take to get this stuff up and running?"

"We can do it tonight, if you're game."

"You bet I'm game. I'll pick you up at eleven. We'll start setting up as soon as it's dark."

"I'll be ready. See you then."

Rafe hung up the phone and called Sam back. "We're setting up cameras. Going over there tonight. Zach Carver's idea. It's kind of his hobby."

Since Zach worked for Great Alaska Charters and Sam was in the fish-packing business, Sam knew Zach. They'd been talking together on the boat that afternoon.

"Zach's real smart," Sam said. "That's a

257

great idea. You know what else we need?"

"What's that?"

"GPS tracking device. I got one I use for hunting. We can put it somewhere in their car and it'll track wherever they go."

"I've got one of those, too. Should have thought of it. You two guys are making me feel old."

"The only trick is getting it inside the car."

Rafe felt the smile before it curved his lips. "Or on it. We can tape it under the bumper. The battery won't last too long, so we'll have to swap them every night and recharge them."

"I'll bring mine to work. You can pick it up there."

"Thanks, Sam." Rafe ended the call and returned to the living room. Carefully scooping Olivia into his arms, her head nestled against his shoulder, he carried her upstairs and settled her in his bed.

For several moments, he just stood there staring down at her, thinking how beautiful she was with her dark hair spread over his pillow, those X-rated lips relaxed in sleep. Desire slid through him, poured through his veins. Hot blood slid into his groin. Every time he looked at her, he wanted her. He had never felt anything like it.

But Liv Chandler was trouble. In more

258

ways than one.

He'd sensed it the first time he'd seen her in the restaurant, sensed it every time he went into the café after that, but couldn't stop himself from heading straight down the road he was traveling.

His brother's words kept ringing in his ears. She was lying, big-time, had been from the start. He tried to tell himself it was time to bail. He didn't need a woman with her kind of problems.

But it just didn't work that way. Not for him. Since the night she had given herself to him, she was his. Whatever trouble she was involved in was also now his.

As he stood looking down at her, he still couldn't convince himself she was anything but the hardworking, capable, caring woman she seemed. He wished he knew what the hell was going on.

Reaching down, he grabbed one of her black leather boots and started gently tugging it off, didn't quite finish before Olivia stirred.

"Rafe?" She slowly opened her eyes and looked up at him.

"You need to get undressed, darlin'; then you can go back to sleep. I'm going out for a while, but I'll be back."

"Where are you going?" Shoving her dark

hair out of her face, she sat up in bed.

"I've got something I need to do. Go back to sleep. I'll be home before you even know I'm gone."

Her sleepiness faded. "Does that something you need to do have anything to do with Scotty?"

He nodded, resigned to filling her in. "Zach and I are setting up surveillance cameras over at the motel. I want to see who goes in and out of that room. We're also putting a GPS on the bumper of their car. One of them leaves, we'll know where he's been."

"Wow, you've been busy. I want to come with you."

"You need to get some sleep, baby. You've had one helluva day."

She smiled at him softly. "I got a nap, thanks to you. I want to go."

He thought it over, didn't see any real harm in letting her come along. They'd be staying out of sight. As long as she was with him, she'd be safe.

Which made him think again of the information Nick had given him and the need to know more. *Later,* he told himself. *One problem at a time.*

"You need a heavier jacket than the one you wore today," he said. "I'll get you one of mine."

Liv pulled her boot back on, came up off the bed and kissed him. "Thanks."

One of his eyebrows arched up. "Since you suddenly seem so rested, maybe you can think of a way to thank me properly when we get home."

Liv just smiled and walked past him out the door.

CHAPTER TWENTY

Night had fallen. It was midnight and it was dark. Liv stood next to Rafe behind a tree and some overgrown foliage at the edge of the Seaside Motel parking lot. The guys were figuring the best place to mount the night-vision surveillance camera. The Jeep Cherokee was gone. Which was good news and bad.

With the men away, they could mount the cameras somewhere out of sight along the covered corridor, get them up and running. But they couldn't attach the GPS to the Jeep.

It was nearly June, but it was still cold at night. Wrapped in Rafe's warm, fleece-lined jacket, Liv reached up and tugged down the brim of the ball cap he had given her.

"I bought this in the souvenir shop this afternoon," Rafe had said with a grin as he settled it on her head. "Saw it in the window. It'll come in handy tonight."

It was black with gold lettering. MINE was embroidered across the front. Rafe said he liked looking at her while she was wearing it.

She should have refused, been indignant at the male chauvinist implication. Instead her stomach kind of melted. Oh, she had it bad. She was getting in deep with Rafe, and she knew how dangerous falling for him could be. She couldn't afford to let the L-word even cross her mind.

She told herself the cap was just to keep her head warm, but she loved the way he had looked at her when she pulled her ponytail through the hole in the back, settled it on her head, and smiled up at him.

"Perfect," he said, flashing one of his heart-stopping grins.

"I'll wear it tonight — but that's it."

"We'll see," he said smugly, and led her down to the garage.

Now they were outside the motel, standing in the dark, and she was wearing his silly hat.

"Stay here." The sound of his voice brought her back to the moment. Moving quietly, he headed over to where Zach was examining a spot up under the eaves. Ben knew they were out there. Occasionally, he would peek at them through the crack in

263

the curtains at the office window.

She had been standing there less than twenty minutes when the soft, nearly undetectable sound of footsteps reached her. Liv gasped as a broad shadow fell over the spot where she hid among the foliage at the edge of the parking lot.

"It's okay," Sam King said softly. "It's just me." Despite the darkness she recognized his Alaska Native features, the sharp nose and slightly tilted eyes.

She released a slow breath. "I didn't know you were coming."

"I wasn't. Thought I might be able to help. Pretty good hiding spot. It took me a while to track you down."

"Rafe's truck is parked around the corner."

"Yeah, I saw it." He tipped his head toward the men working under the eaves. Rafe was tall enough he didn't need a stepladder to reach the spot where they were placing the cameras. Zach was only a few inches shorter. Ben had turned off the outside lights so they were little more than shadows.

"They need any help?" Sam asked.

"I think they're almost finished. Fortunately, no one's around and the men aren't in their room. Their Jeep is gone."

"Good news, sort of, right? I brought my GPS. Rafe's got one, too. Soon as we get the chance, we're putting one on the Jeep, see where these guys go." He looked up, jerked his chin toward a pair of headlights coming down the road. "That could be them now."

Olivia grabbed the two-way radio, one of Rafe's many toys, and pressed the call button. "Car coming. Could be them. Over."

He ignored her, of course, kept working for several more seconds, making her adrenaline pump faster. The lights came closer. Olivia held her breath. Then Zach tapped on the office window, Zach and Rafe slipped into the shadows, and Ben turned the corridor lights back on just as the Jeep rolled into the parking lot.

The two men got out and started toward their room, one tall with ropey muscles, the other shorter, and from what she'd seen in the motel room, really built. The Asian stopped to get out his room key. The men walked inside and closed the door, and the light went on.

Rafe and Zach appeared out of the darkness behind the wall of foliage. "Looks like a convention out here," Rafe said, spotting Sam King.

"I figured you'd be here," King said. "I

thought I might be able to help."

"We've got the cameras up. We set my laptop up in Ben's living room. Wireless connection to the cameras. From now on, day or night, we'll be able to watch them come and go."

Sam held up his GPS. "We need to get one of these on the car."

"Yes, we do." Rafe took it out of Sam's hand. "I looked these up on the Internet. You can buy all different kinds. I ordered one that works with a motion detector. It goes on when the car starts moving, off when it's parked. Gives it a long battery life. Zach can hook it up to the computer so we can follow them on the laptop."

"How long before it gets here?" Sam asked.

"Had it shipped FedEx. Be in day after tomorrow. If we pick it up at the airport, we should have it by ten a.m. Thursday morning."

"The men might be gone by then," Liv said.

"They told us they'd be here till the end of the week. That should give us a few more days."

The light in the room went out. Liv couldn't see even the glow of a TV screen. Clearly the men had gone to bed.

Rafe pulled Sam's GPS out of his jacket pocket. "Looks like time to move in." Rafe turned to Liv. "Keep your eye on that room. Light goes on, anything moves, give me a heads-up on the radio."

"All right."

He looked at Zach and Sam. "You guys keep an eye out for anything else that might cause trouble. The police driving by, just somebody coming back to his room."

"You got it," Sam said.

Grabbing the small canvas satchel he had brought with him — duct tape, a flashlight, a couple of wrenches, and other miscellaneous tools that might prove useful — Rafe headed through the foliage toward the Jeep. Keeping low, he moved out of the shadows into the parking lot, and slid under the car, out of sight beneath the rear bumper.

Next to Liv, Sam and Zach also kept watch, scanning the area in all directions. Headlights appeared in the distance, and her nerves kicked in, but the car turned off the road before it reached the motel.

She was concentrating on the rooms along the corridor, watching for any sign of movement, when Rafe reappeared beside her.

"That ought to do it," he said. "I don't think they'll be going out again tonight, but you never know."

"How long will the battery last?" Liv asked.

"At least twenty-four hours. We'll retrieve it tomorrow night and replace it with mine, take it home and see what we've got."

"We'll also take a look at the video from the cameras," Zach said. "We'll find out what these guys are up to, see who comes and goes."

"I've got a half-day trip tomorrow," Rafe said. "The laptop's set up at Ben's. I'll stop by as soon as I get in."

"When should we meet?" Zach asked.

"Let's say six at the Pelican?"

"Works for me," Sam said. "I'm headed home. I'll drop Zach off on my way."

"All right." Rafe's gaze swung to Liv. "You ready to go?" The burning interest in those hot brown eyes sent a curl of heat into the pit of her stomach.

She swallowed. "I'm ready."

"See you tomorrow," Rafe said to the men. He settled an arm around her shoulders. "Come on, darlin'. Let's go home."

Liv just nodded. She was getting used to the idea of spending her nights with Rafe. The thought sent a tremor of worry down her spine.

■ ■ ■ ■

"I don't know about you," Sam said, "but after a shit day like this, I could use a beer."

"Sounds good." Zach sat back as Sam drove his pickup to the Fisherman's Catch Saloon. It was late, but a number of cars still sat in the lot. As he climbed out of the truck, he noticed Jaimie Graham's little red Chevy Equinox parked off to one side beneath a row of trees.

She was only nineteen, but since food was served at the Catch, she could go in. Zach spotted her sitting at the bar the minute he walked through the door, felt a familiar little punch in the gut. He'd probably never know what there was about Jaimie Graham that had intrigued him since the first time he'd seen her, but he was feeling it again tonight.

A smile touched his lips. For once she wasn't wearing the wool cap she kept pulled down over her ears. Her short, auburn curls gleamed in the bar lights, her breasts looked womanly and plump beneath her navy-blue sweater.

She was wearing the same black leggings and dark blue plaid skirt she'd been wearing at the funeral, an outfit that for once showed the feminine shape of her legs and that sweet little behind he remembered from her swimming days in high school. She was underage, but she didn't look it as she leaned across the bar to flirt with the thin-faced bartender who was letting her buy drinks.

On the bar stool next to her, a good-looking, powerfully built man with features that hinted at a distant African-American heritage was giving her a more than interested glance. Zach ignored a fine thread of jealousy and started walking.

Jaimie laughed at something the bartender said. She hadn't laughed since Scotty died. She had to get drunk to do it, which rankled him more than it should have.

The big guy headed for the bathroom and Zach walked toward her, slid onto the empty bar stool on the opposite side. "Feeling better?"

She turned. Her eyes widened as she realized who it was. "Zach. What are you doing here?"

"Same thing you are, I guess. Trying to forget a totally shitty day."

She made a little scoffing sound. "You and Scotty weren't that close. I was surprised to see you at the funeral."

His mouth thinned. "You don't get it, do you? We weren't close because I couldn't stand to see what he was doing to you."

A hint of doubt appeared in her eyes, which he had never seen before. "I don't . . . I don't know what you mean."

"Scott was in love with Cassie, but he didn't make that clear to you. He knew you idolized him. Maybe he liked that, I don't know. It wasn't fair to keep you hanging, and I didn't like it."

She sat up straighter on the stool. "You don't know what you're talking about. Scotty was the best man I've ever known."

"In some ways I'm sure he was. Cassie loved him and that says a lot. But he wasn't fair to you, Jaimie. You deserve a man who'll treat you like a woman instead of just one of the guys."

Her jaw went tight. She grabbed her purse and threw some money down on the bar, slid off the stool and started for the door, weaving a little as she crossed the room. She was drunker than he'd thought, which ratcheted his irritation up another notch.

Zach slid off the bar stool, signaled to Sam, who was talking to a little brunette he seemed to know, and followed Jaimie out of the bar.

He caught up with her just outside the door. "You aren't driving," he said.

"Yes, I am. You aren't the boss of me."

He grabbed the car keys out of her hand. "Maybe Scotty would have let you drive drunk, but I'm not going to." He started walking and she fell in beside him. When they reached her car, he flicked the door locks open. "Now get in and I'll drive you home."

She cast him a murderous glance. "Sometimes I hate you." But she climbed into the passenger seat and slammed the car door.

"Do your parents know you're out getting drunk?" Zach asked as he slid behind the wheel, adjusted the seat, then cranked the engine.

"They're out of town. And I'm not drunk." She cut him a sideways glance. "Well, maybe a little."

Zach said nothing as he drove her back to her parents' house, a nice ranch-style home in one of the better neighborhoods. He parked in front, came around and helped her climb out, then walked her up on the porch.

"How are you getting home?" she asked.

"It's not that far. I'll walk."

She unlocked the door, turned and gave him a slow, sexy smile. "You . . . umm . . . want to come in?"

One of his eyebrows went up. "You want

me to? Or are you just using me to forget about Scott?"

"What difference does it make? Scotty's gone and you're here."

A fresh jolt of irritation slid through him. Urging her inside, he closed the door. "Maybe you're right. I'm here and Scotty isn't."

Uncertainty crept into her features the instant before he hauled her into his arms and his mouth came down over hers. Heat rolled through him. Her lips were soft and full, and she smelled like flowers instead of fish. Her fingers dug into his shoulders and she started to push him away. Then her body softened into his, her arms slid up around his neck, and she kissed him back, her sweet lips parting under his, allowing his tongue to sweep in.

His blood went south, making him harder than he was already. The kiss went on a little longer, not as long as he wanted, before she broke away.

She was breathing hard, upset at herself and angry at him. Jaimie flashed him a look, jerked back and slapped him hard across the face. "You had no right to do that!"

His jaw clenched. "You liked it. Don't lie to yourself."

"Get out."

"I'm not Scotty. You better figure that out." He rubbed his burning cheek. "I'll let you off this time, but you ever hit me again, I'll put you over my knee and paddle your sweet little ass until you can't sit down. Till you realize that a man who cares about you wouldn't ignore you the way Scotty did."

"You're crazy. You wouldn't dare!" She swung at him again, so hard that when she missed she tumbled forward.

Zach smiled grimly, caught her around the waist, dragged her over, sat down on the couch, and hauled her across his lap. "I'd dare a lot of things for you, Jaimie. This is just the first."

With that he jerked up her little wool skirt and his hand came down on her bottom. A couple of hard swats, then he lifted her up and tossed her on the sofa.

"I'm nothing like Scott, Jaimie Graham, and I'm exactly the right man for you. It's past time you figured that out."

"Get out of my house!"

"I'll see you tomorrow at work. Think about what I said." Something shattered next to the door as he pulled it open and walked out on the porch.

Zach didn't look back. He had made his opening salvo and it was a beaut. She'd be mad for a while, but at least he'd made his point.

His mind went back to the way she had kissed him. Hot and sweet, sexy as hell. He wasn't wrong about Jaimie. He was the right man for her and always had been.

Zach smiled as he walked off into the darkness, heading back to his house. He'd need a cold shower before he went to bed, but at least he was no longer invisible.

As Rafe drove into his garage, he noticed Olivia yawning. With the funeral and setting up surveillance at the motel, she'd had a long, emotionally exhausting day. On top of that, she'd spent last night in his bed, which meant he hadn't given her much time to sleep.

She stirred herself enough to make her way into the house and the two of them headed upstairs. When he came out of the bathroom, he found her curled up on his bed in the faded Coast Guard T-shirt she'd worn the night before.

Since he didn't have the heart to wake her, he stripped off the rest of his clothes and pulled back the covers, eased Olivia between the sheets, and climbed in beside her. She didn't even stir when he pulled her up over his chest and wrapped an arm around her.

She just snuggled in, her face pressed into his neck.

Damn, she felt good. Too good. Rafe thought of icebergs long enough to get his body under control, then his thoughts shifted, moved in a direction that kept him awake a little longer.

He needed to collect a DNA sample, could probably get one off the hairbrush Liv had borrowed that morning. It had to be done. He didn't believe for a moment Olivia was a criminal. But there was no doubt she was in some serious trouble. He had to know what was going on in order to keep her safe. His stomach knotted. Just thinking about it felt like a betrayal.

Rafe kissed the top of her head and drowsiness settled over him, pulled him into slumber. He wasn't sure how long he slept before the press of soft lips against his chest awakened him, the sensation of those familiar, perfect lips moving over his skin.

He was hard before she reached his navel, before Liv ran her tongue around the indentation. Her lips moved lower, soft kisses trailed over his skin and the muscles across his abdomen contracted. Desire hit him like a fist.

Sliding a hand into her thick, dark hair, he cupped her head as that warm, sexy mouth enveloped his erection. *I've got to be dreaming,* he thought as the blood raced through his veins and heat burned into his groin. Just another of the erotic dreams he'd had for weeks before he'd begun his determined pursuit of Liv.

His head went back and he groaned. He was close to release. Reaching down, he caught her shoulders and hauled her up his body. "That's enough. I want to be inside you when I come."

She made a little sound of protest, then started nipping the side of his neck. When he reached over to grab a condom, she caught his wrist.

"I'm on the pill. Irregular this-and-that. You don't have to worry."

Rafe kissed her long and deep as he moved her into position on top of him and buried himself in her soft, warm heat.

"Jesus, Liv, you feel good."

She arched beneath him, wanting more, straining his control. Gripping her hips, he started to move, drove deep and didn't stop. He could feel her inner muscles tightening around him, heard her quick intake of breath, and knew she was close to the peak.

"Rafe . . ." Matching her rhythm to his, she drove him to the brink.

Rafe dug for control, hung on long enough

to push her over the edge, then followed her to release. He came hard, his jaw clenched, and, Jesus, it was good. He let the rush drag him under, hold on to him for seconds that felt like hours, before the pleasure began to fade.

Easing away, he rolled onto his back and drew her up on his chest. She tucked her head into his neck as she had done before, and a few minutes later, she was asleep.

Rafe ran a hand over her hair and drifted for a while, his mind returning to the problems he'd be facing in the morning.

He tried not to think of the DNA sample he'd be sending to his brother. Or the GPS and security cameras he'd set up tonight in an effort to discover the truth about Scotty's murder.

Instead, he kissed the top of Olivia's head and tried not to want her again.

CHAPTER TWENTY-ONE

Rafe got the phone call as he stepped off *Scorpion* after his half-day charter. Not recognizing the caller ID, he pressed the phone against his ear. "Brodie."

"It's Rusty Donovan, Rafe. I've got an update for you on the Ferris case."

"What's going on?"

"Forensics came back. No blood or fibers, nothing in Chip Reed's pickup or apartment. No blood on the clothes in his closet."

In a way Rafe had hoped there would be. "They gonna let him go?"

"No way. Scarborough and the chief still like him for the murder. They think he could have wrapped the body in a plastic tarp. Wouldn't leave fibers. They think he tossed his bloody clothes somewhere on his trip to Fairbanks."

"Could be, I guess."

Rusty must have heard the doubt in his voice. "But you don't think so."

"I don't know. Did Scarborough get anything from the two guys in the motel room closest to the office? I know he talked to them at least once."

"Interviewed them a couple of times. According to what they said, they were over at the Catch earlier that night — which the bartender verified. Bartender said they were watching ESPN and nursing light beers. They claim they went back to the room and crashed before midnight. Didn't hear or see anything."

"Yeah, I talked to them, too. Nevin claimed they were drunk. Nursing a light beer isn't the same as being drunk."

"You think they might be involved?"

"Might have heard or seen something. No way to tell." *At least not at the moment.* He didn't mention the cameras or the tracking device. Rusty was a friend but he was still a cop. Cops didn't like civilians messing in their business. Rafe didn't want to push his luck.

"I'll let you know if anything else comes up," Rusty said.

"Appreciate it." Just as Rafe hung up, his phone rang again. Ben Friedman spoke from the other end of the line.

"Hi, Rafe. Figured I ought to call. I took a look at the video recording from last night just like Zach showed me. The men didn't leave the room till late this morning. Probably went for something to eat or some sightseeing. Haven't come back."

"Thanks, Ben. Keep me posted."

"Will do."

Ben was a quick study. He was watching the live feed as well as checking the recorded images. Tonight, Rafe planned to go in after dark and replace the GPS under the back bumper of the Jeep with a fresh one. Tomorrow, if the FedEx arrived on time, he'd have a more sophisticated device that could be accessed wirelessly in real time.

With things mostly under control, he headed for the Pelican. He was done for the day and he hadn't had anything to eat since morning. The bell rang as he stepped through the door. His gaze automatically went in search of Olivia, but he didn't see her.

He sat down in one of the booths and started perusing the menu, then looked up to see Cassie walking toward him, her light brown hair swinging along her jaw. A little of the color was back in her face.

Rafe stood up as she approached. "Hi, honey, how you doing?"

She shrugged. "Better and worse. Better with the funeral over. Worse because now it

281

seems so final."

"I know."

"You never said, but I know you lost someone you loved."

He nodded. "It was a long time ago."

"A woman?"

"Yes."

She smiled. "And now you have Liv."

Pressure rose in his chest. He thought of the information his brother had given him, thought that Olivia wasn't Olivia at all. "I hope so."

"I . . . umm . . . really hate to ask, but would you do me a favor?"

"Sure, what is it?"

"I've got a doctor's appointment in about fifteen minutes. Mom was supposed to take me, but she isn't feeling well. Liv took Khan for a walk, and Nell's running the café. I hate to go alone. Scotty always went with me. Do you think you could take me?"

He smiled. "Be my pleasure to take you, honey."

"You want a sandwich or something? I could fix it real quick."

"That'd be great."

"You like ham and cheese, right?"

He nodded.

"I'll be right back."

Good to her word, Cassie returned a few

minutes later, holding on to a Styrofoam box. Rafe dropped enough money on the table to pay for the sandwich plus a tip, opened the box and took out half, ate it as he walked Cassie out to his pickup.

He finished the other half on the way, pulled up in front of the doctor's office and turned off the engine, rounded the truck to help Cassie down. Short as she was, getting in and out wasn't easy. Not like it was for Liv. He smiled to think of Olivia's long, pretty legs, remembered how they'd felt wrapped around him that morning.

He walked Cassie to the front door of the gray clapboard building and pulled open the door. She flicked him a grateful smile as she walked into the office. Her stomach was still flat and apparently she wasn't having morning sickness, or at least she hadn't said anything about it if she was.

Two women sat in the waiting room, one cuddling a pink, blanket-wrapped bundle, the other one very pregnant, urging the little girl beside her to fill in the spaces in a kid's coloring book.

"I shouldn't be long," Cassie said, glancing toward the nurse behind the counter. "If you feel like reading, there's some magazines on the table, but they're pretty old and they're probably not your thing."

He glanced down at the dog-eared stack of *Good Housekeeping, Redbook, Parenting,* and *Cosmopolitan,* and his mouth edged up. "I'll make do."

As a nurse led Cassie down the hall, he grabbed the *Cosmo,* sat down in a gray vinyl chair, and read the cover. His eyes widened at the articles inside: "Sixty Sex Tips: Love Tricks That Will Make Him Want You," and "The Sex Position That Increases Female Orgasms."

Feeling the heat creeping into his face, he glanced around to make sure neither of the women in the waiting room was watching, then started flipping toward the last article. Not that Olivia seemed to have any problem.

Still . . .

He was turning pages, flipping through ads for hair products and makeup, when one of the pages caught his eye. It was an advertisement for lipstick, a Revlon ad that showed a portion of a beautiful woman's face, just the jawline, chin, and a pair of sultry lips covered in a dewy shade of deep, dark red.

Rafe felt the zip of adrenaline begin to pump through him. He knew those lips. Knew them intimately. It was funny how the human computer worked. He'd seen it done on TV: A specific feature of an actor was all you got to see, yet strangely, it was obvious who that person was.

In the ad, he could see just enough of the lower portion of the face to know who it was — and he was certain. Those X-rated lips belonged to Olivia Chandler.

He checked the date on the magazine. It was October three years ago. Very carefully, he ripped out the page and set the magazine back down on the table, folded the ad and stuck it in the pocket of the denim work shirt he was wearing.

His mind was still spinning when Cassie walked out of the doctor's office. Rafe stood up from the chair. "Everything okay?"

She smiled. "All good." Her smile slowly faded, her eyes filled, and he knew she was thinking of Scott.

"Don't go there, honey. You're having Scotty's baby. He left you the greatest gift he could give you, yes?"

She nodded, wiped her eyes, managed to recover some of the smile. "You're right. I'm sorry. It's just . . ."

"I know." He took her arm and led her toward the door.

"Thanks for coming with me." She hung on to him as they walked out of the office. "It was easier knowing you were out here waiting."

His chest felt tight. Scott should have been the one waiting for her.

Guiding her back to the truck, he helped her climb in, then drove back to the café. The lunch crowd was gone. When he walked through the door, Olivia was restocking supplies under the breakfast counter.

His jaw tightened. Rafe couldn't wait to see the look on her face when she saw what was in his shirt pocket.

Olivia glanced up to see Rafe walking toward her. God, he was handsome. Stomach-melting handsome. Toe-curling handsome. With that thick, dark hair and those golden-brown eyes, long legs, broad shoulders, and that lean, hard-muscled torso, he was just flat-out the sexiest man alive.

Well, at least to her.

He stopped in front of her and she tried to blank her mind against the memory of what she had done to him in bed. He had teased her about a proper thank-you. Well, she had certainly given him one.

She fought back a grin. Of course, Rafe always gave as good as he got in return.

"Hi," she said, looking up at him, fighting a sudden urge to drag him into the storage room and have her way with him — again. "What's going on?"

"Looks like the lunch rush is over. You got a minute to talk?"

Unease slid through her. There was something in his eyes, something that put her on alert. "Sure." She started for one of the booths, figuring they would have a cup of coffee, but Rafe caught her arm.

"Upstairs."

Tension coiled in her stomach. "Is this about Scott?"

"Upstairs," he repeated, making her uneasiness build.

She led the way up to her apartment and Rafe closed the door behind him. Olivia led him over to the cream-colored sofa, and they sat down in front of the sleek, dark-wood coffee table. Across the room, a view of the Sound stretched out beyond the windows. The dismal gray clouds of an impending storm did nothing to calm her nerves.

"What is it? What's going on?"

In answer he reached into the pocket of his shirt and pulled out a folded, glossy sheet of paper, opened it on the coffee table, smoothed it out flat.

A chill slid down her spine when she recognized the ad. "What's that?" She looked up at him, trying to bluff her way through it.

A muscle ticked in his jaw. "You know what it is and so do I. You had that mouth on me this morning. Don't even think about trying to tell me that isn't you."

Panic shot through her. She had done the photo shoot before she'd fled New York. What were the odds the magazine would still be lying around? Of course it could have been reprinted. Revlon had really liked the ad.

Her mind spun, searching for the right thing to say, tossing aside one answer after another, finally deciding on bold and slightly bitchy. "All right, it's me. So what?"

He relaxed a little. He'd been ready for a fight. Clearly she'd made the right choice. "You were a model before you moved up here?"

"Not a runway model, no. I did magazine ads, just like the one on the table. Lips were my specialty." She forced herself to smile. "At one point they were insured for a million dollars."

His mouth kicked up. "Million-dollar lips. And worth every dime."

Her confidence was building. Maybe she could tell him part of the truth, enough to satisfy his curiosity. "I made a lot of money at it. Enough I could afford the café."

"Where are you from?" he asked casually, though she could tell it was far from what he was feeling.

"I was born in Massachusetts, a little town called Medfield. I went to the U of Mass, then moved to New York. I was a dancer for a while before I started doing ads." The last part was true. She hoped it wasn't too much information.

His smile was gone. There was a hard glint in his eyes. "What about your husband? You said you were married."

"Yes, well . . . I was married for about a year before Tom died."

"Tom Chandler? That was his name?"

"That's right." Total bullshit. She'd made that up when she got to Valdez. It had satisfied everyone else. For the love of God, why wasn't it enough for Rafe?

Liv stood up from the sofa. "Is the inquisition over or do you have something else you want to know?"

For several moments he didn't answer and her heart sank. The more he pressed, the more likely he would find out something that would put them both in danger.

He shrugged his shoulders as if it were no big deal. "I saw the ad. I knew it was you. I was surprised you never mentioned it.

Seems like we ought to know each other well enough by now."

"It was a long time ago," she said.

"Three years isn't so long." The date of the magazine.

Her stomach squeezed. "Sometimes it is." It was an eternity to her, another incarnation. Another lifetime.

Rafe just nodded. "You'll be at the meeting, right? Six o'clock downstairs?"

"I'll be there."

She walked him to the door. "I'm taking Khan for a run. I'll see you later."

Rafe paused in front of her as she opened the door. "It's natural for people who are sleeping together to want to know a little about each other."

She forced herself to smile. "You're right. I'm sorry."

He gripped her arms and drew her close, settled his mouth over hers. It wasn't a gentle kiss. It was hard, and intrusive, and tinged with a hint of anger. He wanted more from her, but she couldn't afford to give it to him.

"I'll see you tonight." He turned and walked out of the apartment.

Olivia released a slow breath. She hated to lie and especially to Rafe. But there was no other choice. She didn't want to leave

Valdez. She was making a home for herself here, making friends. She loved the remoteness, the beauty, loved running her own business. More than that, she didn't want to leave Rafe.

It was crazy. She was falling for him and that wasn't good. But it was happening and she couldn't seem to find a way to stop it.

Ignoring the tightness in her throat and needing to clear her head, Olivia walked into the bedroom to change into her running clothes. A few minutes later, she was headed back downstairs.

Running always made her feel better. She hoped it would work today.

Chapter Twenty-Two

Rafe headed for the FedEx shipping center on Airport Road. He'd been reluctant to send Nick the DNA sample he had retrieved from the hairbrush in his bathroom that morning, a few strands of glossy dark hair that smelled like Liv and made him think of sex.

But she had lied to him. Looked him straight in the eye and lied. She wasn't born in Medfield. She hadn't gone to the University of Massachusetts.

A thread of anger burned through him. He wasn't a man who put up with a woman out-and-out lying to him. If he wasn't pretty sure she had a damned good reason, he would end things with her now.

His chest clamped down at the thought. Which told him he was in up to his neck with Liv and had no choice but to see this thing through. He sent the hair sample via FedEx overnight to Seattle, along with the

Revlon ad and the date of the magazine. He didn't think it would take Nick long to track down the name of the model, and even getting the info on her DNA wouldn't take long these days.

On the way back to town, Rafe phoned Ben. "Our suspects back in their room yet?"

"Suspects. I like that. Makes me feel like it's okay for us to be spying on them. And no, they aren't back."

"Good. I need to get inside the room, take a look around."

"No way," Ben said sharply. "Surveillance cameras in the corridor outside is one thing —"

"See you in five minutes." Rafe hung up the phone.

When he reached the motel, Ben was in the office, pacing behind the counter. "I can't let you go in there, Rafe. I know you're trying to find Scott's killer, but —"

"I need to take a look, Ben. I won't touch anything. I just want to look around. Maybe I'll see something that'll give us some idea of what those guys are doing in Valdez."

"Maybe they're doing just what they say. Vacationing, just like the rest of the tourists who come through here."

"Maybe."

"Okay, if that's not it, maybe they're gay

or something. They're a nice gay couple renting a room. There's no law against it."

"Their sexual preference isn't the point."

"No, but there's no indication they're involved in Scott's murder, and that is the point. We don't have a single reason to think they are."

"Nevin told me they were drunk the night of the murder. Said they crashed in the room after they got home and that's the reason they didn't hear anything outside that night. Bartender at the Catch says they were barely drinking, just sipping light beers. If that's the case, no way were they drunk. Which means they were lying."

"Maybe they went somewhere else, drank more beer before they came back."

"If they did, why didn't they tell the police?"

Ben ran a hand over his balding head. His eyes slid toward the row of keys in the boxes behind the counter. With a sigh, he reached over, grabbed the key out of box number two and handed it to Rafe.

"Hurry up, dammit. You gotta be out of there before they come back or one of the other guests shows up."

"You've got my cell number, right?"

Ben pulled out his phone. "I've got it."

"Give me a heads-up if they show or

somebody else drives into the lot."

"This is against my better judgment," Ben grumbled. "I'm doing it for Scotty."

"I know that. We all are." Rafe set his phone on vibrate, stuck it into the pocket of his jeans, and headed out the door. There was a maid at work in one of the rooms down the corridor, her cart sitting in front of the open door, but she was busy cleaning inside the room.

Rafe slid the key into the lock on room two, slipped inside, and quietly closed the door. The curtains were drawn, but enough light filtered through for him to see. The twin beds were unmade since the maid hadn't reached that room yet, but the place was neat.

He did a quick visual survey, then pulled his shirttail out of his jeans and used it to open the dresser drawers so he wouldn't leave fingerprints. The suitcases had been unpacked, clothes neatly put away.

The bathroom was relatively clean, wet towels hung up, shaving gear neatly arranged on the counter. He returned to the bedroom, started prowling. No liquor bottles in the trash. No condoms in the nightstands. They weren't having wild monkey sex, or if they were, they were doing it somewhere else.

There was something rolled up in the corner. He walked over to take a closer look. He could feel the what-the-fuck? vibes even before he realized what he was looking at.

Prayer rugs. Had to be. He had seen them on TV. He wrapped his shirttail around his fingers to examine them, saw one was red and gold, the other blue and brown, both Middle Eastern patterns with paisley designs. He made sure they were rolled up exactly the way they had been before, and turned to take a last look around.

No sign of blood — not that he'd expected to find any — or anything that might have to do with Scotty's murder.

He moved to the window, checked to make sure no one was around, stepped out the door, then eased it closed, and strode down the hall back to the office.

Ben was waiting, nervously shifting back and forth as he looked out the window. Rafe tossed him the key.

"So did you find anything?" Ben asked, walking behind the counter and setting the key back in box number two.

"They're Muslim. Found prayer rugs in the room. One's Middle Eastern. That's the accent I couldn't quite place. I don't have a clue what that means, but there it is."

"That's it? That's their big secret?"

"I don't know if it's a secret. It just is what it is. One more bit of information to put with everything else we've got — which is zilch."

"Unless Chip Reed killed Scott like the police are saying."

"That what you think?"

"No, it isn't. That's why I let you into that room."

"I appreciate your help, Ben, I really do. I know you're an ethical guy and that was asking a lot."

He relaxed, smiled. "It's okay. I'm kind of glad you didn't find anything, though. Would have been hard to explain."

"Yeah. Thanks again."

Rafe left the office and headed for his truck. He needed to think, and swimming was a good way to do it. He checked his watch. Kids were out of school by now. He kept a suit in his go-bag behind the seat. Rafe headed for the pool up the hill.

Olivia was jogging, Khan clicking along beside her. She'd been gone for more than an hour, her feet pounding the dirt at the edge of the road, her legs carrying her in no particular direction.

If she'd been paying attention, maybe she would have felt it sooner. Maybe she would have noticed a shadow here or an outline there, something concrete that proved it wasn't her imagination.

But the sky was dark and the clouds were thick and a mist had begun to settle over the town. The uneasy feeling persisted, shifted and changed, but stayed with her. Even as her awareness sharpened, she didn't see anyone.

She was just jumpy, she told herself. Nervous after Rafe had found the ad in the magazine. There was no one there, no reason to believe they had found her. And if they were still searching for the person she was before, the last place they would look was remote Valdez, Alaska.

She came to a halt at a stop sign, felt that odd tingle of paranoia again. "Sit," she said to Khan, who sat down close beside her. "Good boy."

She scanned the area around her, but saw no movement, just a dark green Subaru driven by a woman with a couple of kids in the back.

Several people hurried past, pulling up the hoods on their jackets and heading off down the street. The clouds were getting thicker, the sky darker. A light rain had begun to fall. She needed to get inside before a full-fledged downpour set in.

"Heel," she said to Khan and he fell in beside her, quickly matching his pace to hers. "That's my sweet, smart boy."

She didn't see anyone on the way back to the café and the uneasy feeling began to fade. She wondered if she would always be this paranoid, hoped that someday she could actually feel safe.

She turned the corner, saw the sign for the Pelican up ahead, felt that little tug of pleasure at seeing the business she had built and the apartment she considered home, something she hadn't thought she would ever have again. When she released Khan back into his yard, she was surprised to see Tuxedo's black-and-white face peeping through the doorway of the storage shed doghouse, waiting for Khan to get back.

Tux was not a rainy weather cat. On days like this, she usually stayed home. Her whiskers looked wet, though she was inside the door enough to keep her black-and-white fur dry.

Khan saw her, barked, and galloped over to greet her, and they disappeared inside the shed. Liv smiled as she turned away, went inside and climbed the stairs to her apartment.

She couldn't help thinking how good half an hour in Rafe's hot tub would feel, but settled for a nice warm shower and dry clothes — a clean pair of skinny jeans, blue this time, and a lightweight burgundy sweater. She twisted her hair up and put on big silver hoop earrings, told herself it wasn't because Rafe would be coming in at six.

At least she'd been honest with him about coming from the East Coast — a small town in upstate New York, not Massachusetts, but still . . . Being raised in a cold climate was good, because the weather here didn't really bother her.

Though she'd be glad when it warmed up a little.

Thinking of New York sent her thoughts back to the magazine ad. Revlon had liked the ad and used it quite a bit. She hadn't thought of it in years, certainly hadn't expected it to turn up here. She prayed Rafe wouldn't press her for more information, prayed he wouldn't still be mad at her.

But a few hours later when he walked into the café, the dark look on his face said her pipe dream had just blown like smoke out the window.

Rafe's gaze went to the woman walking toward him. She had the sexiest way of moving, all long legs and an easy, swivel-hipped grace. She said she'd been a dancer, and that part of her story had a definite ring of truth. Aside from that, it was all a load of crap.

His jaw tightened. He watched her pause next to a booth where Melissa Young and her baby daughter were being seated. When Melissa struggled with the high chair, Olivia rushed over and took the little girl, propping the baby on her hip. The smile she beamed down on the child was so warm and sincere, so sweet and yearning, Rafe felt a tightness in his chest.

Once the seat was in place, Liv handed the baby back, reached out and touched the child's soft cheek one last time. He wanted kids. He wasn't in a hurry, but he figured he'd have a family when the right woman came along. Clearly, Olivia would make a good mother.

His mind shot back to the lies she had told him and his anger flared again. He managed to hold on to his temper enough to stand up as she approached and politely invite her to join him, Sam, Zach, and Ben in the round corner booth.

Liv slid in across from him, a wise choice at the moment. She was reading him loud and clear, even though he hadn't said a word. She got him. One more thing he liked about her. *Damn.*

"Okay, so where are we?" Sam asked, his solid physique taking up a good portion of the booth. Katie arrived with a fresh pot of coffee, refilled all their cups, flashed a look at Sam that Rafe couldn't read, then zipped away.

"Ben?" Rafe prodded to get them back on track. "Anything new on the cameras since our last conversation?"

"I wish I had something to report," Ben said. "The men went out midmorning and didn't come back till late in the afternoon. They were still in the room when I left to come down here. Maybe you guys will get something off the GPS."

Rafe glanced over at Zach. "I could use a lookout tonight when I go in to switch out the device. Ben'll be inside watching the cameras, but I need someone outside watching the lot."

"You got it."

"I have one thing that might be interesting," Rafe continued. "Wong and Nevin told the cops they were drinking over at the Fisherman's Catch the night of the murder, got drunk and crashed hard in their room. Rusty Donovan says the bartender backs up that they were there, but says they were only nursing light beers."

"So they weren't drunk," Olivia said.

"Doesn't look that way. And I think I know why. These guys are Muslim. I found two Islamic prayer rugs in their room. Muslims don't drink alcohol."

"You broke into their room?" Sam's black eyebrows shot up in disbelief and what appeared to be approval.

"Let's just say I thought I heard a noise and went in to check, make sure everything was okay."

"And you happened to see the prayer rugs," Zach said.

"That's right."

"There wasn't any blood," Ben clarified, still worried about giving him access to the room. "Nothing else that could tie them to the murder."

"No, nothing like that."

Olivia set her coffee mug down on the table. "Wait a minute. If these guys are Muslim, why were they drinking beer in the first place?"

"Maybe they like beer," Zach said. "Lots of American Muslims are seriously Westernized."

"Lee Wong is Asian-American," Rafe said. "Talks like he's corn fed, born and raised somewhere in the Midwest. The other one, Nevin, has an accent. I couldn't place it at first. Now that I've heard him talking a little more, my guess is he's Middle Eastern. Which explains one of the prayer rugs."

"I caught a hint of British in his speech," Liv said. "Maybe that's why his English is so good."

"Lots of Middle Eastern men study in England," Zach said, stirring an extra spoonful of sugar into his cup. "Oxford or Cambridge. Maybe that's it."

Olivia shook her head. "That doesn't sync. They told Rafe they were college roommates."

"Maybe Wong was also educated in England," Ben said.

"Could be," Rafe agreed.

Sam straightened in his seat. "So they're Muslim. I still can't figure why they would lie to the police."

"Because they heard or saw something that night," Zach guessed. "That's all it could be."

"Or one of them killed Scott Ferris," Olivia said.

Silence fell around the table.

"There was no evidence of anything like that," Ben reminded them.

"Something's going on," Rafe said. "I don't know what it is, but it's something. I'm going to give their names to my brother,

304

see what he can come up with."

Sam spotted Katie and held up his coffee mug. "Your brother? He's a cop, right?"

"Not anymore. Nick's in Seattle, working as a private investigator. Maybe he can help us figure this out."

"It could be nothing, you know," Ben helpfully pointed out.

Olivia's gaze sliced in his direction. "It could be nothing, or, as Rafe said, it could be something."

Katie arrived at that moment to top off Sam's cup, then refill the others. Sam winked at her. Her pretty mouth flattened out and Rafe bit back a smile. Looked like she had the kid's number.

Olivia picked up the thread of the conversation where they had left off. "These guys are the only lead we've come up with so far. We need to follow it, see where it goes."

"I agree," Sam said.

"Me too," said Zach.

"Ben?" Rafe asked.

The smaller man blew out a breath. "I've known Chip Reed since he was a kid. He can be a jerk, but I don't think he'd murder anyone. I'm in."

"All right, that's it, then. Zach, you and I go in after dark and change out the GPS."

He turned to the others. "If the device gives us something, or anything else turns up, I'll call, set up another meet. In the meantime, we need to keep this quiet. The police find out we're running surveillance on these guys, we'll be the ones in jail."

CHAPTER TWENTY-THREE

"I'd better get back to work." Olivia slid out of the booth.

"Anyone hungry?" Rafe asked. "I could really use a Pelican burger. I'm buying."

"I'm in." Zach's grin dug a dimple into his cheek. Zach Carver was pretty-boy handsome, though he didn't seem to notice.

"I could eat the ass-end out of a bear," Sam said, and Ben nodded his agreement.

"I'll get some menus." Olivia started toward the counter, but Katie arrived just then, menus in hand, tuning in to the customers' needs the way she always did. She passed around the plastic-coated tri-folds with the flying pelican in a blue-and-white circle on the front, the café logo.

Olivia had too much on her mind to eat, but, as if he could read her mind, Rafe cast her a warning glance.

"You need to eat something, too," he said with a look that reminded her of the night he had carted her out of the restaurant over his shoulder. A memory arose of the hot sex they'd had, and heat rushed into her cheeks and places lower down.

Embarrassed at her thoughts, she glanced away. She didn't look at Rafe. He was still angry, though he was managing not to show it, at least not to the others. A quick scan told her Nell had things under control, and since she was trying to soothe his ruffled feathers, she sat back down in the booth.

It only took a few minutes for Katie to get their orders. Mostly Pelican burgers and fries. Everyone in town knew the menu by heart. Liv ordered a small chef's salad with bleu cheese dressing.

"I'll get these started and be back with more coffee," Katie said. Hurrying over to the kitchen, she hooked the orders up on the wheel behind the counter, grabbed the coffeepot, and returned.

As she refilled the heavy china mugs for the umpteenth time, she turned to Liv. "Oh, I forgot to tell you. A funny thing happened while you were out running. One of our customers came in — you remember Sarah Andrews? Her husband owns the gas station? Bob threw a birthday party for Sarah last week, took over the banquet room."

"I remember."

"Well, some of the guests took pictures and posted them up on their Facebook pages. I guess one of them has a friend somewhere in upstate New York and they tweet and Pinterest, keep up with each other on Facebook."

A tremor of unease slid through her. "So?"

"So, apparently you were in the background of one of the photos, and a friend-of-a-friend saw it. She thought you were an old college classmate, some woman named Fiona Caldwell. I guess she and this Fiona went to Columbia University together, BFFs and all that."

Olivia could feel the blood draining out of her face. Her ears started ringing so loudly she could barely make out the sound of Katie's voice. *Fiona Caldwell.* Just silently repeating the name made her stomach roll.

"I can't remember the woman's name," Katie rambled on, "but she wanted Sarah to say hello to you, ask you to friend her on Facebook." Katie laughed. "I guess Sarah told her she had the wrong person, but I thought it was interesting how far stuff travels on the Internet these days."

Olivia swallowed, forced out a laugh that sounded brittle and hoarse. "Yes, it is. Good story, though. I'm sure Sarah and I will get a chuckle out of it the next time she comes in."

Katie turned to check the kitchen service window. "Looks like your orders are up. I'll be right back." As Katie sailed away, Olivia glanced over at Rafe. His features had turned even darker than they were before and there wasn't a trace of gold in those hard, brown eyes.

Dear God, she felt like running away. Wanted to just slide out of the booth and start walking, keep going wherever her legs happened to take her. Instead she pasted on a smile and was grateful when Katie arrived with an armload of platters heaped with burgers and fries.

The men dug in, even Rafe. Liv forced herself to fork up a few bites of lettuce, but they stuck in her throat. Her mind shot back to her outing with Khan that afternoon. What if it hadn't been just paranoia? What if they'd found her again?

Her stomach knotted so hard the bile rose in her throat. For an instant she thought she might gag. No way could she force down another bite of salad. She had to get out of there, no matter what Rafe thought.

She stood up, grabbed her salad plate. "Sorry, guys, I just remembered something I've got to do. I'll take this with me. See you all later." She didn't look at Rafe, just turned and started walking toward the kitchen. She dumped the salad, left the plate, and headed upstairs to her apartment.

She had to think this through, had to figure things out.

As she stepped through the door, she took a deep breath. She had to calm down, had to get herself under control. Just because her once-best-friend, Gloria Rinehart, thought she'd recognized her in a tiny photo on the Internet — which Sarah had already denied — there was no reason to think the people looking for her had found her.

During her run today, her uneasiness was likely nothing but her imagination. She wasn't ready to leave Valdez. No way was she running away unless she had to. There was too much at stake.

She started to relax. The only person who knew anything at all about her was Rafe. She could handle Rafe Brodie. She was a woman and he wanted her. That gave her an advantage. When his knock came at the door a few minutes later, as she had figured it would, she was ready.

Olivia took a deep breath and pulled open the door.

"Hello, Fiona," Rafe said.

The name sliced right through her. Rafe

was no fool. She had known immediately that he'd picked up on her reaction to the name. Still, aside from his determination to know more about her and the magazine ad he had found, he had no way of knowing she was actually Fiona Caldwell.

She laughed. "You think that's my name? Why, because some woman saw a photo on Facebook and thought she recognized an old friend in the background?"

Those dark eyes drilled her. "It upset you. I could see it in your face."

She shrugged. "This whole thing with Scotty upsets me. I just got to thinking about it, that's all. I needed some time to myself."

His hard look didn't soften. "I know you aren't Olivia Chandler. You aren't from Medfield, and I know you didn't go to the University of Massachusetts."

Her stomach balled into a knot. "What are you talking about?"

"You heard what I said downstairs. My brother's a detective. He ran a check on you. You aren't who you say you are."

She fought not to tremble. How could his brother possibly have found that out? She'd paid a fortune to establish a new identity. Surely, Nick Brodie couldn't figure out it was a fake. Or could he?

She thought of everything she had to lose and pulled herself together, slid into the part of seductress she had prepared herself to play.

"Does it really matter, Rafe?" She dragged the clip out of her hair and tossed her head, letting the heavy strands fall loose around her shoulders. She slid her arms around his neck. "We all have secrets. Whatever I was, whoever I was, I'm not that person anymore. I have a new life here and that's all that matters." She went up on her toes and softly kissed his mouth. "If you care for me at all, you'll accept the person I am now."

She pressed herself full-length against him, felt the coiled tension in his hard-muscled frame. Leaning closer, she kissed him again, a slow melding of lips that got not the least response. She kissed the corners of his mouth, set her lips over his again. Rafe shackled her wrists, dragged them from around his neck, and set her away from him.

"If you're trying to seduce me, I'm not in the mood. I want to know what the hell is going on."

Panic threatened. Her heart was hammering, her throat so dry she could barely speak. She reminded herself how important this was, how much she had to lose.

Snuggling back against him, she kissed the side of his neck. "I'm asking you to let this go. I'm asking you to take me the way I am. I don't think that's too much to expect." She nipped his ear, kissed him, nipped his bottom lip, then kissed him again, urged his mouth open and slid her tongue over his.

She knew he was aroused. She could feel his erection pressing against the front of his jeans.

"We do this now," he warned, "it's just sex, Liv. And the way I feel right this minute, it'll be a damned hard taking."

Her stomach clenched. His words shouldn't have turned her on, but they did. "I don't care. I want you." To prove it, she curled her fingers into the front of his denim work shirt, leaned up and kissed him deeply.

Whatever reserve had been holding Rafe back tore free. His tongue was in her mouth and hers was in his. He caught the hem of her sweater, tugged it off over her head and tossed it away. He palmed her breasts, scraped his thumbs over her nipples, deepened the kiss. Heat rolled through her and a greedy hunger stronger than anything before.

Rafe bent his head to her breast and suckled her hard, rolled his tongue around the tip. She slid her hands into his hair to hold him in place, and his teeth clamped down, sending a coil of heat burning through her.

A moan escaped. She was wet and scorching hot. What had started as a desperate game had escalated into something more, something darkly fierce and erotic.

Kissing her all the while, he walked her backward into the living room. As she came up against the arm of the sofa, she felt his hand at her waist. He popped the snap on her stretchy jeans and dragged them down over her hips. One of his big hands found her sex and he began to stroke her. Shivery need raced over her skin and an ache began to throb between her legs.

When Rafe buzzed his zipper down and freed himself, she was ready. More than ready. She was always ready for Rafe.

He kissed her deeply, his tongue in her mouth, kissed the side of her neck, then turned her around and bent her over the sofa, forcing her to prop her hands on the cushion for support. She whimpered as his big hands gripped her hips and he positioned himself, drove himself inside. Rafe took her deep and hard, just as he had promised. Olivia started coming and couldn't stop.

She cried out as another climax hit,

burned through her. She called Rafe's name as his own release struck, felt his big hands tighten around her waist, holding her in place as he spilled himself inside her.

For several long moments, neither of them moved.

Eventually their breathing evened out and he eased her back against him. He dragged a handkerchief out of his pocket, reached around and handed it to her. When she'd finished, he pulled her jeans up, turned her into his arms and just held her. His hand smoothed gently over her back, and his tenderness, in contrast with the hard way he had taken her, made her eyes sting.

"I know you're in some kind of trouble," Rafe said softly. "Let me help you, darlin'."

She looked up at him and the tears in her eyes slid down her cheeks. "Please, Rafe. I can't . . . I can't do this." Her throat ached. Her heart was squeezing. "I don't want to go, but if you keep this up, I'll have to leave. You have . . . have to let it be."

Rafe studied her face. "Tell me what's wrong. Let me help you."

She brushed away some of the wetness and just shook her head. "Promise me you'll stop what you're doing or . . . or . . ." She swallowed. "Or it's over between us."

His eyes, dark and searching, found hers.

"Are you sure that's the way you want it?"

Her heart jerked. He was going to end things. End their relationship before they ever had a chance. She couldn't have imagined the fierce stab of pain that hit her at the thought of losing him.

Her throat swelled with a fresh lump of tears. "That's . . . that's the way it has to be."

Rafe cupped her face in his hands, bent his head, and very gently kissed her. "All right. Then we'll leave the past behind. I'll take you the way you are. Olivia Chandler, owner of the Pelican Café."

A sob tore from her throat. Olivia curled her fingers into his shirt and leaned against him, pressed her face into his chest and started crying.

Rafe's arms tightened around her. "It's all right, baby." His hand slid down her back, rubbing gently. "Everything's going to be okay."

"Rafe . . ." She only cried harder, her body shaking with the force of her tears.

"It's gonna be all right, baby, I promise."

"Oh God, Rafe . . ."

"Easy . . ."

With a shaky breath, she forced herself under control. "I'm sorry. I don't . . . I don't usually . . . I never cry."

He eased her a little away, tipped her chin up. "Listen to me, Liv. I said it's going to be okay. You believe me, right? You trust me? You know I'd never do anything to hurt you?"

She swallowed, managed to nod. Rafe wouldn't hurt her. She knew that deep down. Knew it soul deep. "I know."

He caught her face between his hands and very softly kissed her.

That was the moment she knew, the moment her heart squeezed hard and she knew.

She had done the most awful thing. She had let herself fall in love with him.

Rafe left Olivia's apartment and headed back to his house. He needed to talk to his brother. He had made a promise tonight and he was a man who kept his word. He had told Olivia he would take her just as she was and he meant it.

He had already considered the consequences of digging into her past, asked himself how he would feel if he discovered secrets from a time in her life when she had been a different person than she was today.

What if she'd been a drug addict? A thief or a prostitute? How would he feel? But whatever dark secrets lay in her past, Olivia wasn't that person anymore. She was Olivia

Chandler, owner of the Pelican Café, a woman whose face had filled with yearning when she'd held that baby girl.

He knew she was desperately afraid. No way could he miss the fear in those big gray eyes. If trouble followed her here, he had to be ready, and the only way he could do that was to find out the truth.

He remembered the way she had cried in his arms. He knew her now, knew crying was a weakness she rarely allowed. She had let down her guard with him. She had let him in and he would not fail her.

Rafe drove his pickup into the garage, parked next to the Expedition, and went inside the house. He had a business to run, schedules to prepare, trips to arrange, ledgers to go over. Later he needed to pick up Zach and go over to the Seaside Motel, retrieve the GPS from the bumper of the Jeep.

He had plenty to do, but first, he had to call Nick. Unless he was working a case, his brother would be home by now.

The phone rang. "Hey, bro," Nick said, a smile in his voice as he answered. Married life obviously agreed with him.

"I've got her name," Rafe told him, skipping the preliminaries. "Fiona Caldwell. She all but admitted it."

The humor went out of Nick's voice. "What else did you find out?"

"She's in trouble. She didn't say it, but there isn't any doubt. You'll get a FedEx in the morning. DNA and a glossy page out of a magazine. She was a dancer, posed for makeup ads. The page you'll get came out of the October issue of *Cosmopolitan* three years ago. I'm pretty sure you'll find her this time."

"Sounds like. You okay?"

"Got something else for you," Rafe said, avoiding the question since he didn't feel okay at all. "This has to do with Scott Ferris's murder."

"Hey, who needs clients when I've got you to fill up my workday?"

"Very funny. Two guys, Lee Wong and Michael Nevin, were staying in the motel room closest to the crime scene the night of the murder. They're playing see no evil, hear no evil, but it's beginning to look like they heard or saw something. Wong's Asian American, midtwenties. Nevin's about the same age, appears to be Middle Eastern. They're both Islamic. I want to know their story, if they have one."

"Interesting. You're thinking they may have a reason for not wanting to get involved."

"Could be. If they do, I want to know what it is."

"That's not much info, but I'll do my best."

"Thanks, Nick."

"What about your lady? Fiona, is it now? You're not falling for her, are you, bro? Because it's sure beginning to sound like it."

"Whoever she was before, she's Olivia now and she needs help. I'm trying to help her, Nick."

"I hope to hell that's all it is. I'll call you back as soon as I can." Nick rang off and Rafe headed into his office.

He had work to do until the sun went down, then he was heading over to pick up Zach. As he sat down in front of his computer, he did his best not to think of Olivia and what his brother might find out.

CHAPTER TWENTY-FOUR

Olivia paced in front of the window of her apartment. It was black as pitch outside, dark enough for Rafe to go back to the motel and retrieve the tracking device he had put on the Jeep last night.

He wouldn't be back for at least an hour, maybe more. Now was the time for her to leave.

Her stomach churned. She couldn't believe she had all but admitted she was Fiona Caldwell. If Rafe looked for her now, he would find out who she was. If he found out the truth, he could destroy her. Destroy them both. She needed to pack a bag, sign ownership of the restaurant over to Nell, get into her Subaru, drive out of Valdez and never look back.

Her throat ached as she stared into the darkness. Fiona Caldwell, the name she was born with, the maiden name she had returned to after her divorce. Fiona was the bail-jumping defendant in a homicide, a woman formally charged with the murder of her ex-husband, Stephen Rothman.

The only reason the crime hadn't become national news was her claim that his mistress, a congresswoman and prominent political powerhouse, had actually been the woman who had shot him.

In three short days, the media had moved on to other news, falling under the spell of a political machine that manipulated them as if they were children. The media had backed away, never even mentioned the woman's name, not wanting to smear one of their favorites.

Instead, they had convicted Fiona even before the charges had been filed. She'd had no other choice but to run.

She needed to run now.

She thought of Rafe and how close she had come to telling him everything, baring her soul and begging him to help her. She still couldn't believe she had broken down that way in front of him. That she had cried so hard she had soaked the front of his shirt, cried as she hadn't allowed herself to do in years.

Maybe, in some small way, the release had helped clear her head. She was back in control and able to think. Valdez wasn't

New York and Rafe wasn't an assistant district attorney, a man running for election, someone willing to throw an innocent woman to the wolves to achieve his goal.

She glanced at the doorway. Rafe was gone. After what had happened, she had no idea whether he would come back tonight. Or ever. There was a better-than-average chance he would use the time away from her to dig for more information, dig until he found out she was wanted for murder.

But Olivia was tired of running. She had made something good here. She wasn't ready to give up her home, her business, and the life she was building. On top of that, now there was Rafe. She'd told herself it wasn't possible to be in love with him, that it had happened too quickly, that she barely knew him.

But she knew everything about Rafe Brodie. In a town this size, there were very few secrets. She knew the kind of man he was, knew he was intelligent and loyal, respected and admired. Since they had started seeing each other, she knew he was a man of deep conviction, a man of his word.

A man worth loving.

She thought maybe she had fallen a little in love with him the first time he had stepped through the door of the café. Maybe right then, she had recognized the fierce pull of attraction as the danger it was.

Outside the window, quiet hovered over the landscape, and Olivia felt a calm stillness settle inside her. She was staying, fighting for what she wanted. What she deserved.

She steeled herself. The life she had made for herself was worth fighting for.

Rafe was worth fighting for.

Ignoring the weight pressing down on her chest and the panic at the edge of her mind, Liv walked into the bedroom and started to undress. Rafe would be finished at the motel by now. He would come back or he wouldn't. The police would arrive at her door, or they wouldn't. By morning, she would have a better idea where she stood.

Wishing it was the faded T-shirt she wore at Rafe's, Olivia pulled on an old sleep-tee, and crawled into bed.

It didn't really matter that she wouldn't be able to sleep.

It was a few minutes after midnight when Lee Heng slid behind the wheel of the Jeep. Mikal Nadir climbed into the passenger seat beside him. The meeting at Trent Doyle's rented house in the mountains was set for twelve thirty. It wouldn't do for them to be late, but Lee didn't want to be early, either. He didn't want to spend any more time with Doyle and his Russian mistress than he had to.

He wasn't a fan of the New York entrepreneur, but Doyle had supplied the money for their mission. He'd put together a very viable plan and made all the arrangements, which had been extremely expensive.

Lee had no illusion that Doyle's motive was anything other than money. Lee had done a little digging, discovered the man who lived like a king was teetering on the edge of bankruptcy — or worse. For running the same kind of operation, Bernie Madoff was rotting in prison.

Lee wasn't sure how the disaster would pay off for Doyle, but he knew the profits would be big or the man wouldn't be involved. Trent Doyle wasn't working for a higher purpose, a cause he'd committed his life to, not like Lee and Nadir.

Lee's Indonesian parents had immigrated to Columbus, Ohio, and raised him in their Islamic faith. He couldn't help being Westernized, since he'd gone to high school in Columbus and attended Ohio State University — go Buckeyes! But after he'd graduated, his worldviews had begun to change.

In time, he'd become a full-fledged member of JAT, the Jemaah Anshorut Tauhid, Indonesia's number-one terrorist group. Through their teachings, he saw the injustices committed by the West against Muslims, and a fire had begun to burn in his heart. Today that fire burned even hotter. Lee was determined to do something that would bring about change.

He glanced at the man beside him. Mikal Nadir was Iraqi, brought to the United States by presidential edict along with thousands of other Iraqi Muslims. Only a handful were militant, but even a few could affect the course of history, as had happened with the terrorists on September eleventh.

The third man in the group, Darius Cain, was a convert to Islam brought into the faith by the death of his brother, who had converted in prison. But since Cain didn't pray to Allah, drank alcohol, and took up with lewd women, he was as far from a true believer as anyone Lee had ever met.

Aside from the crucial job he fulfilled, Lee had no use for him. How Trent Doyle had found the three men and brought them together, Lee had no idea. It didn't matter as long as the mission went off as planned.

He pulled up the driveway, turned off the engine, and both men got out of the Jeep.

Doyle and his Russian woman waited in the entry. This time, Lee and Nadir were invited into the den.

Cain was already there, sipping from a glass filled with liquor from the bottle of Jack Daniel's sitting on the bar. Lee worked to keep his lip from curling into a sneer. He had no respect for Cain, no matter what religion he professed. He wondered if the man would survive the mission, or if Allah would see fit to martyr him. Or perhaps dole out some other form of punishment for his nonbeliever ways.

Whatever happened, Lee didn't care.

"Would you like something to drink?" Doyle asked. "There's coffee in the kitchen."

"No, thank you," Lee said.

"I do not care for anything," said Nadir.

They sat down on furniture arranged around a maple coffee table; a simple beige sofa and chairs matched the carpet.

"I called you here to go over final preparations for the mission. Before that happens, do any of you have anything to report?"

Lee glanced at Cain and wondered if the man had been in town again. He was supposed to be at the pipeline terminal or in his trailer in the RV park, but Cain was never good at following orders.

"What about the woman?" Doyle asked

when no one replied. "Is she still asking questions?"

"She hasn't been back," Lee said. "But if she shows up, we have the information we need to keep her quiet." He was in his element here. His American upbringing had won him a scholarship in the computer field. Combined with his years at Microsoft, he was a hacker extraordinaire.

"Would you like to share?" Doyle asked.

"Her name is Fiona Caldwell. She's wanted for the murder of her ex-husband."

Surprise flickered in Doyle's blue eyes. Then a slow smile slid over his too slick features. "Is that so? A shame we didn't find out sooner. She might have proven quite useful."

"Like I said, she hasn't been back to the motel and the cops are still holding Reed. We should be finished and out of here before the Ferris murder has a chance to become a real problem."

Cain pushed away from the bar, his big, hard frame an imposing presence in the room. "Why don't I just take care of her? Make sure she keeps quiet for good?"

An instant of disgust appeared in Doyle's face; then it was gone. He drilled Cain with a glare. "Stay away from the woman. We don't need more trouble. A few more days, this is over, and all of us get what we want."

He turned to include the rest of them. "Now, let's get on to more important matters, shall we? Starting with news. The ship, *San Pascual,* out of San Diego, is due to arrive on schedule. That puts us within days of completing our mission."

Lee gave an inward sigh of relief. They wouldn't have to wait much longer.

"Within twenty-four hours after the ship's arrival, one-point-five million barrels of oil will have been loaded into the *San Pascual*'s double hull — enough to cause a spill five times as bad as the *Exxon Valdez*."

Lee thought of the havoc it would cause and excitement trembled through him. JAT wanted to make a statement. News of the terror attack on the pipeline would make waves around the world the size of a tsunami.

"Our man is aboard the ship and so are the explosives. Cain should have the rest of the explosives in position on shore by then." He looked over at the big, light-skinned black man. "You *will* be ready on time?"

"I'll be ready."

Doyle nodded. "A few hours after the bombs are detonated, the ship, along with the terminal, a portion of the pipeline, and as many of the storage tanks as possible, will be destroyed. You gentlemen can take credit for the attack in whatever form you wish."

Lee's excitement grew to a fierce joy pumping through his veins. His goal was in sight. His position in JAT would be elevated to glorious new heights. He shared a glance with Nadir. Nadir had his own dreams of justice and glory. Aside from their faith, they had little in common. But this . . . this was a vision that united them as nothing else could.

"Any questions so far?" Doyle asked.

No one spoke. Lee's excitement made it hard to breathe.

"Time is getting short," Doyle said. "We'll meet again tomorrow night to go over final preparations."

The meeting broke up and the men left the house. Neither Lee nor Nadir spoke on the way back down the hill. But the joy Lee felt continued to warm him. His greatest accomplishment loomed just two days away.

Rafe awakened in bed with Olivia, who slept curled against him. Sweet Christ, he liked the feel of her there, liked that she had been waiting for him when he had come back from the motel last night.

He hadn't been sure he'd return to her

apartment, not after the conversation they'd had, not until he heard what Nick had to say. In the end, he remembered the way she had cried in his arms and he couldn't stay away.

They hadn't spoken again of her past or her tears. Until something happened, they were moving forward, just as he'd promised.

Though he'd been tired after his hectic day, he and Liv had spent a few minutes checking the GPS he had taken off the Jeep. The device revealed the car's movements the night before and during the day as it zipped along the roads in town, stopping here and there with what appeared to be no rhyme or reason. At least nothing he could figure out. Maybe they'd have more luck with the device they retrieved tonight.

He glanced at the clock on her nightstand. He had a charter this morning, a full day with a full boat. He needed to get moving. Careful not to wake her, he kissed the top of Olivia's head and eased out from beneath the covers. Grabbing his clothes, he pulled them on and started for home to shower and change.

"Rafe . . . ?"

He turned to look at her, saw her pretty gray eyes open and watching him.

"I'm glad you came back last night."

He nodded. Why he'd returned was hard to explain and he wasn't completely sure himself. "I've got to go. Long day ahead. Any chance you could pick up that FedEx I'm expecting? It should arrive at the airport by ten."

"Your spy-version GPS? Sure, I'll pick it up."

"Thanks. I'll see you later."

She smiled. "What, no good-bye kiss?"

His mouth edged up. "If I go over there, I'll want more than a kiss, and I can't afford to be late. I'll see you when I get back."

She gave him a sexy little smile and he grinned. Actually grinned. *Damn.* With everything going on, what the hell did he have to be happy about? But when he was with Olivia, he just felt good.

He left her in bed, wishing he could go back and join her, make love to her before he headed downstairs to his pickup, but there wasn't time for that. By the time he showered and changed and drove down to the harbor, Jaimie was working on deck and Zach was checking the equipment in the cabin.

The smell of fresh-brewed coffee reached him as he stepped inside. Jaimie would have sandwiches in the fridge for lunch. A box of donuts sat open on the galley table.

Rafe reached in and grabbed one. "Thanks for your help last night," he said to Zach.

"No problem. You find anything on the GPS?"

"Nothing that means anything." He took another bite of donut. "They just drove around town, made a trip out Richardson Highway, drove up Dayville Road a ways."

"Something any tourist might do."

"That's right. If they went out last night after we put the new one on, we'll see their movements when we retrieve the device tonight."

"You still think these guys know something?"

"At the moment, it's just a hunch. I keep telling myself this is going nowhere, but I can't seem to convince myself."

"Then we should stick with it."

Rafe nodded and finished his donut. The discussion ended as Jaimie walked into the cabin. She flicked a dark, petulant glance at Zach, whose jaw went tight. The two of them hadn't spoken all day yesterday. Zach had made a couple of overtures, which Jaimie had nastily rebuffed. It looked as if she had every intention of continuing her snit today.

He didn't know what had caused the rift between them or who was in the wrong, but he wasn't putting up with it any longer.

His gaze went from one to the other and turned into a glare. "Okay, you two. This bullshit between you ends right here. We've got passengers coming aboard. They've spent a lot of money and they're looking forward to a great day of fishing. That isn't going to happen with the two of you looking like you want to strangle each other."

Zach said nothing. Neither did Jaimie.

"Okay, fine. You go out on the deck and make peace, or start looking for another job. What's it going to be?"

Jaimie hesitated, then turned and started walking, flicking a backward glance at Zach as she marched out onto the deck. Zach followed, his expression dark, his jaw set.

Rafe wasn't sure what was going on between the two, but they needed to figure it out. He almost smiled. If they did, it might even turn out to be something good.

Zach walked to where Jaimie stood at the rail. "Okay, I'll go first if you want."

She just nodded.

"I'm sorry you're mad. I'm sorry things went as far as they did the other night. I'm not sorry about what I said."

She looked up at him and something shifted in her features. "You shouldn't have spanked me. I'm a grown woman."

He fought against a smile he knew would be disastrous right now. "That's the point. You're a woman but you weren't acting like one and you weren't being treated like one."

"And that gave you the right to manhandle me?"

"Sometimes when you care about someone you have to go further than just words."

Her big brown eyes ran over his face. "When I was in high school, I . . . ummm . . . used to have a crush on you. Just like all the other girls."

Surprise filtered through him. "Did you? I wish I'd known."

"You went to college and a few years later so did I. In the summers I worked for Rafe and I met Scotty. He was always so nice to me."

"He was nice. But he wasn't interested in you as a woman. I am. I've been interested for a long time."

"Why?"

He smiled. "Because you're smart and you're pretty and you're different from any other woman I know. I don't know any female who works as hard as you do, who takes the toughest job and makes it look easy. And you even make it fun."

She started to smile. She was really pretty when she smiled. "You're good at your job, too. I've never said so, but it's true."

"Thanks."

"Maybe we could, you know, start over," she said.

"That would be great."

"No more spanking."

He smiled. "Not unless you deserve it."

She laughed. "Next time you try it, I won't be drunk. I'll fight you and I'll win."

He traced a finger down her cheek. "I might even let you."

Her smile widened. "Truce then?"

"Absolutely — if you'll let me buy you a pizza when we get back to the harbor tonight."

Jaimie grinned. "You're on."

Heavy footfalls pounded on the deck. Zach turned at the sound of Rafe's deep voice coming from behind them.

"Okay, you two. You're both grinning. That's good. Now get back to work."

Zach nodded, his eyes still on Jaimie, whose eyes remained on his.

Working with her that day, watching her smile instead of frown, was one of the best days Zach could recall.

CHAPTER TWENTY-FIVE

With Rafe not due back from his all-day charter till six, and it being Nell's day for the dinner shift, Liv suited up and went down to get Khan and go jogging.

She felt better today. Rafe had returned to the apartment last night. On the surface at least, he seemed resigned to accepting her as she was, leaving her past behind. As far as Liv was concerned, the past belonged in the past, as it had since she left New York.

There was no way she could ever prove her innocence, not against the powerful forces who had conspired to convict her. Moving forward was her only option. If Rafe was willing to do that, it could still work between them.

She was in love with him. She wanted to make a life with him. She wasn't sure what Rafe felt for her, but she had to believe he wanted more from her than just sex and friendship. If she was wrong, she would deal with it when the time came.

In the meanwhile, today was a glorious day in one of the most beautiful places on earth. Liv took that as a hopeful sign. Grabbing the leash off the hook on the back porch, she pulled open the door and held it up for Khan to see. Lying in the sun with Tuxedo sprawled on top of him, the big dog bolted to his feet and raced toward her. Tux tumbled off, collected herself, and sat down. With a yawn, she started grooming herself, then curled back up in the sun.

Liv snapped on Khan's leash and gave the command. "Heel." The shepherd positioned himself beside her and they took off out the side gate.

The sun felt warm as it soaked through her hooded sweatshirt. The last days of May could still be rainy, but more and more the sun was beginning to make its presence known. She jogged through town and turned toward the mountains. There were some great trails up off Mineral Creek Road.

She thought of Rafe and wondered if he might want to go on an overnight hike up there sometime. He was in great physical condition and he really liked the outdoors. She smiled to think how much they had to look forward to. If only he would stand by his decision and accept her as the person she was now.

She was smiling, enjoying herself, when she heard the sound of a vehicle approaching, turned to see an older model, brown Chevy beater driving up beside her. Unease filtered through her. She shook it off. Old habits were hard to break.

She started to relax, but as the car drew near, the feeling returned, more intense than before. She didn't recognize the driver, a good-looking, light-skinned African American man wearing a sweatshirt with a hood that wasn't pulled up. He had close-cropped black hair and earrings in his ears.

Liv fought an urge to run as he pulled over to the edge of the road and rolled his window down, drove the car slowly along beside her.

"Get in the car, Fiona."

Her heart jerked so hard, she nearly stumbled. Her mouth went dry and her knees started shaking. *Oh, dear God.* She forced herself under control, kept jogging along the road.

"My name is Olivia Chandler." She picked up her pace as she glanced around, looking for an avenue of escape. "You must have me confused with someone else." No houses in sight. She had run past the last residences

340

on the road and there was no one anywhere near.

She glanced back at the car, saw a black semiautomatic pistol appear in the man's big hand. He pointed it directly at her heart and stepped on the brake, bringing the car to a jolting stop. "I said get in the car."

She looked down at Khan. Reading her fear, his fur was standing up, his teeth bared. A low growl rumbled from his throat.

"Make a wrong move," the man said, "I shoot the dog. Now get in the car."

He wouldn't hesitate. She could see it in his hard black eyes. The stun gun rode in the pocket of her sweatshirt, a comforting weight against her body.

"Sit," she said to Khan, then leaned down and unhooked his leash. "Stay." He'd go home eventually. Nell would see him and know something was wrong. She prayed by then it wouldn't be too late.

Her hand went into the pocket of her jacket and her fingers wrapped around her weapon. She needed to get close enough to the man to use it, yet far enough away from Khan so the man wouldn't kill him. She walked around to the passenger side of the car and slid into the worn plaid seat. The interior was dirty, littered with sandwich wrappers, beer bottles, and empty paper cups.

She frowned. Somehow the rusty old beater didn't fit with the image of a high-priced executioner hired by her powerful enemies in Washington.

She slammed the door and as soon as it closed, his foot stomped down on the gas and he drove away, continuing farther up the hill. She needed to get out, but she didn't want to jump until he slowed down. The area grew more and more remote. There was nothing up ahead but the end of the road and the beginning of a set of trails.

Fear rolled through her, clawed at her insides. "If you think you can kill me and just walk away, that isn't going to happen. I have friends here. I own a business. When I disappear, they'll come looking for me. The police will come looking. They'll find you and they'll put you in jail."

One of his thick, black eyebrows went up. "Why would I want to kill a pretty little thing like you?"

The words surprised her. And that they actually sounded like the truth. Surely that was the reason he was there. They had tried to kill her before. They needed her dead. Surely he had been sent to do the job. She didn't understand what was going on.

"What do you want?" she asked, trying to brazen it out as he pulled up at the end of the road and turned off the engine.

He just smiled. He had straight white teeth and if he wasn't so big and menacing, if she couldn't see the evil in his empty black eyes, she might have said he was attractive.

"I know your secret, Fiona. I know you're a murderer. I know you're a wanted woman, hiding out way up here in Alaska, living under some phony name. I don't care who you killed. I don't care if you kill someone else. I'll keep your secret. But I want something in return for my silence."

Her heart was hammering. Sweat rolled between her breasts. "You want money? I-I can pay you. How much do you want?" If she could bribe him, buy a little time, she could still get away.

He chuckled, reached over and touched her cheek. "You're a beautiful woman, Fiona. I've been watching you. I know you keep yourself fit. I'm guessing beneath those clothes you've got one helluva body. For weeks, I've been living up here like a monk. I don't want your money. I want to fuck you. I want to have you any way I can think of. Any way and every way I want. You get me?"

She started shaking, couldn't push a sound past her frozen lips.

"I won't be here much longer," he said matter-of-factly. "Only a few more days. I'm off work today. You do me right, I keep my mouth shut. I leave and no one's the wiser. Now climb over into the backseat and take off your clothes. I do you right here, then we'll go back to my place and I'll do you again."

Her stomach was churning. Olivia shook her head, fighting not to panic, telling herself she would only get one chance, telling herself to wait for the opportunity she needed. "I said I'd pay you. I'm not having sex with you."

He backhanded her hard, the force of the blow slamming into her cheek before she realized what had happened. Pain shot through her head and for an instant she was afraid she would pass out.

The pistol pointed at her temple. "You don't seem to get it, Fiona. I'm fucking you whether you like it or not. What are you going to do — go to the cops? I don't think so."

"Who are you?"

"Nobody. At least not today. Soon, though, I'll be somebody." He grinned. "A man you'll know real, real well."

Her cheek was throbbing, but she'd settled a little, more angry now than afraid. He was still grinning when she eased the stun gun out of her pocket.

"Go on," he said. "Get your ass in the back like I told you."

Her fingers tightened around the plastic. With a breath for courage, she jammed the stun gun into his ribs. The weapon crackled, a million volts of electricity made contact, and a scream tore out of his throat.

Liv gritted her teeth and stunned him again, then one more time for good measure. No way could she tie him up. He was big and heavy and she had no rope, nothing to use.

She shot out of the car and bolted down the road, racing against time and the danger behind her. Adrenaline roared through her and she ran faster. She could dart off the road, but running through the grass would slow her pace and a bullet could travel a whole lot quicker than she could. Staying on the road was the fastest way back to town, the quickest way to safety.

Panting hard, counting the seconds, knowing it would only be minutes before her attacker could recover and come after her, she pounded downhill as fast as she could go.

She knew one thing. She wasn't going to get the second chance she deserved. She wasn't going to have a chance to make it work with Rafe.

Olivia Chandler had died back in that car. She was as dead as her ex-husband. Liv barely noticed the tears washing down her cheeks.

Rafe was sitting in a booth at the café when his iPhone started playing. Liv was out running with Khan, Nell had told him. She was due back any minute.

He looked down at the caller ID and his stomach twisted. "Hey, Nick," he said, pressing the phone against his ear.

"Where are you?"

"In the café."

"Walk outside."

He got up and headed for the door, the knot in his stomach twisting tighter. He stopped in the patio area and sat down at one of the empty tables. A couple sat at a table across the way. It was the warmest day they'd had this year, pushing toward sixty degrees. Soon the patio would be filled with people outside enjoying the weather.

Rafe took a steadying breath. "What is it?"

"You better brace yourself. This isn't good."

His hand tightened around the phone. "Tell me."

"Three years ago, Fiona Caldwell was arrested for the murder of her ex-husband. Happened in an apartment in Manhattan. Upper East Side. Expensive neighborhood. She had a place of her own nearby. Which jibes with her high-paying job as a makeup model. It was a big story at first, appeared in all the papers. Jesus, Rafe, you could have Googled her yourself and found her."

It hadn't even occurred to him. He wasn't a high-tech kind of guy. Or maybe he didn't really want to know.

"You're the detective, not me. She confess to the murder?"

"No. Claimed there was another woman in the apartment that night. Claimed the other woman was the one who shot Rothman."

"That's the husband's name? Rothman, not Chandler?"

"Ex-husband. Stephen Rothman. Caldwell's her maiden name. She took it back after she and Rothman divorced. Fiona was arrested at the scene —"

"Olivia," he corrected. He had no idea why.

"Olivia was charged a couple of days later. Since she had no criminal record and claimed she was innocent, she made bail. Big dollars but she had the money to make it happen. Three weeks later, she disappeared. She's never been seen or heard of since."

"Until now."

"That's right. Listen, Rafe, I'm really sorry."

He shook his head. "Not your fault. You're just the messenger."

"I know you wanted to keep this quiet, but this is murder, bro."

"I need to talk to her. Get her side of the story."

"You really think she'll tell you the truth? She's been lying to you all along."

He glanced back toward the restaurant, his mind sorting through the mountain of lies Liv had told him. "I know."

"Sooner or later, you'll have to do what's right."

"You gave me your word, Nick. I'm holding you to it."

"It's still your call. Be careful, yeah?"

"What if she's innocent?"

"What if she's innocent?" Nick repeated. "If she was innocent, she wouldn't have run."

Rafe gazed off toward the boats bobbing in the harbor across the street. Nick was right. Wasn't he? "What about Wong and Nevin? You come up with anything there?"

"Not enough info. I need a photo or DNA sample. Something."

"I can do that. We rigged security cameras in the corridor outside their motel room. Got 'em on video. Zach Carver's a whiz at that stuff. He's the kid who took Scotty's place. I'm betting he can isolate their pictures and e-mail them to you."

"Great, I'll watch for them."

"Listen, Nick, I really appreciate your help. I'll stay in touch." Rafe hung up before his brother could launch into another warning.

For several long moments, he just sat there. Then the front door to the café burst open and Nell rushed out, broad hips swinging, salt-and-pepper hair flying around her face.

"Rafe, thank God you're here! Something's happened to Liv!"

Rafe came up off the chair. "What's going on?"

"Liv and Khan went running, but Khan came home alone. He was making a racket at the gate. I heard him, went out and let him in. Now he's scratching to come inside. I think he's looking for her."

He strode through the café, not bothering

to reply to the friendly hellos from some of the customers, Nell hurrying along beside him. When he reached the back door, Khan looked frantic. The dog barked and ran back toward the gate, barked and ran up to the porch.

"He isn't wearing his leash," Nell said as the frenzied animal rushed back and forth. "Liv must have let him go."

"Why would she do that?"

"I don't know."

Unless she planned to leave town and the run was just a distraction. "I need to go upstairs. You've got a key, right?"

"Yes, but what about Khan?"

He started climbing the stairs. "In a minute. First, I want to look around, see if she packed her clothes."

"Good heavens, why would she do that?"

"Just do it, Nell. Open the door."

Nell pulled out a ring of keys, unlocked the apartment door, and turned off the alarm. Rafe went straight to the bedroom. The bed was made, nothing disturbed. Aside from Olivia not lying there naked beneath the sheet, smiling at him as she had been that morning, it looked exactly the same as it had when he'd left.

A chill ran through him. If she hadn't left town, where was she? Turning, he ran back downstairs. Khan was still frantically pacing in front of the porch. The dog had gone with her and clearly come back on his own. Liv was in trouble and Khan was trying to help her.

Rafe strode toward him. "Let's go, boy! Find Liv! Come on, Khan. Find Liv!"

The dog whirled and took off for the side gate. Rafe followed him, opened the gate, and Khan shot off down the road as if he knew exactly where he was going.

Rafe ran after him, picking up speed until they were both flat-out running, first along the road, then heading up the hill toward the mountains.

Rafe looked ahead. Someone was running down the hill in the opposite direction, running hard and fast. Tall, slender, graceful. *Olivia.*

He intercepted her, stepped into her path and she collided with his chest. Her face was streaked with tears. A bruise had begun to form on her cheek and she couldn't catch her breath.

A jolt of fury tore through him. "What the —"

"Rafe, oh my God! We have . . . have to go. He . . . he's coming. He'll catch us." She grabbed his arm and started tugging him back down the hill the way he had come. Rafe caught her and swung her around to face him.

"Tell me what the hell's going on."

"We don't have time! We have to run! He's got a gun!" She turned to the dog. "Come on, boy, let's go!" She started running and this time Rafe didn't stop her. Together they sprinted off down the hill, Khan racing along beside them. At the corner, they turned.

"That's him!" Olivia pointed toward an old brown Chevy roaring down the hill. It shot around the corner, turning in the opposite direction, and careened off down the road, gathering speed as it moved farther out of sight.

Rafe tried to get the license number off the bright yellow plate, but the shrubs in the area were dense and he only got the first three letters. ETU.

"I have to go," Olivia said, slowing only a little. "God, Rafe, I'm so sorry." She started to turn away, but he caught her arm.

"I know everything, Olivia. I know about the murder. I know all of it. You aren't going anywhere."

Her eyes shot to his. Her lips trembled, and a sob escaped. She swayed unsteadily. Rafe wrapped an arm around her, pulling her close as she collapsed against him. If he

352

hadn't been holding her up, he wasn't sure she could have stayed on her feet.

She was trembling all over, her eyes still wide with fear. She glanced off down the road, took a shaky breath. Her eyes slid closed a moment before she looked up at him. "I'll do whatever you say. I just don't care anymore."

He caught her chin, studied her face. "He hit you. Who was he?"

She shook her head. "I don't know. I really don't. He knew my name. My old name. Knew about the murder. I offered him money, but he wanted . . . he wanted . . ." She swallowed and glanced away.

He studied the bruise on her cheek and a fresh wave of fury rolled through him. "What, baby? What did he want?"

Olivia's gaze locked with his. "He wanted me to trade sex for his silence." She managed a wan half smile, reached into her pocket and pulled out her stun gun. "He got a jolt of something a lot hotter than sex."

Relief washed through him, along with a hint of respect he didn't want to feel. She dropped the weapon back into her pocket and his arms tightened around her. Olivia buried her face in his neck, and his chest clamped down. It was insane to feel such a powerful surge of protectiveness for a woman who'd committed murder. And yet there it was.

"Come on." He took her hand. "Let's go back to my place. We'll call Nell, tell her you're okay. Then we'll talk."

CHAPTER TWENTY-SIX

They brought Khan with them to Rafe's house, put a blanket down for him in the living room. The big dog had been frantic to save her. Olivia couldn't bear to leave him behind.

She showered and slipped on a pair of Rafe's sweatpants, pulled on the faded Coast Guard tee she had borrowed from him before.

Rafe was waiting for her in the living room when she went downstairs. She was surprised he wasn't standing guard outside the bathroom door.

Why had she ever believed he would be able to accept her as just Olivia Chandler? No past, only the present and the future they might have created. It was a crazy, stupid fantasy. One she would now be paying for.

She reached the bottom of the stairs, and he stood up as she entered the room, handed her a snifter of the single malt they had enjoyed together before. She sat down in the chair instead of sitting next to him on the sofa.

Those days were over. The two of them were over. She might as well get used to it.

Rafe left for a moment, came back with a bag of ice wrapped in a towel, handed it over. She pressed it against her cheek.

"You want to start or you want me to?" he asked.

She just shrugged. What did it matter?

"My brother found out who you are," he said. "Once I gave him your name, he said it was easy."

She nodded dully. At least the ice was having the same dulling effect on her cheek. "It was a big story for a while. The media killed it in a couple of days. They didn't want the real murderer to get bad press. They didn't believe she'd done it, of course. They were sure I was the one."

Rafe leaned toward her. "Look at me."

She let her hand drop and looked him straight in the face.

"Did you kill him?"

She shook her head. "No." She was through lying. She had never really fooled him anyway.

"Did you murder your husband, Stephen

Rothman?"

"No, dammit."

"Do you know who did?"

"Yes. But your brother didn't see her name in the papers, did he?"

"Why not?"

"Because her name is Julia Stanfield. Julia Stanfield? Married to Phillip Stanfield the Third? Ring any bells?"

He frowned. "You don't mean the congresswoman? The woman who's likely going to run for president after Hillary Clinton?"

"That's her. The darling of the press."

"You're telling me Julia Stanfield killed your husband."

"Ex-husband. Stephen Rothman. He and I had a relatively congenial divorce. Stephen was older. We were friends before we married. He cheated. I ended it. Eventually we became friends again. That's what I was doing at his place that night. Stephen asked me to come over. He said he needed someone to talk to. When I got there, he told me he'd been seeing the Stanfield woman, but it wasn't working out and he wanted to end the affair."

"What happened?"

"Apparently Mrs. Stanfield doesn't take well to being dumped. She showed up at the apartment while I was in the bathroom. I heard a shot. Scared me to death. I thought it was a robbery. I cracked open the door so I could see what was going on and recognized her, saw her fire another four rounds into Stephen's chest. He was dead after shot number one."

"You're innocent," Rafe repeated as if he couldn't quite believe it. And why should he? No one else did. "You didn't kill him."

"No, I didn't kill him. I stayed in the bathroom until she was gone, came out and called the police. But by the time they got there, her people had set things in motion. The cops didn't believe a word I said. The gun was there, wiped clean but lying next to him on the rug. Her people fed the police and the press a bullshit line about how I was still in love with Stephen and I wanted him back. When he refused, I went over there and shot him. They kept her name out of the papers, the story died, and I was charged with murder."

"You had money. You could afford a good lawyer. Why did you run?"

She scoffed. "You really have to ask? Julia Stanfield is one of the most powerful women in the country. She's married to one of the most powerful men. I didn't decide to run until someone shot at me while I was leaving my apartment building. They found me one more time after that, shot at me in the parking lot next to the office where I was working in Dallas. I got away, spent more money, paid big to reinvent myself, and came up here."

She swallowed past the knot in her throat. "I love it here. God, I don't want to leave."

And I don't want to leave you, Rafe. But she didn't say that.

"You aren't going anywhere," Rafe said. "You're innocent. We're going to figure this out."

She shook her head, feeling a rush of sorrow so deep an ache throbbed in her heart. "I'm leaving, Rafe. You saw what happened today. That guy knows who I am. People know who I am. Word will get out. They'll come after me again and when they do, someone is going to get hurt. It could be Nell or Cassie or Katie. It could be you, Rafe. I won't let that happen. So choose. Either turn me over to the police, or I'm leaving. What's it going to be?"

Rafe came up off the sofa, took the towel-wrapped ice from her hand and set it on the table. Bending, he scooped her out of her chair and sat down with her in his lap. Indulging herself in these last few moments with him, she didn't protest, just let herself lean against his chest.

"You can't run for the rest of your life," Rafe said. "You have to take a stand sometime and it might as well be here. You have friends here, people who care about you. We just need time to figure this out."

"Rafe . . ."

"I'll talk to my brother, see what he thinks. He knows people. He has a friend in the FBI in Fairbanks. Dylan has a friend who's a high-powered criminal lawyer in Anchorage. We'll find a way."

Her heart squeezed. She turned to look at him, reached up and gently cupped his cheek, felt the rough shadow of his beard. "I never would have guessed. You are just the sweetest man."

He grunted. Lifting her off him, he set her beside him on the sofa, slid an arm around her waist to keep her there. "I'm not sweet. I'm determined. I believe in justice and I know there has to be a way to find it for you."

She sighed. How could she fight a man like that? One of the few people in the world who stood up for what he believed in.

"All right, I'll wait a couple of days. But it's risky. That guy could already be on the phone calling someone."

Rafe seemed to mull that over. "Or maybe

not. You said you offered him money but he wasn't interested. If he wanted you that badly, maybe it's personal. Maybe he'll come after you again." He cast her a glance. "From now on, you're with me, twenty-four-seven."

Olivia shook her head. "You don't have to do that. I told you I wouldn't run. I won't, Rafe, not without telling you. I give you my word. I know it isn't worth much, but —"

"Dammit, that isn't it. I want you safe. I said we're going to figure this out and we are. Until we do, you're staying with me."

Emotion tightened her chest. "You're serious. You actually believe you can help me prove my innocence."

Rafe came up off the sofa, turned and looked down at her. "I know you, Olivia. Day after day, I've watched you in that café, watched how you treat people, how they respond to you. I know the kind of woman you are. No way are you a murderer. There has to be a way to prove it."

She rose and went into his arms, hung on to him as hard as she could. He was her anchor in a world that made no sense. A rock in a sea of troubles that constantly threatened to drown her. She wished she could tell him she loved him.

She couldn't do that. And even if she

could, asking Rafe to believe she meant it was simply too much for one day.

Rafe left Olivia on the sofa in his living room, curled up in a pair of his sweatpants and one of his faded T-shirts. She was exhausted. And scared. More for him and her friends than for herself. He spread a blanket over her, went into the kitchen and pulled out his cell phone.

His first instinct was to call his brother, tell him what had happened, tell him about the man with the gun, that the guy knew she was Fiona Caldwell and had tried to blackmail her for sex, maybe even meant to kill her.

But Nick could be a hothead, and like all the Brodie men, protective when it came to family. Rafe needed time to think, to figure the best way to handle the situation.

Instead of calling Nick, he phoned Zach.

"Hey, Rafe," the kid said. "We still going in tonight to get the GPS?"

Finding Scotty's killer was no longer his top priority, but from what the men in the motel had said, they would be leaving town in just a few more days. Rafe was convinced they were somehow connected to Scott's murder.

He hated the amateurish tracking system

they were using, but this was Valdez. There was no Apple Store on Main Street. Tonight, however, things would be getting a little more twenty-first century.

"We're going to get it and take a look, see if there's anything useful. Olivia picked up the new device this morning." They had stopped at her apartment on the way to his house and retrieved the FedEx package she had picked up that morning.

At the time, it hadn't been his main concern, but it had kept his mind off the conversation they needed to have, the fact that her troubles had followed her here, and the rage he'd felt when he realized she could have been killed.

"If you can get the new GPS hooked up to a computer," he said, "we'll be able to follow these guys in real time."

"I can handle it."

"There's something else I need you to do. I need photos of these two guys. Can you get them off the video? Something I can e-mail my brother?"

"Wow, cool. Your brother's a detective, right?"

"That's right."

"He's planning to use facial recognition," Zach guessed. "We really are going high-tech."

"Can you get them?"

"Depends what the cameras caught. I'll call Ben Friedman, go over and do it right now. Give me your brother's e-mail address."

That was easy enough. "Nick Brodie at g-mail dot com."

"Got it. It's getting late. This might take a little while. I'll walk on over, start checking the video, and wait for you there."

"Thanks, Zach."

A few hours later, the photos had been retrieved and sent to Nick in Seattle. By midnight, the old GPS had been retrieved, and the new, high-performance device attached to the bumper of the Jeep. No mishaps, not a soul around. During the process, Olivia had waited for him in his pickup.

Her attacker was still out there. They didn't know who he was or what they were dealing with. If the guy had been watching Olivia, undoubtedly he knew about Rafe. There was no way he could leave her alone. And no matter what she'd promised, there was still a chance she would run.

As soon as he was finished, he returned to his truck. Olivia scooted into the middle while Zach climbed in on the passenger's side for a ride back to his apartment. Rafe

364

pulled up in front and turned off the engine.

"This is interesting," Rafe said, looking down at the screen of the old GPS. "Last night, right after we taped this under the bumper, the men made a trip. Looks like the car left the lot at 12:10 a.m."

"Where'd they go?" Olivia asked.

"Someplace up in the mountains. Looks like they drove straight there, spent less than an hour, and came back to the motel."

"We can follow their route," Zach said, "drive right up and see what's there."

"We could, but it's late and we've got a charter tomorrow. It's only a half day. Soon as we get back to the harbor, I'll drive up and take a look."

Zach nodded. "You're still convinced something's going on with these guys. Something to do with Scotty."

"I think something's going on. I'm not sure anymore what the hell it is. But I'm going to find out."

Zach seemed satisfied. He cracked open the door. "I'll see you in the morning," he said to Rafe as he climbed down from the cab. "Night, Olivia."

"Good night, Zach."

Rafe waited till the kid got inside, then turned to Liv. "You were attacked today. The guy who came after you is still out there. I want you to know, you're what's important in all of this. Keeping you safe. Solving your problem. Not finding Scotty's killer or anything else. Nothing is more important than you. You understand that?"

Tears gleamed in her eyes before she blinked them away.

"You understand what I'm telling you? Answer me."

She swallowed and nodded. "Whatever happens, I'll never forget you, Rafe."

"Bullshit. We're going to figure this out."

"Okay." She looked up at him, gave him a tremulous smile. "In the meantime, we have to keep going. We have to find the guy who killed Scotty. We're getting close, Rafe. I can feel it. We promised Cassie. I don't want to stop now."

His eyes found hers in the dim light inside the cab. "That's it, isn't it? The reason you were so determined to help me find Scott's killer. You couldn't get justice for yourself so you wanted to get it for Scotty."

"Yes."

"All right, we'll keep going. But remember what I said. You come first. Tomorrow we make a plan. We figure out who we can trust. Who can be the most help to us. How to reach them. How to convince them you're innocent."

She shook her head. "All that takes time. What happens when the guy comes back? He's going to, Rafe. He isn't just going to give up."

"He comes back, we'll be ready." He leaned over and softly kissed her, reached down and cranked the engine. "In the meantime, let's go home. We both need to get some sleep."

As he put the truck in gear, she rested her head on his shoulder. Olivia trusted him. Funny thing was, even after all that had happened, Rafe still trusted her.

Trent Doyle surveyed the small group gathered in the den. Cain lounged negligently next to the bar, taking up more than his share of space, sipping Jack Daniel's. He was a convert to Islam, but he was hardly a true believer. Trent had tried to keep him on a short leash, but so far that hadn't worked.

Lee Heng and Mikal Nadir were far more dependable. They were committed to their cause. They would do whatever it took for the mission to succeed.

"Anything new to report?" Trent asked, allowing his gaze to wander over the men.

"We've located our targets," Heng said. "We've planted explosives in a fish-packing plant down at the harbor, and also at a local beer joint, a place they call the Catch, that'll be full of people that time of night. The detonations should be enough to create the diversion we need."

"Excellent. Cain?"

"The last of the terminal explosives are in place."

"They're secure? No one's going to stumble over them?"

"Not a chance."

"Very good. All right, let's go over the plan. The *San Pascual* arrives around three a.m. day after tomorrow. The loading arms will be put in place and they'll start pumping crude oil into the tanker. Within twenty-four hours, the ship should be fully loaded, carrying a million barrels and ready to depart."

"Too bad it'll never leave the dock," Heng said with a smile.

"No, it won't. Well before the ship's departure, our man onboard will have the detonators in place belowdecks. He'll leave the ship and make contact with Cain at the designated location at exactly twelve forty-five. Are you clear on this, Darius?"

"I'll be where I'm supposed to be," Cain said darkly.

"You'll pick the man up — Yousef is his

name — and the two of you will drive out of the terminal to the rendezvous point."

Trent turned to the others. "By that time, Heng and Nadir will be in position outside the terminal, close enough to disarm the security system. No alarms will go off, the gates will open, but —"

"But the cameras stay on," Heng finished with barely concealed excitement. "So the world can watch exactly what happens."

"At that point," Trent continued, "Cain and Yousef should be clear. Accessing the Internet through the terminal cell tower, Mikal will detonate all of the explosives. The storage tanks, a portion of the pipeline, and the *San Pascual* will all be destroyed."

"You better not screw this up, Cain," Heng warned.

Cain flipped him a bird while Trent ignored them both. "The terminal will be in chaos, but by then the four of you will be on your way to meet up with the escape vessel, which will be waiting offshore. Are we clear?"

"Yes," Nadir said. Heng just nodded.

"You have not explained the escape plan," Nadir said. "I am ready to die in the name of Allah, but not unless it is his will."

"Arrangements have been finalized. As I said, a boat will be waiting just offshore. It will pick you all up and transport you to Tatitlek. That's a small airport on a landmass about thirty nautical miles south of the terminal. There you'll catch a seaplane for your journey inland. You'll cross overland into Canada and disappear."

"What about you?" Heng asked. "How will you get out?"

Trent flicked a glance at Anna, who sat quietly in one of the overstuffed chairs. She'd been with him through all the preparations. He was grateful to have her there.

"Anna and I will be flying out earlier in the afternoon. Unfortunately, we'll have to miss all the fireworks."

"You can always watch the video replays on TV," Lee said with a grin.

"What about our money?" Cain asked.

"Your money will be transferred into the bank account numbers you've provided, available to you on completion of the mission." He glanced around the wood-paneled den. "Are there any more questions?"

They'd been over the plan half a dozen times, in far greater detail. All but the escape route, which Trent had arranged after he'd arrived and familiarized himself with the area and surrounding terrain. He had men who would handle the job.

"No questions," Lee said. "I'm ready."

"As am I," Nadir agreed.

" 'Bout time we got this fucking show on the road," Cain growled.

They all came to their feet.

The meeting was over. It was a waiting game now. If the operation went off as planned, the terminal would be destroyed. The oil spill created would be devastating.

Trent looked over at Tatiana and both of them smiled.

CHAPTER TWENTY-SEVEN

Billowy clouds, white as the snow that clung to the distant mountains, hovered above the rising peaks. Overhead, the sky was a brilliant azure blue. Only a slight chop tapped against the hull of *Sea Scorpion* as it skimmed over the crystal clear water.

Standing at the rail, Liv tugged down the brim of her hot-pink ball cap against the breeze. LIFE HAPPENS was printed on the front. But even in her lightweight jacket, she wasn't really cold. A warm sun offset the morning chill while the day was picture-perfect. She was grateful to be out here, away from her troubles, at least for a while.

On the deck at the stern of the boat, Jaimie and Zach worked together to keep the passengers' hooks baited and handle any trouble they had with the lines. Four men and two women smiled and laughed, enjoying their morning at sea while Rafe expertly guided the boat to the best fishing spots in the Sound.

Liv loved watching him work, the skillful way he handled the craft, the way he spoke to the passengers, patiently answering their endless stream of questions, never growing tired of the time he spent on the water.

Once he walked out of the cabin, came over and spoke to her. The fish were biting. Lots of laughter out on the deck. *Scorpion* was bobbing gently, the engine turned off, giving Rafe a breather.

He smiled as he tipped his head toward Zach and Jaimie, who were laughing together as they changed the rigging on one of the fishermen's poles. "I guess they've settled their differences."

"Looks like. I saw them that day at the funeral. I could tell Jaimie resented Zach for taking Scotty's place. I knew how she felt about Scott. Everyone knew it. It's good she's getting interested in someone else."

"Zach understands her. I think Jaimie's coming to trust him." Olivia felt Rafe's dark eyes on her. "Trust is a hard thing for her. She's a little like you that way."

"Trusting someone isn't easy."

"No, it isn't. In Jaimie's case, I think the problem is learning to trust herself."

Olivia looked up at him. "I trust you, Rafe.

I've never trusted anyone as much as I do you."

He reached out and cupped her cheek. "I won't let you down, Olivia."

Her heart pinched. "I know."

Rafe walked back into the wheelhouse and Olivia continued to enjoy herself. Zach spotted a pod of whales and everyone crowded around to watch them until they disappeared.

For a while, Liv continued to distract herself from the problems waiting back in Valdez, but as the morning wore on, she found herself thinking of the man in the rusted-out Chevy, the light-skinned black man who would have raped her without a qualm.

He'd said he wasn't there to kill her. But that didn't make sense. Her enemies needed to silence her. They had tried two times before.

Her mind kept replaying the scene, going back over his words, remembering things she'd been too rattled, too frightened, to recall before.

Why would I want to kill you? he had said.

How had he known who she was? How had he known she was in Valdez?

But Nick Brodie had found her. Which meant she wasn't nearly as far off the grid as she had believed.

Get in the backseat and take off your clothes . . . The words made her stomach roll.

She remembered something else . . . a shadowy impression that was probably nothing, but kept nagging her as if it were important.

She wandered into the cabin.

"Hey," Rafe said when he saw her, flashing one of his sexy smiles. Her pulse kicked up. One look from those hot brown eyes, one little smile, and she was gone.

"Hey, yourself," she said.

"You doing okay, darlin'?"

She ignored the little tug on her heart at the endearment. "I'm glad you made me come with you today." He'd said he wanted her safe and clearly he meant it. "I forgot how good it feels to be out on the water."

"Yeah, it does. Kind of God's remedy for whatever ails you."

She nodded. "It's given me time to do some thinking about what happened yesterday, sort out the whys and the hows."

"And?"

"The man who attacked me . . . I know it's going to sound crazy, but there's something that keeps niggling at the back of my mind."

"You never can tell what's going to be important and what isn't. Could be any little thing. That's something I learned from Nick when he was working homicide."

"Remember the third guy in the motel room?"

"The one you might or might not have seen?"

"That's the one."

He frowned. "You aren't thinking this could be the guy?"

"He's big, he's dark. Same thick-shouldered build."

Rafe seemed to mull that over. "Okay, let's assume you actually did see a third guy in the room that day. You said he disappeared into the bathroom, like he didn't want you to see him."

"That's right."

"The guy who showed up on the video camera down at the harbor . . . big guy, kind of hulking. Wearing a hoodie. You told me the guy yesterday had on a sweatshirt with a hood, right?"

"Yes, but it wasn't pulled up. I remember he said something about leaving in just a few days. That's what Wong and Nevin said, too. They'd only be staying till the end of the week."

"Interesting coincidence, I'd say."

"Yes, plus he seemed surprised I would think he was there to kill me. Which is weird because why else would he be in Valdez?"

"You told me he didn't fit the image of the professional hit man your enemies in Washington would have hired."

"That's what crossed my mind at the time."

"Put all that together and maybe the attack on you had nothing to do with Julia Stanfield and your ex-husband's murder. Maybe it has something to do with Scott Ferris's murder."

"Oh my God. If he's the guy who killed Scott and he saw me that day at the motel, he could have been afraid I might try to find out who he is. Maybe he tracked me down just like Nick did and found out I was wanted by the police. That knowledge would give him a great deal of power. It could have made him feel safe enough to come after me, try to blackmail me into giving him sex."

Her eyes widened as another thought occurred. "Something else I just recalled. He said that for weeks he'd been living up here like a monk. That was the reason he wanted sex."

"So he's been here a while, working or

just living up here, but he's getting ready to leave."

"Just like Wong and Nevin."

Rafe started nodding. "I've been following a hunch all along. Right now, my instincts are screaming. Something's going on with those guys in that motel room, and whatever it is, it's looking bigger all the time."

She bit her lip. "If it weren't for me, you could go to the police."

"With what? Aside from the attack on you yesterday — which would bring you under police scrutiny — we still don't have a damned thing. I got a text message from Nick this morning. He got the photos Zach e-mailed and he's running them through facial recognition. If he finds something, we'll reassess the situation, decide on our next move."

"God, I hope he does."

"So do I." Rafe's jaw hardened. "We need to figure this out, and soon."

The rest of the morning was tense for both of them. Olivia had no idea if her attacker was connected to Julia Stanfield, or Scott Ferris, or if the attack had been motivated by something else entirely.

Like a juggling act, they needed to keep all the balls in the air at one time.

Leaving Rafe to do his job, Liv went back

out on deck, hoping the crisp, clean air would clear her head as she waited for the trip to end so they could get back to Valdez.

They'd just arrived back in port. The town was beginning to entertain a steady flow of tourists. The ferry dropped passengers, cars, and RVs off at the ferry terminal and the visitors milled around town, hitting souvenir shops or eating at local restaurants.

Jaimie and Zach busied themselves with the clean-up work on *Scorpion,* getting the passengers' catch off-loaded, hosing off the decks, and putting equipment away. Olivia felt Rafe's big hand close over hers as he led her down the dock toward town.

"Where are you going?"

"We're going to follow the route Wong and Nevin took up the hill, see where they went."

Olivia stopped and turned to look at him. "I'd love to go with you, but I can't. I need to go to the Pelican, make sure things are going smoothly, check on my employees, do some scheduling."

"That guy's still out there, Liv. What if he comes into the café?"

She thought it over, didn't see it as a viable threat. "You really think he'd be that bold? I promise I'll stay inside. I won't go anywhere until you get back."

Rafe shook his head. "I don't like it."

Liv reached up and touched his cheek. "You asked me to stay and fight for the life I've made here. Well, the café is part of that life."

Rafe let out a slow breath, realizing she was right. "Okay. But you've got to stay in the restaurant until I get back. You can't go anywhere else."

"I won't. I promise."

"This shouldn't take long. I'll follow the GPS track up the hill and come back. We'll make plans, figure some of this out. Then I'll call Nick, maybe ask Dylan to intercede with Peter Keller, the attorney I told you about."

A tremor went through her. She was taking a risk, a huge leap of faith. Once they started, there would be no turning back.

Rafe walked her to the door of the café, did a visual sweep of the area outside, bent his head and very thoroughly kissed her. "Stay away from the windows," he said gruffly. "I'll see you when I get back."

Liv went inside and closed the door, resisted the urge to walk over to the window and watch him drive away. Instead she headed for the kitchen. She needed to check in with Nell, make sure her manager had things under control.

As Olivia approached, the worry in Nell's face was clear. She spotted the bruise on Liv's cheek and her eyes widened. "Oh, my Lord — what happened to your face? Are you okay?"

"I ran into some trouble on my run yesterday, but I'm fine now."

Nell planted her hands on her hips. "Okay, missy. What's going on?"

Liv almost smiled. Nell Olsen was the only employee in Alaska with the nerve to address her boss as *missy*.

"We aren't too busy. Why don't we go upstairs?" That morning, Rafe had stopped by her apartment on the way to the boat so she could dress for a day on the water and pack a few things to take over to his house, since she would be staying there until they could straighten things out — as if that could actually happen.

She and Nell climbed the stairs. Olivia unlocked the door and turned off the alarm, then reset it when the two of them got inside. The gesture didn't go unnoticed.

"What happened to your face?" Nell asked. "Honey, you've got a bruise the size of a dinner plate on your cheek. Rafe called and said a man attacked you. He said you were okay, but you don't look okay." Nell's gaze ran over her. "Tell me what happened."

"A man followed me when I went running. He pulled a gun and demanded I get into his car. He hit me but I got away before anything else bad happened. I was running back down the hill when Khan showed up with Rafe." She smiled. "Khan saved me. He's the best dog in the world."

"Yes, he is. What do you mean before anything else bad happened?"

"The guy . . . he wanted me to . . . he was going to rape me, Nell."

"Oh, good Lord! Did you recognize him? What did the police say? Are they looking for him? Have they caught him?"

"I didn't call the police. The thing is, Nell, I was in some trouble before I moved up here. It was a few years back, but I just . . . I didn't want to stir it up all over again."

"You were in trouble? I can't imagine you doing anything bad — it just isn't in you."

Emotion moved through Olivia's chest. "If you want the truth, I didn't do anything, but the police believed I did. Now I have a new life, and I just want all of that left in the past."

She didn't tell Nell she was still a wanted person. She would deal with that when the time came.

"Well, that doesn't seem right. If the

police made a mistake, you should —"

"Nell, I'm asking you as a friend. Can you leave it alone?"

Nell straightened. "Well, of course I can. If that's what you want, I won't say another word about it."

Olivia leaned over and hugged her. "You're a good friend, Nell."

"What about the man who attacked you? You don't think he'll try it again?"

"I'm staying with Rafe for a while, just in case. You know how protective he can be."

Nell seemed mollified, though she kept eyeing the bruise on Olivia's cheek. "Speaking of Rafe . . . how's it going with the two of you?"

How was it going? There was no way to know for sure. She was still wanted for murder. Rafe had vowed to help her, but at this point anything could happen.

"He's a good man," she evaded.

One of Nell's silver-black eyebrows went up. "That's it? He's a good man?" Nell's knowing gaze searched her face. "You aren't falling in love with him, are you? We talked about that. You're supposed to be having an affair."

Liv shrugged. "Rafe's hard not to love."

Nell started frowning. "Yes, I'm sure he is." Her frown deepened. "He better not hurt you. I warned him. He better treat you right."

She felt the pull of a smile. Rafe was right about one thing. The life she had here was worth fighting for. The friends she had made. Especially Nell Olsen.

"I'll do my best not to hurt him, either," she teased, though she really had no idea how Rafe would feel if she packed her bags and left town.

At least the subject of her past was over.

"Rafe had an errand to run," she said. "He won't be back for a while. You covered for me this morning. You're off tonight. Why don't you go home a little early?"

"You sure?"

Liv nodded. "Positive. I've got some scheduling to do, plenty to keep me busy."

"All right." They headed back downstairs. Nell took off her apron and left the café, and Olivia went to work. It felt good to be busy. She liked that about the restaurant business. She liked keeping things organized and at the same time being creative, exploring new ideas, new recipes, new ways to make things better.

She was back downstairs, cleaning up with Katie, getting ready for the dinner crowd that would be coming in a little later, when Cassie walked into the café. She headed straight for Liv.

"I was hoping you'd be here. Oh my God, what happened to your face?"

Even the makeup she'd dabbed on couldn't quite hide the bruise. "I had a run-in with a broom handle. No big deal." Sounded better than the usual *door* explanation, and around the restaurant, accidents were always happening.

Cassie just nodded. "I've done that myself. Have you got a minute to talk?"

"Sure." They sat down in one of the booths. Through the window, the sun was still shining, the blue sea glittering in the distance. She thought of her day on the water, remembered how good she had felt being out there.

"I went to see Chip this morning," Cassie said, regaining Liv's attention. "I know you probably think that's terrible, but I just . . . I don't believe he killed Scotty and I just feel so sorry for him."

"I don't think it's terrible at all. I'm proud of you for following your conscience. If you think Chip's innocent, then you should stand by him. That's the right thing to do."

"A few of the guys have gone to see him. His boss. Ben Friedman and Sam King."

"What about Marty Grossman? He was a close friend, wasn't he?"

"They were friends. Marty's married. I think he's afraid to stand up for Chip because of what people might say."

"That's what happens when trouble comes knocking. You find out who your real friends are." And there weren't that many, Liv had discovered. None who were really there when she needed them most.

"Chip says they're moving him to the correctional facility in Anchorage. That's where his trial's going to be held. He thinks he's going to be convicted. He's sure he's going to prison."

Cassie rested her elbows on the table, gripped her hands in front of her. "He looks awful, Liv. He can't sleep. He isn't eating. He's lost tons of weight. I was wondering, you know, hoping maybe you and Rafe might have found something that could help him prove his innocence."

A wave of empathy washed over Liv. She remembered how she'd felt when she had been wrongly accused. The desolation, the hopelessness. If Chip was innocent, she knew exactly how he felt.

"We're following a lead," she said. "You can tell Chip that, if you think it will help. It may be nothing, but we're going to find out. That's all I can tell you right now."

Cassie pulled a Kleenex out of her purse

and dabbed it against her eyes. "It does help. Chip needs something to hold on to, something that'll give him hope." She tucked the Kleenex away. "Thanks, Olivia."

Liv just nodded. When she'd been arrested, no one had stood up for her. She'd thought that Stephen would have, if he had been alive. In death, he was her silent accuser. Her attorney had come to believe strongly in her innocence. After the attempt on her life, he'd been the one who had helped her escape.

"We're doing everything we can," she told Cassie. "Rafe is working on something right now. Tell Chip not to give up. Not yet. Okay?"

Tears filled Cassie's eyes and the tissue reappeared. She blew her nose and tucked the Kleenex back into her purse. "I'll tell him." Rising from the table, Cassie reached over and squeezed Liv's shoulder, turned and walked away.

Olivia watched her disappear out the door, thinking that whatever happened, Chip Reed was lucky to have a friend like Cassie Webster.

He'd been a fool to ever let her go.

Chapter Twenty-Eight

Rafe checked the GPS sitting on the seat beside him. The Jeep had driven all the way out Egan Drive across Mineral Creek to the far west side of town. He turned on Front Street, followed the map on the screen to the end of the road, then turned onto Dewey Court.

There weren't many houses out here. The Jeep had pulled into the driveway of a two-story, wood-frame home at 16530 Dewey Court. The oversized property was located on a cul-de-sac with only a solitary house across the way.

Rafe pulled up behind a thicket dense with spring foliage. There was no name on the mailbox. As soon as he got back to town, he'd look up the property records, see who owned the house.

He wondered what he'd see if he walked up to the windows and looked inside. He glanced at his surroundings. No one anywhere near, not on the street or the house across the way. He reached into the door pocket on his side of the truck and pulled out a pair of binoculars. This being Alaska, he kept a pair in each vehicle. You never knew what interesting sights you might see.

His truck was parked where it couldn't be seen from the house. He cracked the door and stepped down, started quietly walking toward the back of the property, careful to stay out of sight behind the foliage.

Crouching in the bushes, he focused the binoculars on the back windows, slowly scanning from one room to another. Movement in the kitchen caught his eye. A woman stood at the sink in front of the window. Black-haired, late twenties, early thirties. There was something familiar about her.

A man walked up behind her, turned her into his arms and kissed her. For an instant, Rafe couldn't make out the man's features.

He held the binoculars steady. The kiss ended, the pair broke apart, and the man smiled down at her. Decent-looking guy, dark hair touched with silver, blue eyes.

Jesus. The couple who had taken the sightseeing trip aboard *Scorpion.*

What the hell was his name? Trent

something or other. Trent Petersen, that was it. The wife's name was Anna.

He watched them through the binoculars until they left the kitchen and disappeared out of sight. Then he turned and headed back to his truck.

The Petersens had been aboard *Scorpion.* So had Wong and Nevin. The coincidences were mounting.

What the hell was going on?

Rafe walked back into the café, relieved to see Olivia waiting on a couple of young tourists, a girl and a guy, their backpacks on the floor beside the booth. Liv was laughing at something one of them said, and the sound warmed his heart.

She had dealt with so much, most of it by herself. But she had him now. She wouldn't be so alone.

He settled himself in a booth by the window and stretched his legs out in front of him. He was still trying to sort out the information he had discovered up at the house, make some sense of it, but nothing had jelled so far.

Katie spotted him and waved, but didn't come over to take his order, leaving the job to Liv. Olivia belonged to him and everyone seemed to know it. He figured even Sally

Henderson had heard. He was glad Sally had found someone else. Rumor was the guy, a businessman who lived in Anchorage, had asked her to marry him and she had accepted. Rafe was happy for her.

He knew the moment Liv saw him. He liked that her cheeks flushed, liked that she didn't look away or hide in the back, the way she used to.

Olivia was his and he was going to keep her. A thought he'd done his best to ignore, but so far it hadn't worked. Even knowing the trouble she was in hadn't changed that.

His phone started ringing as she walked toward him with that elegant grace that had attracted him from the start. Rafe pulled the phone out of his pocket and read Nick's name on the screen.

He hadn't told his brother about the bastard who'd come after Liv. He knew Nick would go into Ranger–cop mode if he did. But things were happening all around them. Rafe needed to unscramble them into something that made sense. To do that, he needed his brother's help.

Sliding out of the booth, he walked toward the back of the restaurant, motioning for Liv to follow him, heading out onto the porch behind the café where she wouldn't be a target. She was part of this — whatever the hell it was. She deserved to know what was going on.

"Hey, Nick."

"Hey, bro, I've got something for you."

"Go ahead." He held the phone so Olivia could hear.

"I got a hit on one of the photos Zach sent. The Asian, the guy who calls himself Lee Wong? His name's Lee Heng. Indonesian American. No criminal record. On the surface he's squeaky clean. His photo popped up in a college yearbook. Went to Ohio State on a scholarship. Worked at Microsoft for a while. I couldn't figure why the guy would be using an alias so I enlisted a little help to go deeper."

"I'm listening."

"Ian's got a friend, does work for him off and on, a real computer guru." Ian was one of the many Brodie cousins. He owned Brodie Operations Security Services, the company Nick worked for in Seattle.

"The guru . . . some young kid about twenty, right?"

Amusement crept into Nick's voice. "Middle-aged woman with two grown kids. Husband died. Took up computers when the kids left home. Turned out she had a real knack."

"So I guess there's still hope for me."

Nick chuckled. The amusement slid from his voice. "Here's the bad news, bro. Dig deep enough, the guy's got ties to JAT. I can spell the name but no way can I say it. JAT is Indonesia's number-one terrorist group."

Beside him, Olivia sucked in a breath. Rafe whispered the F-word under his breath.

"You got that right," Nick said.

"What about the other guy? Michael Nevin?"

"Angle of the photo was wrong. Couldn't get a clear enough image. We need to call Homeland, Rafe. But the truth is, this guy isn't on any no-fly list, nothing like that. He hasn't had any recent contact with the group, or at least nothing Sadie could find. He's on Homeland's radar but it's pretty distant."

"Sadie? That's your computer whiz?"

"Yeah."

"Good lady to know."

"Especially when it looks like you could be up to your ass in alligators. I'm thinking if something's going down, likely it has to do with the ferry system or the pipeline. Only two things in Valdez big enough to interest a terrorist organization."

"Hundreds of folks on one of those big ferries."

"Yeah, and an attack on the pipeline would cause an environmental disaster. Either one would be very bad news."

"It's a pretty big leap from a couple of prayer rugs to a terrorist attack," Rafe said, playing devil's advocate.

"You really think so?"

He shook his head. "I don't know. It feels big, but it's just a hunch. Either of those things would be a disaster. Ferry would be a whole lot easier to pull off. The pipeline terminal has all kinds of security."

"That's what I was thinking. Blowing up one of those boats and killing five hundred people would be huge. When's the next ferry in?"

"This time of year there's one damn near every day."

"So it could happen any time. You're supposed to call nine-one-one to report suspicious activity, but that might pose a problem since there's no way you could legally know anything about these guys."

"Something's going down, Nick. And it's going to happen soon. This afternoon I followed the route those two drove the other night. Wound up at a house out on the west side of town. I don't know who it belongs to, but I recognized the couple inside, a man and his wife who took a cruise on *Scorpion*. So did Heng and his roommate. The four of them know each other. I can't think of a single reason why they should."

"What's the couple's name?"

"Trent and Anna Petersen, but I've got a hunch their names are as phony as Wong and Nevin."

"I'll run it, see what comes up. What's the property address?"

"It's 16530 Dewey Court."

"I'll find out who owns it. Soon as I get a little more information, I'll call Charlie Farrell, give him what we've got."

"Farrell's your FBI buddy in Fairbanks, right?"

"That's right. But Homeland gets tips like these every day, so don't expect them to come running down there. Heng and his friend could just be on vacation, you know? Then again, it might cross with something Homeland's working on."

Rafe took a deep breath. "There's something else." He glanced over at Liv, who nodded. "Yesterday a guy came after Olivia. Knew her real name, knew she was wanted. Tried to blackmail her for sex."

"Jesus, Rafe. Haven't you got enough trouble? You need woman trouble, too?"

"She didn't kill that guy, Nick. I don't have time to explain everything now, but I'm telling you she's innocent and I'm going to help her prove it."

"Christ."

"You're really going to hate this, but there's a chance the guy who attacked her might be part of this thing."

"You've got to be fucking kidding me."

"I've got to go, little brother. I'll talk to you soon." Rafe disconnected, ending his brother's next rant before it got started. Whatever happened, Nick would do everything he could to help them. Rafe would be waiting on pins and needles till his brother called back.

It was after ten p.m. The restaurant was closed, and Rafe and Olivia were settled in at his place for the night. They still hadn't come up with a plan to clear Olivia's name. At the moment, they were too focused on trying to prevent a terror attack.

Or maybe not.

What had started as a murder investigation had morphed into a mystery that was going nowhere. Maybe it was all just a series of coincidences that meant nothing. Until they came up with something new, there was no way to know for sure.

Heading for bed, Rafe draped an arm around Olivia's shoulders and led her toward the stairs. Both of them were beat, but with Liv tucked against him, her soft breasts brushing his side, need stirred inside him. When he glanced down, she was looking up at him, the same need mirrored in her lovely gray eyes.

Need turned to hunger. At the top of the stairs, he turned her into his arms, pulled the ball cap off her head and the band holding back her hair. Sliding a hand into the silky dark mass, he wrapped a fist around the long strands, pulled her head back, and his mouth crushed down over hers.

Heat burned through him, settled in his groin. He was hard and aching, wanting her with the same unrelenting need that had only grown more powerful since the first time he'd had her.

"Rafe . . ." she whispered, urging him to take the kiss deeper, her fingers digging into the muscles across his shoulders.

He wasn't sure how many times his cell phone played before the sound penetrated his sex-fogged brain.

With a sigh, Rafe ended the kiss, his forehead tipping against hers for the instant it took both of them to catch their breath. Pulling the phone out of his jeans, he read the name.

"It's Ben," he said to Olivia, and pressed the phone to his ear.

"You aren't going to like this," Ben said.

"Tell me." Rafe put the call on speaker so Liv could hear the conversation.

"I went out to get some supper and just got back. I found two room keys on the counter in the office. Both were for room number two. The room was paid through Sunday so the men didn't owe anything, didn't need to check out. They just packed their stuff, loaded it into the Jeep, and took off."

"Have you looked at the video? Maybe there's something there."

"I looked at it. Ran it back until I saw them walk out of the room earlier in the evening, ran it forward and saw them return, probably after they'd had supper. They were in there a while. When they came back out they were carrying their bags and something that looked like a laptop case."

Rafe had noticed the computer sitting on the desk when he'd gone into the room, but it was turned off and closed and he'd left it that way.

"The Asian guy was on the phone when they got into the Jeep," Ben said. "They drove away and that was it."

He had the plate numbers, but the Jeep was a rental from Hertz in Anchorage, probably rented in a fake name, so he hadn't pursued that angle.

"What time did they leave?"

"Eight forty-five, according to the data on the video."

"So they left the motel. Doesn't mean they left town. Thanks, Ben. I'll keep you posted."

Rafe hung up and phoned Zach. They'd decided to rig the new GPS they'd attached to the Jeep last night to Zach's computer, since he knew how to download the program they needed to track the car's movements and how to handle the system if a problem came up.

"The men checked out of the motel," Rafe told him. "Can you take a look at your laptop, see where they are right now?"

"Let me go check. It's been a couple of hours since the last time I looked."

Zach was gone a while; then he came back on the line. "The GPS isn't moving, Rafe. The last location before it went dead puts it in the ocean off South Harbor Drive."

"They found the bug," Rafe said.

"Looks like," said Zach grimly. "Probably the reason they checked out of the motel. They found out they were being tracked, got spooked and took off."

"Sounds right."

"Sorry, Rafe."

"Yeah, me too. I'll see you in the morning." Rafe hung up the phone.

"The GPS was hidden under the bumper," Olivia said. "How could they have found it?"

"I don't know. It was a more sophisticated device. Nick said Lee Heng worked for Microsoft. He's got to be good with computers. Maybe the signals from the GPS triggered something. If we could pick them up, maybe he could, too."

"So they found the device and left the motel like Zach said. Maybe they drove up to the house on Dewey Court."

"It's possible, but I doubt it. If they know we've been tracking them, they know we know about the house. Odds are Trent and his wife have packed up and left just like their friends did."

"If they're actually involved."

"Yeah. Another one of our many ifs."

"What do you say we take a ride? A little trip up the hill to Dewey Court?"

He started to tell her no. No way was he driving her into what might be a hornets' nest, and after the attack yesterday, it wasn't safe to leave her in the house alone.

His phone rang, postponing the argument he figured they were about to have. He glanced down, didn't recognize the caller ID. "Brodie."

"Noah Devlin. I flew down with Derek Hunter. We're out at the airport. We could use a ride into town."

Rafe knew Devlin and Hunter. They were good friends of Nick's. Ex-military. Boot-leather tough and as loyal to family and friends as a pair of old hounds. "I take it my brother called."

"That's right. He's worried about you. Said you might need a little backup."

"I might. I might not. Depends on how things shake out."

Derek took the phone out of Noah's hand. "From what Nick says, you're in some deep shit, buddy. Now come and get us so we can help."

Rafe chuckled. "On my way. If I didn't say so before, I'm glad you're here." Rafe hung up the phone. At least now he'd have men he trusted to help him keep Olivia safe.

"What's going on?" she asked.

"You wanted to go for a ride. Help just arrived out at the airport. Noah Devlin and Derek Hunter. Friends of my brother's."

She stopped on her way back down the stairs. "Cops?"

"Ex-military. A couple of real badasses. You definitely want them on your side, not the other way around. Derek flew them down. We're picking them up at the airport."

CHAPTER TWENTY-NINE

Olivia climbed into the Expedition next to Rafe. He'd chosen the bigger vehicle, which had more room to haul the men and their gear. She leaned back as the big SUV rumbled over the road toward the airport, told herself it was good the men had come. Still, her nerves were buzzing again at the thought of what their arrival might mean.

First Scotty's murder and trying to find out who'd killed him. Then being attacked and nearly raped by a man who knew her most terrifying secret. Now they were in the middle of something that might involve terrorism. She wasn't sure how much more she could handle.

It was dark by the time they got to the airport, parked, and walked out on the tarmac. Rafe introduced her as Olivia Chandler, said she owned the Pelican Café. The solid arm he slid around her waist and the way his dark eyes claimed her, made it abundantly clear she was his.

As much as it should have annoyed her, instead it made her feel safe.

"Nice to meet you, Olivia," Noah said politely, taking her hand in one the size of a ham. He was huge, six-five, she figured, his chest and arms bulging with muscle. He wasn't just handsome, he was gorgeous. Dark brown hair and blue eyes, even a set of dimples. Every bit as hot as Rafe.

Derek Hunter was about six-two, equally great-looking, with a lean, hard-muscled build, dark hair, and green eyes.

While the bigger man was all power and dynamic movement, Hunter was more laid back, taking things in stride while those green eyes never missed a thing. The way he was sizing her up marked him as a ladies' man, but when he shook her hand, she sensed the respect he felt for Rafe, and that he wasn't a guy who would poach on a friend's territory.

As handsome as they were, Liv preferred Rafe's sexy good looks and calm control, the feeling that no matter what happened, he would take care of it. That she would be safe as long as she was with him.

She wondered how much Nick had told the two men, wondered, with everything going on, how much longer she would be able to keep her secret. She wondered how long it would be before the police showed up at her door.

"It's nice to meet you both," she said, "and it's okay to call me Liv, like everyone else."

Noah grinned, showing off his dimples. He and Derek tossed their duffels into the back of the Expedition, then loaded a heavy rectangular box they took out of the plane.

"I don't even want to know what's in there," Rafe said.

"If we need it, you'll be glad we brought it."

Rafe's mouth edged up. "I'm already glad. Where we're going, we might even need it tonight."

"Yeah?" Noah said. "Where's that?"

"House on the other side of town. Could be these guys' headquarters."

Rafe told them about the GPS that had been located and destroyed, told them the men had checked out of the motel. "Security camera showed one of them making a call. I figure they were warning their friends. By now they're probably long gone. We'll just take a look and see."

He didn't mention Olivia's attacker, though she caught them eyeing the bruise on her cheek. She wondered if Rafe was worried they'd climb back in their plane and fly off the way they'd come if they knew.

Though she had to admit, they looked like they could handle whatever trouble they ran into. Noah's worn camouflage pants molded to his powerful thighs as if he wore them every day. Beneath his jacket, Derek was dressed in jeans and an Army-green, long-sleeve T-shirt, his long legs encased in high-topped leather boots. Both had the quality she had recognized in Rafe. They were men who knew how to handle themselves.

Unconsciously her hand came up to her cheek and she remembered the hard, dark, evil man who had attacked her. She thought of Scotty lying dead with his head bashed in, thought of Rafe getting hurt or killed, and her chest squeezed.

Whatever happened, she was also glad the men were there.

Rafe drove the Expedition toward the west side of town, Noah riding shotgun, Derek in the backseat with Liv, where she would be safer if they ran into trouble.

"We'll just do a drive-by," Rafe said. "See if it looks like they've bailed. If they're still there, we'll come back, set up some kind of surveillance, take shifts, keep track of their movements from now on."

"Sounds good," Derek said. "How 'bout

you bring us up to speed on the way?"

"Be best if you'd start at the beginning," Noah added. "Your brother told us as much as he knew. Filled us in on the guy named Lee Heng, his background, and his connection to JAT. We need to hear the rest."

"All right." As they drove toward the house, Rafe laid out the information they had gathered, their suspicions and possible conclusions.

He left out the attack on Olivia. He wasn't sure it was connected and he wanted to protect Liv's secret as much as possible.

"There's something you aren't telling us," Noah said. "You're working hard to skirt around it. We know about Olivia's past. Nick wouldn't risk our lives by withholding that kind of information."

He should have known. His brother trusted these two men with his life. He wouldn't put them at risk without telling them everything he knew.

"Sorry," Rafe said. "We still aren't sure that what happened to Liv is connected." Rafe flicked a glance in the mirror. Even in the dark he could see the pale hue of her face.

"We can't work blind," Derek said. "We can't help if we don't know what we're up against."

"Liv . . ." Noah's deep voice sounded oddly gentle as he turned in the seat to face her. "If Rafe believes you didn't kill that guy in New York, that's good enough for me and Derek. For now, let's concentrate on stopping these people from doing whatever it is they have planned."

She took a deep breath and nodded. "All right. Yes, we have to do that."

"Good girl. Just tell us what happened."

"Yesterday while I was out running, a man attacked me. I thought he was there to kill me."

"Why is that?" Noah asked.

"I didn't kill my ex-husband. There are people willing to kill me to keep me from telling who did. The man knew my real name, knew about the murder. I assumed he was some kind of hit man, but all he wanted was sex."

"What'd this guy look like?" Derek prompted. "Can you describe him?"

She concentrated, trying to bring back details. "He was big. Powerful, you know? Light-skinned African American. He wasn't a gangster type, though. He spoke well, seemed intelligent, but there was something really scary about him. He was totally sure of himself, sure he could force me to do whatever he wanted."

"How'd you get away?" Derek asked.

Rafe grinned, caught Derek's eye in the mirror. "She stun-gunned the bastard. Gave him a jolt of something a helluva lot hotter than sex."

Noah boomed a laugh and Derek grinned.

"I'm starting to like this lady," Noah said.

"The thing is, if he wasn't supposed to kill me, why did he come after me?" Olivia filled them in on as much of the details as she could recall.

Rafe hadn't realized the men were armed until he heard the sound of metal as they dropped the clips on their semiautos, shoved them back in, and racked the slides.

"Rafe . . . ?" Olivia's uncertain voice floated toward him from the backseat.

"Take it easy, sweetheart," Noah said before Rafe could answer. "That bruise on your cheek ought to be enough for you to know these guys are dangerous. Always better to be prepared."

"Yes, of course. I'm sorry."

"So I guess you think this guy is part of it," Rafe said, voicing the notion he had been mulling over himself.

"If he'd been paid to shoot her," Noah said, "he could have done it. I say there's a good chance he's here for something else."

Devlin and Hunter asked a few more

questions, then something in the distance snagged Rafe's attention.

"What's that?" Noah asked, his gaze going up the hill.

As Rafe drove over Mineral Creek, he could see the orange-red glow in the sky above the mountain. "I've got a hunch I know."

He turned off Egan onto Front Street, slowed at the turn onto Dewey Court, saw the house at the end of the road fully engulfed in flames. "Sonofabitch."

Fire licked out the windows. The front porch blazed. Streamers of red licked up the walls into the black night sky. The roof was a wall of solid red flame.

The fire trucks were already there but the firemen were fighting a losing battle. The fountain of water they poured on the blaze turned into columns of thick, black, choking smoke.

"Looks like they took off with their buddies," Derek said.

"Burned down the house and any evidence they might have left behind," Noah added.

"Evidence of what?" Rafe said grimly. "We don't even know why they're here."

Noah's big frame shifted in the seat. "And they've just made sure we won't find out.

No fingerprints, no DNA, nothing that could give us a clue as to what, when, why, or where."

"This all just seems so surreal," Olivia said, staring at the blaze.

"So I guess your brother made the right call getting us down here," Derek said.

"Looks like," Rafe agreed, somewhat grudgingly, since as good as Nick was, he was still Rafe's little brother.

They watched the fire for a while, in case anyone showed up who looked suspicious. But clearly there was no one in the house, and the only people on the street appeared to be neighbors or firefighters, most of them volunteer.

Certain they wouldn't gain anything by staying, Rafe backed up the SUV, turned around, and drove back down the hill to his house.

Olivia brewed a second pot of coffee. It was after one o'clock in the morning, but no one was sleepy. She carried the pot into the living room and refilled the guys' mugs. The men were going over the information they had discussed before, reviewing it in even more detail.

Olivia refilled her own cup, returned the pot to the burner, then went in to join the

411

others, taking a place next to Rafe on the sofa. His arm slid comfortingly around her.

"Any chance they scrapped the mission — whatever it was — and just took off?" Rafe asked hopefully.

"Not likely," Noah said. "My guess, they've got a bugout pad somewhere. A place to go if something came up and they needed to change locations."

"So they're going ahead with whatever it is they've got planned."

Noah nodded. "I was in Afghanistan and Iraq. If they're fanatics, they're committed. They won't get this close and back away."

"You think that's what they are?" Olivia asked, her fatigue fading under a shot of adrenaline. "Fanatics?"

"Heng is connected to JAT," Noah reminded them. "They're bad motherfuckers. So, yeah, I think they could be."

"You still think the guy who attacked Liv is part of this, right?" Rafe said.

Noah took a drink of his coffee. That it was scalding hot didn't seem to bother him. "Let me lay it out the way I see it. Your friend, Scott Ferris, gets murdered. Good guy, from what you said, no enemies. They arrest some local but it doesn't add up. Which is why you and Liv got involved."

"More or less."

"But you still don't think the guy in jail killed him," Noah said.

Rafe set his coffee mug down on the table. "My hunch says no."

"So there's a chance the killer is the big guy who tried to rape Olivia."

"He fits the fuzzy image on the security camera of the man seen leaving the dock after the body was dumped."

"Also similar to the hazy figure Olivia spotted in the motel room," Noah said, "next to where the murder was actually committed. The same place Heng and his buddy were staying."

"That's right."

"Best guess, your friend Scotty stumbled onto something he shouldn't have. He heard or saw something, the big guy killed him and dumped the body. You with me so far?"

Rafe nodded. It was something they had talked about, but when Noah said it, it seemed to make the pieces come together.

"Heng worked for Microsoft," Noah said. "Guy's a college grad, computer nerd. When Olivia goes back to the room asking questions, he gets nervous, starts digging into her past, looking for a little insurance, something they can use to get her to back away. He hits the jackpot. Heng tells the killer — a member of the group — that she's

413

wanted."

"Sounds good so far," Rafe said.

"Here's where the theory takes a twist. Big Guy, desperate for a piece of ass since he's been 'up here for weeks' — his words — goes off the reservation and tries to blackmail Liv for sex."

Derek grinned. "Instead Liv stuns his sorry ass, but he keeps his mouth shut since what he did could have fucked up the mission."

Noah's amazing dimples popped out as he smiled at Liv. "Nice work, by the way."

She felt a trickle of warmth at his approval. "Thanks."

"Your theory makes sense," Rafe said, nodding as he thought through the rest. "Even after Big Guy screws up, everything is still going along fairly smoothly until Heng and his roommate find the GPS on the Jeep. They call the house to warn their buddies, then pack up and get out of Dodge."

Rafe glanced at Noah. "What I can't figure are the Petersens, the couple staying in the house. Anna, the wife, had some kind of an accent, but it didn't sound Middle Eastern."

Derek shrugged. "Somebody's got to run the show. Since the digs up on the hill are a lot nicer than the rooms at the Seaside

Motel, I'd say Petersen's our man."

"I met him," Rafe said. "I don't see him as a Muslim terrorist. If not, what's his motive?"

"Could be anything. Love. Money. Revenge. The usual stuff," Derek said.

"After the fire, it's clear they're involved," Noah said. "Nick may turn up something on the owner of the house. He'll be looking hard. He needs all the info he can get before he calls Charlie Farrell. I figure we'll hear from him in the morning."

Derek grinned at Rafe. "Unless he shows up at your door."

"God, I hope not," Rafe said.

Noah sipped his coffee. "Nick's on a case. Missing kid. He couldn't bail on the family or he'd already be here."

"He's got a pregnant wife and he's a long ways away," Rafe said. "This could be over by the time it takes him to get here."

"That's what we told him," Derek said.

Rafe scrubbed a hand over his face, praying that for once, Nick would control his impulsive nature. On the other hand, he was extremely grateful for his brother's help.

"Okay, let's go with the theory we've got," Rafe said. "With the Petersens, Big Guy, Heng, and his friend, we've got four men and a woman, all here to wreak havoc on something. What is it?"

"Nick says you think it could be the ferry," Derek said. "Five hundred souls aboard."

Rafe's jaw hardened. "I think it's the pipeline."

The room fell silent. Olivia's chest clamped down.

"Fuck," Noah said. "So do I."

"I do, too." Derek stood up and began to pace back and forth in front of the window. "We've got nothing. No way to prove it."

"They have to be extremely organized," Rafe said. "The place is a fortress."

Derek turned toward them. "Since we can't find hide nor hair of them, I'd say they've got things pretty well worked out."

"We've got to call the police." Olivia's stomach began to churn. *The police.* She could almost see the prison doors closing around her. But the devastation an attack on the pipeline would cause, the massive oil spill, would destroy Valdez, destroy the animals and fish, the sea, the harbor, everything for miles around.

She turned to Rafe. "The police are in charge of the pipeline, aren't they?"

He nodded. "It's their jurisdiction, but there's only eleven guys on the force."

"Yes, but there's lots of security out at the pipeline. And the police can call Homeland.

The cops will be able to convince them to help."

"The question is, how do we convince the police?" Rafe said.

Noah leaned back in his chair. "We need something more than speculation. Not to mention our intel was all illegally obtained."

Her stomach rolled.

"The Jeep's a rental," Rafe said. "The plate was in a Hertz Anchorage frame. Probably rented in Wong or Nevin's fake name. I don't think that'll help us."

Derek paced away from the window. "We know what it looks like, right?"

Rafe nodded. "Dark blue, newer model Jeep Cherokee. First three letters on the plate are ETU.

"As soon as it's daylight, I'll go up, do a little aerial surveillance. I'll find the damned thing. Once we know where these guys are, we'll come up with a plan. If we have to, we'll go in and handle it ourselves."

Olivia shot up from the sofa. "What! You can't be serious!"

Rafe caught her waist, drew her gently back down beside him. "Maybe we won't have to. Nick's talking to the FBI. Maybe they'll step in and make this end."

"Don't count on it," Noah said darkly. "We haven't got jack shit. By the time we do, this is going to be coming down. We need to be prepared to get it done ourselves."

Olivia's gaze flew to Rafe. The hard look on his face was like nothing she had ever seen before.

It said he completely agreed.

CHAPTER THIRTY

Nick phoned at six a.m. Seattle time, five a.m. in Alaska. Rafe was just rolling out of bed. Beside him Olivia groaned and dragged a pillow over her head, making him smile. Scrubbing a hand over his face, he grabbed his cell off the bedside table and pressed it against his ear.

"I hope you're still in Seattle," he growled, knowing his volatile brother would be itching to get into the action — assuming there was going to be any.

"I'm here. I'm still tied up with a case I just can't leave."

"There is a God."

"Dammit, this is serious and you know it."

"You're right. Thanks for sending in the Marines."

"You better not let them hear you say that."

Rafe smiled. Devlin and Hunter were

Army first, last, and always. Noah was Delta, the elite of the elite. Derek was a Night Stalker helicopter pilot. Flying didn't get any better.

"Tell me Charlie Farrell and the feds are jumping in the middle of this," Rafe said. "Tell me we're out of it."

"Unfortunately, Charlie isn't in Alaska at the moment. He's working a case in California. The guy I talked to wasn't impressed. He took a look at Heng, said the kid was so far down the watch list it wasn't worth worrying about. He said he'd make note of the phone call and Heng's visit to Valdez in case something else came up."

"I was afraid of that. Anything on the rental property?"

"Man who owns the house lives in Anchorage. He rented the place to Trent and Anna Petersen over the Internet, got a very big cash deposit along with two weeks' rent. The address they gave him in Connecticut doesn't check out."

"Since the place burned to the ground last night, I hope he got enough to cover his insurance deductible."

Nick hissed into the phone.

"We think the target's the pipeline."

"Sonofabitch. I was afraid of that. All those oil-covered fish and cute little ducks dying in front of the cameras. It's just the kind of shitstorm those a-holes like to rain down on people. I need to get up there."

"I don't think you're gonna make this party, little brother. Lucky for me your stand-ins are first-rate."

"Yeah, and then some." Nick paused a moment. "What about your lady? She doing okay?"

"She hasn't made a run for it, if that's what you're asking."

"That isn't what I was asking. Listen, you've always had great instincts. If you care about her that much, she's got to be something special."

"She is," Rafe said.

"Tell her to hang in there. We'll find a way out."

Something tightened his chest. When things got rough, he could always count on his brothers. "Thanks, Nick."

"I'll keep digging. Maybe something will turn up."

Rafe ended the call and headed downstairs. He was in the kitchen, getting out the coffee to brew a pot, when he looked up to see Olivia walking toward him, yawning behind her hand.

"What's the plan?" she asked.

"The plan is for Derek and Noah to take

the plane up and do a sweep, see if they can find the Jeep. Since we have no idea when — or if — this is actually going down, and I've got a half-day charter I can't get out of, you're coming aboard *Scorpion* with me."

"I've got to go to work."

"Not today, darlin'. After you went upstairs last night, we talked a little more. We think the guy who tried to rape you is part of this and not working for your enemies. But there's no way to know for sure. We have to be ready in case we've made the wrong call."

She looked like she wanted to argue, but gave up a sigh instead. "All right, I'll phone Nell, tell her I'll be in later this afternoon."

"Good enough."

"I can do this for a while, Rafe, but I can't live this way forever."

"If we're right, you won't have to. With the fire last night and Heng and his buddies on the run, the attack has got to be coming down soon. Till then, I want you where I can keep you safe."

"Fine. In the meantime, why don't I make all of us some breakfast?"

"Not much in the pantry."

"You're right. Wayne'll be in the café by now. He'll be getting the kitchen up and running for breakfast. If I call him, he could whip us all up something to eat and have it ready when we got there."

"Good idea."

"*Great* idea," Noah said as he walked into the kitchen, dressed once more in his camos.

Derek walked in behind him, scratching his naked, very impressive chest. "Man, I could eat a bowl of skunk stew. I haven't eaten since yesterday afternoon."

Rafe chuckled. "You better tell Wayne to double the order."

Liv smiled. "No problem."

The breakfast crew was already hard at work, Wayne Littlefish in the kitchen, Katie making coffee and setting the tables. Nell wouldn't be in for another hour, since she was working a split shift today.

Liv brought the men in through the rear of the restaurant, stopping long enough to check on Khan. The dog was back in his own yard and happy to be home, she thought. Though he'd seemed content in Rafe's big backyard, he'd probably missed Tuxedo.

"Great-looking dog," Derek said as Liv knelt to hug him and give him a back rub. She scratched until he was content, then returned to her feet.

"Sit," she commanded, and Khan obediently dropped to his haunches. Rafe handed her a dog biscuit from the bag next to the door and Liv held it out to Khan. "Okay. Here you go. What a good boy."

"I see you have a guard dog," Noah said, studying the big German shepherd. "Looks like a good one. Extremely well trained." He eyed her sharply. "I guess I know why he's here."

"Jesus, Rafe," Derek said. "You got more problems than your brother." They knew all of it now, the murder Olivia was accused of, who'd done it, and the attempts that had been made on her life.

"Nick got his troubles straightened out," Rafe said. "I plan to do the same."

Liv looked up at him and felt a pang in her heart. He wasn't giving up on her. How could she give up on him?

"Go on inside," Rafe said to the men. Since they were starving, they didn't hesitate. Rafe waited for Liv to finish feeding Khan and then followed her into the café. He joined the men in the big booth in the corner, while Liv went to check on their meals.

Katie swung up beside her. "Oh, my heart be still. Would you look at that? Those three guys have the market cornered on hot."

Liv smiled. "We need to get them fed."

"I'm on it. Wayne's got their orders almost ready. Don't even think of trying to take them over."

Olivia laughed. It felt really good. "I'll help. We're kind of on a tight schedule."

"Good idea. That way you can introduce me."

"You like the sexy one or the big sexy one?"

"Both."

Olivia grinned as they grabbed platters heaped with eggs, bacon, fried potatoes, and toast from under the heat lamp and carried them over to the booth.

Liv introduced Katie. Noah was polite. Derek flicked her a hungry glance but must have realized she was barely old enough to buy a beer. He winked at her, then dug into his eggs.

Katie just sighed and headed off to another customer. Liv's smile faded away. The hours were sliding past. It was going to be a very long day.

Trent Doyle awakened in the comfortable king-size bed at the Marriot hotel near the Anchorage International Airport. Rolling over, he checked the bedside clock.

"Time to get going," he said, gently shaking Tatiana's pale white shoulder. She sat up, shifting her thick, black hair back from her face.

She smiled when she saw the rise of his arousal beneath the sheets. "So . . . you are in a good mood this morning." Leaning over, she began to press kisses on his naked chest, his belly, slid lower, took care of him the way she often did in the mornings.

He was glad he had brought her along.

He groaned as she finished. Sliding out of bed, he headed for the shower, feeling relaxed and ready to face the trip ahead. Since airline connections out of Valdez were abominable, he'd arranged a charter to Anchorage, which was only a short hop away. Though they'd been forced to fly out last night instead of as planned this morning, with the money Trent was paying the pilot, the man hadn't complained.

Thank God they were leaving this god-awful wilderness. He was sick of Alaska, sick of the isolation, and his work here was done. He hadn't been happy when Heng had picked up a signal, then found the GPS on his rental car, but it wasn't a police model, nothing the FBI would be using, nothing as sophisticated as what Homeland might use, at least according to Heng.

Trent's jaw tightened. It was Brodie. Had to be. Brodie and the woman were looking for evidence in the murder of their friend. They had zeroed in on the two men in the motel room. Though it was Cain, not Heng or Nadir, who'd committed the crime, their interference had become a serious problem.

It was Brodie. Had to be. Trent had recognized a dangerous foe when he and Tatiana had been aboard the *Sea Scorpion.* Intelligent and capable, the kind of man who would make a worthy opponent.

The GPS tracker had made Brodie a big enough problem that Trent had ordered his men to abandon the motel and move to the secondary location he'd arranged off Richardson Highway. A big enough problem that Trent had packed up the car he'd rented under the Petersen alias, set a good-sized blaze in the rental house to destroy any evidence, and flown up to Anchorage.

As a final precaution, and perhaps as payback for the inconvenience, he had ordered Nadir to get rid of Brodie once and for all.

It was almost over. This morning, he and Tatiana would be boarding a commercial flight, first-class, of course, from Anchorage to New York City. The attack would begin a little after midnight tonight. The ship, *San Pascual,* a number of storage tanks, and a portion of the pipeline would all be destroyed.

Anticipation rolled through him. Once that happened, oil stocks would soar, and since he'd invested every dime he could beg, borrow, or steal in oil futures, overnight his financial problems would be solved and he'd be an obscenely wealthy man.

His anticipation grew. He didn't have to worry about getting caught. The escape boat leaving the rendezvous point would never arrive at the Tatitlek Airport. A crew of mercenaries had been paid handsomely to handle the job, men who had no connection to Trent or any idea who he was.

Heng, Nadir, Cain, and the fanatic who had illegally entered the States through Mexico and taken a job aboard the *San Pascual* would simply disappear, their bodies tossed into the icy waters of Prince William Sound.

They would be dead. All of them martyred.

Trent smiled.

Allah was good.

Derek and Noah took off for the airport right after breakfast. The first order of business was to locate the Jeep. If there was going to be a terrorist attack, the men in the motel room were the key.

Rafe left the café with Olivia shortly after, crossing the street in front of the restaurant, heading for the harbor to take *Scorpion* out for its scheduled half-day charter.

Liv stopped him just as they reached the dock. "Before we go, Rafe, there's something I need to say."

He looked into her worried face. "What is it, baby?"

"I've been thinking about all of this. We have to stop those men. You and Noah and Derek, you guys are extremely competent, but the best way to end this is to bring in the police."

"Nick called the FBI. There isn't enough evidence to convince them to get involved."

"I'm not talking about the FBI. I'm talking about Chief Rosen and the police here in Valdez. They can speak to pipeline security, put them on notice that something might be in the works."

"Same thing goes. We don't have enough information."

"It's because of me, isn't it? You're afraid if we call the cops, it might trigger something that'll bring them down on me."

Rafe took a calming breath and slowly released it. "That's part of it. I won't lie about it. We're going to need some time to figure out how to clear your name. We get the police involved in this, anything could happen. The man who attacked you is still out there. He knows who you are, knows your real name. If they arrest him —"

"Stopping this is more important. I couldn't live with myself if the pipeline was destroyed. If there was a massive oil spill because we didn't do everything in our power to stop an attack."

Rafe cupped her face in his hands. "Have I told you how important you are to me? How much you mean to me?"

"Rafe . . ."

"I'll call Chief Rosen, if that's what you want. But until we locate Heng and his friend, we don't have anything to give him. What do I say? That Wong's real name is Heng and he and his friend are Muslim? The information has already been given to the FBI and they weren't interested. Do I say that the house that burned down last night was a place the two of them had visited? At this point, the police may not even be able to confirm it was arson. It isn't enough, Liv."

She sighed. "I don't know . . . maybe you're right."

"Rosen's going to want to hear how we know any of this, and if he calls the FBI, they're going to say they've already checked it out and there's nothing to worry about. Rosen will be pissed we made him look like a fool. What little credibility we have will go straight down the drain and that will be the end of it."

"So what are we going to do? We have to do something."

"What we do is hope like hell Hunter and Devlin find that Jeep." They started walking down the long, wooden dock toward the boat.

"You know, the guy who attacked me said he'd been up here for weeks. Maybe he works at the terminal. That would make sense."

"It would. Trouble is, more than three hundred people work there. More like eight hundred if you count employees who live outside Valdez. How do we find him?"

Frustrated, she lifted her ball cap a little, then tugged it back down on her forehead. Today the cap read I'D RATHER BE IN PARIS.

Rafe stopped when they reached the boat. "We aren't done with this yet, baby, not by a long shot. We've only got a half-day trip so we'll be back early. I talked to Mo this morning and rearranged the schedule so we won't have a trip tomorrow. In the meantime, we take the boat out and show our passengers a really great time."

Olivia managed a halfhearted smile. "Okay, then."

Rafe climbed aboard, reached back and took Liv's hand to steady her as she climbed up on deck. Zach and Jaimie were already aboard and had everything in order. Both of them were laughing at something one of them said. They looked good together, Zach with his olive complexion and dark good looks, Jaimie with her pretty face and Scots' red hair. Rafe couldn't remember seeing either of them smiling so often.

"Passengers ought to be here any minute," Zach said, walking toward him.

"Got a call this morning. It'll only be two instead of the four who paid for the trip. I guess the others had a problem of some kind and couldn't make it."

"Should be an easy day then," Zach said.

Rafe just nodded. *An easy day.* Except for his worry about what might be going to happen that they were still unprepared to stop.

CHAPTER THIRTY-ONE

The boat was getting ready to head back to the harbor when things went sideways. In the far distance, beneath a mantle of white, the lower slopes of the mountains rising up from the Sound had begun to turn a rich bright green.

The day had been spectacular. Everywhere Olivia looked was blue. Blue sky, blue water, blue shadows cast by the sun onto the melting snow. Even with the swirl of intrigue around her, the open sea and obvious pleasure of the people aboard was contagious. Liv could feel the pulse of attraction between Zach and Jaimie, feel that same hot pull between her and Rafe.

And the passengers, an older couple from Los Angeles in their early fifties, were so clearly in love with Alaska and having the time of their lives on the water, there was no way to have anything but fun.

They stopped at one of Rafe's favorite

fishing spots, where the black cod, lingcod, and snapper were practically leaping out of the sea. While the boat bobbed gently in the ocean, Connie Neiderman, a buxom blonde whose hair was silvering with the years, boomed out a throaty laugh as she worked to reel in one big fish after another.

Her husband, completely gray but still handsome, was having an easier time and just as much fun. While Zach and Jaimie worked with the pair, Rafe came out from behind the wheel to join Liv on deck. He must have seen her watching them with a trace of envy.

"You've got a license, right?" As if it were impossible for anyone who lived in Valdez not to have a fishing license.

Liv grinned. "I do. I bought one over at the sporting goods store on one of my afternoon runs. I figured if I was involved with a fisherman, sooner or later he'd want to go fishing."

Rafe glanced over to make sure his passengers weren't watching, slid a hand down inside her jeans to cup her behind, and pulled her flush against him.

"Oh, you're involved, all right." He nibbled the side of her neck. "The next time we're alone, I'll show you just how involved you are." A gentle squeeze sent a pulse of heat into all her womanly places.

Olivia laughed and pulled his hand away, though she didn't really want to.

Rafe just smiled. "Let's get you rigged up. We can use a nice catch in the freezer." At Rafe's nod, Jaimie rigged a pole, and for the next half hour, Olivia reeled in fish, so many her arms began to ache from hauling them up on deck.

The sun was climbing. "It's getting toward noon," Rafe said. "Time to go home." And though she'd loved every minute out on the sea, she was ready.

He turned to his first mate. "Go ahead and take her in, Zach."

Zach grinned ear to ear, went inside and stood behind the wheel. The engines rumbled to life.

In another few seconds they would have been underway, skimming at twenty knots over the surface of the water. The explosion in the bottom of the bow would have blown backward, into the center of the boat, killing everyone on board.

Instead, as the boat idled in the ocean, the bomb blew off the lower front portion of the *Scorpion,* shooting a geyser of water and debris into the air, pitching the boat so violently, Jaimie and Connie Neiderman flew overboard into the sea.

Olivia's ears rang as she struggled up from the deck, head pounding, fighting to gather her senses. A wet trickle of blood ran down the side of her face from a flying chunk of debris. The deck tilted wildly. Icy water rushed in. It was already up to her knees as she struggled to her feet and sloshed toward where Jim Neiderman lay groaning, his arm tilted at an odd angle, obviously broken.

Zach was on the radio, frantically calling the Coast Guard, shouting a mayday and relaying their position. She heard a splash and turned to see Rafe dive into the sea. Connie Neiderman had gone under. Ten yards away, Jaimie was treading water, her head above the surface, but just barely. Something was wrong. Jaimie was in trouble.

Liv didn't take time to think, just dragged off her sneakers, turned and dove into the ocean. She wasn't prepared for the shock of forty-degree water that hit her like a brick. While Rafe dove under, searching for Connie, Liv swam toward Jaimie.

She caught a glimpse of Zach, hauling out the bright yellow inflatable life raft, grabbing life rings and tossing them out in the water, doing exactly the right things. Liv was a good athlete, always had been. She was a good swimmer, not nearly as capable as Rafe, but as she powered through the water, in seconds the icy cold began to sap her strength.

She reached Jaimie and locked an arm around her neck. "It's okay, I've got you. Just relax, sweetie. Let me get you over to the boat."

Sea savvy, Jaimie weakly nodded and let Liv do the work. As the boat began to sink, she saw that Zach had put a vest on Jim Neiderman, but hadn't had time to grab one for himself. As soon as they went into the water, he started swimming, pulling Jim toward the life raft with long, confident strokes. He left Jim holding on to the raft and turned to look for Jaimie.

There was panic in his voice as he called her name, didn't see her at first. "Jaimie!" He spun around in search of her. "Jaimie!"

"She's here!" Liv called back. She knew he'd wanted to go after the girl himself, but he'd stayed, done what had to be done. Zach spotted them, started swimming toward them. He took over with Jaimie, soothing her as he swam toward the life raft, then began helping her and Jim into it.

Treading water, Liv turned in a circle, searching for Rafe, the chill turning her body sluggishly numb. When she didn't see him, fear gripped her.

She hadn't seen him surface. Not once. There was no sign of him or Connie. How long had he been down there? Dear God, maybe he'd been injured in the blast. Maybe he'd gone too deep and his oxygen had run out.

A fresh rush of adrenaline hit her and she started swimming toward the last place she had seen him. She dove under when she got there, frantically began to search for him beneath the surface of the sea.

She stayed down as long as she could, shot up for air, took in a big gulp, and dove under again. Searching madly, she caught no sight of him. Frantic now, she took a deep breath and turned to dive under again when his dark head broke the surface of the water. So did Connie Neiderman's.

He shook his head like a big wet dog, and a sob burst from Olivia's throat. "Rafe!" He was alive. He was okay.

"Liv! Dammit, why aren't you in the boat?"

"I had to find you. I had to."

Something shifted in his eyes, something wild and fierce. He had Connie Neiderman in a carry position, but the woman wasn't breathing. "Keep moving. We've got to get out of the water."

She didn't realize how exhausted she was

until she saw how far the life raft had drifted from where they were now. Zach was manning an oar, paddling like crazy to reach them. Rafe was a stronger swimmer and he soon outdistanced her. As soon as he reached the boat, he and Zach loaded Connie aboard.

"Start CPR," Rafe said. "I've got to get Liv."

She could make it, she told herself. She wasn't that far away. But she was completely exhausted, her muscles weak and unresponsive. When Rafe swam up, hooked a powerful arm around her middle and started towing her the short distance left to the boat, she could have cried with relief.

Zach helped Rafe load her aboard, then Rafe used those strong arms to hoist himself into the rubber raft, where he quickly took over drowning CPR from Zach, blowing life into Connie Neiderman's lungs.

Time seemed to slow. Rafe just kept working over Connie. Two breaths, then thirty chest compressions. Two breaths, then thirty compressions. Liv wondered how long he'd continue before he gave up. Next to him Jim Neiderman was praying, his lips moving as he silently repeated the words again and again.

When the woman took a deep breath and

coughed up a mouthful of water, Jim started crying. Liv blinked against the tears blurring her vision, swallowed past the lump in her throat, reached over and gripped Jim's hand.

"She's going to be okay, Jim. We're all going to be okay."

He just nodded, a little embarrassed. Liv squeezed his hand. After being so terrified for Rafe, she understood exactly how he felt.

While Zach checked Jaimie and pronounced she had a concussion but otherwise seemed okay, Rafe moved Jim Neiderman so his broken arm would be in a more comfortable position. The entire time, Jim held his wife's hand and never let go.

"I saw what you did," Jim said as Rafe dug blankets out of a waterproof bag. "You saved her. She wouldn't have made it if it weren't for you."

"I'm the captain. I did what I'm supposed to do."

"You did more. A lot more."

Rafe's mouth edged up. "I've had some practice." His beautiful brown eyes came to Liv. He reached out and cupped her face, leaned over and softly kissed her.

"You're amazing," he said. "I already knew it, but today proved just how incredible you are." His gaze held hers and her heart swelled.

Turning away, he spoke to Zach. "I assume you got the Coast Guard off their duffs and on their way to pick us up."

"I made contact. They know the boat was yours. Cordova's not that far. It shouldn't take them long to get here."

"What happened?" Jim wanted to know.

For an instant before he answered, Rafe's gaze locked with Liv's. "I'm not sure. It could have been a problem with the propane in the galley. Until the Coast Guard checks out the wreckage, we won't know for certain."

But Olivia was certain. And so was Rafe. Someone had tried to kill them. It could have been Heng and a group of terrorists. Or it could have been someone from her past, someone who wanted to keep her quiet.

As Rafe dug into the emergency kit for something to use to splint Jim's arm, Olivia closed her eyes and leaned back against the rim of the inflatable raft. As they floated gently in the water, exhaustion settled over her. She felt Rafe's hand brush her cheek, opened her eyes and looked up to see his steady gaze on her face.

"Everything's going to be okay," he said.

Her throat tightened.

Olivia couldn't force out a single word.

After what seemed like hours but was more like thirty minutes, a chopper appeared overhead. The door in the side of the helicopter slid open, and a man in an orange COAST GUARD RESCUE uniform stood in the doorway with a bullhorn in his hand. "Hey, Brodie. How's it feel to be on the other end of the rescue?"

Rafe's dark eyes crinkled at the corners. "I'd rather be up there with you!" he shouted over the *whop* of the rotors.

A two-way radio was lowered into the raft along with some blankets. A Coast Guard boat was on its way. Rafe told them there were two people in the raft with injuries severe enough to require air transportation.

The two-way crackled. "You're a legend around here, Brodie. You still remember how to do this, right?"

"I remember."

The basket came down and Rafe went to work, loading and securing Connie Neiderman inside. Once she was hoisted up and brought aboard the chopper, the basket returned and Jim was hauled up.

"Nice work," the guy on the radio said to Rafe. "Boat's almost here. I can see it on the horizon. Just hang tough."

"Will do. Great job. Thanks for coming to the party."

The guy on the radio chuckled. The chopper swung away and the small group settled in to wait. They needed to get warm and dry, but the Coast Guard boat would be equipped for that.

Olivia thought of Rafe's prized *Sea Scorpion* scattered in bits and pieces across the ocean and felt a sharp pang for the loss he must be feeling.

She couldn't help hoping some kind of equipment failure had caused the explosion. She prayed it wasn't her fault.

But she couldn't make herself believe it.

CHAPTER THIRTY-TWO

It was early evening by the time Rafe, Liv, and his crew were released from the Providence Medical Center, where they had been taken after the Coast Guard boat arrived in Valdez.

Liv's cell had gone missing, but Rafe and Zach kept theirs in waterproof cases, and Rafe's had been stuffed in the pocket of his jeans. He phoned Noah as soon as he got to the hospital. They were out at the airport, refueling Derek's plane. So far they hadn't found a damned thing.

"I've been calling," Noah said. "No answer. I was starting to worry."

"You weren't far off the mark. I'm at the hospital. Everyone's okay, but *Scorpion*'s in a jillion pieces out in the middle of the Sound."

"Jesus, Rafe. What happened?"

"Somebody blew us up. That's not the official version, but there it is."

"But everyone's okay? No one got hurt?"

"One of the passengers damn near drowned. She's okay, but it was a close thing. Her husband's got a broken arm. One of the crew wound up with a concussion."

"I don't like this. We're coming in. Take Liv and we'll meet up at your place. If you get there first, make sure no one's paid you a visit while we've been gone."

"I've got to talk to the chief of police. He's due any minute."

"You gonna tell him about our friends?"

"We could use his help. Maybe now that the boat's been blown sky-high, the police will believe we've got a credible threat."

"You sure what happened out there wasn't about Olivia?"

He blew out a breath. There was no way to know for sure. "No," was all he said.

Noah swore softly. "Good luck, then. We'll see you back at your place."

Rafe hung up the phone. Liv borrowed it to phone Nell and tell her what had happened before news of the explosion spread all over town. Zach walked out just then, an arm draped over Jaimie's shoulder. Since their clothes had been wet, all of them were wearing the disposable green scrubs they'd been given by the Coast Guard crew.

"How are the Neidermans doing?" Zach

asked as he and Jaimie walked up.

"Doc says they're both going to be fine. Jim's in a cast. Connie's got a concussion. They're keeping her overnight for observation." Rafe turned to the redhead tucked beneath Zach's arm. "How about you, Jaimie? They letting you go home?"

"The concussion wasn't bad. My folks are on their way, so I'll be okay." She flicked a glance at Liv, then looked back at Rafe. "I was pretty scared out there. I was nauseated and dizzy and I couldn't get my bearings. If Olivia hadn't come after me, I don't know what would have happened."

"If Liv couldn't have made it, Zach would have come for you. I know he wanted to go as soon as he saw you hit the water. Instead, he did his job, maybe kept all of us alive."

Rafe swung his attention to the dark-haired kid who had done as well as any man twice his age. "You were great out there, Zach. Smart and in control. You did exactly what needed to be done. I'd crew with you any time, any place."

A smile broke over Zach's handsome face. "Thanks, Rafe." The smile faded. "Do you really think the propane in the galley exploded?"

"You heard what I told Jim. Until they examine the wreckage —"

"I think it was a bomb," Zach said. "I think one of those guys in the motel room killed Scotty. We were getting close, so they tried to kill us. That's what I think."

"I'd appreciate it if you didn't speculate too much at this point."

"Are you kidding?" Zach looked appalled. "We could get arrested for putting the GPS on that Jeep. I'm not saying a word."

"Me either," Jaimie vowed. "Whatever happened, I don't want any more trouble. The boat blew up. That's it. You can tell them whatever you want."

Rafe nodded. "Thanks. You kids go on. Without a boat, we aren't working tomorrow or any day soon. Mo can take some of *Scorpion*'s passengers. I'll arrange for another company to handle the rest. You two are on paid leave until I can find us a new vessel."

"I really liked that boat," Zach grumbled.

"So did I. But it's people who matter. And when the time came, *Scorpion* did her job. She stayed afloat long enough for you to get off that mayday and get the raft in the water. She'll be hard to replace. Now get going."

Zach smiled. "After a day like today, I could use a little time off."

"Me too," Jaimie said, unconsciously moving closer to Zach.

Arms around each other's waists, the two of them walked away. Jaimie's parents were outside waiting to drive them home. Rafe watched them disappear through the door just as Chief Rosen walked in.

"I understand one of my officers has already taken an incident report," the chief said, his eyes going over Rafe, who stood there in a pair of scrubs. "Looks like you came out unscathed aside from a few cuts and bruises. How about you, Ms. Chandler?"

"Cuts and bruises. Except for those and being a little shook up, I'm fine."

"What about everyone else? No overnight hospital stays for anyone?"

"Mrs. Neiderman suffered a concussion. The hospital's keeping her for observation. Her husband has a broken arm."

"What happened out there?"

He shook his head. "No way to know. Not at this point. Propane leak in the galley, maybe."

"Or maybe it's something else. There's an empty office we can use down the hall. We can talk in there."

Rafe flicked a glance at Olivia as they started in that direction. He could feel the tension in her body as they made their way along the corridor and went into the empty

448

room. Rosen followed them in and closed the door.

The office was hospital sterile, with seasonal photos of Prince William Sound on the walls, a metal desk, and a couple of stacking metal chairs.

"I got a call a few hours ago from the FBI," Rosen said, taking a seat behind the desk, motioning for them to sit down on the opposite side. "I don't know your brother Nick, but apparently he has a friend in the agency. Since his friend wasn't there, he spoke to Special Agent Brian Bunting. Your brother called in regard to possible suspicious activity that might or might not affect the pipeline terminal. I presume you know something about that."

"Nick's a private investigator. I gave him a couple of names to run in regard to the Scott Ferris murder. One of them showed former connections to a terrorist group."

"Special Agent Bunting checked out the information, but came up with nothing of any real consequence. That being said, as a precaution they called and alerted me, and also gave a heads-up to the security people out at the terminal."

Rafe felt a wave of relief.

"Is there any chance this accident today could in any way be linked to the information the FBI received?" Chief Rosen asked.

How much should he say? The police department and the terminal were already on alert. At this time, there was no way to verify what had actually happened to the boat.

And anything he said might wind up getting Olivia arrested — or killed.

"The boat exploded, Chief. At this point, that's all I know."

"Good. Because I'm not in the mood to go head-to-head with the FBI unless I'm in possession of hard evidence that proves there's a problem. Tips come in every day — Bunting's words, not mine. So unless you have something more to add, we'll leave things as they are, and you can both go home."

"Thanks, Chief."

"You need a ride?"

"One of the girls at the restaurant is picking us up," Olivia told him. Liv had spoken to Nell, told her what had happened. Katie was picking them up and dropping them back at Rafe's truck, parked at the café.

The chief nodded, smiled as he walked out from behind the desk. "All right. One last thing. From now on, it'd be a good idea if you left the investigating to the police."

"Good advice," Rafe said as he and Liv

stood up, too.

"I'd advise you to take it." The chief walked out of the office.

As soon as the door closed behind him, Olivia went into Rafe's arms. He could feel her trembling. "They know there might be an attack," she said. "We've done everything we can."

Rafe's hold tightened. "We'll see," was all he said.

It was late but still light outside when they arrived at Rafe's house. The Expedition, which Noah and Derek had driven to the airport that morning, was parked out front. Noah had used the house key Rafe had given him and the two men were already inside when Rafe guided Olivia up the stairs from the garage.

Seated on the couch, Noah eyed their baggy green scrubs with a hint of amusement. "A little old to be playing doctor, but at least you've got a pretty nurse."

Derek grinned, and Rafe felt a smile tug at his lips. The humor faded as the men fixed worried eyes on Liv.

"When Brodie takes a woman on a date," Derek drawled, "it's one she won't soon forget."

"You okay, sweetheart?" Noah asked.

"You should have seen her," Rafe said. "Swims like a fish, and that ice water didn't faze her. She brought Jaimie in, then swam back to rescue me."

One of Derek's dark eyebrows went up. "That so?"

"He didn't need my help," Olivia explained, flicking Rafe a glance. "He was busy saving Mrs. Neiderman's life. I was just . . . I was afraid he might have been hurt in the explosion."

Noah smiled, deepening his dimples. "I want you on my next fishing trip, lady, just in case the boat sinks."

"That's for sure," Derek said.

Noah looked at Rafe, his features turning serious. "We checked the house. No sign of a break-in. No explosives."

"Whoever blew up the boat is probably sure the explosion took you out," Derek said.

"It's a miracle it didn't."

"You talk to the police?" Noah asked.

Rafe nodded. "No way to determine the exact cause, at least not yet. I didn't press the issue, since we don't know any more than they do. The good news is, all the agencies have been alerted to the possibility of a terrorist attack — FBI, local cops, terminal security. The bad news is, they don't have enough info to view the threat as entirely credible. I was really hoping we could locate that Jeep."

"I'm going up one more time before it gets dark," Derek said. "We were working a grid. We cut the pattern short and came directly back here after Noah talked to you. We've got one more area left to search."

"The Jeep could be parked in a garage somewhere," Olivia said. "You wouldn't be able to see it from the air."

"Could be, but it's worth another try," Derek said.

Rafe nodded. "After what happened, I don't think we can afford to overlook anything." He turned to Liv, spoke to her softly. "Why don't you go upstairs, darlin'? Maybe take a soak in the hot tub, yes?"

Her whole body seemed to sigh at the notion. "Okay."

The three of them watched as she wearily climbed the stairs in her baggy, borrowed clothes and disappeared down the hall.

"I'm beginning to understand why you're determined to fight for her," Noah said.

"She's worth it," said Rafe.

"We'll do what we can to help," Derek said, "but we need to solve this problem first." He glanced out the window toward the still-light evening sky. "I'm heading back to the airport, take a look at that last search area."

"I'm with you," Noah said. "Four eyes are better than two, and I'm still convinced these guys are going after the pipeline." He turned to Rafe. "That said, you need to stay alert. If we're wrong and Liv is the target, they may come after her here."

Rafe nodded. He'd already considered that. "I've got the S&W .45 I carry when I'm hiking, a .38 revolver, and a couple of hunting rifles. I'll get them out of my gun safe."

"Our gear's in the back of the Expedition," Noah said.

Rafe walked them to the door. "You spot the Jeep, you call. I'll move in, keep an eye on them till you can get there."

"You got it." Derek and Noah headed out of the house.

Rafe went upstairs to retrieve his weapons: his semiautomatic pistol, two hunting rifles, and the .38 revolver his dad had given each of his sons for Christmas one year. He laid them out on the bed.

Shedding the scrubs, he grabbed the semi-auto and padded naked down the hall to the hot tub. Olivia was floating on her back with her head against the rim, her eyes closed, dark hair drifting around her face.

He set the gun on the edge of the tub and quietly slid into the water, intending to let her doze. The warmth soaked into him, began to wipe away some of the tension. He swam often enough that today's adventure hadn't really tired him, but the hot tub thawed the chill that lingered deep in his bones.

On the opposite side of the tub, Olivia's eyes slowly opened and a soft smile curved her lips. "Feels good, doesn't it?"

"Amazing."

She pushed away from the edge and drifted toward him. He could see her slender curves, naked and pretty beneath the water. If she came any closer, she would realize he was aroused and all his noble intentions would fly right out the window.

She pressed up against him, flicked a glance toward the rim of the tub where he'd set the pistol within easy reach. "I see you brought your gun." She smiled, slid her hand down to his groin. "Both of them."

Rafe couldn't stop a grin. "I'm trying to behave, but you're making it hard."

"Oh yes," she said. "I can see that." The tips of her breasts teased his chest and the hand in the water wrapped firmly around him. Figuring he had given her fair warning, he swooped down to capture those plump, million-dollar lips. The world around them might be spinning out of control, but the next few moments belonged to them.

Liv returned his kiss, her fingers sliding into his hair, her tongue in his mouth, his over hers, going deeper, turning wild and erotic. Life was precious. Coming so close to dying stirred basic survival instincts. The instinct to mate was strong.

Backing her up against the side of the tub, he lifted her a little, wrapped those long, sexy legs around his waist. She was wet and hot and he drove deep.

Olivia moaned. With a long, hot kiss, she arched against him. Rafe gripped her hips and took what he wanted, what he so desperately needed. Gave Olivia what she needed, too.

Time seemed to slow, their troubles somewhere far away. He took her again before reality seeped in and he reluctantly prepared to leave the water.

"We need to get dressed," he said, pressing a last soft kiss against the side of her neck.

"I know." With a sigh, she angled away from him, climbed out of the hot tub, grabbed a towel, dried off, and headed down the hall. Rafe grabbed another towel off the stack and followed, enjoying the elegant sway of her hips beneath the towel as she moved toward the bedroom, reminded himself it wasn't a good idea to have her again.

Ten minutes later, Liv was dressed in jeans and a dark green sweatshirt with tiny embroidered pink tulips on the front. Rafe wore black jeans and a black, long-sleeved T-shirt. If something went down, he didn't want to stand out as a target.

They headed down to the living room. It was almost dark when Rafe's phone began to play.

CHAPTER THIRTY-THREE

"We got 'em," Noah said. "Spotted them leaving a cabin off Richardson Highway just as it was getting dark. We followed their headlights. Couldn't get a fix on the plate, so we can't be one hundred percent, but I'm betting it's them."

"Where are they now?"

"Drove out Dayville Road toward the terminal, pulled off on a dirt lane just before the entrance. Road weaves back in a ways, runs along a creek."

"Allison Creek."

"They're about a mile off the main road, pulled in under some trees. We'll be landing at the airport in five minutes. We'll head out as soon as we're wheels down."

"I'm on my way." Rafe grabbed the semi-auto he'd set on the end table next to the sofa, stuffed it into the holster he'd brought downstairs, and clipped it onto his belt.

Olivia came up beside him. "Where are

you going?"

"They found the Jeep. Do you know how to shoot?"

"I can, yes. I took lessons after the first time someone tried to kill me. I'm better with a handgun than a rifle."

Rafe felt the pull of a smile.

Olivia stared down at the weapon on his belt and frowned. "You're not going after those men?" Accusation deepened the tone of her voice.

Rafe walked over to the table and picked up his revolver. The hunting rifles leaned against the wall. He pressed the revolver into Liv's hand. "If someone comes after you, don't be afraid to shoot."

Olivia took the weapon, looked into his face. "If you're going after those men, I'm going with you. We've been in this together from the start. That's not going to stop now."

"No way. You're staying here. I'll be back when this is over."

"You aren't leaving without me."

"You can't come, darlin'. You'll only be a liability."

"I'll stay with the truck and keep watch. You might need an extra pair of eyes out there. As I said, I know how to shoot."

"Goddammit, Liv, I want you safe!"

She gripped his arm. "I know you do, but look what happened today. We still don't know who tried to kill us. You really think I'll be safer here than I will be with you?"

"Dammit!"

"You're wasting time, Rafe. Let's go."

He clenched his jaw. *Damned woman.* But arguing wasn't going to change her mind and they needed to get on the road. And there was always the chance she was the target, or maybe two things were happening here at once.

"If this comes down, promise me you'll do what I say."

"I will. I promise."

With both of them armed, Rafe urged her toward the door.

Olivia leaned back in the seat of the pickup. She was strapped in nice and tight and it was a good thing, since Rafe was barreling a jillion miles an hour down the road. She prayed he wouldn't hit a moose.

She picked up the revolver, pulled it out of its black nylon holster, flipped open the cylinder and checked the load. Five bullets loaded and ready to shoot.

As her instructor in Texas had said, "They ain't much good if they ain't loaded." She shoved the pistol back into its holster. She had an extra handful of shells in her jacket pocket.

On the road ahead, the pickup headlights cut through the blackness as they careened along the pavement. The vehicle hit a pothole, but Rafe didn't slow.

"Why aren't we calling the police?"

"Because we aren't completely sure it's them and even if it is, they haven't done anything wrong — at least nothing we can prove."

"So we're going after them to see what they're up to? That's it?"

Rafe cast her a sideways glance that spoke volumes. They were armed. So were Noah and Derek. The men would do whatever it took to stop a terrorist attack.

Olivia kept pressing. "But we'll call them, right? We'll call the police if we're sure this is going to happen. We'll call, right?"

"Yes, absolutely. We need help with this. We just have to be sure we've got the information we need to get them involved."

"Okay, then. All right." It made sense. One thing about Rafe. He was solid as steel. He wouldn't go all macho and try to take matters into his own hands. Would he?

She didn't think so, but she couldn't say the same for Noah and Derek, who were even more overloaded with testosterone than Rafe and looked to be spoiling for a fight.

"Derek gave you their location?"

"Approximate, yes." He slowed the pickup and turned onto a narrow dirt road. "They pulled out of sight beneath a cluster of trees. They can't just drive into the terminal unless they have some kind of clearance, and obviously they don't. If we can find them before they can launch whatever they have planned, we can stop them."

A chill slid through her. "Stop them how?"

"Just keep looking. There aren't that many places they can be."

"What if they see us?"

"The idea is to see them first." Rafe slowed again, checked his mileage, pulled over to the side of the road out of sight. He rolled down the windows and turned off the engine, reached up and popped the bulb out of the overhead light, then quietly cracked open the door.

"Stay here. I'm going to scout ahead, see if I can spot the Jeep. Derek and Noah should be here any minute. Keep your eyes and ears open."

He didn't give her time to argue, just slipped off into the darkness and disappeared. Fear coiled in her stomach. What if he was spotted? What if something happened to him? She remembered her awful, sickening terror when she thought he had drowned.

He was raised here, she reminded herself. *He was in the military. He knows how to handle himself.* But her fingers curled around the pistol just in case.

The night sounds began to creep in, the rush of the sea against the rocky shore, the breeze rustling through the foliage, new leaves jostling against one another in the darkness. In the distance, the low rumble of an engine reached her. No lights appeared, just Rafe's big, dark SUV with big, bad Noah Devlin behind the wheel.

He pulled out of sight a little off to the right of where the pickup was parked. No overhead light went on. She didn't hear a door open or the sound of footfalls. They were just there.

"Easy," Noah said. "It's us. Don't shoot."

They were both dressed in black, wearing black tactical vests, and armed to the teeth. A long, ugly knife was strapped to each man's thigh, and their faces were streaked with black grease paint, making them look like villains out of a horror movie.

Olivia fought not to panic. Rafe and the others were supposed to be following Heng and his friend, not confronting them.

"Where is he?" Derek asked, forcing her to concentrate.

"Rafe's looking for the Jeep. He should be right back."

He stepped out of the quiet just then, a tall, familiar shadow that sent a little pang of relief sliding through her.

Rafe walked over to the men, tipped his head back the way he had come. "Quarter mile down the road. Computer set up in the back of the Jeep. Looks like state-of-the-art equipment. Whatever they're planning, they're ready to roll."

"How many?" Noah asked.

"Two."

"Where's the big guy?" Derek asked.

"Inside," Rafe said without the slightest doubt, though there was no way to know for sure.

"Got to be," Noah agreed, sticking to the assumption that the man who had tried to rape her was part of the group.

"Shit," Derek muttered. "And there may be more."

Noah turned his head, his gaze shifting farther down the dirt track toward where the Jeep was hidden. "Explosives. Just like the boat. My guess, they're planted and ready to blow. The destruction will be massive."

"We've got to stop these guys now," Rafe said.

Olivia felt faint. "You said you were going to call the police. That's what you said."

He stepped in front of her, reached out and caught her shoulders, forcing her to look at him. "Soon as we take these guys down, we'll call. But we can't let them blow the terminal, and that's what they'll do the minute they know the cops are on to them." He leaned over and kissed her quick and hard. "Damn, I wish I'd left you home."

"We need a few things before we go in," Noah said, striding over to the Expedition. Lifting the back without the light coming on, he opened the case, took out a black tactical vest and tossed it to Rafe, who slid into it as if he did it every day.

He joined Noah at the back of the SUV, rubbed greasepaint on his face, then Noah handed him a second semiautomatic pistol and a couple of extra clips. Derek passed an ear piece to each man, who stuck it into his ear.

"Keep your revolver handy and stay out of sight," Rafe told Liv.

Noah walked up and tossed her his cell phone. "It's on vibrate. Derek and Rafe are both programmed in."

"The keys are in the ignition," Rafe added.

"If we don't call or get back in fifteen minutes, get the hell out of here."

Olivia's heart throbbed with fear as the men disappeared out of sight.

Moving silently through the shadows, Rafe spotted the Jeep, pointed it out to the others, and they fanned out into the darkness around it. The rear door was up. Two men worked in the back of the vehicle in front of a laptop screen that was lit up like a NASA control room.

Rafe recognized Heng and the man he knew only as Michael Nevin.

He heard Noah's voice in his earpiece. "We need to separate them from that laptop. They can use it to detonate the bombs."

"Roger that."

"Copy," said Derek.

The wind kicked up and Rafe moved closer, the rustle of leaves and the soft, damp earth covering the sound of his footsteps.

Heng typed a command into the computer. "Security's disabled," he said, his voice clear in the quiet of the night. "From now on the cell tower won't respond to anyone but us."

"Very good," Nevin said.

"Two minutes till detonation, then we're

out of here." Heng's smile looked demonic in the light of the computer screen.

Noah spoke softly into his mic. "Let's move." As a unit, they silently ran forward, appearing like specters out of the night. Being the closest, Rafe body-slammed Heng, knocking him away from the keyboard. Noah grabbed the Arab, spun him around and crashed a meaty fist into his face. Nevin flew backward, sprawling into the wet grass and mud, his body going still with the impact.

Derek went straight to the laptop, used his body to block access, turned to examine the screen.

"One of the lights is blinking. It's asking if it's okay to proceed."

"It's asking to detonate," Noah said. "Forgodsake, don't touch anything."

Heng took off running, Rafe on his tail. Just as Rafe reached him, he whirled and went into a martial arts stance, crouching down, angling both hands up in front of his face. Rafe smiled grimly, his eyes locked with Heng's. The Asian never saw the kick Rafe aimed between his legs, doubling him over, or the hard blow that knocked him backward flat on his ass.

Writhing around in the grass, Heng moaned and clutched his crotch.

467

"Next time, Jackie Chan, don't bring a knife to a gunfight." Striding over, Rafe dropped down on top of him, flipped him on his belly, and twisted his arms up behind his back. Derek tossed him a plastic tie and he used it to bind the Asian's wrists.

"We've got to call this in," Rafe said. "Those bombs are rigged to blow. We can't afford to take any chances."

"I need a couple of minutes." Noah leaned down, grabbed the front of the Arab's shirt and hauled him to his feet. "Where's the big guy?"

Nevin was nearly as tall as Rafe, lean, hard, and fit. He spit into the dirt next to Noah's boot. "Infidel dog. You will get nothing from me. You can kill me. It will make no difference."

Noah must have believed him. Spinning the Arab around, he bound his hands with a plastic tie, then tied his feet and shoved him back down on the ground. He strode over to Heng.

Noah grabbed Heng's bound wrists and hauled him up off the wet grass. "The third guy? Is he still inside?"

"Go to hell," the kid said.

"That's where you're about to go if you don't answer my question." Noah pulled his big semiauto out of the holster at his waist and pressed it against Heng's right thigh. "One more chance. Where's the big guy?"

"Fuck off."

Noah pulled the trigger and the kid shrieked in pain.

"College graduate, right? Scholarship, right? Nice Midwest family? You really want to die for this shit? Now . . . where . . . is . . . the big guy?"

"He . . . he's heading for the rendezvous point," Heng sobbed out.

The Arab started cursing. All the words weren't in English but their meaning was clear. "You will be punished for your betrayal, filthy traitor," he said, spitting at Heng.

Noah kicked him, knocking him back in the grass, then returned his attention to the Asian. Blood soaked the side of the camouflage pants he was wearing. Noah was Delta. Rafe figured if he'd wanted the kid to die, he'd be dead.

"What's his name?" Noah asked.

"Cain. Darius Cain. I can't believe you fucking shot me!"

"Where's the rendezvous point?" Noah asked. When the kid didn't answer, Noah pressed the muzzle of his gun against Heng's left thigh. "Where is it?"

"Wait!" Heng started crying. "There's a

boat at the turnout off Dayville Road. They . . . they're waiting for us there."

"Is Cain by himself?"

Heng looked down at the barrel of the gun. "He's with our inside man. His . . . his name is Yousef. He rigged the explosives on the ship."

Noah's jaw went iron hard. "Which ship?"

"The *San Pascual.*"

Noah looked at Derek, who had his pistol trained on the Arab. "You got this?"

"I got it."

"You can make your call on the way," Noah said to Rafe. "Let's go." They started running back the way they'd come. Rafe phoned Liv, who answered on the first ring. "Don't shoot, we're coming in."

A few seconds later, they reached the pickup. "You drive," Rafe said to Noah. "I'll call the cops." Noah slid in behind the wheel and Rafe jammed into the passenger seat, forcing Olivia into the middle.

"I heard a shot," she said as Noah cranked the engine. "What . . . what happened?"

"We stopped them from blowing up the terminal but the big guy wasn't with them. Darius Cain. We need to find him."

Noah shoved the truck into gear, and they took off down the dirt lane back toward Dayville Road. Rafe had his cell in his hand when it started playing. He wasn't sure the Coast Guard song would ever bring the good memories it had before. He checked the screen, saw Sam King's name, figured it might be important.

"It's a bad time, Sam."

"Somebody blew up the packing plant, Rafe. There's cops all over the place."

His fingers tightened around the phone. "Tell them it's a diversion and there may be more. Tell them the pipeline terminal is rigged with explosives." He gave the location of the Jeep, off the road near Allison Creek, and told them Derek Hunter was there guarding the men. "Make sure you get word to Chief Rosen. Do it now, Sam."

"You got it."

As the pickup flew down the highway, Rafe turned to Liv. "They blew up the fish-packing plant. Sam King is calling the cops, bringing them up to speed, but I'm guessing they're up to their necks in their own problems at the moment."

Noah pointed toward the water. "Out there. That's the pickup boat."

"The turnout's around the corner," Rafe said as they headed toward the wide spot in the road.

A few seconds later, Noah jammed on the brakes, bringing the truck to a sliding stop

471

in the grass and shrubs on the opposite side of the lane, hidden out of sight. The men's attention was fixed on the light of the boat approaching the turnout.

Both doors swung open and Rafe turned back to Liv. "Get down and stay out of sight. Keep your gun out."

Before she could argue, he hauled her down off the bench seat onto the floor of the truck, then he and Noah started running.

CHAPTER THIRTY-FOUR

Rafe and Noah slowed their pace as they neared the turnout on the opposite side of the road. Crouched low and moving quietly through the grass, Rafe followed Noah toward the parked vehicle. Two men stood in front of the hood, staring at the boat moving toward them across the water.

Thirty-footer, Rafe guessed, heading for shore at about ten knots. He couldn't tell how many men were aboard. At least two shadowy figures, maybe more.

Noah pointed to the right and Rafe eased off in that direction. The .45 felt comfortable in his hand. His second weapon, Noah's borrowed semiauto, was holstered behind his back. The mountain side of the road opposite the water was lined with thick shrubs, trees, and foliage, making it easy for them to stay undercover. Trouble was, it was open between there and the ocean side of the road, where the men were parked.

Noah slid into position behind a boulder at the edge of the mountain, while Rafe moved behind a telephone pole.

"Put your hands in the air!" Noah shouted. "Do it now!"

Instead, both men whirled and pulled their weapons, ripped off a barrage of bullets that had Noah ducking behind the boulder and Rafe jerking back out of sight. A bullet slammed into the pole beside his head and chips of wood when flying. He pulled off a couple of quick rounds, Noah fired a double tap, then another. Rafe squeezed off two shots, which pinged loudly off the side of the car, the same brown Chevy beater he had seen the day Olivia was attacked.

One question answered. Not a hit man from D.C.

Using the car for cover, the two gunmen fired round after round. They didn't seem worried about running out of ammo. Rafe fired off a barrage and so did Noah. No way could they step out into the open.

More shots were fired. One of the gunmen took off running. Noah cracked off a round that hit him from behind and knocked him forward a couple paces before he landed flat on his face. He was shouting obscenities, and though only part of them were in English, Rafe understood where the man had been hit.

He almost smiled.

"Toss your weapon!" Noah shouted. The man sent his pistol flying sideways and stretched out facedown on the ground. There was only one shooter left across the road. Rafe laid down cover fire as Noah ran toward the man on the ground. The other man must have dropped over the embankment and slipped out of sight along the edge of the water.

The Chevy wasn't going anywhere now that Noah was there. The pickup was the only other means of escape. Rafe felt a jolt of fear, followed by a shot of adrenaline. He signaled to Noah and started running back toward his truck.

Olivia crouched on the floor on the passenger side of the pickup. Gunshots sounded in the distance. Short bursts, then return fire, another short burst, and then another.

She wanted to put her hands over her ears to block the sound, block the thought that Rafe or Noah might be killed. Instead, she steadied herself, held the cell phone against her ear and listened to the dispatcher's steady voice.

Sam had already called the police, but she and Rafe were the ones who had talked to Chief Rosen. As soon as the men had left, she had phoned to be sure the cops understood what was going on.

"Olivia, are you still there?" the dispatcher asked.

"I'm here."

"Chief Rosen can't be reached. I've got officers on the way. Just stay on the line."

"I've got to talk to him. It's a matter of life and death." She had already given her location, a spot on Dayville Road near the turnout closest to the pipeline terminal. She had told the female dispatcher that men had tried to blow it up. Some of them had escaped and were shooting, and she and the two men with her needed help.

She was still holding for Rosen when the driver's-side door burst open and the big, light-skinned African American who had tried to rape her slid in behind the steering wheel.

Darius Cain.

A lecherous smile curved his lips. "Hello, Fiona."

Olivia's heart jerked, but she didn't hesitate. The phone dropped out of her hand as she grabbed the revolver off the seat, aimed, and pulled the trigger.

Shock and fury widened Cain's black eyes. "You bitch!" He clutched the bullet wound in his shoulder. "I'll fucking kill you!"

"Move an inch and I'll shoot you dead. I swear it." Her palms were sweating but she held the pistol steady, gripped in both hands as she had been taught. She was shaky, but in control. Olivia eased up onto the seat across from him.

Blood oozed between Cain's fingers. Pure evil stared at her out of his black eyes. Icy calm settled over him. "You shot me," he said. "I'm no threat to you now. It'd be smart if you just let me go. They bring me in, I'll tell them who you are and what you did. Let me drive out of here and I won't say a word."

Her mouth tightened. "Maybe I should just pull the trigger. You can't talk if you aren't breathing."

A smile lifted his lips. "If you were gonna kill me, lady, you'd already a done it."

"I'm warning you." When he didn't say more, she risked a glance through the windshield in search of Rafe. She wasn't prepared for the sudden movement, the leap of Cain's big body over hers. Olivia screamed as the pistol fired and went flying. She started fighting, hitting Cain as hard as she could, trying to shove him off her.

The next thing she knew, Rafe was dragging the man out of the pickup, spinning him around and smashing a fist into his face. Cain fought back and the two of them struggled. Olivia searched wildly for the pistol, but it must have flown out of the truck.

Heart pounding, she jumped down from the pickup and ran to where the men battered each other back and forth, rolling around on the ground, first Cain on top, then Rafe. Cain was bigger, heavier through the chest and shoulders, but he was injured. Both were swinging powerhouse punches, Rafe's tinged with a fury that seemed to give him an edge.

Cain was on top one minute, then Rafe rolled him onto his back and came up over him, started punching Cain in the face, hitting him hard. Rafe rocked to his feet, grabbed Cain's shirt and dragged him up off the ground, hit him again, drew back and punched him so hard his head bobbed uselessly at the end of his neck.

"Rafe!" Liv called out. "He's unconscious! You'll kill him!"

The way his fist shook with the effort not to punch the man again told her how much he wanted to do just that.

Rafe let go of the front of Cain's bloody

shirt, and Cain sank like a stone onto the ground. Reaching into his tactical vest, Rafe pulled out a plastic tie, rolled Cain over and used it to bind his hands behind his back, another to bind his ankles; then he stood up and strode toward her. He didn't stop until he reached her, pulled her into his arms.

Olivia started trembling.

"I've got you," Rafe said, his cheek pressed against her hair. "It's over. Everything's going to be okay."

She wanted to cry. Just let go the way she had before when he had been holding her this way. Her heart was still hammering and her throat felt tight. With a shaky breath, she pulled herself together, but she didn't move out of his arms.

"Noah?" she asked, looking up at him.

"He's coming in now." Rafe tipped his head toward the two men walking back to the pickup, the gunman in front, hands bound together, Noah behind him, his gun pointed at his captive's back.

Rafe eased away from Liv enough to pull out his cell and call the police. She couldn't hear what was being said on the other end of the line, but it sounded as if he was having better luck than she'd had. He was nodding, seemed relieved when he ended the call.

"What about the boat?" Liv asked as he shoved the phone back into his pocket.

"Coast Guard's on its way. They spotted the boat. They'll pick the men up and bring them in."

"We need to call an ambulance for Cain."

His dark eyes softened as he looked in her face. Cain knew her secrets. It was all going to come out.

"Noah called. Ambulance is on its way. Good ol' Yousef took a bullet in the ass as he was trying to escape."

"You didn't —"

"Noah doesn't like terrorists."

At the *whop, whop, whop* of helicopters moving toward them overhead, Olivia looked up, saw a pair of dark spots traveling low through the night.

"Looks like the good guys are here," Rafe said. "I don't know where they came from, but I'm damned glad to see them."

Noah walked up just then, shoved his prisoner down on the grass next to Cain. Police vehicles began roaring up and slamming on their brakes. Officers streamed out all four doors.

One of the choppers set down in the turnout and men with FBI tactical vests jumped down from inside. The other helicopter kept going, heading, Liv presumed, for the spot where Derek was waiting. A man walked toward them, bulky, with silver-touched brown hair.

"Special Agent Charlie Farrell." Farrell extended a hand to Rafe. "I'm a friend of Nick's."

They shook. "Nick's brother, Rafe. Nice to meet you. This is Olivia Chandler and Noah Devlin. Glad you could make it. How's it happen you're here?"

"Nick tracked me down. Some kid named Zach sent him another batch of surveillance photos off the cameras at the local motel. We knew about Heng. Facial recognition identified the second man as Mikal Nadir. Nadir's an Iraqi national living in Detroit. Lately, he's been popping up on some of the watch lists. The coincidence of him and Heng traveling together to a primary target like Valdez was enough to convince the Bureau to take another look."

Thank God they had, Liv thought. Another siren cut through the night. An ambulance roared up, and EMTs jumped out, rounded the vehicle, and threw open the doors at the rear. Liv watched them go to work on the injured men on the ground.

She only glanced at Cain once. The look of pure hatred in his face told her he would do everything in his power to destroy her.

Olivia shivered. She swallowed past the lump in her throat. It was only a matter of time now. Her days as Liv Chandler were over.

The rest of the night passed in a blur. Cops everywhere. FBI. Questions asked, statements taken. The injured men were transported to the hospital.

One thing she knew. When she'd fired that bullet through Darius Cain's shoulder instead of his heart, she had made an irreversible decision.

It was time for her to run.

The sun was coming up by the time Rafe pulled his pickup into the garage. Noah and Derek drove in beside him. The men would be leaving that morning unless there were follow-up questions. Rafe told them they could stay as long as they needed. He could spend his nights with Liv above the café.

Rafe dropped her at the Pelican just before noon. Though both of them were exhausted, they had businesses to run. With the town in an uproar over the averted attack, media and law enforcement everywhere, they needed to keep an eye on things.

The good news was, a second bomb location, given up by Lee Heng, hadn't exploded. It was set to blow up the

Fisherman's Catch Saloon, but apparently the timer was faulty. Rafe didn't want to think how many people could have been killed if the bomb had gone off as the men had planned.

Things in Valdez were under control. His big worry now was Olivia. Darius Cain was in the hospital, soon to be released into FBI custody. Rafe had no idea how much he had told the police, but if he hadn't already turned Olivia in, there was no doubt, sooner or later, he would.

It was a hole card he would play whenever it gained him the most. Rafe had talked to Liv about it as they'd drunk coffee before he'd taken her to work.

"While you were in the shower," Rafe said, "I spoke to my brother Dylan. Dylan called his attorney friend, Peter Keller, and filled him in. I talked to Peter a few minutes ago. He's flying down from Anchorage, Liv. He's agreed to represent you."

She just looked at him. Then she nodded. "Thank you."

He didn't like whatever it was that moved across her features, but he figured with everything that had happened, he needed to cut her some slack.

"I've got to go to work," she said, setting her coffee mug on the table. "We can talk about it tonight, okay?"

"You're working all day?"

"I've got to. Everything's been a mess since Scotty died. I need to get things straightened out." *Before the police arrest me* were her unspoken words.

Rafe's chest tightened. It was true, and both of them knew it. The police wouldn't have any choice.

"Which reminds me," he said. "I need to talk to Rosen. I figure by now he knows Darius Cain killed Scotty, not Chip Reed. But I want to make sure."

She smiled at him softly, and he saw that flicker of emotion again. He wished he knew what it was.

"It's good to know we accomplished what we set out to do," she said. "We caught Scotty's killer."

"Maybe Cassie will finally be able to move on with her life."

"I hope so."

He left Liv at work and headed back home. He called Chief Rosen and they talked about Chip Reed. Rosen was on the same page. Reed had already been released. Next Rafe made arrangements for the passengers on the rest of the charters he had booked that summer. Some people he could move onto *Sea Dragon* or *Sea Devil,* but the balance required booking with another charter company.

Once things quieted down, he'd begin looking for another boat. Which could take a while, since he wasn't going to settle for less than he'd had before.

In a way it was good he had the time off. He had no idea how to approach the problems Olivia was facing. He knew Nick had already started digging, trying to find something that would help them prove her innocence. He figured he'd know more after he talked to Keller.

Thinking of Olivia had him smiling. Despite everything that had happened and everything they would have to overcome, he knew he had found the woman for him. He thought maybe he'd known as he'd watched her all those weeks in the café. Since they had been together, it was something he had never really doubted.

Olivia finished packing a second suitcase, zipped it closed, and set it by the front door next to the first. Satisfied she had packed everything she needed but would still be traveling light, she went into her bedroom office.

There were two things she had to do before she could leave Valdez. The first was to sign over the restaurant to Nell. She couldn't tell her friend she was leaving. Nell would ask questions Liv didn't have the time or the strength to answer. Nell would try to stop her.

But after Cain's arrest, Olivia couldn't possibly stay.

She glanced at the clock. It was already one thirty in the afternoon. Rafe would be back at the café for supper, figuring to take her home with him after she finished work. By then, she had to be as far away as her little Subaru would carry her. She had to be somewhere Rafe couldn't find her.

Where no one could find her.

Once she got on the road, she'd have time to figure out a destination where she would be safe. She'd done it before. She could do it again. This time she would change her appearance completely, bleach her hair, wear colored contacts, blend in so thoroughly no one would remotely consider she was Fiona Caldwell.

She wouldn't look like herself. She wouldn't *be* herself. She would give herself up completely.

Liv swallowed past the ache in her throat. She had only just found herself here in Valdez.

She bit back a sob. She had to go before

she weakened. Before the police showed up at her door. Even if she had the courage to stay and face the charges against her, she couldn't bear to think what seeing her in prison would do to Rafe. She knew the kind of man he was, knew he wouldn't abandon her. It could take years to prove her innocence, might never even happen. Rafe would be wasting years of his life. He might even be in danger.

She sat down at the desk and wrote a letter to Nell, thanking her for everything she had done. Telling her what a wonderful friend she had been. She asked her to find a good home for Khan, someone who would love him as much as she did.

Then she took the ownership papers she'd had drawn up a few weeks back in case she ever needed to leave in a hurry. She signed them over to Nell, put the papers in an envelope and licked the seal.

For a moment, she held the document against her heart. She loved this place. Loved the business she had created, loved the friends she had made.

She loved Rafe.

Her hand shook as she picked up the letter she had written him earlier. She had thanked him for everything he had done, told him how much she appreciated his friendship, told him how sorry she was that she had to leave.

The letter ended, *You're the best thing that's ever happened to me, Rafe Brodie. I wish things could be different, but sometimes that's just the way it is. If you care for me as I believe you do, please don't come after me. Have a great life. Liv*

She didn't tell him she loved him. She didn't say that leaving him was tearing her in two. She didn't because she knew if she did, he would search for her no matter how long it took, no matter how much of his own life he would be giving up.

She slid the note in an envelope and wrote his name on the front, left it on the sofa where it was easy to see. Next she took the ownership documents in the envelope marked with Nell's name and headed downstairs. Leaving the envelope on the office desk, she went out back to finish the last thing she had to do before leaving town.

Khan was lying in the sun in front of his doghouse, Tuxedo curled up beside him. When he saw her, his ears perked up and he shot to his feet. Tuxedo stood up, too. Both of them looked at her expectantly, then Khan jerked forward in a burst of speed and slid to a halt at her feet.

One great bark told her he was ready for his run.

Liv swallowed past the painful knot in her throat. "Hey, boy." Kneeling next to him, she buried her face in his soft, warm fur. "Not today, sweetheart. We can't go today. From now on, someone else will be taking you out." She brushed at a tear that slid down her cheek. "I have to leave. I'm sorry, but I can't take you with me this time."

She rubbed his fur, kissed the top of his head. She had to change her life completely and that meant giving up Khan.

She scratched his ears and rubbed his head and handed him a dog treat. He downed the treat politely, turned to look at Tuxedo, but didn't leave. He cocked his head, watching her, made a little sound in his throat. He could tell something was wrong. He was such a good dog.

"Good-bye, boy," she said, wiping at the wetness that continued to roll down her cheeks. "Bye, Khan." Her throat ached. Her chest hurt. Turning, she hurried back up the stairs to check a few last-minute things and retrieve her suitcases. Once they were loaded into the back of the Subaru, she would be gone.

Her life as Olivia Chandler was over. She

released a shaky breath. Fiona was once more on the run.

CHAPTER THIRTY-FIVE

Something was nagging him, chipping away at his good mood. Rafe didn't know what it was, but instead of finishing the work he had started, he left his house and headed down to the café.

He needed to see Liv, make sure she was okay. A lot had happened in the past few days. She had to be upset. Hell, she had shot a man last night.

He smiled grimly. If he'd had any doubts she was innocent of murdering her ex — which he didn't — they would have disappeared last night. As he'd hurried toward the pickup, he'd heard Cain's voice, heard him threatening to expose her. She could have shot him right there and saved herself. But Cain was right. Olivia wasn't a killer.

And because she wasn't, there would be a lot more to face ahead.

The bell rang as he pushed through the door into the café. Nell spotted him and started forward, set a hand on his chest and shoved him back outside onto the patio before he knew what was happening.

She clamped her hands on her hips. "All right, what did you do to Liv?"

"What are you talking about? I didn't do anything to Liv."

"You promised me you wouldn't hurt her. I warned you, but you wouldn't listen."

"Dammit, I didn't do anything. I wouldn't hurt her." He grinned. "I'm going to marry her — though it'd probably be better if you don't say that to her. At least not yet. I'm not sure she's ready to hear it."

"You're gonna marry her?"

"If she'll have me. We've got some problems —"

"You're gonna marry her!" Nell threw her arms around his neck and hugged him hard.

Rafe chuckled as she hung on to him. "So I guess you approve."

Nell stepped back and swiped at the tears beneath her smiling blue eyes. "Of course I approve. You two are perfect for each other. But you need to talk to her. Something's wrong. I don't know what it is, but I'm worried about her."

Rafe didn't waste any time, just walked past her and shoved open the door to the café.

"Where is she?" he asked Katie when he didn't see her right away.

"She was upstairs a few minutes ago."

He started walking, picked up his speed until he was almost running. Something was wrong. He'd felt it all morning. He pounded up to the top of the stairs and tried the door, found it open, which wasn't like Liv.

"Liv! Baby, where are you?"

He spotted the note with his name on it on the sofa, and felt a clutch in his stomach. He picked it up and tore it open. His insides churned as he skimmed the letter, read the meaningless niceties, *thanks for your friendship, thanks for your help, sorry I have to leave,* blah, blah, blah. He looked for some hint of her feelings, found none.

Then at the bottom. *You're the best thing that's ever happened to me, Rafe Brodie. Have a good life.*

His chest clamped down. He knew her now, knew the way her brain worked, knew she was afraid if she gave him the least indication of her feelings, he would follow her no matter how far she ran.

You're the best thing that's ever happened to me.

It wasn't *I love you,* but it was enough. He crumpled the note in his hand, turned and walked out of the apartment. If he hadn't heard Khan bark, he might have turned the wrong way at the bottom of the stairs and gone back into the café. Instead, he walked out on the back porch, saw Khan at the gate, and started across the yard to the garage where Liv parked her car.

He paused at the gate and lifted the latch, saw the garage door was open. The trunk of her Subaru was up. Liv was loading a piece of luggage in next to another bag in the back.

When she spotted him, her face went deathly pale. "Rafe . . ."

His jaw hardened. Rafe started walking.

Olivia's heart was pounding. All her careful planning had just gone out the window. Rafe was here. Dear God, what should she do?

She took a step backward into the shadows, wishing she could just disappear.

"What do you think you're doing?" he asked, but clearly he could see she was leaving. He just kept coming as she inched back, stalking her and reminding her of the lion she'd called him.

"Please, Rafe. I have to go." Her voice was trembling. She hoped he wouldn't notice.

"You're running," Rafe said darkly, and she could read the anger in his face.

494

"I'm going, yes. I'm sorry. I don't have any choice."

Rafe made no reply, just kept closing the distance between them, driving her back till she came up against the wall. She gasped as he bent and slid an arm beneath her knees, scooped her up against his chest, turned and started striding back the way he had come.

"Put me down. What are you doing?"

He ignored her, of course, carried her inside, climbed the stairs and strode into her apartment, kicked the door closed with his boot. He sat down on the sofa with her in his lap.

"Rafe, please . . ." She tried to stay calm, tried to think of a way to soothe his temper, tried to think what she should say.

"You're not leaving," Rafe said. "You might as well accept it. I love you. I'm crazy in love with you and I'm not letting you go."

"What?"

"I said I love you, and you aren't leaving. Even if you aren't in love with me, I'm still not letting you go. I promised you we were going to fix this, and that's what we're going to do."

Her heart was pounding, her chest squeezing so hard she could barely breathe. He loved her. The words filled her heart. Rafe loved her, and dear God, she loved him. It was the reason she had to let him go.

She leaned into him, rested her head on his shoulder. "Don't you see?" She wiped away a tear she hoped he wouldn't see. "If I stay, your life will be ruined. You might even be in danger. Please, you have to let me leave."

He just shook his head. "No."

"It could take years to fix this. I don't want my past to destroy your future. It's time for me to go."

His jaw went tight. "No."

Olivia sat up and looked at him, her gaze running over his face. At the hard set of his jaw, the tenderness she was feeling changed to something else.

Her chin went up. "You can't just say no. You don't own me. I'm a free person. I can leave if I want to."

There was something in his eyes, a look of stubbornness tinged with desperation. "You aren't leaving. I won't let you. We're going to find a way to prove your innocence. You're staying here with me."

She stared at him for several long seconds. No matter what she said, he wasn't letting her go.

A soft warmth spread through her body. Dear God, she loved this man. Loved his arrogance. Loved his protectiveness. Loved his beautiful face and his amazing body. She started smiling, chuckling at the audacity that was so much Rafe.

He looked down at her. "What, you think this is funny?"

She reached up, caught his face between her hands and kissed him, a long, wet, hot, thorough kiss that made him groan.

She eased a little away. "It isn't funny. It's wonderful. I love you, Rafe Brodie. All that stubbornness in such a sweet, sexy package. I don't think I could live without you, even if I went away."

She didn't miss the relief that moved over his beloved face. "I want to marry you, darlin'. All we have to do is find a way to prove Julia Stanfield killed your ex-husband — not you."

She started grinning. "That has to be the craziest proposal any man ever made to a woman."

Rafe grinned back. "I'll do better next time," he promised. Then he kissed her, and Liv knew, soul-deep, she wasn't going anywhere.

CHAPTER THIRTY-SIX

A lot went on during the next few days. The media tried to make Rafe, Noah, and Derek celebrities. But the two friends had slipped quietly away, leaving Rafe in the spotlight. Noah was former Delta. For all intents and purposes, as a hero, he didn't exist. Derek was pretty much a loner, a man's man who spent most of his time flying tourists in and out of the backcountry.

Rafe was a local and a businessman. He dealt with the media, kept things as simple as he could, and did his best to steer attention away from Olivia.

Liv spent the week in his bed. She hadn't tried to run again, hadn't even mentioned leaving. He figured she had finally figured out that they belonged together and that wasn't going to change.

Darius Cain still hadn't played his hole card. Rafe figured he was biding his time, trying to cut the best deal he and his attorney could make.

Cain had rolled on Trent Doyle, aka Trent Petersen, and his mistress, Tatiana Valenchenko, but so far hadn't mentioned Fiona Caldwell, keeping his trump card in place. He'd use it sooner or later, trade Fiona's whereabouts for something that would help him.

Whatever deal he made, Cain was going to prison for a very, very long time. So were Heng, Nadir, the mercenaries the Coast Guard had picked up on the escape boat, and anyone else connected with the terrorist plot.

Doyle and his mistress had been arrested in New York, their faces splashed all over the newspapers. The motive for their involvement was money. Big money, according to the FBI. Since Doyle and Valenchenko were considered international flight risks, the judge refused to release either of them on bail.

Peter Keller had flown to Valdez three times in the past week to meet with Rafe and Olivia to discuss the best way to fight the murder charges against her. They all knew it wouldn't be easy. But they'd set a plan in motion and they were determined. Keller had flown back to Anchorage last night.

Nick was in New York, working the Stephen Rothman murder case from where it had happened. Keller had connections in D.C., one of whom was a top-notch private investigator. The man was working the Julia Stanfield angle, treading carefully, since digging into the lives of such powerful people might get him killed.

Keller had been great. The attorney wanted to get all the pieces in place before he made contact with the authorities. They were racing against time, hoping they'd come up with something before Darius Cain told the FBI where to find Fiona Caldwell.

Once that happened, Olivia would have to turn herself in. A better scenario would be if Keller managed to assemble enough information to make a convincing case for her innocence.

Either way, Liv would have to go to prison. Once she was arrested, no bail amount would be high enough, since she had run before. Neither Rafe nor Liv was ready for that. No matter how much they talked about it, no matter how many plans they made, they just weren't ready.

And there was still the fear that once she came out of hiding, the same people who had tried to silence her before would attempt to kill her again.

Thinking about the problem had Rafe brooding that morning as they sat at the kitchen table drinking cups of freshly brewed coffee, Olivia seated across from him, reading a section of the *Valdez Star.*

Watching her, his mood grew even darker, so bad he didn't even reply to the e-mail he received on his iPhone from a guy in Anchorage wanting to sell a forty-three-foot North Pacific that might be exactly the boat he was looking for to replace *Sea Scorpion.*

Telling himself he should at least give the guy the courtesy of a response, he was e-mailing a reply when his cell started playing the Coast Guard anthem. His mood went blacker. Maybe he should change the tune.

Rafe sighed as he pulled the phone out of his pocket and recognized Nick's number. It was almost six a.m. in Valdez. Four hours later in New York. He pressed the phone against his ear. "Hey, bro, what's up?"

"Turn on your TV, big brother. Put on Fox or CNN."

"What's going on?"

"Just do it."

Rafe's worry kicked up a notch. He flicked a glance at Liv. "It's Nick. He says there's something we need to watch on TV."

"Oh God. I hope it isn't another terror attack somewhere."

Rafe headed into the living room, Olivia right beside him. He grabbed the remote and clicked on his big flat-screen, brought up CNN. He didn't recognize the dark-haired woman at first, attractive, late forties, dressed in an expensive tailored suit. But Olivia did.

"That's Julia Stanfield." She stared at the screen. "Oh my God, she's being arrested."

Nick's voice came through the phone. Rafe put the call on speaker and set it on the arm of the sofa.

"You see that, big brother? FBI just arrested Julia Stanfield. I guess her husband got tired of her many affairs and demanded she stop fooling around. Julia got tired of her husband. She tried to hire a hit man to take him out. Trouble was, the hit man was an FBI undercover agent."

Rafe's gaze was fixed on the screen. They were loading the Stanfield woman into an unmarked police car, an officer shoving her head down as they settled her, handcuffed, into the backseat.

Nick's chuckle came over the phone. "Funny thing is, the feds weren't even targeting her. She just fell into a sting they were operating across the country. The

502

pictures you're seeing are from early this morning. Word is, after the arrest was made, her entire staff turned on her like a pack of rabid wolves."

"We have to call Peter," Olivia said excitedly. "Maybe he can figure a way to get her to admit she killed Stephen."

"I don't think that's going to be a problem much longer," Nick said. "According to Keller's man in D.C., one of her aides has already jumped on that bandwagon. Made a deal to save his own ass. The deal includes information about the murder of Stephen Rothman. Info that it was Julia Stanfield who killed Rothman, not Fiona Caldwell."

A sob caught in Olivia's throat. Rafe reached for her, pulled her into his arms and held on tight.

"Congratulations, big brother," Nick said. "You too, Olivia. I'm on my way back home. Got a sweet little wife waiting for me. I'll keep you posted." Nick hung up the phone.

Rafe felt Olivia's body soften against him. Her arms went around his neck. "I can't believe it. I can't convince myself it's really true."

Rafe kissed her forehead. "Now that it's all out in the open, you'll be safe. There's nothing you can tell the police they don't already know."

She just nodded.

Rafe caught her chin, tipped her face up. "They say bad things happen to good people. That's what happened to you, darlin'. But sometimes good things happen to good people. This is one of those times."

Liv looked up at him, tears in her beautiful gray eyes. "I love you, Rafe Brodie. I love you so much."

He ran a knuckle over her cheek. "Will you marry me?"

Olivia smiled at him through her tears. "That's the second time you've asked. It was yes the first time."

Rafe bent his head and very thoroughly kissed her.

EPILOGUE

It was a perfect late June day, the water in Prince William Sound smooth as glass, the sky even bluer than the ocean. The forty-three-foot North Pacific that Rafe had bought and named *Sea Scorpion II* was bigger and newer than the first boat.

"There's two of us now," he told Liv as they stood on deck looking out at the sea. "We'll be using it ourselves more. I wanted a roomy cabin, a stand-up head with a separate shower. I wanted a galley where you'd be able to cook. This thing's got that and everything I need for fishing, got twin diesels and all the latest electronics, and it's built solid and safe."

He missed the Mac. He'd loved that boat, but this one was fast becoming his favorite. Since he'd reassigned all *Scorpion*'s summer charters, he planned to take some time off, take Liv and go exploring.

Peter Keller had worked tirelessly to get

all the charges against her dropped and exonerate her completely from any wrong-doing in the murder of Stephen Rothman. Finally the job had been accomplished.

Today they were out on the water with Zach and Jaimie, just getting used to the boat and its equipment, its capabilities, learning the best ways to handle her. Tonight the gang at the Pelican was throwing a small engagement party for the two of them.

Standing next to Liv, he glanced down at the brilliant marquise-cut diamond he had picked for her. After losing Ashley, he hadn't been sure he'd ever get to buy a ring for the woman he loved.

"It's beautiful," Liv said, admiring it. "Exactly what I would have chosen. I love it." She leaned toward him, pressed a soft kiss on his lips.

They hadn't set a wedding date. Rafe was ready, but he figured Liv deserved at least a few months of being courted.

He rested a hand at her waist, and she looked up at him. They were both wearing the matching red-and-black baseball caps he had bought at the souvenir shop. Liv's said HIS on the front. Rafe's said HERS. Every time they looked at each other, they grinned.

"Nice day," he said, and though it was the

best God had to offer, it was the lady standing beside him that made it so.

"Perfect," Liv agreed and he knew she was thinking the same thing.

"You ready for the party tonight?"

"I'm still not used to being the center of attention, but I'll handle it."

"Nell and Katie have been planning it for a couple of weeks."

"I know."

"I guess we'd better head back in, give you time to work up your courage."

She looked up at him and smiled. "Long as I have you on my arm, I'll be fine."

The party was in full swing. Just the people who worked for Liv, the guys who worked for Rafe, and a few close friends.

At least that's how it had started. But word had leaked out and now the restaurant, closed for the occasion, was packed.

Along with Nell, Katie, Cassie, Wayne Littlefish, and Charlie Foot, Cassie's mother, Lois, was there; Mo Blanchard and his daughter, Cindy; Josh Dorset; Zach and Jaimie; and the rest of the Great Alaska Charters crew. Ben Friedman, Sam King and his latest girlfriend, even Chip Reed. Half the Valdez police force was there, including Chief Rosen, Lieutenant Scarborough, and Rusty Donovan.

Olivia stood next to Rafe, his arm around her, looking out at the group eating mounds of raw oysters and fresh shrimp, heaping platters of roast beef and chicken, and big pieces of the CONGRATULATIONS LIV AND RAFE chocolate cake that Nell and Wayne had baked. Everyone was drinking spiked fruit punch, wine margaritas, and beer.

Liv smiled as she looked out at the group, her heart trembling. She had never had friends like these, people she could count on, people willing to stand by her through thick and thin. She had never known a man like Rafe.

He was laughing at something Zach said, and Jaimie was blushing. He glanced up when the door opened and two familiar faces strode into the café.

Noah Devlin and Derek Hunter. Noah looked big and powerful in pressed blue jeans and a white western shirt with pearl snaps on the front. Derek wore black jeans and a black leather jacket, both men just as hot as the last time they were in town.

Noah enveloped Liv in a big bear hug. "Congratulations, both of you." He shook Rafe's hand, clapped him on the shoulder. "First time I met Liv, I figured you'd find a way to keep her."

Derek bent and kissed Liv's cheek. "Looks like everything worked out okay. Only problem is, now that your life's back to normal, things won't be nearly so much fun."

Olivia laughed.

"Welcome to the family," Noah said, and she realized that's what these people were. Maybe not by blood, but family just the same. And she loved them all.

"Zach left a car for us out at the airport," Noah explained. "We figured you wouldn't let us in if you knew we were coming."

Rafe grinned.

The door opened again and a tall, ruggedly handsome man with incredible blue eyes, and a beautiful woman with gorgeous red hair walked into the restaurant. Rafe smiled so big the air in the room seemed to warm.

Dylan strode toward him. "Hey, big brother." Their man-hug lingered a few extra moments. "Congratulations."

"Thanks."

The redhead hugged Rafe, then Rafe turned to Liv. "Dylan and Lane, meet Olivia. She made the mistake of saying yes, and I'm holding her to it."

Liv smiled at the amazing man she was

going to marry. "I'm lucky he picked me. Luckier than you could ever imagine."

"One thing about my brother," Dylan said. "He finds something he wants, he goes after it. Once it belongs to him, he keeps it. Welcome to the family, Olivia." Dylan kissed her cheek.

"Thank you."

Lane hugged her. "We didn't bring our little girl, Emily, this trip. We thought . . . we figured we'd make it a romantic weekend."

Olivia smiled. "I'll meet her next time." More family. Even a little niece. A year ago, she couldn't have imagined being anything but alone for the rest of her life.

"Nick couldn't make it," Dylan said. "He wasn't happy about it, but Ian and Meri are away on a belated honeymoon. Nick's running the office. He says he'll see you at the wedding." Ian was a Brodie cousin, the owner of BOSS, Inc., where Nick worked.

"Which wedding?" Rafe asked with a smile. "Mine or yours?"

"Mine, since it's coming up first. He and Samantha send their love."

Lane smiled at Liv. "Samantha can't wait to meet you. She's pregnant, you know, so you'll have another niece or nephew in the fall. I hope you like kids."

"I do. I love kids."

Rafe gazed down at her and she didn't miss the hot look in his eyes. "We thought we'd practice for a while before we got serious about having a family of our own."

Something melted inside her. They had never talked about children, but she had always wanted a family. If she hadn't been standing in a room full of people, she would have thrown her arms around his neck and kissed him.

She gave him a brilliant smile. "Rafe thinks we should just keep practicing until we get it right." She grinned. "Which, considering he's already mastered his part of the job, shouldn't take all that long."

Rafe laughed. So did Dylan and Lane. Derek grinned and Noah chuckled.

"I'll drink to that," Derek said. "Where can a guy get a beer around here?"

Katie sailed up just then, took his arm and laced it through hers. "Why don't I show you?" she said.

And the party was on.

AUTHOR'S NOTE

I hope you enjoyed Rafe and Olivia in *Against the Tide,* book three of the Brodies of Alaska series. If you haven't read Dylan's story, *Against the Wild,* and Nick's story, *Against the Sky,* I hope you will.

Next meet Ethan Brodie, one of the hot Brodie cousins, and catch up with Nick and Samantha. Ethan works in Seattle with Nick at Brodie Operations Security Services. His current assignment at BOSS, Inc. — providing security for the *La Belle* lingerie fashion show tour — is the last thing Ethan wants. He's already got more woman trouble than he can handle.

But when the models receive threatening notes and one of them is murdered, Ethan must go into bodyguard mode to protect them. And there is the promise he made to Nick's wife, Samantha, that he'll protect her supermodel friend, Valentine Hart, which makes the bombshell blonde Ethan's

513

first priority.

It's a high-action, romantic adventure filled with passion and intrigue. I hope you'll watch for *Into the Fury*.

Till then, very best wishes and happy reading.

Kat